THE
EMPEROR'S
GENERAL

THE
EMPEROR'S
GENERAL

A Novel

JAMES WEBB

BROADWAY BOOKS

New York

BROADWAY

Broadway Books titles may be purchased for business or
promotional use or for special sales. For information, please write
to: Special Markets Department, Random House, Inc.,
1540 Broadway, New York, NY 10036.

BROADWAY BOOKS and its logo, a letter B bisected on the
diagonal, are trademarks of Broadway Books, a division of
Random House, Inc.

Library of Congress Cataloging-in-Publication Data
Webb, James H.
The emperor's general : a novel / James Webb. — 1st ed.
p.   cm.
ISBN 0-7679-0076-6 (hardcover)
1. MacArthur, Douglas, 1880–1964—Fiction.   2. Yamashita,
Tomoyuki, 1885–1946—Fiction.   I. Title.
PS3573.E1955E46   1999
813'.54—dc21   98-23143
CIP

FIRST EDITION

Designed by Pei Koay

99   00   01   02   03   10   9   8   7   6   5   4   3   2   1

During the writing of this book, life's rhythms claimed their casualties and the mourning of those passings could not help but find their places, however subliminal, in the words that the author chose. And so I must especially lament:

JAMES HENRY WEBB, SR., 1917–1997, my hero, mentor, and forever friend. Fierce but shyly tender, self-educated singer of grand poems, proud to the grave of the uniform in which he served our nation as pilot and missile pioneer, he constantly amazed me with a mammoth intellect that was never fully recognized or adequately rewarded, other than through its impact on those he left behind. I miss you, Dad.

PETER BRAESTRUP, 1929–1997, quiet, gruff, and earnest, possessed of an unbending honesty, among the best and brightest who from Yale served Corps and country and was wounded as a rifle platoon commander in Korea. A fearless combat correspondent, the unsung Ernie Pyle of the Vietnam War, and a great friend.

THOMAS W. MARTIN, JR., 1947–1997, squad leader and truth teller, who fought the enemy in Asia and then the prison of a wheelchair that became its legacy, yielding early into the earth, but, like my father, leaving behind an insistence that the truth can be a majority of one.

And as the days unfold into years that are forever lost, each morning I awaken and remember that bright, faraway Asian hotel, which if life had been different, might have been my refuge in the cruel November that steadily approaches.

And so it goes . . .

"Think now

History has many cunning passages, contrived corridors

And issues, deceives with whispering ambitions,

Guides us by vanities. Think now

She gives when our attention is distracted

And what she gives, gives with such supple confusions

That the giving famishes the craving. Gives too late

What's not believed in, or is still believed,

In memory only, reconsidered passion."

—T. S. ELIOT, "GERONTION"

A SPECIAL ACKNOWLEDGMENT

Many people helped through their encouragement and advice as this book moved forward, but it would not have achieved its full majesty without the continuous support of my agent, Nick Ellison, who brings to his trade a rare combination of intellect, publishing savvy, and personal warmth. I am also indebted to his assistant, Faye Bender, who was generous in her time and honest in her comments as the manuscript moved forward.

This novel is an attempt to bring context to a series of historical events that occurred separately from one another, but became intertwined as the United States and Japan sought to move from the hostilities of World War Two into a new era of cooperation and interdependence. The historical events—the rapes of Nanking and Manila by Japanese troops, Douglas MacArthur's maneuverings as he solidified his role as the proconsul of Japan, the intense negotiations between MacArthur and the Japanese imperial government over war crimes accountability and the drafting of a comprehensive new Japanese constitution, and the trial of General Tomoyuki Yamashita by a hastily drawn military commission—did occur, and the author has labored to recount them with accuracy. The major historical characters who move the novel did exist, and again the author has labored to retell their involvement in historical events with factual correctness.

But the author wishes to emphasize that this is above all a novel. The impact of one set of historical facts on another involves the author's own deduction and surmise. Conversations with the fictional characters, and many of the internal motivations laid out in the novel that drive historically known decisions, are the product of the author's imagination. And all characters, other than the well-known historical figures who inhabit these pages, are fictional. Many people served in the United States Army during and after World War Two. Any resemblance to any other person, either living or dead, is entirely coincidental.

PROLOGUE

FEBRUARY 23, 1997

Morning

I cannot even think of Manila during the war without drawing in my mind a picture of General Douglas MacArthur. And I cannot do justice to the memory of either him or the war without first visiting Manila Bay.

It was my first order of business on Sunday. I had arrived the evening before, heading from the airport to a new hotel in the business district of Makati, six miles from old Manila. The travel agent who booked my trip had urged me to stay in Makati, praising its newfound opulence at the hands of Chinese and Japanese investors. She did not steer me wrong. Even though I had been in Manila only a few years before, the bright lights of Makati amazed me. A sparkling circular pool marked the horseshoe entrance to the Esmeralda Hotel, at the center of which was a brightly lit fountain that spewed its geysers twenty feet into the air. I was greeted by smiling, white-coated attendants and in the marbled lobby was passed along to an entire squad of greeters, bag lifters, and credit card processors.

They were all very pleasant, and indeed well trained. It was as if I had reached an oasis imported from Las Vegas or possibly Hong Kong. Dinner was exquisite. The Esmeralda was a lovely hotel, but to me it was not very Filipino.

The next morning I hired a car, and even on a Sunday we crawled for more than an hour through a vast mass of congestion and construction just to reach downtown Manila. Stuck in the traffic, my heart played little tricks on me. In February 1945 our military forces had come into Manila along the forerunner of this same road. In front of us, the steadily retreating Japanese had burned and raped and murdered in a final orgy of certain defeat, leaving a hundred thousand corpses strewn like foul garbage among pyres that had once been homes. The sight had filled me with hatred. But Manila, fecund and resilient like its people, had recovered, and Japanese businesses had led the way. The metropolitan suburbs had grown into one congealed, metropolitan morass. Ten million people now choked the streets and byways of the city.

Finally I reached downtown Manila and then the American embassy, its high walls and wide lawn and square white buildings connecting me at once to that other era. Not so long ago the embassy had been its very own oasis, an isolated splendor now lost to the glassy modernity of Hiltons and Nikkos and Esmeraldas. After a little negotiation I managed permission to walk along its flat, sprawling side yard to where a low wall overlooked Manila Bay.

I strode quickly in the lush grass, at first near the buildings and then across the helicopter pad, and finally in the rear where it approached the vistas of the mammoth bay. My chin was raised like a bird dog's and my heart was racing with excitement, so anxious was I to be near the bay. My strong gait seemed to surprise the young foreign service officer who had been assigned to accompany me. But I was once a fine athlete and have always been sturdy, even in these later years. And no matter. I was mindless of him anyway, uninterested in contemporary travelogue, caught up in a moment long ago.

He persisted, seeking to make conversation. "Are we in a race, Ambassador Marsh? The bay's not going to disappear, you know."

He was certainly no Asia hand. I pointed to the sky above the bay. "How long have you been out here? Can you not yet read East Asian weather?"

Indeed, the rain was coming. The air clung to me like a gentle blanket as we walked. The sun fell slowly away behind a thick, viscous bank of pillowy grey clouds, leaving them pink around the edges. The wind started blowing in hot and horizontal from the bay, like the breath of some unseen dragon. I knew from other days that I had better hurry, because soon the sky would become a torrent and the streets would flow like rivers and the bay would disappear from view as completely as if it had become full night.

I had not yet met the new ambassador. A sharp, kind woman who was not yet born the first time I had caught this gaze, she had greeted me in her office despite the holiday, and then insisted that I have full run of the embassy grounds. I am retired now, hardly worthy of such attention, but an unspoken, common bond exists among most ambassadors, present and former, that allows these little courtesies. Since I had represented our country in three different Asian nations over the course of my career, she had graciously overlooked the suddenness of my unannounced arrival and insisted that I tour her grounds, even assigning me this young, irritatingly eager seeing-eye escort. Walking with him toward the wall I decided that his probable assignment was to scoop up my corpse and ring some magic bell should I collapse from the heat.

But it was he who flinched and squirmed under the steaming sky, not I. By the time we reached the wall he was sweat-drenched, working to hide his irritation at having been called away from his air conditioner. He stood impatiently, as if trying to decide how to be useful, then started pointing out hotels and skyscrapers and ships out in the bay, all the proud and promising changes along Manila's new horizons. And finally I could take it no more.

"Young man," I said, folding my arms and turning my face out to the sea, "if you don't mind, I would like to be left quiet and alone."

Somewhere behind me he disappeared, fading like a polyester ghost toward the embassy, no doubt glad to be relieved of this dubious mission. My eyes did not follow him, nor did I say good-bye. Instead I stood transfixed, consumed not merely by what was before me but by all that I had seen and lost since I first had held this vision. I was looking out into the bay, but I was swallowed like Jonah into the belly of a different time, another world, indeed another person who used to bear my name.

Far against the horizon I could see a faint nipple on the sea that I knew was the island of Corregidor. To its right in my vision, now fading through the mist of the distantly approaching rain, was the Bataan Peninsula. The two landmarks are still sacred to me, an old soldier's wailing wall. In the cruel months following Japan's invasion of the Philippines, the over-whelmed American and Filipino soldiers fought a rear-guard action down the peninsula, ending up in a last-ditch defense on Corregidor itself, all the while hoping that reinforcements and resupply might somehow arrive and free them from their devastation. Reinforcements did arrive, but more than two years too late. They had been forced to surrender, then march back up the peninsula under the probing bayonets of the conquering Japanese, and then after that had still waited, starving and tormented in disease-ridden prisoner camps.

If the reinforcements were late, it is fair to say that they arrived when they did only because General Douglas MacArthur had made a promise to these defenders, his own soldiers, when he escaped from Corregidor on a PT boat, and he did not forget them after he traveled to Australia to assume command of the Allies' southern advance. Once the Philippines were reinvaded MacArthur made a point of liberating the archipelago in its entirety, single-handedly winning a debate against more senior officers who were calling for him to take only a chunk of the distant island of Mindanao for bases and then proceed northward to Formosa.

I did not fight in Bataan or Corregidor, never underwent their terrors, but I was with him after the liberation of Manila as we traveled to the filthy, stench-saturated prisons at Muntinglupa and Santo Tomas, where he greeted the survivors among the soldiers he had left behind. They seemed half human as they stood in their hollow-eyed, pointy-boned, gaunt thousands, staring at their old commander as if he had returned from the dead to anoint them for their suffering. He was at his best on those visits, filled with emotion and bold prose, and when MacArthur was at his best he was better than anyone then alive. They lined up in a pitiful formation for him at Santo Tomas and as he toured their ranks and heard their ragged cheers I understood at least a part of his obsession.

Nearer to me as I stood looking at the bay, perhaps only a mile up to my right, was the elegant old Manila Hotel, which for many years before the war had been MacArthur's home. Another memory leaped out at me as I peered up the coastline, watching it—the General running up the hotel steps toward his old penthouse as the battle to recapture Manila still raged around us, joining a machine-gun team that was retaking the hotel. His eyes were on fire with fear. It was not fear of death that shone on his face; I was with him constantly during those long months and I never saw him flinch from the thump and crackle of enemy guns. It was the kind of nauseating dread that one feels when the symbols of his very life are being destroyed.

The Japanese, who had taken over his penthouse and used it as a command post, had set it afire as they retreated. Smoke billowed down the stairs as we climbed them. Gunfire erupted steadily, without warning. Bodies of shot enemy soldiers tumbled and fell down the landings. MacArthur had raced forward, impervious. In the living room of his former home the General stepped over a just-dead Japanese colonel who was oozing blood onto the charred carpet and surveyed the rubble and ashes that once had been his defining treasures. He had labored for three years to save them and had arrived only a few minutes too late. Pointing to the smoldering library, where not one book had survived, he managed a wry and yet prophetic observation.

"All the treasures that define us have been destroyed, Jay. Do you understand what I mean? It will never be the same after this war is over."

I did not understand him then, but I do now. For it was also MacArthur who insisted that the history of the world for the next thousand years would be written in Asia. Looking at the burned books, he had seen beyond all our lives.

I turned yet again, my eyes searching beyond the embassy buildings and then further landward, knowing that nearby were Sampaloc and Quiapo and after that Quezon City. And for the first time I felt the weight of my years and the utter loneliness of a dream that but for my own foolishness would certainly have happened. Yes, I was a young man here. And yes, I was in love. And I did not handle it well. It is an old story, unless you've never lived it.

And so I had a mission to fulfill on this trip, one that I had struggled with for more than fifty years. Now that my bones were rattling and my life was mostly lived, I was finally going to see her again. I held no great hopes for this visit, other than perhaps to catch a glimpse of what had been my better self.

Thinking of her I found myself again becoming angry, and I knew the anger was directed within. It was a recent phenomenon for me, this bitter disappointment with the man I had become. Make no mistake, I lived an enormously successful life after World War Two. But there were prices to pay, and I began paying them at Quezon City.

And I paid further at Los Banos. I turned to look southward, where perhaps thirty miles away at a camp near that town, in the middle of the night five months after the war was done, I had been forced to witness the hanging of General Tomoyuki Yamashita. It had been my price for questioning MacArthur's almighty judgment and his motives. I had seethed mightily as the trapdoor sprung, but it was indeed a brilliant way of reinforcing his infallibility, that I should be ordered to watch and report on all the minutiae of the very action that I had dared to question, and then be rewarded for my acquiescence and continued silence.

Fifty-one years ago, to this very day.

Yes, I learned the importance of symbols and anniversaries from General Douglas MacArthur. And of arrogance and intimidation, both useful tools.

Facing Los Banos, I noticed that my polyestered, seeing-eye foreign service officer escort had returned and had been waiting for me under the eaves of the white embassy building. The young fool caught my gaze and jogged out to me as if summoned. There was a new respect or at least a curiosity in his limpid, moonful face as he reached me.

"I was just talking with the ambassador," he said breathlessly. "She tells me that you actually knew Douglas MacArthur."

"I worked for him," I answered, turning away and looking at the approaching rain.

"What was he like?"

"I just felt a drop of rain," I said, avoiding his question, for it is one that I have seldom seen fit to answer.

My silence proceeds from a small but insistent conceit. Many people have claimed that they knew Douglas MacArthur. I knew him better than any of them and so I must say that all of them were wrong. Because I knew him not at all.

The General, as he demanded to be called, had no friends. Born like a crown prince to an earlier and equally mighty general, he was from his first breath a creature of the army's rigid structure. People came in categories. There were superiors, who must be wheedled, impressed, and at the proper moment defied. Next came peers, to be intimidated, secretly probed, and then defeated in pursuit of rank and honors. Below them were subordinates, who owed the Great Man flawless performance, unquestioning loyalty, and frequent adulation.

Then out beyond the khaki-sentried gates, on the other side of the bugles and the camp fires, lived the grey, foreign "other world," a place never, even in his dotage, to be actually lived in but always to be tolerated. For who but they could paint his glory upon the canvas of the nation's history? These Other Worlders were in his mind a mixed and unhappy bunch, all in need either of his blanket or his sword—unknowing and undisciplined civilians, scheming, malleable politicians, oppressed peoples with their rice bowls and empty hands stretched hopelessly into the air. And the blood enemies—the most honorable of them marching toward him through fields of muck with their weapons at the ready, the truly contemptible among them armed only with cameras that needed to be tricked or notepads to be lied into.

And finally, always in his waking thoughts like the summer sun's warmest aurora, was his mother, Pinky. Pinky was the only person who had ever truly known MacArthur. Indeed she was the very force that created him, not merely in the flesh but in the always unsettled, reaching maw of his yearning and domineering spirit. She had lost her two other sons, one to disease and the other to war, and through most of the General's life seemed to compensate by compelling him to be large enough for all three of their youthful dreams.

And certainly he was more than one mere man, although perhaps not in the manner that Pinky had imagined. He was a brilliant and tormented child, Douglas MacArthur, even at age sixty-two, when I first met him. Even yet when I saw him for the last time more than twenty years later, a few weeks before he died.

I rode with him, flew with him, sat through his peacock tirades, lived for his praise, and suffered his abuse as if I were some eager young Polonius. Each day was a roller-coaster ride. I ran the gamut of emotions—ever happy to be near his greatness, fortunate to be treated to the wonders of his mind, distressed from time to time at my inability to comprehend the centuries that passed before his eyes even as he studied the mindless mire of a rain-driven rice field, thrilled on the rare occasions he would pat me on the back and tell me how important were my small, throbbing contributions to the advancement of the war and thus the universe.

Yes, a young Polonius. Not at the hot gates, where the war belched its ugly, temperamental fury, but in the jeep, on the plane, five people down from the Great One, reading his mail, taking his orders, running his secret errands, even on occasion venturing a phrase of carefully considered advice. Deferential, as they say. Devoted, to a fault. Glad to be of use.

We did have a few things in common. We both were born in Arkansas—he by the mischance of army assignments, in Fort Dodge, near Little Rock, where his father served frontier duty as an infantry officer, mine by the sad inevitability of four generations of misguided meanderings, in a tenant house fifty miles to the north, where my own father sharecropped someone else's cotton along chopped and sunbaked rows of powdered earth scratched from the snake-filled forest. We both were seduced early in our lives by East Asia, gone green and willing like stupefied young lovers to its clamoring energy, its swelter and odd rhythms, and then never shaking its seduction, forever after finding euphemistic reasons to return. We both made careless choices in our women, coming painful and naive to romance and paying a lifelong price for our hesitations. And of course there was the army, that frail gossamer which by the accident of necessity bound us together for three dazzling but terrifying years.

And there was also much to divide us. But that came later.

Out in the bay the rain approached swiftly, making a wide cat's paw on the water that crept ever closer. A few drops splashed against my face. I knew I must hurry or be drenched. I began jogging toward the embassy building, my escort in tow. As we reached the building a ragged curtain of rain roared across the yard behind us, pulling a full storm behind it as it moved with fury into old Manila beyond the embassy walls. I found myself laughing as the storm passed within arm's reach of my haven under the building's eaves. Its timing was perfect, the ideal final welcoming moment of my return.

"I'll leave now," I said. "Thank the ambassador for her courtesies, will you?"

He had a new mission, though, as if he deserved some payment in kind for having interrupted his Sunday siesta to accompany me.

"They say he was a genius?"

I watched his expectant face, knowing he would not understand, and sighed out a small reward. "He was brilliant when he spoke of war and history, but he could be stupid with people who manipulated his ego. He was kind, but in the end I found him cruel. He helped me more than any other person. But in truth, he did it for himself."

The young man looked at me as if I had uttered the Riddle of the Sphinx. I ignored his further curiosity, heading into the building and cutting along the corridors until we reached the front portico, where my car still waited.

I reconsidered as we walked, and at the car I surprised him. I shook his hand and then held it firmly, watching his eyes grow ever rounder as I spoke.

"He killed a man. I could say murdered, but what would be the use? He killed a great man because of his jealousy and his ego."

"Who?" he said, delicately trying to loosen my grip on his hand.

"MacArthur."

"No, sir. I mean, who did he kill?"

"Why, General Tomoyuki Yamashita," I answered. "He killed him, with the full blessing and encouragement of the Japanese imperial government. They wanted one thing, he wanted another. And Yamashita became the sacrificial lamb that served them both. I watched it. I was a part of it."

He was looking at me as if I were a different person, not an eminent retired ambassador who had made a fortune on Wall Street but an old man who had brought a bad rain, given over to a vengeful paranoia.

"But—I've read about this, sir. A military court convicted Yamashita. And the Japanese wouldn't have wanted him dead—he was one of their greatest war heroes. And anyway, the imperial government was dissolved by the time MacArthur took over the occupation."

"A *court?* It was not a court. And the imperial government? It never truly dissolved. So, you see, you know nothing," I finally let go of his hand. "And Yamashita? The imperial court hated him! They had other people to protect, you know."

He chuckled to himself, turning his head for a moment to hide a smile, and I knew that in his eyes I now had become an old fool. Diplomatically changing the subject, he pointed to the deep scar that to this day jags across my right cheek like an ugly bolt of lightning.

"I hope you don't think I'm rude, sir. But did you get that in the war?"

Now, that was indeed rudeness. I opened up the car door. "I got it here in the Philippines." I climbed into the car. "Good day, young man. I really do have to go!"

I left him puzzled and speechless in the driveway, waving slightly as we pulled out into the still-ravenous rainstorm. As usual I had said as little as possible, and as always it was misunderstood. Not that it mattered. It all would have taken too much energy to explain, and it would not have been in his bureaucratic training to comprehend.

I urged the driver onward. The rain would soon stop, but the traffic had already been brought to a waterlogged standstill. I had an appointment in Quezon City that had taken me more than thirty years to arrange. And I had no desire, ever again in my life, to try and explain to resistant ears what led up to those final hours that left Tomoyuki Yamashita dangling from a rope at Los Banos.

PART ONE

OCTOBER 1944–AUGUST 1945

CHAPTER 1

For two days we zigzagged north and west up from Hollandia, making a snaking column one hundred miles long. The sea was heavy with us, frothing in our wakes. Two fleets of warships plowed the waters—aircraft carriers, battleships, cruisers, destroyers, oilers, cargo ships, personnel carriers, minesweepers, landing craft—seven hundred of them belching their smoke and churning their screws, heading unknowingly into perhaps the greatest naval battle of all time. Two hundred thousand soldiers waited puking and nervous in the holds and on the decks of the transport ships, ready to be offloaded and thrown against enemy positions in yet another steaming jungle. At night they cleaned their weapons, said their prayers, and wrote letters home. We were heading for Leyte.

I had embarked as the junior member of General MacArthur's staff on the cruiser USS *Nashville*. Our journey filled me with an almost superstitious dread. I did not like warships and in fact had enlisted in the army to be away from them. They too-often sank, and when they did they brought their sailors with them, making cold, steel, barnacled coffins deep in the yeasty surges of the still-volcanic, ever-erupting Pacific. For those of us who had not aspired to military careers, such unhappy conclusions had been the subject of much conversation in the uncertain days that followed Pearl Harbor. Viewing our choices, the war boiled down to different ways of dying. Would it be worse to sink and drown, or to fall like a shot quail from the air, or merely to crumple into the sweet grass from a bullet or artillery round?

In January 1942 I had weighed these options and finally acquiesced to facing death in the dirt. Luckily for me, the army took note of my ability to speak passing Japanese. Starved for such talent, they had sent me to language school instead of infantry training. I was then shipped immediately to the Pacific, where I spent five months as an interrogator-translator and then was ordered to MacArthur's staff. I was a good staff officer, something of a natural diplomat, enthusiastically obedient and always thorough. A recent top college athlete, I carried myself with a rugged self-confidence that seemed to accentuate my obeisance. MacArthur and his top generals had grown to like and trust me completely.

But behind my smiling facade was a profound sense of unworthiness. Every morning as I reported to the General's headquarters for my day's orders, I reminded myself that if it had not been for this stroke of luck by which I had learned to speak Japanese, my war would have been more predictable and far more dangerous. Indeed, my younger brother had taken the more traditional family route, his eight years of school and dumbifying Arkansas dialect ensuring him a role as an infantry private. As with my father and his father before him, he had turned into a brave and competent soldier. And he had died in June 1944, in a little town I had never heard of, during the invasion of France.

No, I was not born to this. I had never even seen a city until the age of fourteen, when one bleak rainwinter morning my mother awakened and announced to us that my dead father had come to her in a dream and told her that we should leave Arkansas and go to California. The corn shucks in my makeshift mattress rustled under me as I rubbed my eyes awake, watching her busily pack four cotton bags. It was obvious, watching her lined and furious face, that Daddy had meant for us to leave that very day.

My father's grave lay in a small cemetery just above a thickly wooded cow pasture, marked only by a favorite rock. We visited it together before we departed. Mother said a prayer for all of us and then promised Daddy that she wouldn't leave him buried in this lonesome field, that she would move him to California once things got better. He had been dead less than a year and I could still feel his presence, warm as a woolen sweater and filled with a knowing kindness that had irreplaceably disappeared from my life when they lowered his pine coffin into the hole.

As I stood over his grave for perhaps the last time, my father seemed alive again. Two hundred yards in front of me a thin herd of cattle grazed on winter grass. Off in the distance a squirrel gun went off, bagging someone's lucky supper. I tried to listen to his voice. I thought I heard him tell me that he had made a big mistake by staying in this cruel backwater place, that if he had only left instead of fighting its ugly reality, he would never have been laid into an early grave. I looked at the plain jagged rock of a tombstone that would not long remember him and I decided that he had told Mother the same thing in her dream the night before.

I had never seen even a picture that was as beautiful as the California coast. The morning after our bus arrived in Santa Monica I stood on the vast pier and smelled the salt air and the seafood cooking and watched the lazy pace of people walking and fishing, and I looked back toward the bluffs at the waves breaking over the sand and then the rows of lofty palm trees that disappeared northward toward Malibu and I will admit I cried. It had been beyond my capacity even to imagine such beauty and contentment. I was ragged and longhaired and laughed at but I felt my father's warmth surround me, and I vowed that I would never let my mother leave.

There were schools. I was smart. And just as important, at least for me, I discovered that I had a knack for carrying this nearly weightless leather object called a football and knocking people over when they tried to bring me to the ground. Mother objected fiercely, arguing that I should be working, but I found it to be great fun. Three years later she was stunned beyond amazement to find that top universities throughout the state were vying for the right to pay my way through college, asking only that I continue to show up in the afternoons after classes and play for a while with the other boys and on the weekends do the same before large crowds.

I chose the University of Southern California because it was near Mother and I could still help her on the weekends. She found work in a defense plant, and after mobilization worked twelve-hour shifts as a riveter, her small size ideal for climbing into the narrow nose sections of military aircraft. My brother was studying to become an electrician, knowing he would soon be called into the army.

Life was good in California, and the coming war only helped us.

Just off the campus, on a side street near Exposition Park, a Japanese family ran a grocery store, specializing in fresh fruits and vegetables brought in from the valley by other Asian immigrants. I was nineteen, in

my second year at Southern Cal, when I first saw Kozuko. She was standing in front of her father's store, arranging a sidewalk display of fruits and
vegetables. She was wearing a full white apron, tied tight around her tiny
waist. A red bandanna pulled her hair away from her face and clutched it
long and flowing down the center of her back. Her face was downturned,
frowning from some inner debate. She went about her work with such a
proud and careful delicacy that she might have been placing lush, exotic
flowers into a grand vase. But when she looked up and saw me, she
smiled.

I was enormously shy, still conscious of my full-voweled Arkansas accent and my unvarnished social etiquette. Southern Cal had actually
increased this shyness, despite my quick notoriety on the football field. It
was a high-tuition, sophisticated school, and I was not yet sufficiently
facile to turn my ragged journey into a party joke. I finally smiled back. I
had no reason to talk to her other than my awkward appreciation of her
beauty, but I finally mumbled that I wanted to learn to speak Japanese.
She told me she wanted to speak better English. We agreed to teach each
other. And within two weeks, over the objections of both our parents, we
were inseparable.

We fell together naturally, more as playmates than lovers, both outsiders, immigrants from different kinds of remoteness. And as I struggled to
please her, Kozuko opened up for me a fascination with Asia and its many
cultures. On the weekends in Santa Monica she and I would look out into
the vast, emptying darkness of the Pacific, practicing Japanese and talking
of the intricate culture that defined her parents' homeland. I began reading constantly, at times deep into Asian history and at others following the
trail of Japan's ongoing military conquests.

And then Pearl Harbor was attacked. Kozuko and her family were sent
to camps in Texas. I reported to the army. Japan became the hated enemy.
Indeed, its army and its rulers were vicious, unyielding, cruel to those they
conquered. But I never lost my fascination for its ancient greatness, and I
could never hate the Japanese as a people after I had known the sweetness
of Kozuko and seen the strength of her family.

I knew that the campaign for the Philippines would be long and
bloody. After two years in the Pacific I was already mind-weary, ready to
leave the army. And so as we proceeded toward Leyte I invented my own
little escapes. As the *Nashville* sliced and turned through the gleaming
royal blue waters I spent my free hours standing alone on its holy stoned
wooden main deck, under the long tubes of the eight-inch guns so that I

could not see them, and pretending I did not hear the boatswain's pipings as I peered out into the incessant waves. In those moments I imagined I was a tourist, on a luxury liner headed not to the France where my little brother had just died but to the old and glorious Paris where he somehow might still be alive.

I could not deceive the sea, though. It was all Pacific Asia, surging and playing, rocking the giant warship like a toy, entertaining us with escorts of flying fish and swirling, multicolored giant eels. Behind us were the festering, swampy jungles of New Guinea, where MacArthur had feinted, prodded, bombed, enveloped, and eventually bypassed a frustrated multitude of Japanese soldiers whose greatest desire had been to die for the emperor but who now were useless to the war. He was at his military best in those battles, cutting off the enemy from their sea lanes, dwindling their supplies rather than crushing them with the brutal, costly frontal assaults that Nimitz and the Marines were using in the central Pacific. He had left the enemy, as he put it, "dying on the vine."

The correspondents liked to write that a lot of soldiers hated MacArthur for his arrogance and showmanship, and in truth he was at times unbearable. But a multitude of them would not have been alive to feel these resentments had he not planned and directed their battles with such undeniable genius.

Ahead of us was fresh grist for all the passions MacArthur had conjured, and some new ones as well. The sprawling islands of the Philippines were indeed a military challenge, defended by four hundred thousand Japanese soldiers. But much more than that, they were MacArthur's great obsession. No place in the world, not even in America, so claimed MacArthur's emotions. He had begun his military career here, more than forty years before. His father had served here before him. He had spent another tour here as a general officer, between marriages and before he became army chief of staff. He had been rescued from the anonymity of early military retirement by becoming field marshal of the Philippines in 1936 when his regular army career was over. He had met his present wife on a ship as he headed to that assignment and had married her here. His son had been born here. His mother had died here. He had a singular place among the people of these islands, large and small, and he had promised them personally that he would return.

And there was something else. By now we knew the war had turned, that it would be won, if not in months, then soon, someday, inevitably. When that day came, we who had been reluctant but dutiful soldiers would go thankfully home. But what would our General do? Some, including Franklin D. Roosevelt in his darker moments, thought MacArthur might run for president, but we knew instinctively that he could never endure the indignities of true democracy. He had not even set foot in the United States since 1937. Some odd and unpredictable karma awaited him, a future that would be set in motion on the coming beaches. This was his true moment, the eve not of his retirement but of his enthronement, the day he had dreamed of during nearly three years of wandering through his own personal wilderness.

But he had to do much more than win a military campaign. He could not be truly great unless he was without enduring stain, and the Philippines had stained him deeply. He had suffered his most humiliating moment right here in the land that had always fed his greatest hungers.

Sometimes we were his stooges, at others we played the whore, but one could not rationalize, sympathize, or euphemize away the simple fact that he had been defeated by the Japanese in 1942. Not simply beaten but routed. Washington might be blamed, but MacArthur had not been ready either, despite four years of preparation. His air force had been bombed into uselessness on the ground twelve hours after the debacle at Pearl Harbor, the pilots and ground crews improperly forewarned, at first unable to believe that the attacking formations were Japanese and that they were in reality at war. His armies had been pushed back inches at a time down the Bataan Peninsula and then onto the rocks and caves of Corregidor. He himself had escaped the humiliation of capture, torture, and imprisonment that had been visited on his soldiers only by fleeing on a small PT boat to a faraway airstrip, where a plane carried him and his wife and child to Australia.

He had been defeated. And worse, he had abandoned his men under fire, in their most desperate moments.

But from Australia he had planned and implemented his personal and military revenge. He had taken it out a campaign at a time, his soldiers leapfrogging from one jungle battle to another, ever northward, always aiming at the Philippines. Because for a general who viewed himself as the greatest mind that had ever lived, the only retribution could be found not simply in victory but in an unholy excess of genius. And finally on these beaches and in the ensuing months the Japanese would taste and feel that kind of retribution in its full and flowery fury. With the move from Hollandia to Leyte, he was determined to leap from mere fame to a historic place no general had ever dreamed of.

For who was Napoleon but some poodle with hemorrhoids who wasted an army in the frozen tundra of the steppes? And who was Caesar, who in the end had pampered himself with such vanity that he could not control his own murderous staff? And who, particularly, was Yamashita, this bump in the road in front of MacArthur's charge toward immortality, this so-called Tiger of Malaya who had humiliated Percival in Singapore and then sent British prisoners of war parading through all the streets of conquered Asia to show the weakness of the soldiers of the West?

Who, indeed. This was MacArthur, cold and brilliant and in control, knocking on the door of greatness.

Leyte was a centerpoint in the Philippines archipelago, one of several midsized islands with names like Samar and Panaon and Dinagat that were clumped between the Philippine and Sulu Seas. Since it was far smaller than the main islands of Mindanao to the south and Luzon to the north, many questioned its strategic value. The Joint Chiefs of Staff had argued that MacArthur should establish bases in Mindanao, then leave the rest of the Philippines to "die on the vine" as he moved north to beachheads in Formosa and eastern China before the final assault on Japan. Others had called for a more cautious approach, a Mindanao landing in November, then a series of leapfrog moves northward to Luzon, home of Manila, the final, most important prize.

But MacArthur wanted Leyte, and he wanted it in October. He had chosen to invade here, he told us, because strategically it would cut Japan's shipping lanes in two, severing them from their petroleum and other resources that flowed from Borneo or through Singapore, while tactically it would divide the Japanese ground forces in the Philippines themselves. That may have been true. The president and Joint Chiefs finally bought this logic, and the navy had concurred. But I had been with him continuously for more than a year, and I knew there were other reasons.

Leyte was personal. It held the charms and ruins of his youth.

And so MacArthur had formed his strategy, badgered the government, tilted the ocean, and in the end swung whole fleets and armies into motion toward this small and little-known island, because it was from these beaches that he could best glorify the magnitude of his second coming. It seemed so obvious to me that I wondered why the rest of the government wasted its energy on weeks of complicated debate. Do not great men, the very few chosen by history to be remembered a thousand years hence, seem always to find in their crowning moments some mystifying event that appears to be a portentous coincidence of fate?

The evening before the invasion, he summoned nine of us who served on his personal staff to the *Nashville's* wardroom. The ship now gently undulated with what the sailors called ground swells, echoes of some nearby surf that told us we were approaching shore. As I walked down the darkened tunnels of red-lit passageways toward the wardroom I could hear and feel the distant rumblings of the big guns from our fire support ships and escort carriers as they unendingly pounded Japanese coastal defenses. The day before, army ranger battalions had taken two small islands guarding the entrance to Leyte Gulf, thus securing the flanks of our coming invasion. At that very moment, minesweepers and underwater demolition teams were already inside the gulf, clearing obstructions from the beachheads. For the last several days Allied aircraft had struck repeatedly at Japanese air bases far to the north in Formosa and China, to the east in the Marshalls and Carolines, and to our south in Mindanao and the East Indies, isolating Leyte from air attack.

The *Nashville* was in Condition One. Its sailors had become tense, preoccupied and electric. In a few hours they would go to battle stations. And at first light we would steam into the gulf, beginning the assault.

In the wardroom, MacArthur sat at the head of the large, cloth-covered dining table. Navy stewards slipped quietly in and out, bringing us ship-made cookies and great pots of hot coffee. The stewards placed their trays soundlessly at the center of the table and disappeared back into the kitchen. We just as soundlessly took our seats. As the most junior officer on his staff, I took my customary chair at the far end of the table, furthest from the General.

MacArthur lit his favorite corncob pipe, surveying us. He was smiling like a young boy. He twitched nervously in his chair, unable to contain his excitement. He was a handsome, gallant man who had no need to so carefully manufacture his charisma. At sixty-four his hair was still dark, his face thinly lined and his energy palpable. And back in Australia he had a much younger wife and a son just out of infancy. He had never consented to live in the world of his peers, and because of that MacArthur would never grow old with them.

I had met with him every day for more than a year, but I still felt a thrill when I heard him speak. His bearing and his choice of words were the same with an audience of one as they were in front of thousands. The world in which he lived was right-angled, erect and classical, and it took no respite from privacy. For a young man of twenty-three, to be in his presence was to be swept behind a magic screen into a royal court where centuries did not matter. I admired him boundlessly. And unlike others I took no jealousy from his egotism, for I knew that I would never seek to equal him. I was Jay Marsh, happy to be this close to greatness, and anxious to be done with war. Only God and Pinky could create a MacArthur.

"Get me a cup of coffee, Jay."

"Yes, sir."

Thrilled as ever to be recognized by my first name in the presence of these battlefield luminaries, I rose quickly, leaning over the center of the table and pouring him a fresh cup of steaming hot coffee. Then I placed it carefully before him with both hands, as if delivering him a treasure.

He nodded, blessing me with a rewarding smile, and sipped his coffee as I hurried back to my seat.

"Excellent coffee," he said, as if only his words would make it so.

He surveyed the array of senior officers who awaited his wisdom. "Well, gentlemen, the moment we've all dreamed of has finally arrived."

He went through a small list of details, making them seem grand. He ordered us to wear our helmets once the invasion began. He told us to remember to take our malaria pills. He held up the pages of a speech he would deliver into a Signal Corps radio microphone once he arrived onshore and sought our reactions to his proposed words. We nodded our agreement to each dictate, quibbled with a few phrases in his speech, took a few careful notes, sipped our coffee, ate our cookies, lit a cigarette or two, and waited for the main event.

Suddenly he stood and began pacing, his chin against his chest, and I knew we had reached the MacArthur Moment. As he paced, he reached into his trouser pocket and pulled out a small derringer. The derringer was old and scratched, small enough to disappear inside his hand when he closed it. MacArthur theatrically studied it and then produced two bullets, slowly loading them into its chambers. He displayed the pistol to us as he spoke.

"Most of you remember my father for having won the Medal of Honor as a very young man at Missionary Ridge in the Civil War, or perhaps for having been the senior general in the army before his retirement. But I consider his greatest days to have been here in the Philippines, both as a combat soldier and as military governor some forty-five years ago. He was the first senior American official to argue convincingly for the importance of these islands. He risked his life many times here and ended up with a price on his head. And he carried this derringer always, on the streets of the cities and into dozens of vicious battles against Filipino rebels, vowing that if he ever faced the prospect of being taken prisoner, he would kill himself first."

MacArthur stopped pacing and faced us. "The Japanese know where and when we are landing. Tokyo Rose has even broadcast to the world that I am on this very ship and am going ashore with our forces tomorrow. The enemy knows I am back, and they know what that means to those loyal Filipinos who have waited patiently through years of suffering and defiance for my return. If General Yamashita is wise, he will send a suicide squad to the beaches to try to capture or kill me. Think of it! Could there be a greater victory for the Japanese cause than to capture MacArthur and parade him through the streets of Manila as the battle rages behind him? But it will never happen. Because tonight I make the same vow to you that my father made: *I will die first!*"

He held the pistol loosely for another second, then slipped it quietly back into his pocket and resumed his pacing.

I sat amazed and enthralled, watching him walking back and forth, his chin down to his chest again as if he were in a trance, his lungs sucking in new inspiration from the dank and smoke-filled wardroom air. My logic told me that with the pounding the Japanese were already taking and with the ferocity of the invading soldiers who would precede us onto the beaches, what he had posited was a near impossibility. And yet one could not disagree that if MacArthur were indeed killed or captured on the invasion beach tomorrow, the impact on the Philippines campaign would be irreversible.

And that was his real point. In two short minutes, the General had reminded us that the coming campaign would not have taken place without his dogged insistence and would never succeed without him. And he had performed this feat by pulling from his pocket a symbol of courage and defiance that tied him to his father's heroic lore. This gesture itself was a subtle reminder that he and his father were the only father-son Medal of Honor winners in our nation's history, and at the same time refreshed our memories of his family's long historical ties to the Philippines. He had given us a near-perfect, metaphoric poem.

Now he stopped pacing and lifted up his head, facing us again. His voice became strong and urgent, like a football coach's during a halftime locker room talk.

"Tomorrow we strike. We will land just down the beach from Tacloban. This will be a very full moment for me. It was at Tacloban that I reported for my first duty assignment after leaving West Point. And as fate would have it, I reported to Tacloban forty-one years ago, on the very same day I will return! This is a symbolic omen that the Filipino people will understand. It is the kind of sign they look for in their own lives! When they learn I have returned they will rise up in the cities. They will unleash their guerrilla forces from the jungles. And we will deal the Japanese the swiftest, ugliest retaliation they have suffered in this long and costly war."

He started pacing again, looking at every one of his staff in turn as if wishing to bond personally with each of us. "There is more than a battle at stake here, gentlemen. I must seal our future with the most important islands in the Pacific other than Japan itself. And after that I must tame Japan. But the future does begin with battle. And in battle, brave men die, no matter how well the plans are conceived and no matter how flawlessly they are executed. So now I will return to my stateroom and read from my favorite biblical passages and pray to the Almighty that He will grant our gallant soldiers a swift and merciful victory. Good night."

We rose to our feet, standing at attention as he abruptly departed. After that we slowly retook our chairs, remaining alone with our coffee and cookies and small conversations. The usual, defensive cynicism of the lesser generals and senior colonels floated across the wardroom in little taunts, for by now they were used to his vanity, and comfortable with one another.

"You're welcome, General. Anytime, sir."

"Wait a minute, let me get this straight. Is he going to pray to God, or is God going to pray to him?"

"How's anybody else going to get shot when he's fighting this war all by himself?"

The sarcasm was short-lived, though. For behind the quick asides that protected other egos, they all knew that there was no better place to view a war than from the backseat as Douglas MacArthur steered our army through it.

I say "they" instead of "we," for I was a very junior officer, a note-taker, errand-runner, and coffee-pourer among very senior colonels and generals. As was my careful practice, I had said nothing as they ventilated their emotions. To some of these more senior officers, my mere continued presence after the meeting had ended was an act of presumption. And so within minutes I left also.

I needed to write another letter to my mother, who was unnecessarily worried about my safety in the wake of my brother's death. I was not really at risk, not like the infantrymen who tomorrow would busy themselves with slaughter. But I was also young and nervous, sick with the thought of battle.

D awn revealed a horizon of lush and epic grandeur, soon embellished by the sounds and smells of carnage. We had entered the gulf. Its serene and emerald waters were now cluttered with the imposing majesty of our armada. I awoke early and rushed from my stateroom to the main deck and began walking toward my favorite place just underneath the eight-inch guns. As I neared them the guns suddenly erupted with black smoke and ugly tongues of flame, spewing shells onto the whispery, smoking beaches with a series of explosions that cracked my ears and sent me stutter-stepping to catch my balance. The guns continued and I retreated, walking along the main deck toward the wardroom. Dozens of ships now joined in this heavy, thunderous barrage, until Leyte before us seemed to shift and reverberate from explosions and fairly disappeared behind a veil of smoke and haze.

After breakfast I stood on the bridge for hours. The *Nashville* laid to, and the barrage continued on the beaches, leaving trees stripped and broken and setting hundreds of buildings ablaze. Nearby the troopships dropped their heavy nets over the sides until the nets reached the sea and then an unending stream of burdened, struggling soldiers began to crawl down the nets toward the water. The soldiers worked the nets like ladders and then dropped down into rectangular landing craft that bobbed next to the troopships in the gentle sea. The small landing craft were lined up behind and beside one another in the water like waiting taxis. Each in its turn took on a load of assault troops and then powered away to the open waters. The craft gathered at their rallying points, circling and circling until all the other boats in their wave had joined the curling column. Finally the assault flags raised from the mother boats, signaling the invasion. The landing craft straightened out side by side into lines of assault waves, leaving long white tails of foam behind them as they churned toward the shore. Half of them went toward Red and White Beaches, near Tacloban. The other half approached Violet and Yellow Beaches, a few miles away, near Dulag.

On the beaches the shells still fell steadily, the drifting clouds of smoke and phosphorous continually replaced anew as explosions saturated the tall trees and the grass huts and tore into the enemy's positions. Lush, sharp hills rose abruptly behind the beaches. Now the shells crumped and flashed inside those tangles of rocks and trees and vines. The ships were "lifting" their guns away from the beachhead as the soldiers poured from their landing boats and seized positions just off the water. We knew that most of the Japanese would now be moving back from the beaches, seeking to draw our army into the hills and jungles, where artillery would not favor us, where rifles and grenades informed the battles, and where they could best attempt to take a life for every one they gave.

The skies filled also. Throughout the morning, dogfights burst into my vision like dancing kites. Enemy fighters suddenly would appear from behind the distant hills as they attempted to strike the ships in the gulf, only to be intercepted by American planes launched from nearby aircraft carriers. The Japanese had preserved their forces until MacArthur made his final move, wanting to fix his positions and to stall the ships. Now that much of the navy was at anchor they would try to confuse the assault and lure our guns away from the beaches. We did not yet know it, but the Japanese navy would soon make its boldest move of the war, in an effort to cripple our navy and to cut off support to the invasion force as it struggled to keep its beachhead ashore.

Through much of the morning, MacArthur stood on the bridge, flanked by a small group of senior officers. His mood alternated between serene self-confidence and childish anticipation. But his face became lit with undeniable ecstasy when the early sun rose above the smoking, belching beachhead and he could finally see the small town of Tacloban. He walked over to me and grabbed my shoulder, pointing toward it as if we were tourists, immune from the violence that surrounded us.

"Tacloban, Jay! There it is! It looks not a bit different from when I first saw it forty-one years ago this morning!"

I thought I noticed a rather obvious difference, so I ventured a careful response. "It's on fire, General."

He waved my irrelevant observation away as if he were swatting a mosquito. "Of course it is. The fires are the price of freedom. They'll go out, and the lights will go on. And Tacloban will be free!"

In great spirits, the General returned to his cabin for a quick lunch. When he returned on deck he was wearing a freshly pressed khaki uniform and his trademark sunglasses. He was ready to again set foot on the Philippines, and he wanted to do so in a crisp uniform while the guns blazed and the smoke still rolled down off the flaming hills.

A landing craft bobbed below us in the gentle waves, lashed to an external ladder that ran down the side of the ship. Our small staff boarded it along with a handful of war correspondents, followed by the beaming, effervescent MacArthur. Sunglassed, starched, and scrubbed, he looked picture-perfect. He even wore his famous soft military cap, after having ordered us to wear our helmets. Standing near him as the boat powered away toward a nearby ship I noticed that he was so adrenalized that his hands were trembling.

American aircraft now patrolled the skies overhead. Our small boat lashed up to a landing at the bottom of the troopship *John Land*'s external ladder. On the platform awaiting us were the leaders of the Philippines' government-in-exile, which MacArthur would reestablish at Tacloban. Its president, Sergio Osmena, its secretary for national defense, General Basilio Valdez, and the president's aide, Brigadier General Carlos Romulo, were pictures of mixed emotions as the boat's coxswain helped them aboard. Osmena descended slowly into our boat, nervous and visibly burdened by his coming tasks. He was trapped between the memory of the wildly popular Manuel Quezon, who had served as president of the exiled government until dying of tuberculosis a few months before, and a future with the near-spiritual presence of MacArthur, who was sure to overshadow his every move during the coming months. Osmena stifled a frown as MacArthur embraced him once he stepped inside the boat. And then we were off, powering toward the still-uncertain battleground of Red Beach.

The beaches in front of us were no longer contested, the bulk of the assault forces having gone further inland toward the smoking hills. But our bombardment had blown away most of the docks and piers, and those still standing were choked with supply boats and landing craft that were busily loading wounded soldiers. MacArthur noticed this as well. He called to our coxswain, asking him where he was going to land. The coxswain, a petty officer about my own age, searched frantically to his front for a place along the shore. Then suddenly the boat ground to a halt and it did not matter. Fifty yards from the beach we had run aground.

"What is the problem, Sailor?"

The coxswain threw his hands helplessly into the air, an apology. MacArthur scowled back at him, furious. Then as if to rebuke the lowly sailor he marched to the bow and ordered the boatswain to drop the front ramp of the landing craft. It fell slowly forward and MacArthur walked down its ramp, resolutely stepping out into the waves, followed by our little coterie of liberators. The General had dreamed long and worked hard for this moment, and no fool coxswain or mushy sandbar was going to deprive him of its fullness.

A newspaper photographer on the beach raised a lucky camera and caught it all: the perfect, redemptionist scowl and the jutting chin underneath the sunglasses and the ruination of the General's just-pressed trousers as he waded toward the beach from a few yards offshore. The picture became instantly famous, dramatizing the moment of MacArthur's return far better than speeches and maps ever could. The world did not know that the General's fierce frown was mostly the product of his pique at the careless coxswain for having dumped him off on the edge of a sandbar at the very moment of his prophesized and acutely choreographed return.

But it was his moment, and he seized it with relentless purpose. The island, the anniversary, the exiled Filipino leaders, even the ongoing battle itself provided mere backdrop for the message MacArthur was intent on sending by standing on the invasion beach only hours after the first wave of assault troops had poured from their boats. The message went worldwide, but the symbols MacArthur was piling up hour by hour were meant to be digested here. In East Asia, myth and bravado were the building blocks of power. MacArthur was showing them the very omnipotence of his return. He had not been driven out, he had escaped in order to find and energize the reinforcements. He had not sent the liberating troops, he had brought them. He was not afraid to die in battle, he was like his father before him bred to it, at home under fire.

Throughout the afternoon he treated the world to a one-man standup theater. Sniper rounds cracked overhead as he strode the fresh battleground. Japanese soldiers could be heard in the near distance, calling out insults in broken English. He brought us forward, calmly seeking the sound of the guns, unflinching under fire, surprising many infantry soldiers with his sudden appearance.

Near one foxhole he turned over the bodies of two freshly killed

Japanese soldiers with his foot, identifying their unit insignia. "Good," he said, making sure his infantrymen as well as the correspondents heard him. "These soldiers are from the regiment that did the dirty work at Bataan." For even on Leyte, even in the midst of another battle, the humiliation of that campaign was never far from his mind.

As evening approached we returned to the relative calm of Red Beach. MacArthur took a seat on the log of a newly fallen coconut palm. For the first time showing the edges of weariness, he stared for a long moment into the yeasty, smoking jungle.

"Jay," he finally called, summoning me.

"Yes, sir." I jogged up to him, nervous and exhausted by the enormity of our day.

"My field message pad."

I reached into my knapsack and handed him a notepad and a pen. Sniper bullets still visited the beach area. In the distance a fierce firefight erupted. Mindless to the sounds of battle, MacArthur scrawled out two letters. Once finished, he rose from the log. Nearby a group of soldiers and the exiled Philippines leaders waited for him at a just-off-loaded truck. They had hooked up the Signal Corps microphone. He would soon broadcast his announcement throughout the Philippines that the Americans were again on Philippines soil.

He handed the letters to me as he passed me on the way to the waiting microphone. "Post these."

"Yes, sir."

I could not contain my curiosity. Walking behind him, I quickly read over the letters he had written. The first was to President Roosevelt, who over the years had been alternately a friend and fierce rival. The note was subtly boastful yet also shrewdly ingratiating, as if his warrior father had written the note and his calculating but wise mother had carefully edited it. He informed the president that he was writing from near Tacloban and that this was the first message sent from the "freed Philippines," adding that it might be appropriate for his "philatelic collection" and that MacArthur hoped "it would get through" from the battlefield. He then protected himself from his critics by reinforcing the strategic value of the invasion. Aware that the letter would no doubt be leaked, he asked that Roosevelt consider granting the Philippines immediate independence. He finished with more self-congratulation by apologizing for the writing equipment, noting that he was "on the combat line with no facilities except this field message pad."

The second, shorter note was to his wife, Jean, back in Australia. He told her he had returned, and that he hoped soon they would be together in their former home in Manila. He signed the note, "Love, MacArthur."

Love, MacArthur. I snickered quietly despite my almost fearful regard for the Great Man. It was as if I had just peeked into the privacy of his bedroom. Did she call him MacArthur when they made love? Did he ask her to get MacArthur an aspirin when he had a headache? Or did he perhaps think she might not recognize the handwriting if he had merely signed it, *Love, Doug?*

As MacArthur neared the waiting Signal Corps microphone it began to rain. This was his most important moment of the day. His hands were trembling again as he took the microphone. He started to speak and then took a step back, looking down, testing his voice, for the first time that day seeming almost unsure of himself. The rain attacked us now, East Asian rain, torrential and insistent. In the foothills the fighting holes would fill with water tonight. MacArthur nodded to the technician and began speaking into the microphone. I struggled mightily to listen to his words in the rain with the sound of gunfire in the distance and the big shells from the ships still screaming over us and crunching into distant hills.

"People of the Philippines," he began, "I have returned. By the grace of Almighty God, our forces stand again on Philippine soil." He faded in and out of my helmeted earshot, but his voice grew stronger as he spoke. "Rally to me," he was saying. "Let the indomitable spirit of Bataan and Corregidor lead on. Rise and strike. Strike at every favorable opportunity. For your homes and hearths, strike! For future generations of your sons and daughters, strike! Let no heart be faint!"

President Osmena and General Romulo followed MacArthur to the microphone, and in a few rainwashed minutes the ceremony was over. The weather whipped us as we headed down the beach to find the boat that would take us back to the *Nashville*. We did not yet know it, but the Japanese fleet was riding in behind the rain. In a few days the Japanese would bet almost their entire navy on knocking us off the beaches and out of the Pacific. The Battle of Leyte Gulf would begin in terror but would end with the virtual destruction of the enemy's fleet.

On the boat heading out to the *Nashville* the General cast a longing eye toward Tacloban, still smoldering despite the rain. He smiled broadly, his face now serene and confident. MacArthur was on the move. It had been a complete day for him. He had not only reclaimed his past but had laid down a stake for his future, the final leavings of a life well fought, with much to do after wars were over. MacArthur had always clung to a vision of himself as the great spiritual benefactor of the Philippines, but it was clear to me he believed his understanding of the ways of these islands transcended their sprawling reach. His grasping, cunning intellect sought now to embrace all of Asia.

In the landing craft the moon was for a moment shining through the rainful sky, casting us in a pale and eerie glow. It reflected on MacArthur's wet face. And in his eyes I saw a look that told me he had made a secret vow.

CHAPTER 2

At Leyte our soldiers continued to pour ashore and press into the rain-
soaked jungle. Soon we left the ship and joined them, stopping at
the water's edge. As was his practice, the General chose for our
headquarters Tacloban's most beautiful mansion, which the Japanese had
used as their officers club. Its owner, an American businessman named
Walter Price, was at that time imprisoned at Santo Tomas, outside Manila. His Filipina wife, who had been tortured by the Japanese earlier in
the war, was living in the jungle with their children.

When told that MacArthur wanted to use her house, Mrs. Price was
reported to be flattered, insisting that we stay as long as we liked. And so
MacArthur, ever courtly, ever chivalrous in his decorum, gratefully sang
her praises as he seized her house and left Mrs. Price and her children to
their own devices. And we stayed at her mansion in Tacloban for three
more months.

Out at sea, a once-great navy died. Just after the invasion the Japanese
launched a bold but eventually disastrous naval attack, trying to dislodge
our fleet and destroy our transports and thus regain control of Leyte. For

three days the waters around us were filled with the sounds of heavy guns and droning aircraft as hundreds of ships converged from distant points. Their energies spent, the Japanese precipitously retreated, leaving four aircraft carriers, three battleships, six heavy cruisers, three light cruisers, and eight destroyers at the bottom of the sea. Leyte Gulf had been a spike through the imperial navy's heart. Their navy would continue to fight, but it would never again pose a serious threat.

In the jungle all was mud. Out in the rain our soldiers endured an earthquake and three typhoons. Beyond the beaches the troops moved forward underneath leaking ponchos and the Japanese stood firm in insect-laden mud holes and both sides fought until they died. The General ordered airfields to be built but the slick, mud-covered ridges mocked him. Whole convoys of trucks lost their way, sliding door-deep into mucky road banks.

Each afternoon the mud-smeared trucks passed in front of the Price mansion on their way back from the front lines, having exchanged their loads of food and ammunition for that day's tally of dead and wounded soldiers. The soldiers who could still stand and see peered numbly from the truck beds down at us in our clean and pressed uniforms and our mudless boots, telling us all we wanted to know of life on the other side of the mountain.

Thus motivated, I thankfully shuttled about my little tasks, happy to be a few miles from the blood and drek. We who shared this beachfront headquarters communicated our good fortune to one another without words, as if to mention it would cause us to be taken from our lovely sanctuary and sent out to die. Combat engineers who might otherwise have been building pontoon bridges or blowing up captured ammunition grinned conspiratorially as they daintily patched bullet holes in the stucco and followed MacArthur's orders to level off the lawn so that his view might be improved. He did love the view as he paced the wide veranda and looked out at the mountains and the sea. Enemy soldiers hid in those mountains, but old memories laced them too, warm reminders of his youth.

The weeks passed. We took Dagami and Burauen, then pushed against the Japanese positions in the central mountains, capturing the key towns of Baybay and Carigara. More Japanese arrived to fight. Against his wishes, General Yamashita had been ordered by the general staff in Tokyo to reinforce Leyte from faraway Luzon, thinking he might turn the island into a decisive battlefield. Half of the Japanese replacements were drowning at sea as our navy sank their transports. But three divisions of reinforcements had already entered through the port of Ormoc and joined the battle. So we attacked and closed the port.

I knew all these intricacies even then, because MacArthur loved to talk about them to anyone who would listen. And now that the beachhead was secure, a constant stream of media and dignitaries began arriving at Tacloban. It was one of my main duties to be their escort. The General was fond of showering them with elaborate, map-filled briefings. He was at his grandest when pacing before a ceiling-high situation map and pointing out the pivots and the turns of battle, his hands making sweeping gestures that brought a grandeur to the muddy, small-unit brawls. It was his favorite place also to compare his brilliance with the more mundane trudgings of Eisenhower's European effort and the numbing casualty counts from the Marine Corps assaults to our north in the central Pacific drive. To MacArthur, Eisenhower was still the soft-voiced, baby-faced subordinate who tended to his ego years before in one staff assistant job after another, while the Marines were a mindless bunch of overpromoted sergeants, wasting their people in frontal assaults because they lacked his finesse.

He had a knack for luring visitors into certain questions and then springing his own verbal ambush. He was behind his own schedule for retaking Leyte, but when the question came up he would stiffen with a form of irate majesty. "I could retake Leyte in two weeks," he would assure his questioners. "But I have too great a responsibility to the mothers and wives in America to do that to their men. I will not take by sacrifice what I can achieve by strategy!"

Despite our successes MacArthur seemed lonely, given to fits, often deeply depressed. During the Leyte campaign Congress awarded him a fifth star, making him one of only a handful ever to reach that rank, and not even that seemed to cheer him. Something else was bothering him, something deeply personal, beyond the ability of his uncanny acting talents to conceal. I knew instinctively what it was, though I would never have dared to speak this truth even to another staff member: having returned to Leyte, the General was indeed looking into the distant mirror of his youth. And there was a sense of loss in this four-decade journey that had troubled him.

Slowly, despite my admiration and my fear, a part of me had come to pity Douglas MacArthur. Gaggles of sycophants crowded around him, competing for his graces. Some sought to flatter him and to copy his mannerisms. Most looked to him for solutions. But secretly they envied

him his eminence and in private loved to trash the very vanity that ineluctably propelled his greatness.

And some of it he brought upon himself. There is a tragedy that comes
with MacArthur's kind of fame. When one measures a life by the enemies
he has conquered rather than the friends he has made, it becomes important never to run out of battles. For what then is peace but a debilitating
emptiness?

But that was not all of it. What was it, I kept asking myself, that this
great man so deeply wished for as he stared out from the veranda of the
Price mansion at the mountains and ridges that had informed his youth?
And then one night in early November I decided that I knew.

Just after dinner I was summoned outside the mansion by a military
policeman who told me a young Filipino man wanted to talk to the
General. I greeted the young man fifty yards down the road, where he
waited in front of a nearby house. Shafts of light from the house illuminated a clear-eyed, serious face. I could tell that he was about my age,
tight-skinned and muscular, with the close-cropped hair of a disciplined
guerrilla fighter. Behind him, under the fragrant purple blossoms of a
frangipani tree, an older woman watched us expectantly. She was wearing
a beautiful yellow dress. The dress seemed to shimmer from the distant
light like a low, reflected moon. I could not take my eyes off of it. It
seemed incongruous, too beautiful and elegant for the rain and mud and
war that then surrounded us.

The young man's eyes grabbed mine unblinkingly, and he squared his
body before me, clearly regarding me as an equal. "Who are you?"

"I'm Lieutenant Jay Marsh," I said. "I work for the General."

"How do I know that?"

His bluntness both impressed and offended me. I towered over him,
and my rank was clearly visible on my uniform, even in the dim light. But
neither my size nor my having just left the inside of the General's personal
residence fazed him. It finally occurred to me that he was on a mission,
and that he would lose great face if he failed.

"I guess you'll just have to trust me on it," I finally answered.

He thought about that for a moment, looking at me and then back at
the woman underneath the frangipani tree. Finally she nodded to him, an
approval.

"All right," he said. And then he caught himself. "Does MacArthur
trust you?"

"So far. I'm still here, aren't I?"

He continued to stare seriously at me, apparently not getting my little joke. For it was common knowledge on MacArthur's staff that if the General lost his trust in a junior officer, a day would not pass before the unlucky subaltern was out in the mud, chomping on K rations, slapping away mosquitoes, and waiting to be shot. Finally I began walking toward the woman, sensing that she was in control.

"Let's put it this way," I said as the young man walked alongside me. "You're not going to do any better than me, so you can either talk to me or go back where you came from."

She moved toward us as we walked, and soon the three of us were gathered at the edge of the sweet-blossomed tree. Her hair was pulled back behind her face. She wore small gold loops of earrings. She was fair-skinned and oval-faced, of mixed blood, probably from some Spanish priest or soldier of long ago, as were so many in these islands. She had a strong face and a certainty in her eyes that made me think of the great women of history who had suffered and endured and somehow prevailed. She seemed nearly as old as MacArthur, but like him she had held her age well. And she was not in the least bit afraid.

"This is my nephew Ponce," she said, as if trying to excuse his rude-ness. "He is a very famous fighter here and on Samar. And you must not be offended by him, he is sometimes too loyal."

"This is my aunt," said Ponce, returning the favor. "Her name is Con-suelo Trani. MacArthur wants to see her."

"How do I know this?" I asked.

She smiled slowly. "Maybe you should ask Douglas."

Douglas, I thought, walking alone toward the mansion. She calls him *Douglas*? No one except for presidents and royalty, not even his wife, called MacArthur "Douglas," at least not anymore.

He was on the veranda, pacing slowly, smoking his pipe and looking out toward the sea. That afternoon five reporters, including the publisher of the *New York Times*, had visited him. Waving at the ever-present maps, he had walked them through the Philippines campaign in intricate detail. Then he had surprised them by holding forth grandly on the future of the war with Japan and Germany and of the growing threat of the Soviet Union once the war was finished. He had stunned them by announcing that the key to Asian stability after the war would be a peaceful and prosperous Japan and that only a strong relationship between Japan and the United States would limit Soviet expansion. He had teased them by saying he already was designing a seven-point program to be put into place once Japan was defeated. Even here, in the wilderness of Leyte where he had first served as a young lieutenant, he could see beyond the carnage and predict where next his country would be threatened.

As I had escorted the men out of his room one reporter had blurted out to another, almost without thinking, "He is the most arrogant man I have ever met in my life."

"Yes," observed the other. "And the most brilliant."

They were common observations, MacArthur's yin and yang. And yet now he stood alone on the veranda, far from the power centers where such subjects were being debated, his very arrogance and brilliance having brought him here to this jungled, isolated epicenter of his own personal returning. He seemed oddly peaceful, though, so lost in thought that he did not even hear my approach.

"General?" I spoke quietly, as if awakening him from sleep. I was still uncertain if I should bother him, and embarrassed at my unnoticed arrival.

"Yes, Jay?" he answered, having recognized my voice without even turning to see me.

"There's someone here to see you, sir. Her name is Consuelo Trani."

Far behind us on the other side of the mountains we could hear the muffled booms and cracks of a distant battle. More soldiers were dying in the mud, and tomorrow more bodies would be trucked in from the front lines to be buried in the new cemetery we had started just down the road. Out in the bay a flight of navy planes droned by. MacArthur continued to watch the sea, silently puffing on his pipe. I began to wonder if he had heard me. Then finally he spoke.

"An old friend," he said. And then he turned to me, as if catching himself and searching for something more officious. "From a very good family, by the way. Her father was helpful to me after the massacre at Balang Higa." He saw that I had no memory of Balang Higa and smiled. "Forty years ago, Jay. In another life. Where is she?"

"I'll get her, sir."

As she stepped onto the veranda he greeted her with a pained and awkward stare, not even speaking. In her eyes I could see the pride that comes from a possessive, long-held certainty, as if he had fulfilled his destiny just for her. Ponce and I were both too young to understand the full dimensions of their silent greeting and too foreign to each other even to converse in depth. But it took neither age nor an interpreter to know that something powerful and yet hopeless was passing between them as

MacArthur took Consuelo's hand and welcomed her to his temporary home.

As if by silent command, Ponce and I left them on the veranda and walked together back toward the road in front of the mansion. Ponce glanced behind his shoulder as we walked, as if he might somehow still see them. Then he stared up into my face.

"He wrote her many letters," he said. "I have read them."

I remained silent, trudging uncomfortably toward the road. In truth, I preferred to keep my vision of MacArthur simple and military. I did not want to know any more of what Ponce so clearly wanted to share with me.

"His mother would not let them marry," said Ponce, still searching my face for some reaction. "What future would an American officer have, married to a Filipina? Tell me that. They would think he had lost his mind. And maybe he would want to run for president. How could he do that with a Filipina wife? What do you think of that?"

MacArthur with a Filipina wife? I did not know what to think of that. Because Ponce was right. In the army they would have talked quietly about him in sad murmurs, noting that the brilliant young officer had irretrievably "gone Asian." He would never have been promoted to general, much less made army chief of staff. And so he would never have become MacArthur. I dismissed the thought, pulling out a cigarette from my breast pocket and lighting it as we walked.

"Lucky Strikes," said Ponce, pointing to my cigarette pack as we continued to walk. "Lucky Strike Green has gone to war, isn't that what they say? I read it in *Life* magazine. An advertisement. But that was two years ago. Maybe three. Do they still say that? May I have one?"

I gave him mine and lit another. We had reached the road. On the far side of the mountains the battle had begun again. Ponce inhaled deeply, savoring the rich tobacco flavor of an American cigarette. "I am not lying," he finally said. "We are of a good family."

"The General told me that," I answered.

"So you know?"

"No," I said, not only uncomfortable with what he had told me but suddenly fearful that MacArthur might be angered or even threatened by my very knowledge. "I only know what the General tells me, and that is all he told me."

"She never married, you know. She never will. That is the way of our people, at least here in the Visayas. He took her. She is his."

"He is married," I finally replied. "He's been married twice."

"Married or never married, it doesn't matter," said Ponce, his eyes resting protectively on the distant, darkened veranda. "Did you know the Spanish were here for three hundred years? Yes, I think you must know that. And the priests could never marry. But if a priest took one of our women and he loved her and she loved him, then she was his. No one else's, do you understand? Who could take a priest's lover for his wife? What would God think? MacArthur came and he was more powerful than a priest. His father was governor general! So who would she marry after she was with MacArthur? She has loved him for forty years. She will always love him. It is the way of our people. To the last breath. To the last drop of blood. It is how we fight—*waray waray*. And how we love."

"I don't understand that," I said.

"You don't have to," said Ponce, almost absently. "It's not your burden." In the house across the street I could see people watching us from the now-darkened porch. I found myself wondering if they also were listening. "Anyway," said Ponce, "He did not bring his wife."

"She's in Australia," I said. "We're fighting a war here."

"He will bring her to Manila, even if there's fighting," continued Ponce, as if presenting evidence. "My aunt is here in a piña dress, even though there's fighting."

"That doesn't prove anything."

"I don't have to prove anything," said Ponce, giving me a suddenly sly look. "Who are you? Why are you here at the headquarters in Tacloban instead of fighting in the jungle?"

"Because MacArthur trusts me."

"So far," he answered, now winking to show he had indeed gotten the import of my earlier joke.

"So far," I agreed. I understood his unspoken point and resolved to keep my mouth shut about Ponce and Consuelo and all the rest of it. At the same time I began to wonder if this incident might be my undoing simply because I had observed it.

Ponce stood silent for a moment, then looked over at my breast pocket. "May I have another cigarette?" I handed him the full pack of Lucky Strikes. He took only one and abruptly forced the pack back into my hands, his urgency telling me I had threatened his pride. He cupped his hands around the cigarette as I struck my lighter for him, as if he were still in the jungle and was worrying about snipers. Then he pulled away, looking again toward the veranda.

"MacArthur came back here for her." He spoke with a certainty that I knew had come from many conversations, as if it were now common knowledge in the islands.

"I told you, Ponce, he's married."

"Not to marry her. Not to keep her." Now he seemed irritated, as if I were too naive to understand. "To honor her. We all know that."

"He came here to win the war."

"I know," said Ponce, dragging on the cigarette and blowing smoke toward the Price mansion. "He is almost like Christ to us."

He paused, considering my face as if looking for signs of intelligence, then again looked away. "Six thousand islands in our country and he chose Leyte. Mindanao? No. Luzon? Not yet. Leyte. The whole American army, right here. To win the war. And also to honor my aunt. He will always love her but he can never have her. So this was his gift, that he came back to liberate her first."

It somehow embarrassed me to hear Ponce say those words, but I also found myself believing that they might be true. Standing on the road with Ponce I tried to imagine MacArthur at twenty-three, the same age as I myself at that moment, posted from the unforgiving social bridle of West Point to this jungled yet seductive outpost, for the first time away from an ever-dominant mother and falling in love with this still-beautiful mestiza who was now visiting alone with him on the back veranda of the Price mansion. Real love. Not the society-page, wear-the-right-furs love of his first wife, whom he did not marry until age forty-two and who shortly thereafter humiliated him with her blatant trysts and wanderings. Not the furtive, almost pornographic love of the Eurasian movie actress he kept in downtown Washington while he was army chief of staff, providing her with a limousine and dressing her in black-lace lingerie in her secret apartment while he lived with his mother at Fort Myer. Not the mature, dinner-hosting, "Love, MacArthur" love he surely felt for Jean, whom he married at fifty-seven after his mother had died in Manila.

Real love. Was this another secret that America's greatest living actor kept hidden as he earnestly portrayed not the MacArthur who lived but the MacArthur he wanted history to remember?

Had this chiseled, preening Hannibal ever felt the kind of love that left him gasping but certain as he pressed her hard against him in the sultry darkness while the gentle wind blew in from the sea and caressed their joined and naked bodies, carrying with it the warm perfume of plumeria and the glorious night-blooming jasmine? Had he awakened in her arms when the sky began to blue and the roosters crowed and the water bulls began to stir, then walked happy and fulfilled in dawn's light to the village well, soaping and laughing as he towered above yapping puppies and the stares of delighted children? Did he bring back two buckets of fresh water so that she might wash herself and then make him breakfast? Had they fed each other jackfruit and *macapuno* and sweet golden papayas, laughing as the juice dripped from their chins onto their naked chests, all the while lost inside each other's eyes, wanting only to fall again into each other's arms? When he was with her did she make him feel as though there were no other place but Leyte and Samar?

That kind of love. The kind that opened up to him a world both wonderful and forbidden. The kind that would in the end force him to choose between mother and lover, between the destiny he owed his father and lost brothers and the happiness he might dare to ask for himself. The kind of love, once lost, that made it impossible ever really to love again.

At that moment I could see MacArthur swept along by that kind of love and then harshly pulled away from it by his mother—or who knows, perhaps even pushed away by a wiser and somehow more knowing Consuelo Trani—so that after it was lost, there was only a career to be made and a destiny to be pursued. And yet never losing that passion when he thought of her, indeed never allowed to see it ripen into the mundane rhythms of the decades, so that this love grew all the more powerful and exotic because he knew he could never really have it. So that in the end the final gesture to the love he was never allowed to keep and the life he had chosen not to live was to bring his army back to Leyte, freeing Consuelo and her family first, and in that way assuring her that what the two of them had been forced to give up somehow was for a purpose, that as they slid toward their dotage on separate islands or continents there had been meaning in their sacrifice.

I could not have you, and after I could not have you my fate became only to have my army, so now I will truly return, not only to the Philippines but to the very embryo of all that made me not only great but half fulfilled. I will bring my army to Leyte, to Tacloban, to you, rescue you and elevate you in the eyes of your people as a symbol of the impossible love that reason and fate forced us to throw away.

Yes, I thought. I did not know if it was true, but with MacArthur it was so grand and preposterous as to be eminently possible. And this to me explained his darkest moods. On Leyte he was surrounded by the dreams that he had dealt away like a young Faust in exchange for a glorious career, while at the same time he was separated from the wife and toddler son that had eventually replaced them.

Ponce and I waited on the road for another hour. Then again as if by silent command we walked together back to the house and slowly approached the veranda. MacArthur and Consuelo were not there. Hesitantly, I peeked inside the house but saw nothing in the darkness. Then I heard Ponce, whispering behind me.

"There!" he said.

I turned and saw him pointing across the wide lawn to the beach. Following his finger, I finally saw a tall silhouette standing underneath the coconut trees, next to the lapping waves. But I could not see her.

"Where is she?"

Ponce grinned, as if vindicated. "They are together!"

Looking more closely, I saw that he was right. They were embracing. As we watched, MacArthur suddenly turned, looking toward us, and then took Consuelo's hand and walked further down the beach.

Watching them walk away I felt soiled and voyeuristic. I was ashamed of myself for watching, and despite his power and greatness I felt sorry for the General. Because I now believed Ponce's story.

"I'm going to bed," I said. And I left Ponce alone on the veranda.

The next morning after breakfast, MacArthur called me into his room. He was pacing, clutching a stack of papers, cables from Washington and reports from the field. When I entered he fixed me with a look that almost dared me to disagree.

"She was telling me about the death of her father," he said.

"Yes, sir," I answered.

"I was very close to their family."

"That's what Ponce told me," I said, wanting to be done with it.

"Yes, Ponce," said MacArthur, scrutinizing my face, his eyes telling me what his words had no need to say. "A very brave soldier, famous among the guerrillas. They're a very important family, both here and in Samar. And they're welcome here at any time, Jay. Take care of it."

And so I did, several times a week.

CHAPTER 3

★ ★ ★ ★ ★

On December 15 our soldiers invaded the island of Mindoro, giving us air bases only two hundred miles southwest of Manila. The day after Christmas MacArthur announced that the Leyte operation was over, except for what he termed some "minor mopping up." In his announcement he proclaimed that "General Yamashita has sustained perhaps the greatest defeat in the military annals of the Japanese." Both of these observations were at once odd and premature, for he knew it would take several more months of rugged, exhausting fighting to finish off the thirty thousand Japanese still dug in at Leyte. And he had yet actually to face Yamashita at all.

On January 9, 1945, we landed at Lingayen Gulf, just down from the very spot where the Japanese had invaded three years before. But now both sides were playing on a much larger scale. We had approached Luzon with nearly a thousand ships, and 280,000 soldiers—more than had landed at Sicily, and more than would fight in the battles of Iwo Jima and Okinawa combined. Yamashita waited with 262,000 men, more than twice the number that would defend the home island of Okinawa and more than ten times the forces on Iwo Jima, by far the largest army the Americans would face in any of the Pacific campaigns.

But Luzon was as large as Ireland, a vast strategic canvas laced with mountains and jungles. Rather than allowing his forces to be bottled up in the cul-de-sac of the Bataan Peninsula, Yamashita withdrew most of his army into the Zambales Mountains west of Clark Field and far away to the north in the mountains near Baguio. A smaller, principally naval force stayed behind in Manila.

From our landing place at Lingayen Gulf, Yamashita was to the north and Manila was to the south. General Walter Krueger, the field commander, was carefully deploying his forces in both directions. But MacArthur wanted Manila. Daily, sometimes hourly, he was pushing Krueger to advance. MacArthur, never particularly cautious but usually clever, was now impelled by his emotions, ready to burst with frustration. He sullenly marked his sixty-fifth birthday on January 26, without having budged Krueger and without entering Manila.

"Get to Manila! Get to Manila!"

But the Prussian-born Krueger would not budge. Now wearing four stars, he had first served in the Philippines as a private under MacArthur's father. Krueger knew the terrain of Luzon better than anyone, and he also knew MacArthur's mercurial moods. He realized all too well that he would be blamed if the attack went wrong.

On January 29 General Robert Eichelberger, another of the leaders some had facetiously come to call "MacArthur's Germans," landed south of Manila, making an immediate, daring dash toward the city. That same day Krueger finally ordered the just-arrived First Cavalry Division to race southward, creating a double envelopment of the capital. On their way in, Krueger's forces liberated prisoner of war camps at Cabanatuan, Muntinglupa, and Santo Tomas. And on February 3 our soldiers finally entered Manila.

MacArthur had thought the city would be left undefended. Instead the imperial navy garrison left behind by Yamashita, bent on fighting to the last man, resisted our soldiers in one of the most suicidally destructive battles of the entire war. The Japanese mined the streets. They made bunkers out of houses. They took naval weapons and turned them into point-blank artillery pieces. And for a month they fought the advancing Americans until the last of them had died.

Worse, in the midst of the battle the Japanese went on a sick and murderous rampage. The port facilities and the entire business district were deliberately destroyed, as were most of the factories, utilities, and housing areas. By the time the last Japanese had been rooted out of the last room in the last rubble of what used to be downtown Manila, one hundred thousand Filipinos had been killed. Hospitals had been set afire with patients deliberately strapped to their beds. Men had been routinely mutilated. Women and even young girls had been raped. Small children and babies had been slaughtered and desecrated.

There would be no victory parade, no joyous celebration, no garlands of *sampaguita* thrown around the necks of marching soldiers by thankful, smiling, slender-waisted Filipinas. Unlike Leyte, MacArthur's return to Manila could not have been more devastating. Personally, he had lost most of the treasures in his prewar home at the Manila Hotel. Strategically, the heart of the country's government and economy was in ruins. And as a military leader he had to take moral responsibility for putting into motion an assault that led to a level of suffering greater than any other American ground attack on any city in the entire war.

And it was not just any city being attacked by any American. It was the city in which he had spent long years of his life, the city whose people revered him above all other places on earth. In many ways, MacArthur had just attacked and seen the destruction of his own hometown.

I t is almost embarrassing to repeat this, but as I have said, my own war was different. For it was in the midst of all this carnage, on a road filled with death, that I fell in love. Her name was Divina Clara Ramirez. I met her in early February during the First Cavalry Division's dash toward Manila.

Unlike in Leyte, where he rarely left the mansion in Tacloban, after the landing at Lingayen Gulf, MacArthur was constantly agitated, always in motion. He inspected infantry units even as they fought. He went up in a B-17 bomber to observe an airborne drop. At one point he personally rallied a regiment under attack by Japanese tanks when the American forward positions began to lose their nerve. He wanted to be everywhere at once. We were forever on the roads, with him or behind him, like the tail of a dancing kite.

MacArthur had quit for the day, and I was taking a jeep back to a temporary camp near San Miguel. The road was moonlike, cratered and broken by bombs, washed into gullies by a recent incessant rain. Traffic was unending, dominated by rumbling, surging tanks and military trucks. On both sides of the road our aircraft were making repeated bombing runs. Overhead, the skies danced with dogfights between Japanese and American planes. All around me was a terrible destruction that on the one hand was ubiquitous and on the other had assumed an odd normality: nipa shacks and markets aflame, churches and schools knocked to pieces, cars and trucks ripped open and burning, and everywhere the bombs and artillery that seemed never to end. And far to the front as I drove, like a false dawn on the grey horizon, I could see the pulsing of more bombs and the orange tongues of reaching flames as Manila began to quake and burn.

She was beside the road, sitting inside a brightly colored *caratela*. The small pony that had been pulling the little two-wheeled cart had been startled by a passing tank and had slipped into a mud hole, breaking its leg. The pony was now lying on its side, snorting and struggling, hopelessly trying to regain its footing. Its eyes were bulging with fear. It was still harnessed to the *caratela*. The *caratela* swayed dangerously as the pony twisted and whinnied. As I neared her in my jeep I watched a young Filipino walk up to the pony, shaking his head apologetically as if the animal could understand what was about to happen, and then shoot it between the eyes.

I pulled off the road behind the *caratela* and walked up to her. She was still sitting in the cart, her knees together, clutching a wooden box protectively against her. The box was as wide as her shoulders, and as high as her chest. It was intricately and beautifully carved from *narva*, the Philippines' most precious wood. She was crying, more from anger than despair, all the while shouting commandingly in Tagalog to the young man, who now was holding his hands helplessly up into the air and shaking his head as if denying responsibility.

I could tell not only that she was beautiful but that she had taken great pains to hide her beauty. She wore no makeup or earrings. Beneath her plain brown cotton dress it appeared that she had bound her breasts to minimize their fullness. Her hair was pulled back and down, tied severely in a bun at the base of her neck. And she did not look particularly happy to see an American officer leaning inside her cart.

"Are you all right?" I asked.

"Are you blind?" she answered, angling her head toward the dead pony, her eyebrows arched rebukingly.

"Is there anything I can do?"

"If you were Christ, I would ask you to resurrect my horse," she said. She stared for a moment at the young man, who by now I could tell was her servant, and then down at the wooden box. Then she crossed herself quickly, as if apologizing to God for her sacrilege, and looked back up to me. "I'm sorry, I should not have said that. But it was our last horse. Maybe you can take me to Pampanga."

"I'm not going to Pampanga," I said. "I'm going to San Miguel."

"After Pampanga I'm going to San Miguel," she said. "I live in San Miguel. But first I have to go to Pampanga."

I checked my watch. She picked up on it intuitively, raising her chin and looking away from me. "Never mind."

"No," I said. "It's OK. I have time."

"I will not be put in a position of begging," she said firmly, staring straight ahead at her dead pony and clutching the box to her. Her eyes now averted, I scrutinized her features for the first time. I decided that she was the most naturally beautiful woman I had ever seen. And more than that, she emanated a certain fearlessness that illuminated the contrast between her delicate profile and the strength of her determined eyes.

"You should go with me," I said. "You can get hurt out here."

"Out here, in there, it's all the same." She glanced at me as if to preempt my next question. "We only stay in San Miguel because if we leave someone will steal our house."

"Why do you need to go to—"

"Pampanga," she reminded me, finishing my sentence. "There is food there. I'm to trade this box for a *caván* of rice."

"How much is a *caván*?"

"Two bushels."

"Two bushels of rice for that? It's one of the most beautiful boxes I've ever seen. It must be an antique."

"Yes, it's been a family treasure for more than a hundred years. But you can't eat it. And we are feeding seven people."

I found myself smiling in admiration. She was so strong, so sure of herself in the midst of all this chaos, that I wanted to stay near her. That was all. If I left I would never see her again, and that thought made me sad. "Come on," I said. "Get in my jeep. I'll take you to Pampanga and then to San Miguel."

"All right," she said, as if granting my petition. "But afterward I will pay you. And give your name and your military number to my boy."

"My *what?*"

"You're a soldier. You must have a military number."

"Why would you talk to me like that? I'm offering to risk my life to take you to Pampanga."

She leaned toward me in the cab, fixing me with a polite but powerful stare. "I'm very sorry if I am offending you, but these are not normal times. I don't know you! If I don't come back, my boy can help my parents find me. Or you. Doesn't that seem fair?"

A half mile up the road a Japanese aircraft suddenly swooped low and lobbed a bomb into a truck. The huge explosion sent the vehicle sideways, where it did a double roll and landed upside down in a nearby field. A half dozen bodies had flown from the truck bed into the air. The truck was a flaming shell. I crouched for a moment behind the *caratela*, then came up shaking my head. She had not budged from her place on the seat.

"What do you think I'm going to do?" I said. "Nothing's going to happen to you."

"If anything did happen, my family would kill you."

I was enormously attracted to her, and her stubbornness only increased her magnetism. But it seemed to me that she had crossed over to impudence.

"You've insulted me," I said, beginning to walk back to my jeep. "Get somebody else to take you."

"Wait!" she called. I stopped and turned to face her again. She gave me a small, scrutinizing smile. "Why are you afraid to give my boy your name?"

"I'm not," I said. "But all I did was offer to help you, and now you're threatening to have me killed!"

"Give him your name," she said, as if the issue were now decided. "And I promise you won't be killed."

"You're a very strong woman," I said, smiling my surrender.

"Give him your name," she answered. Only now it sounded like a lilting invitation.

I wrote my name and service number on a piece of paper and gave it to the boy. As I walked back to the jeep she instructed him to unstrap the dead pony and pull the *caratela* back to San Miguel himself. He carried her box and loaded it behind my front seat. And when she joined me in the jeep she gave me her first true smile.

"I like it that you were going to leave," she said as I steered the churning jeep through mud gullies back onto the road. "It shows me that you have pride. Gallantry without pride is nothing more than servitude, don't

you think? I mean, I have been thinking about this. All men of true honor
have a point beyond which they will not bend."

"Was that my test?" I teased, gaining the road.

"Oh, no." She smiled. "True tests are never obvious."

That was the way she talked, and that was the way she thought. We had
not traveled a mile before I was certain that she was better educated and
more intelligent than I and probably more firmly principled. It was as if
she had thought everything through. Nothing seemed to surprise or intimidate her. She was only twenty-two, but somehow she had acquired the
gift, or perhaps the curse, of wisdom.

In Pampanga the war seemed far away. She directed me down narrow
side roads until we found a large warehouse. Fierce little dogs barked at us
as we drove up, and along the edges of the warehouse building I watched
two huge rats scurrying inside. The warehouse was guarded by a dozen
armed Filipinos who appeared to be guerrilla soldiers.

A well-fed older man met us as I braked the jeep. He was wearing a fair
amount of his wartime profiteering, four gold rings, a fine wristwatch, and
a thick gold chain around his neck. He eyed Divina Clara's *narva* box and
they spoke rapidly in Tagalog, bargaining. I could see her becoming
angry, and finally the old man waved at her and began walking away. She
shouted at him, an obvious insult, and he waved at her again, not even
turning his head.

"What's going on?" I asked.

"He'll only give me half a *caván*. I traveled all the way from San Miguel
and now my horse is dead. He is a despicable liar."

I walked toward him, calling to him. "Sir!"

He turned to face me, looking back at her for one quick moment with
an exultant grin, and greeted me in English. "She called me a liar. I heard
her say that. So let her find rice from someone who tells the truth."

"Let me talk to you," I said. He hesitated, so I took him by the shoulder
and moved with him toward the warehouse. As soon as I touched him a
half dozen rifles were raised to the ready position by nearby bodyguards,
but I ignored them.

"Over here," I said. "I'd like to make you an offer."

"You will not talk to him!" called Divina Clara from near the jeep.

"Stay there!" I commanded, and she did. For the second time that
afternoon I saw a look of respect flash across her face.

The old man and I walked to the doorway of the warehouse. Tons of rice were stashed in a series of bins inside. I took out my wallet and showed him my military identification card.

I spoke quietly. "My name is Jay Marsh. I work directly for General MacArthur." Seeing the look of disbelief in his eyes, I gestured toward the jeep. "How do you think I have my own jeep? You should check this through your people. Jay Marsh. Remember my name. I will be seeing General MacArthur tonight, and I will be with him all day tomorrow. I want to be able to tell him that you are helping his effort to bring assistance to the people of San Miguel. I would like to tell him that you gave this woman a *cavần* of rice as a way to thank him for liberating Luzon."

As I spoke, the man's eyes continually shifted, from the inside of the warehouse to my identification card to Divina Clara, who was still standing impatiently near my jeep. He was calculating. If I were lying, he would lose some face and be out a *cavần* of rice. If I were telling the truth and he did not give me the rice, who knew? Perhaps MacArthur could seize the warehouse itself and even arrest him.

"How do I know you are telling the truth?" he finally said.

"Because you are a very smart man. And if I were lying you could read it in my eyes."

"I can't give away rice," he decided. "I am in business."

I took out an American five-dollar bill. "You're right. You deserve payment."

The money, although not a great sum in the black market, would at least save him some face. He thought about it for another moment, then called inside the warehouse, speaking rapidly in Tagalog. In seconds, two men jogged outside to my jeep, each placing a heavy cloth bag of rice behind the front seats. Divina Clara started to hand over the *narva* box and I called to her.

"No! Keep it! I made a deal with him."

And for the first time I saw something else in her exquisite, intelligent almond eyes: a surprised admiration.

As we drove back toward the city I told her what had happened. She began to lecture me once again. "Now you own my box!"

"I don't own your box," I said, beginning to laugh at her earnestness.

"Yes, you do! And you bought it for only five dollars!"

"I didn't buy your box, Divina Clara, I bought rice."

"I can't take your rice unless you take the box."

An idea came to me. "How did your horse break his leg?"

"When the tank went by it startled him."

"Exactly! An American tank! And was your horse worth five dollars?"

She looked at me, a smile slowly growing until it lifted her entire face. Its glow warmed me, and I smiled back. Now she relaxed back into the seat, and her voice took on a new, vibrant tone.

"Thank you, Jay. Thank you."

Darkness was approaching. The battle in Manila illuminated the far horizon, like a wide, pulsing sunset. She was watching me as I drove and I could sense that she had decided she liked me. We passed the place in the road where the truck had been blown up earlier, and then the spot where her horse had died. And she grew melancholy.

"My country is so cursed," she said, looking at the ravaged landscape. "Why do my people have to die?"

"You should stop taking it so personal," I said, looking over at her. "This isn't the only place where people die."

"That was a cruel thing to say. I think being a soldier has killed a part of your spirit."

"People don't only die in wars. You're talking about trading away your family treasures for food. My family owns nothing. My sister died when she was seven because there was no doctor. And my father died because he tried to help a black man read a contract."

"Where was this?"

"In Arkansas. In America."

"Then America must be a terrible place."

"No. Terrible things can happen, but it's a wonderful place. My mother escaped to California. I got to go to college. And now I'm an officer."

In front of us, Manila pulsed again from new explosions. "In the Philippines, dropping bombs," she retorted, as if I were responsible for the war itself. "If the Americans had not made us a colony, then the Japanese would not have come."

"Oh, I see. Like they wouldn't have come to China? Or Korea, or Malaya, or Borneo or Java or New Guinea or Indochina or Singapore?"

Finally she relented, staring again at me in the jeep. "You're right. I'm sorry. I'm being upset about my horse. The Japanese have been terrible. I'm glad the Americans came back. I only wish it would be over. And the rest of it, your—Arkansas. I'm sorry but it's not my problem."

"Why is France my brother's problem?"

"I don't know anything about France."

"Neither did my brother. And now he's buried there."

"He died in the war?"

"Yes," I said. "We've died everywhere, you know. All over the Pacific. North Africa, France, Belgium, Italy, Germany—" I looked over at her. "In Leyte. In Manila."

"Yes," she said, almost as if she were ashamed. "I didn't mean what I said. I'm sorry I was being selfish."

"You're not selfish. I think I was being hard on you." I glanced at her as I drove. "I watched you when the plane blew up the truck. You're one of the bravest people I've ever seen."

I felt her eyes, heavy on me as I drove. Then finally she touched my shoulder. "Since you bought the rice," she said, as if needing to sum it all up in order to maintain some measure of control. "Then you must let us feed you dinner."

"But you're feeding seven people."

"Yes," she said. "But there's enough for you. Do you like vegetables? I will mix the rice with *kangkong* and there will be plenty."

"I can't take food from your family."

She was laughing warmly now. She punched me on the shoulder. "It's your rice, Jay!"

It excited me that she called me Jay. "I have two cans of Spam in the back of my jeep."

"Then we'll have a feast!"

I looked over and saw her grinning and I knew she was enjoying me. "Will your family like me?"

"If I do, they will."

"Do you like me?"

She thought about it for a moment. "No." She laughed. "I think it's more complicated than that."

She lived in a huge old two-story house surrounded by high walls and protected by an ancient iron gate. Inside, it had the air of a living museum that somehow connected her family to a faraway Spanish past. I walked past antique furniture through immense, dark, high-ceilinged rooms. My heels clicked on exquisite brick parquet flooring framed by thick slabs of rich mahogany. And so even before I met her family I understood the caution she had shown when I first met her on the death-splattered road. Her father, Carlos, still in the jungle with the guerrilla forces, had been a prominent businessman before the war. Her older two brothers were in the jungle with him. She was living with her mother, two aunts, two sisters, and a fifteen-year-old brother.

The servant boy had not yet returned with the *caratela,* and they had been certain she was dead. They gathered joyfully around her as we entered the sitting room, hugging her and chattering as the bombs and guns echoed from across the distant river. As was their custom, they welcomed me as an honored guest. Divina Clara's mother insisted that I treat myself to a bath as they prepared dinner. When I arrived for the meal they sat me at the head of the table and decided that as the oldest man present I should lead them all in blessing the food. I did my best, offering a stumbling Arkansas backwater Protestant prayer that nonetheless seemed to please them.

Divina Clara watched me possessively as we ate. She had unbound her breasts, put on gold loop earrings, and combed out her hair. All of her unfolding was like a delicate flower that had gone from bud to gorgeous blossom in the space of one hot tub-soaking. I had never seen anyone so beautiful or listened to one so smart By the time dinner was over I had completely fallen in love with her. And I knew that as long as I lived, I would never fall out of love with her.

Yes, I know this sounds overly romantic. Yes, I was young, and I had been lonely through the dark months from New Guinea to Hollandia to Leyte. Yes, the war's incandescent drama fed all our passions, heightening emotions and leading us to blunder in our souls from time to time. Think what you wish. But MacArthur had no trouble believing me. When I awkwardly told him the story the following morning, I saw a flash of envy in his eyes, followed by the flickering shadow of a personal memory. Then he laughed softly, teasing me.

"Jay," he said. "I'm serious, now. Be careful with this. You have discovered one of the world's great secrets."

"Secret of what, sir?"

I watched him with innocence in my eyes, as if he were my father. He had tantalized me and I wanted more. What was it that this great man knew of secrets? Was he thinking of love? Of the Philippines? Or maybe simply of war itself? Looking at his suddenly averted face I knew that he had meant something far more personal, and in my heart I wanted to yell it. *Consuelo!* But what? He said no more, his face quickly becoming clouded with the reality of the terrible, ongoing destruction of his most treasured city.

And yet—it was the only time I had seen him smile for weeks.

On February 27 the General reinstalled the Philippines' government, turning it over to President Osmena. Pockets of Japanese resistance still fought on in central Manila. We could hear the sporadic stutters of point-blank firefights inside the high walls of the old Spanish fort Intramuros as we drove toward Malacanang Palace. In the car I watched him surveying the wreckage that surrounded us. For the first time since I had been with him he seemed weary, truly broken, even old.

Malacanang Palace, once the residence of Spanish governors, was scarcely touched by the war. Inside, its carved *narva* woodwork, lush furniture and carpeting, crystal chandeliers, and historic paintings were a reminder of the elegance of prewar Manila. General Krueger and his commanders stood dutifully by, in front of a throng of Filipino leaders and a bigger gathering of newspapermen. Filipina women milled among the dignitaries and reporters, dressed in traditional butterfly-sleeved gowns hand-sewn from piña, a linen painstakingly woven out of pineapple fiber.

MacArthur stood before the crowd, gathering himself. They grew silent, watching him. His lips shook as he began to speak. He talked about the years that had passed since he had evacuated Manila, leaving it free of military destruction, and predicted the doom of the Japanese for having so wantonly violated "the churches, monuments, and cultural centers that might, in accordance with the rules of warfare, be spared the violence of military ravage."

Vowing revenge for this destruction, he read the simple but legalistic words that restored governmental powers to President Osmena and the legislature. And then, as hundreds watched, the General lowered his face and wept into his hands.

CHAPTER 4

★ ★ ★ ★ ★

Father Garvey walked into my bedroom, turned on a light, and started singing. He had a nice, trilling tenor of a voice, but it was one o'clock in the morning. He was singing an irritatingly happy, bouncy prewar favorite, something about rolling out of bed in the morning with a big, big, smile and a good, good morning, and having a grin so that the sun could shine in. He was altogether too happy. I could tell that he had been drinking. I wanted to strangle him. Finally I indeed rolled in my bed, and then managed to sit up, staring vacantly at him.

"If you weren't a priest, Father, I'd deck you."

He laughed breezily at me. "And if you weren't always so hard to wake up, I'd whisper in your ear, Jay."

"Have you considered that I went to bed an hour ago?"

"Yes," he said, laughing again. "But we have been called upon to perform vital missions, you and I."

Father Garvey held up a golden signet ring. He was a small, muscular man with bright blue eyes and a square Celtic face. His thick brown hair had already begun to grey. As he laughed I could see that his teeth were stained by tobacco and tea. But his voice was young and rolling, rich in a knowing cynicism that caused his words to wash over me like a calming hand. Sometimes it was the only reason I listened to him.

"This ring belongs to Lord Mountbatten." Conscious that as an Irishman he was not being suitably anti-royalist, he suddenly corrected himself, speaking with a polished acidity. "Excuse me, then. It belongs to Admiral Lord Louis Francis Albert Victor Nicholas Mountbatten, Supreme Commander, Allied Forces, Southeast Asia, great-grandson of her majesty Queen Victoria, and a handsome, dashing ass to boot."

I was sitting on the edge of my bed, rubbing my face, still trying to wake up. "So why do you have this ring, Father?"

"Because after we peons left the General's reception, the big boys went swimming in MacArthur's pool. And Admiral Lord—et cetera, you know how it goes—Mountbatten lost his ring. Everyone looked for it for an hour. They even had servants swimming along the bottom of the pool. And finally Admiral Lord et cetera had to return to Clark Field, from whence he will fly back to Burma tomorrow morning. Or perhaps they said India, I can't remember for certain. The whiskey, you know."

I pointedly checked my watch, now teasing Father Garvey. "You mean this morning."

"Exactly," said Father Garvey. "This morning. And then when the servants were removing the towels from the bathhouse, one of them found the ring underneath a towel. So congratulations, Jay. You, young captain that you are, baby of the General's staff, have been elected to bring the lord admiral his ring. And I am coming with you. Because I—"

"—have had a bit to drink. Right, Father?"

Father Garvey waved a small, thick hand into the air. "Ah, well, I can't get into that. But I have ecclesiastical duties to perform. So, let's go, Jay! Put on a uniform. Check the shine on your shoes. The driver is waiting downstairs! The sooner we begin, the sooner we'll be back."

In five minutes we were on the road, heading through dark, musty streets that would lead us out of the city and onto a narrow highway that went all the way to Clark Field. Once awake, I did not really mind the trip. It would take most of the day to travel to Clark and back, and thus I would be relieved of my other chores. And as unlikely as it seemed, over the past six months Father Garvey had become my best friend. So it was as if we were setting off together on a lark.

We were also housemates. In March after the battle for the city ended I had moved with Father Garvey and several other officers who worked directly on MacArthur's staff into a beautiful villa just east of Malacanang Palace, a few blocks from the Pasig River. As befitted our duties, we were just down from the General's own temporary home, which of course was the most exquisite house still standing in Manila.

That had been five months ago. Now, in early August, we all knew that this grand and horrible adventure would soon end. In Europe the war was already over. In the Philippines, Yamashita's soldiers were still fighting hard in a costly war of attrition but had been pushed far back into the mountains near Baguio. Elsewhere, Japan's empire had disintegrated. Its military was beaten, dying on the vine all over Asia. Its major cities were scorched from months of intense firebombings. Okinawa, the first Japanese population center to be attacked, was now in Allied hands. And so my daily duties had become—well, easy. No, make that embarrassingly easy.

In the mornings I usually toured the plush mansions and exotic villas where MacArthur's senior officers now dwelled, gathering up messages and edicts to return to the General's office. At other times I was MacArthur's delivery boy, reversing my route. I sometimes was asked to do follow-up interviews with the few Japanese we were able to capture alive if our interrogator-translator teams thought a prisoner might have information useful to the General's staff. But more than any other function, since we had settled into our Manila mansions I had become, as the other officers like to tease, the General's SLJO—shitty little jobs officer.

Unspeaking, unhearing, unseeing, in this role I became the witness to an odd and sometimes embarrassing array of secrets. The dozen or so senior generals who surrounded MacArthur had come to trust me, not only with classified information but with all the blunt evidence of their own indiscretions. Perhaps it was the grand sense of infallible power the years of war had brought to them, or perhaps it was merely their accumulated carelessness. I did not complain, and I swore to myself I would never tell. Happy to be trusted, delighted with the comforts this trust had bought me, I enjoyed the unfettered nights of freedom with Divina Clara that were the rewards of my simple chores.

If life had been good in Tacloban, it was heaven in Manila. As completely as I had fallen in love with Divina Clara, I had fallen thoroughly and passionately in love with this wounded city. Manila, from its centuries under Spain and its decades with America, was not completely Asian anymore, and yet not Western at all. It was its own place, sui generis, as the lawyers liked to put it, a thing unto itself. And it was as if I had unknowingly waited all my life to find its harmony.

But at night it pulsed and throbbed from the destruction the war had brought it. Father Garvey and I drove through miles of unlit, still-rubbled streets, past thousands of families still camped on the sidewalks and in the vacant lots where homes had stood before the February battles. People slept in the dirt, and even in crude hammocks strung from broken trees. The air was dense, filled with the aroma of flowers and cook fires. Father Garvey watched the city silently as we drove, as if taking in every scar and making it his own.

Finally he spoke, his face worked up into a scoffing, remembering grin. "I've never seen anything like that reception for Mountbatten, have you? It was like some last, big hurrah—all the four-star generals preening and clucking and sulking, jealous of each other every time MacArthur noticed one in favor of the other. What are they going to do when this war is over, Jay? What do you think?"

I chuckled, thinking of the reception, where a collection of now world-famous generals had gathered in one small room to drink wine and make small talk—the surest sign that the war was nearly finished. "Did you see General Kenney, Father? Do you think he wants this ever to end? What's he going to do, bomb Toledo? He knows what peacetime is like. After World War One he spent the next seventeen years as a captain, except for one year when they demoted him to first lieutenant. This war catapulted him from lieutenant colonel to two stars overnight. And there he was last night, a four-star general with his very own villa, kissing the ass of Queen Victoria's great-grandson."

"And Krueger and Eichelberger, still so jealous of each other that they move around a room like the opposite ends of a compass needle." Garvey laughed at his own little joke. "Krueger will never get over Eichelberger's telling the press he was 'molasses in January' during the invasion of Manila. And Eichelberger will never get over Krueger's getting most of the media coverage."

"MacArthur likes it like that," I said. "As long as everyone is fighting each other, he keeps a separate line of loyalty from each one of them to himself. He even uses General Sutherland to stir the pot and make sure the others keep arguing."

Father Garvey sneered at the mention of MacArthur's famously arrogant chief of staff, shaking his head with irritation. "I've always thought

MacArthur kept Sutherland around because he's the only officer in the army who is more disagreeable and arrogant than MacArthur himself." He hedged, remembering my loyalty to the General, an ironic grin creeping across his face. "If you will forgive my forthrightness, that is."

"You're half right, Father. The General likes it that they spend all their energies hating Sutherland. It makes him grander, because then only he can fully resolve their fights."

"You're smarter than I thought," mused Father Garvey.

"That's just the General's style, Father. It's like the spokes of a wheel, with MacArthur in the center."

"And does he know how observant you are?"

I laughed lightly. "I don't know what you mean, Father. I'm just little Jay the monkey boy, riding out the war."

"Ordinarily I would feel it was my duty to encourage you to be more honest, Jay. But MacArthur is no ordinary man."

The jeep cleared Manila. We were almost alone on the black, straight highway that led to Clark Field. "He's sure the war is going to end soon," I finally said.

"I would have to agree," said Father Garvey. "I cannot truly imagine him carrying out this invasion we're planning for November. The Japanese will quit before then. I will grant them that they've been impressively brave on the battlefield, but their leaders must know they've lost. They can't possibly be so barbarically stupid as to order all their citizens to fight hopelessly to their collective deaths from town to town and house to house throughout the country. I mean, the imperial government does not seem to be a logical enterprise, but it wouldn't perpetrate a form of genocide upon its own people."

"I hope you're right, Father. Our cable traffic shows that the Japanese are trying to convince the Soviets to help negotiate an end to the war. But General MacArthur is trying to bring the Soviets in on our side, in case we do have to invade the main islands. He estimates that a million Americans will be killed or wounded if we have to invade Japan."

"They wouldn't be that stupid!" Father Garvey thought about it for a few seconds. "Then again they might not think of it as being stupid. You heard MacArthur tonight, didn't you? He called them brilliant barbarians. Highly skilled, minutely organized, deeply superstitious, *barbarians*. And I've read about their religion myself, you know. It's one of my duties as a Jesuit to understand other systems. Think about it. They worship the emperor as their God. They say he is directly descended from a union with a mystical figure they call the Sun Goddess, which took place at about the time of Christ. They would die for him, Jay!"

"And so," I said, speaking slowly, half teasing. "At the time of Christ God came down from heaven and—took some action—with a mere mortal named Mary, and from this union came Christ the savior. And you do not dispute this, Father. But in Japan at the time of Christ came another union with a spirit called the Sun Goddess, resulting in an uninterrupted series of emperors. And you simply wish to pass off its continuing impact over two thousand years as barbarism?"

"What do you believe?" challenged Father Garvey.

"I don't know," I answered. "I'll tell you after we get there. But it doesn't sound like barbarism to me."

"I'm going to take a nap," he announced suddenly. "I've had a bit too much to drink, you know." It was his usual way of dismissing me when I pushed too hard against his religious beliefs. And I will admit it was much better than fighting.

Father Garvey quickly fell into a deep sleep, and I was left with my own thoughts as the car pressed on toward Clark Field. The war would indeed end soon. We all knew it. The prospect dominated our thoughts. And what, I thought again, would I do, not tomorrow, which was as far as I had been able to plan for the past three years, but for the rest of my life? I might go quickly home, but little waited for me there, and I had grown comfortable in Asia. I liked the way it smelled, I liked the way it felt. And I had become useful to the General. Rumor had it that he would be chosen to lead the Occupation of Japan. I began hoping that he would, and that since I spoke Japanese he might bring me with him.

Or perhaps, I thought, he would leave me in Manila for as long as there were Japanese soldiers to interrogate and repatriate. Even if I went to Japan I knew I would eventually come back here. I had asked Divina Clara to marry me, and I was willing to live with her in the Philippines if I could find work after I left the army. Thinking such thoughts, I could not help laughing at myself. For years I had dreamed of escaping the army at my earliest opportunity, and now I was searching for reasons to remain.

Father Garvey dozed beside me, not quite sober enough to be hungover. He had not yet told me why he also had been sent to Clark, but I knew that once he awakened he would be refreshed, ready to dig anew into every aspect of the universe, prepared to tell me everything. In fact, he would tell me things I did not want to hear, mixing in history that I did not understand and biblical passages that I sometimes suspicioned he simply made up. He was an impressive little bulldog, part genius and part fraud. I liked him very much.

I also sympathized with his drunkenness. For Father Garvey clearly admired women, and Manila was filled with world-class beauties. And in Manila, beautiful women could be a problem for an energetic, gregarious priest still in his thirties, no matter how deep his calling. Their traditions from the Spanish had taught them that although it may have been in some form a sin for a priest to take a Filipina for a lover, it was no great shame, and in fact from the female perspective sometimes even an honor. And so daily, sometimes hourly, Father Garvey was tempted beyond his capacity to soberly endure this cruelest of fates that God had forced upon him. And the only refuge when the temptation escalated was to pray mightily, and dull his senses with large doses of strong brew.

The city was now far behind us. We drove past miles of lush, torn fields and thick stands of trees. The night air was heavy and perfumed. I tried to doze as the jeep bounced and swayed, but the odor of plumeria kept washing over me and it made me miss Divina Clara. I loved the smell. It made me think of the lilac bushes in the side yard of the only home in which my father had ever been happy. Divina Clara hated the aroma. The *kalachuchi*, as she called it, was used in funerals and reminded her of death.

Finally the jeep began to slow, as the driver looked for his turnoff. Next to me Father Garvey stretched and stirred, bringing me out of my memories. The sky was beginning to grey, and already I could make out the sharp peaks of the Zambales Mountains to our west. Clark Field was only a few miles further up the road.

"I feel rather refreshed," said Father Garvey.

"You've been out for two hours, Father. You're the only person I know who can sleep for so long in a jeep."

"Yes," he answered, twisting his neck to undo the kinks. "It's a true blessing, isn't it?"

It was Father Garvey's greatest trait, that he found blessings where others merely reveled in good luck.

At Clark we were hastened by a military police escort to the main operations building next to the runway and quickly brought inside. There, in a small waiting room designed for dignitaries, Admiral Lord Mountbatten and his staff were finishing an early breakfast. An aide whisked Father Garvey out of the room, while Mountbatten himself waved me to the breakfast table and offered me toast and coffee.

"Your ring, Lord Admiral."

"Splendid," grinned Mountbatten, taking it and putting it onto a finger as I hungrily downed a piece of toast. "You'll never know how much this means to me. It was given to me on my twenty-first birthday by the Prince of Wales himself. Tell General MacArthur I am greatly in his debt."

Mountbatten was a tall, handsome man with aquiline features and a very straight Nordic nose. I thought again how much he and General MacArthur resembled each other in their style and bearing and the meter of their speech. And it occurred to me that MacArthur had been more at home with Lord Mountbatten than I had ever seen him with his own soldiers. Douglas MacArthur was at heart a royalist, pure and simple.

"Yes, sir," I answered as I washed the toast down with a gulp of coffee. "I will tell him you were pleased."

Mountbatten's face then shifted for a moment, like a rain cloud blotting out the sun. "And tell him—tell him I now understand about Singapore."

I was grabbing a second piece of toast, and wishing there were eggs and maybe even a few pieces of bacon. "About Singapore, sir?"

"Yes," said Mountbatten. He was sounding clandestine, as if he and I were in together on a huge secret. "He told me last night that I would never have to worry about personally liberating Singapore. I thought he was being uncharacteristically mysterious, to be frank, or even teasing me that the Americans would beat me to it. But tell him a courier arrived here last night to explain to me, and that I understand what he said about Singapore."

"Yes, sir." I had no idea what he meant.

Mountbatten smiled somewhat defensively. "I wouldn't want him to think I didn't know."

"Yes, sir." I was finishing my third piece of toast.

Father Garvey reappeared. It was time to leave. Mountbatten walked us to the door and handed me a small cardboard box. Someone had wrapped twine around it, as if it were a ribbon.

"Sorry there aren't medals for retrieving signet rings, Captain. But I do appreciate your having come out here in the middle of the night. And I guarantee that finer scotch will never pass through your lips again."

"You're very kind, Lord Admiral," I said as Father Garvey and I headed for the door. "Please have a safe flight."

"And thanks for the omelette," muttered Father Garvey as the door closed behind us and we headed toward the car.

Two bottles were in the box. In the car, I gave one to the corporal who was my driver, as compensation for his own lost evening. It was still morning when we cleared the military compound and headed out onto the road back toward Manila. An ugly rainstorm blew in without warning from the distant sea, turning the road to mire and choking the traffic. The road was filled with trucks, jeeps, horse-drawn carts, wagons pulled by sinewy little men, and mud-splattered people of all ages, walking. They were mindless to the downpour, used to it. Women waved to us. Children called happily, asking for cigarettes and gum. I felt comfortable in this chaos, even at home.

"It'll be midafternoon before we're back," mourned Father Garvey.

"No," I said. "With this rain it will be night."

I smoked a cigarette, watching the lush vistas now awash in sheets of rain. The jeep churned and bumped through the mud. Rain splashed us through the side vents and leaked through the roof. Finally I unscrewed the bottle of scotch.

"Let's have a drink, Father."

"And why not," said Father Garvey.

We passed the bottle back and forth. I was already numb from lack of sleep. Mountbatten's unjellied toast sat lightly in my stomach. The whiskey was warm and smooth. We quickly killed half of the bottle. And soon I felt a grand elation as the jeep fought through the rain and mud, as if this journey past the waving, ever-enduring people I had come to love were my very own victory parade.

"I think I want to stay here, Father."

"Don't be a fool, Jay. You don't belong here."

"And where do I belong? My dad and sister died in Arkansas. My brother died in France. And my mom's living in California with a fucking Italian. I think his name is Bachioli or something like that."

"You must learn to control your emotions," said Father Garvey.

"And you know what? My mother will never accept Divina Clara. She doesn't like Asians. I once dated a Japanese girl when I was in college. Kozuko. A beautiful, sweet girl. And you know what my mother said? She doesn't want slanty-eyed grandkids."

"Don't be hard on your mother, now. Tribal passion is a natural phenomenon. Racial pride, religious belief. Even love of war."

"So what tribe do the fucking Italians belong to, that she thinks they're better than Filipinos?"

Father Garvey started laughing, deep in his belly, finally throwing his head back and laughing some more. His bright blue eyes began to water, he was laughing so hard. I forced a frown, stifling my own grin. He was confusing me.

"It wasn't that funny, Father."

He laughed some more. "This isn't real, Jay! Look around you. It isn't really happening, not in the same way that the rest of your life is! You're passing through, do you understand? There's no conscious choice in this. You're here because MacArthur landed an army, and when he decides to leave you'll be gone. And if you were to stay, it would never feel the same. The army will be gone, and it would be just you, here among all the people who were here before. They won't even look at you in the same way. You won't be a liberator then. You'll be an interloper."

I did not believe him. "How do you know that?"

He stopped laughing, holding my gaze for a full five seconds, and then shrugged. "Well I don't, really," mused Father Garvey. "But it's what you needed to hear."

"Father," I said, "you're so honest that you're silly."

We both laughed at each other for a long time. Father Garvey took the bottle from me and drank some more, and then I took the bottle back from him so that he would not take it all. The rain lifted and a low mist covered the ground, like wisps of smoke, and then the rain began again. And all around us the people walked and laughed and waved.

"Why did Mountbatten send for you, Father?"

"Well, now you're intruding into matters of the highest ecclesiastical concerns," trilled Father Garvey. "And wouldn't I be abusing the bounds of my calling if I told you?"

"Well, I don't know," I answered. "My question wasn't particularly ecclesiastical. I'm not even a Catholic."

"Somewhere deep in your heart you are indeed," said Father Garvey. "I once heard you say that your mother was a Murphy, and that proves it." He laughed some more, beaming at me as if I were prey for eventual conversion. "But anyway, all right, Jay. There was an officer on the lord admiral's staff who needed to see me. He wanted to go through confession in case the plane crashed on the way to India."

"Was he carrying a heavy burden, Father?"

"I cannot tell you that."

"I like confessing to you, Father, and I don't even have to."

"That's not the same, but of course you do. There's nothing more difficult than confessing to ourselves, is there?"

"So, what did he do?"

"You're straining our friendship, Jay."

"Oh, come on, Father. I'm drunk and I haven't slept in two days. I won't even remember."

"No," said Father Garvey. "There are limits and I am bound to silence." Then his eyes began to twinkle mischievously, as if he had found another loophole, made another compromise with God. "But I suppose since you do not know him and did not see him, we can discuss this academically, in terms of our spiritual obligations."

"That's actually what I was thinking," I lied.

"There is hope for you, then," teased Father Garvey. "So you can ask yourself, what is it that would make an Englishman want to confess, even if he had to be heard by an Irish priest? You might think it had to do with all the beautiful women on this island. Or maybe I am simply single-minded in my own feelings of deprivation. But no! He has to taunt me with the—" He caught himself and would not finish.

"With what, Father?"

"Consider my dilemma and try to empathize with the human spirit," said Father Garvey, now looking coyly out toward the edges of the war-torn city. "Think broadly, now. I've had many blessings, have I not? But did you know that sometimes I do weep, knowing that I will never have a child of my own, or in the end someone who truly loved me? Other than God, of course. The greatest love of all. But when I see the way some women look at me the thought of what I'm missing pains me beyond even the strength of my faith. Having a child, that is. And I'm not alone in that. A massive confusion, yes? These things reach up from places you never knew were there, and when you're alone and in a foreign land, it happens."

"*What*, Father?"

"I cannot answer that," said Father Garvey. "Not as a priest. But as your friend, let me tell you that I myself am more human than you think. Oh, yes. And I understand personal failure far too well."

"*What the hell are you talking about?*"

"I have nothing left to explain to you!" said Father Garvey, suddenly indignant. "I do not have to make sense, Jay! *I am drunk!*"

Father Garvey laughed mightily at this bit of evasive cleverness, then we both retreated into silence. Without talking, we finished the bottle of scotch. The scotch finally dulled us, and we dozed. It was late when we reached Manila. I went immediately to bed, not rising until late the next morning to make up for the sleep I had lost the night before.

By the time I reached MacArthur's headquarters to begin my morning rounds, the entire staff seemed afire with exultation. Something huge had happened, wonderful and yet terrible, forever changing not only war but the conduct of nations. In the middle of the night an American B-29 bomber had taken off from Tinian in the Mariana Islands. At 8:16 that morning the B-29 had dropped a single bomb that had wiped out most of the city of Hiroshima. One plane. One bomb. One city. Tens of thousands of people, dead. The world was reeling from the news. There was no doubt, now. The war would be over in a matter of weeks.

And I finally understood what it was that had made MacArthur so certain about the imminent fall of Singapore and why Mountbatten had so adamantly wanted me to tell MacArthur that he had been forewarned.

A new certainty washed over me, and its reality suddenly scared me. MacArthur would lead the occupation. We were going to Japan. Soon.

CHAPTER 5

★ ★ ★ ★ ★

The next two weeks were frenetic, often chaotic. Two days after the atomic bomb was dropped on Hiroshima, the Soviets repudiated their treaties with Japan and to MacArthur's delight invaded Manchuria. The next day, August 9, a second nuclear bomb was dropped on Nagasaki. Three days after that, President Truman suspended the bombing of Japan and instead began dropping leaflets over Tokyo, urging the Japanese to revolt, telling them that even as their people continued to die, their government was secretly offering to surrender. On August 14, with the approval of the British, Soviets, and Chinese, Truman named Douglas MacArthur supreme commander of all Allied forces in the Pacific, indicating that the General would oversee the entire Occupation of Japan once the war was over.

On August 15, as confusion and hints of revolution sundered the Japanese capital, the emperor announced Japan's surrender, personally speaking to the Japanese people through a prerecorded radio broadcast. The emperor's broadcast was itself stunning news, as no ordinary Japanese had ever before even heard his voice. It seemed incredible and premature, but with that news we knew that we would be landing in Japan within two weeks.

In Manila, our staff began a twenty-four-hour workday, frantically preparing for the coming trip to Japan. An advance group of a few thousand people would soon drop into the midst of a nation of eighty million, who only a few days before were vowing to die to the last person rather than surrender. Gone were the lazy days of tending to high-level egos, followed by my own somnolent, easy evenings. The General had been preparing himself for more than a year. He had already put together a seven-point plan for dramatically changing the texture of Japanese culture and society. But the nuclear bombs had taken him by surprise, just as they had the rest of us. Ever mindful of his place in history, he knew how vital the first moments of his arrival would be, not only to the future of Japan but to his personal legacy.

I had never seen the General as animated and electric, not even in the early days of the Luzon campaign. At last, here was a role equal to his talents. He had expected to command the military invasion of Japan, and he had hoped to have a role in its postwar reconstruction. But the powers that President Truman had delegated to him on August 14 were as great as those given to any proconsul in perhaps two thousand years. So long as he succeeded, his rule over the Japanese people would be absolute.

And me? I had a simpler problem, one that would never make the newsreels but at the same time threatened to overturn my own life. As the day of our departure for Japan neared, I finally garnered the courage to come to the General with it. Against such a grand historical tapestry as the ending of a war that had taken more than fifty million lives and the occupation of a strange, closed nation that had never before been conquered, I felt close to humiliation as I knocked on his office door, heard his familiar invitation to enter, and began walking toward his desk.

As was the case throughout those weeks, MacArthur's two closest advisers were with him in the room. In a chair to his left was General Charles Willoughby. Born in Germany as Karl Weidenbach, Willoughby was a hulking, thick-accented intelligence specialist. Reticent, introspective, and deeply loyal to the General, he had been with MacArthur for more than six years, and had made it plain to all who would listen that the General's career was his life's work. Willoughby would listen to every word I said but would rarely comment, except to MacArthur after I left the room. To the right of MacArthur's desk sat Brigadier General Courtney Whitney. A genial, well-spoken lawyer, Court Whitney had first met the

General in prewar Manila, where he had made a fortune in business. He was coming to Japan as MacArthur's chief political negotiator. In small meetings Whitney often acted as a provocateur on behalf of the General, drawing out visitors or staff members so that MacArthur might choose the best way to respond.

All three eyed me with familiar smiles. I was going with them to Japan as a special projects officer. I had worked with Whitney and Willoughby almost daily throughout the war, and unlike the churlish General Sutherland both had developed a liking for me. In addition to my mundane chores, because of my youth and junior rank I served the necessary function of relieving pressure on the staff. When times grew tense, I was the designated court jester, the butt of their silly jokes and recipient of their mock derision. But they, like MacArthur himself, had made it clear that with my proven loyalty to the General and my ability to speak Japanese, I would be immensely valuable to their plans once we began the occupation.

"Get in here, fat boy," joked Court Whitney as I stepped inside the General's office. "What do you weigh by now, anyway?"

I had put on weight. It was solid muscle, but Manila had indeed been good to me. "I guess I'm back up around two hundred, sir."

"We need to get you off that Filipino cooking."

"From what I hear that's not going to be a problem, sir."

Willoughby chuckled, for him a moment of extroversion. MacArthur leaned back in his chair. He had been watching me closely as Court Whitney teased me. A boyish smile now crept onto his face, and I knew that he was again going to ask me about Divina Clara.

"And I would imagine that your young lady is not very happy with your leaving, Jay?"

I held his gaze for a moment. Secrets passed between us through our eyes. And then I wondered, *is this how it ended for him?* "No, sir," I said. "In fact I, ah, have a major crisis, here."

Court Whitney chuckled. He had told me that he knew Divina Clara's father from before the war. "A nuclear explosion in the Ramirez household, is that what I'm hearing?"

"Well." I stumbled. "Not yet. But close. The end of the war came so fast that it just, sort of, took us all by surprise, sir. And then with the work schedule I haven't been able to explain everything to her family."

MacArthur preempted Court Whitney's next jibe with a sharp glance, then folded his arms judiciously. "What's the problem, Jay?"

"Her grandmother, sir." I hedged, feeling inane discussing an old woman's hesitations in front of three men who were preparing to pull an entire nation into a new era. "Sorry, sir. I don't mean to take your time with it. But I feel like I've got to do something."

MacArthur had regained his slow, secret smile. "She doesn't believe you're coming back, does she?"

I smiled back, embarrassed at how silly it all sounded once it came out of the Great Man's mouth. "No, sir."

"*Are you?*"

It hung in the air like a disbelieving dare. We both knew what MacArthur was saying, and why two simple words carried so much emotion.

"Yes, sir," I answered. Again our eyes locked. "I'm going to marry her, General."

MacArthur pointed toward the door. "Then don't waste any time, Jay. Go tell her grandmother."

As we drove from Manila toward Subic the road suddenly ended at a wide and swirling river. The bridge across the river had been blown in January by retreating Japanese soldiers, then quickly repaired by our Army corps of engineers so that General Krueger's forces could advance from Lingayen and Subic toward Manila. But the repairs were makeshift, and in the past few days a torrential rain had washed over western Luzon, loosening the bridge's structure until a span had dropped.

I pulled my jeep to a halt at the river's edge, staring with frustration at the damaged bridge. Army engineers were clambering all over the structure as they again worked to repair it. Nearby, a group of Filipinos stood placidly at the muddy edges of the water, waiting and watching. I climbed out of the jeep, into the mud and jasmine morning. Cursing, I slammed my fist into a fender, then checked my watch.

"You're always checking your watch," said Divina Clara. "It was the first thing you did when I asked you to take me to Pampanga the day we met. Do you remember, Jay?"

"This is going to cost us at least an hour each way," I said. "I don't have that kind of time."

"We're on Filipino time." She laughed brightly, climbing out of the car and standing next to me. "My grandmother won't even notice."

"MacArthur will, if I'm late getting back and he's left me a message."

"Then go back to MacArthur, Jay." She had darkened at his name, and now she was daring me with her eyes, her chin held high. "Go ahead. Turn around. Go back."

I had tried to tell her that unlike in her life, I had no control over my time, that my time was indeed MacArthur's, that I was lucky beyond imagination to have been given most of a day to travel with her to her grandmother's home in the first place. I wanted to tell her to stop being resentful, that to admire MacArthur did not mean that I loved or even particularly liked him and certainly did not mean that I would willingly leave her only to follow in the wake of his glory.

But if I told her that, it would reinforce the thought that I was leaving, setting off a whole new downward spiral. In her mind it was MacArthur who was taking me away from her, rather than duty and the army and the reality of Japan's occupation. Yes, he had ordered me to go with him. But he was the army. There was nothing I could do about that.

"He's a five-star general, Divina Clara. I'm a very little tadpole in a very big pond."

"He should not begrudge us this day. It won't be long until he'll have you all to himself in Japan."

"He personally gave me this day off, in spite of everything that is going on. You should stop being jealous."

She spun away from me. "That was a cruel thing to say. Why did I fall in love with you? I won't let you treat me like that."

"I'm sorry, Divina Clara." I moved to her, putting my arms around her. She felt soft and warm against me. And that was another reason I was hurrying. "To be honest, I wanted to make sure we have some time together after we get back."

"Stop that. We'll have time." She put her head against my chest. She would not look at me but I heard promises in her voice. "Jay, this is your only chance to see my grandmother. If you walk into her house checking your watch and talking down to her like a Subic sailor you'll upset her. And if you upset her, it will take her years to recover. Or maybe never."

"I won't upset her."

"She's not happy with this, you know."

"I'll make her happy."

She broke away from me again, turning toward the water. I followed her. I had never seen her so preoccupied. "I don't think so. If she survives to see our grandchildren, and knows that we are still together, and sees that this wasn't another American soldier telling another Filipina girl another lie, then you might make her happy."

"Then I'll make *you* happy."

She suddenly took my hand and held it, staring into the river. Her eyes were far away and very sad. "I already am happy."

We stood together like that for a while, looking out into the river. Suddenly she brightened, her mood changing like the sun reappearing from behind a cloud. She pointed toward the river. "This must be our ferry!"

In the river I could now see an American navy "Papa boat," a small amphibious landing craft, puttering toward us from the far bank. The nearby group of Filipinos started chattering excitedly to one another, moving to the riverbank. One of them was steadying a large water buffalo, holding a rope attached to a ring through the animal's nose.

We returned to the jeep and drove slowly down the riverbank. The Papa boat had now powered its bow onto the bank and dropped its front ramp. The motor was still running and the coxswain was steadying the boat against the river's current. The coxswain, an American sailor, motioned at me for the jeep to board first, yelling at the others to wait. I drove forward and he used hand signals as he positioned the jeep carefully at the Papa boat's center of balance. Then he brought on the water buffalo, signaling the boy who was pulling the huge animal to come aft and center. And after that the half dozen other Filipinos boarded, spreading themselves along the boat's platform to distribute the weight.

Divina Clara and I climbed out of the jeep and stood together next to it. The Papa boat backed out and then carefully powered forward, beginning its slow journey to the other side. We were very low in the water. Divina Clara clutched my hand tightly, afraid we might tip over. The water buffalo pulled his head this way and that, swaying with the boat's movements, his eyes red and wild with fear. The young American coxswain could not keep his own wild and hungry eyes from alternating between Divina Clara's full breasts and her firm hips. But except for him, our obvious closeness drew neither stares nor comment. And in fact our little group on the deck of the Papa boat was a collection of people who had made an immediate and unspoken pact not to judge one another.

Next to us was a small Negrito woman from the savage jungles of the nearby hills. She suckled a tiny baby, all the while holding the hand of a young boy. The boy looked curiously up at me as if I were the first white man he had ever seen. A thin grey monkey sat on the woman's shoulder, its chest pushed into the back of her head. One of the monkey's hands had been cut off. With its other hand and the slender stump of a wrist, the monkey was studiously picking lice out of the Negrito woman's hair and eating the insects as if they were candy. The woman stared blankly out toward the river, consumed by secret thoughts.

On the other side of the jeep an older Filipino couple stood impassively next to a sturdy, round-faced girl who looked to be in her late teens. The girl was obviously their daughter. She was not wearing a wedding ring. She was holding a baby who was unmistakably half Japanese. She kissed the baby, nuzzling it. Her parents gazed dotingly as the baby smiled.

Divina Clara watched all of them for a full minute, as if studying each face. And then she started speaking rapidly in Tagalog. I had no idea what she was saying. At first they were serious, but in moments they all were laughing and chattering back to her. And by the time we reached the far shore it was as if she had known them and they had known her for years.

The Papa boat nudged the shoreline and the ramp fell forward. We climbed back into the jeep. As we began driving off the boat's ramp she pulled my arm, grinning sweetly. "Wait, Jay!"

"For what?"

"We're taking them to Subic."

"Who?" I asked.

"All of them!"

"All of them?"

"Yes!" She laughed. "Except for the *caribao* and his boy. He lives just over there. So stop the jeep!"

Reluctantly, I stopped the jeep. They trundled up the steep mud bank, slipping and laughing and calling to one another as if it had all become a merry game. Then they busily packed into the backseat, stacking on top of one another, shifting babies and the monkey to make room.

I turned to her again. "How did this happen?"

"How could it not?" She continued to smile sweetly, taking the half-Japanese baby for a moment so that its young mother could squeeze into the jeep. "You see, we have room. And it's a long way to Subic."

"You're right," I said sarcastically, gaining the road. I began driving ever more carefully, lest I hit a bump and lose half of Divina Clara's newfound friends. "It's perfectly obvious, isn't it?"

"Now you're being cynical," she teased. Behind us they were laughing and talking ecstatically, as if a jeep ride were one of life's great thrills. "I have thought about cynicism. It is a defensive form of humor, Jay. Usually it comes from resentment, wouldn't you say? So how can you resent filling up an empty space in your car?"

"OK, OK!" I chuckled, giving up, powerless to fight her sweetly rendered logic. We drove for a few minutes more, then I glanced over at her. "What were you saying to them on the boat? Why did everyone start laughing?"

She touched my face, a gesture that somehow served as a happy signal to our backseat guests. "I told them it was time that we became comfortable with ourselves, and that we should help each other after all the sorrow. I asked Maria—that is her name—if she loved the baby's father, and she told me that she was sorry, but that she did love him, and that maybe I should be sorry, because he is now dead."

"But everyone was laughing," I said.

"Well, yes," said Divina Clara. "Because then I told them I was part Spanish, in love with an American, looking at a Negrita with her monkey who was trying to ignore me, and talking to a new mother with a half-Japanese baby while an American military boat carried us across the river! But that we were all Filipinos, do you know what I mean? And that we were all in love. And they agreed, even the Negrita. Out of all the chaos, still there is love! And what is love, that God allows such things to happen? Whatever it is, and whoever God brings us to share it with, we should be glad for it, not ashamed. It's beautiful, isn't it? And so now we are all friends."

I touched her face in the same way she had been touching mine. She said something rapidly in Tagalog. In the backseat I could hear them softly laughing, seemingly urging me on. And then as the traffic slowed, I leaned over and kissed her on the lips.

"Be careful, you'll have a wreck!"

"I love you, Divina Clara."

She pushed me away, laughing. "Then be nice to my grandmother."

Near Subic the road began to wind around high hills and lush, scrubby knolls. Monkeys lolled casually along the edges of the road, as natural to this jungle as tree squirrels were in Arkansas. The hills flattened and the road broke through to a string of small villages. Filipinos lazed underneath the thatch of their nipa shacks, watching with mild curiosity as we passed. Children waved at us and called for chocolates and gum.

The road turned again and dropped down a very steep slope. In the distance far below me I could see the mammoth Subic Bay, where the Americans had kept a naval base since 1898, except for the period of Japanese occupation. Dozens of warships and troop transports were anchored in the bay. As we neared Subic, the roadside paths and the nipa shacks became mixed with an increasingly larger percentage of American soldiers and sailors, until they seemed to dominate our view. Their caps were pushed back. They sauntered when they walked. They laughed loudly and waved money at young Filipinas whose faces were fixed with delighted, devilish grins.

From the outer provinces the young girls came, emptying into Subic in search of money and with dreams of happiness, ready in their youth to believe every sailor's lie, content in their middle years to assuage their sorrows with the color of his money. And if they were lucky enough to live into their older days they spent their wisdom in an effort to convince other unbelieving young girls who found their way to Subic from the same dream-ridden provinces that life would truly have been better if they had spent it harvesting coconuts and planting rice.

I knew all that. But as we dropped off our thankful passengers and absorbed the dozens of hungry stares that bored in on Divina Clara, she reminded me anew with the angry flashing of her eyes.

Isabela Ramirez was Divina Clara's grandmother. She lived with four servants in a large two-story home surrounded by a walled compound on a grand hill that overlooked the bay. From the turn of the century on, the Ramirez family had grown wealthy through its dealings with the American navy. Isabela's husband, Fidel, who had died during the war, had begun as a young man by supplying fruit, vegetables, and meat to the naval base. Later he had expanded into construction and was a major contractor as the base grew larger. He had insulated his children from the raucous conduct of American sailors who took their liberty calls in Subic by sending them to school in Manila, bringing them home on weekends to help him work. Divina Clara's father had taken over the family business, which by the beginning of the war had expanded to include the port of Manila.

Living on the edges of Subic's constant chaos, benefiting from it and yet always threatened by it, had taught the Ramirez family one vital lesson. They had drilled it into every female, from the first day that her hips began to widen and her breasts began to swell. It boiled down to an axiom. Divina Clara had warned me of it when she first told me that her grandmother had demanded that I meet with her before I left for Japan.

In the Philippines, falling in love with an American means that someday you will be left behind.

"I want to ice-skate," said Divina Clara as we drove up the hill on the way to her grandmother's house. "What do you think about that?"

I began to laugh. "What are you talking about?"

"Ice-skating," she said. "I saw this movie last night at the American hospital. Sonja Henie. She is a very famous skater. It looks like wonderful fun. All the men were loving the way she moved on the ice. She had strong legs and a beautiful costume."

"You're far more beautiful than she is, Divina Clara."

"I don't have strong legs."

"You have wonderful legs. I marvel at your legs."

"She has long eyelashes," said Divina Clara, studying my face for a reaction. "I don't have eyelashes. Did you ever notice that?"

"Of course you have eyelashes."

"Not long ones."

I took her hand. "Are you nervous?"

She squeezed my hand, looking toward her grandmother's house. We were almost there. A flash of hopelessness passed across her face like the shadows of an old storm.

"Yes."

A teenaged boy was sitting lazily at the high black gate that led inside Isabel Ramirez's compound. As we drove up he recognized Divina Clara and jumped to his feet, smiling widely and waving to her. They called happily to each other as he slid open the heavy wrought-iron gate, letting us inside.

"She's been expecting us for hours," said Divina Clara as we climbed out of the jeep. "I told him the bridge was out."

"What happened to Filipino time?" I teased, deliberately taking her hand as the houseboy scrutinized me.

"It's different when you're waiting for your children to come, don't you think?"

"I think you just make things up to fit the moment."

"Today I am," she smiled. "Is that a sin?"

Her grandmother's house was a palatial and beautiful mix of Spanish and Filipino, as if its designer had placed brick and masonry around the basic structure of the nipa huts we had seen on the road coming into Subic. Instead of thatch, its high, steep roof was covered with rounded Spanish tiles. Almost the entire second floor was recessed, leaving a wraparound porch that opened out from the bedrooms. The elegant wooden eaves above the porch ringed the house with elaborately carved floral designs.

Isabela Ramirez appeared suddenly in the doorway. She was a smooth-skinned and full-breasted woman. Her grey-streaked hair was pulled tightly behind and then wrapped on top of her head. She was wearing a gold necklace with a matching bracelet and a brightly colored satin dress. Her firm lips told me that she was used to making decisions and that she was already beginning to make one about me. In fact, she was giving me a look that could have cracked a rock.

Isabela moved to us, pushing me back with a hard glance as she embraced Divina Clara. She melted then, lovingly holding her grandchild as she mussed with her windblown hair and teased her about her lipstick and earrings. Without loosening from her grandmother's embrace Divina Clara found my arm and tugged on me, pulling me into their orbit.

"Grandma, this is Jay Marsh."

"Yes," she said, giving me a small, frigid smile. "I know that." Finally she gestured to her doorway, speaking to Divina Clara. "Come in!"

Isabela had every reason not to like me or trust me, and she made that clear to me from the moment I entered her home. The home was cool inside, high as it was on this majestic hill that took its breezes from the bay. A grand mahogany staircase pointed upstairs. Old pottery and heavy wooden artifacts surrounded us as I followed her toward the sitting room. In the nearby *batalan* a tiny, hunchbacked cook who was about Isabela's age was busily preparing us a sumptuous midday meal. She and Divina Clara waved gladly to each other, exchanging hellos in Tagalog as we passed.

We reached the sitting room. The cook brought us juice she had squeezed from green mango, and a pot of jasmine tea. I drank the juice quickly and began to sip my tea. We sat in a nervous triangle, each of us intensely studying the other two. In this land where tests were rarely obvious, I could sense that I was failing mine. Finally I cleared my throat and tried a smile.

"You have a beautiful home," I said. "Far nicer than my own family's in the States."

Isabela nodded her thanks. "Do you have servants?"

"No," I answered. "But I've never *been* a servant."

"You are a servant of MacArthur," said Isabela, unimpressed.

"An aide," insisted Divina Clara. "Important to the General's success! Not a servant."

"Divina Clara has always had servants. I don't think she could live in a house without servants."

"Grandma—" began Divina Clara, forcing a smile and trying to interrupt.

"—and we are very close," said Isabela. "I cannot imagine Divina Clara living far away from family."

"Grandma—"

But Isabela would not be interrupted. Her words began pouring out of her with a force of their own, like a bubbling volcano. "—Divina Clara is young. And you, you are young. And I cannot find fault with this, this— force of nature. But you see, I have watched this for forty-five years already. It is not new to me. It is all around us here. I myself once thought I was in love with an American boy."

"Grandma!" said Divina Clara, laughing and clasping her hands underneath her chin as if praying. "You never told me that!"

"It would only have encouraged you, Divina Clara." Isabela's eyes went far away and brought back a memory, still young in its simplicity. "His name was Wesley Allen. We were not yet lovers, but he said he loved me. He told me he was coming back. I waited for him. I believed him. And he did not come back."

Divina Clara reached over and touched her grandmother's hand. Rather than comforting the old woman, it seemed to bring her to her senses. "But I have had a blessed life without him. And we have more experiences with Americans now. We know things. Americans for some reason are drawn to Filipina women. It is something I cannot fully understand. But when they go back to their own homes in the States they are somehow ashamed. Perhaps it is American women who shame them, I don't know. It doesn't matter if I know. And it is true that many Filipina women have a weakness for American men. Perhaps it is the Lord's work—"

"Yes," said Divina Clara hopefully, "I think it may be the Lord's work."

"—but it does not matter." Isabela said it with a flat finality, and looked directly into my eyes. "I will not trust you to go away and then say you are coming back. Or even to take Divina Clara so many thousands of miles away, into a culture that does not understand us, and that none of us understand. She is beautiful. She is educated—probably far better than you yourself! She has been tutored for years by Jesuits! What do the Americans understand about that? They will only see the color of her skin."

"But Grandma," said Divina Clara, her face lit with a new expectation. "He wants to stay here. He wants to live with us!"

She studied me for a long time, openly and without inhibition, reading my eyes and the set of my mouth and even the way I sat with one leg crossed over the other. "Why would you stay here?"

"I love it here," I said.

"It is hot, and it rains a lot," she protested.

"I'm from Arkansas. I'm used to that."

"What about your family?"

"My father and sister died before the war. My brother died in battle. My mother is living in California, but she has her own life now."

"She's living with an Italian!" volunteered Divina Clara, as if that were full evidence of my independence.

"You would want to work with our family business, then?" I picked up a hint of instant suspicion in Isabela's question, as if my interest in Divina Clara were mercenary.

"Only if you wanted me to," I said. "And only if I liked what it was that you wanted me to do. I'll never have to worry about finding about a job." I could see her beginning to weaken, perhaps even to believe. "I have a degree from the University of Southern California—a very fine college. And I've met many people who've offered me jobs while I've been work-ing for General MacArthur."

"MacArthur does hold great sway in these islands," said Isabela. "Many Filipinos love him, you know." She eyed me carefully. I knew there was a test in these simple words. "How do you find him?"

"He is a genius, of course," I answered, holding her eyes. "And a very difficult man."

"You must try to understand MacArthur," she said coquettishly. "It is a burden to be admired."

"To the contrary, I think he rather likes it."

"Yes," she said, holding back an amused smile. "But once they put you on a pedestal you must live in fear. It is a humiliation to be removed."

"I doubt that the thought of being removed has ever occurred to him."

"Of course it has," she said. She had finally allowed herself to smile fully, but her eyes seemed to hold a glimmer of respect for my honesty.

"He's more human than you think. The Japanese took him off his pedestal at Bataan and Corregidor. Now he must climb back up and stay there, or his life means nothing." She stared at me for another moment, her eyebrows arched with curiosity. "You sound like you don't like him very much."

"I respect him," I answered.

She nodded judiciously, as if she had reached some sort of a decision. "You're very careful with both your criticism and your praise," said Isabela. "Most Americans are not like that. So I will be more open with you. Not all Filipinos love MacArthur. Many are disappointed in him."

She watched me shrewdly for a moment, measuring me, then continued. "My husband is dead at the hands of the Japanese—just down the road from here! My son fought them from the jungle for three years. And what does MacArthur do, once he is reestablished in Manila? He makes a point of taking care of his high-level friends. He even pardons Roxas and all the others who openly collaborated with the Japanese."

Roxas. Her comment surprised me, but I could see its logic. Before the war the widely popular Manuel Roxas y Acuña had been a favorite of MacArthur, who had given him a general's commission in the U.S. army. He was also the protégé of former president Manuel Quezon, who announced just before he died while in exile that Roxas should be his successor. But the war had altered this pristine image. Roxas had at a minimum been used by the Japanese and from the evidence had turned into a willing collaborator. And MacArthur had indeed insulated him and other prominent Filipinos, shielding them all from any legal action by the strength of his own reputation.

"He didn't pardon them," I answered weakly. "He issued statements indicating that it was his opinion that they should not be tried."

Isabela laughed at me. "He exonerated them, Captain Marsh! They will use this. And never forget: they are from the great families. The little Filipinos are in awe of them and afraid of what would happen if they oppose them. Eighty percent of those who were in the Senate when the war began ended up serving under the Japanese in Laurel's puppet regime. They were spoiled landholders who had never worked in their lives. What did they know about fighting? They knew nothing but playing tennis and having parties! And already the suffering of my husband and my son mean nothing to them. They will continue to rule."

I remained silent, unsure of her motives in telling me this. And finally she nodded, as if urging me on. "You must be careful with MacArthur, especially in his new position. He worships power, you know. He will deal you away if it suits him. That is my point."

"I have learned a great deal from him," I finally managed to say. "The Philippines would not be free if it wasn't for his persistence."

She giggled, a vision dancing in her head. "Free, Captain Marsh? With his corrupt friends running the country again? And anyway, you have no memory of him before the war. His rich patrons tolerated him, and the little people loved it, but the rest of us used to laugh at him strutting around in his grand field marshal's uniform. He designed it for himself, you know! All the gold braid and flashy medals and white tunics. He takes himself too seriously. And then when the Japanese came they defeated him, did they not? Perhaps by forgiving Roxas he is forgiving himself."

"Jay is a very important adviser to the General," interrupted Divina Clara, leaning forward hopefully and taking my hand. "He speaks perfect Japanese." She squeezed my hand. "Jay, you should tell Grandma how you changed the words on the surrender document when the Japanese delegation visited Manila last week." Before I could begin she sat straight up, putting an arm on my shoulder as if presenting me for evidence. "Jay prevented a major international incident!"

Divina Clara was being a bit dramatic, but she was not incorrect. The week before, I had worked as an interpreter when sixteen representatives from the Japanese government had been flown into Manila. Arriving on an American C-54 with "BATAAN" emblazoned on the side, the delegation had been summoned by MacArthur to discuss the terms of Japan's surrender and to begin preparations for his arrival at Atsugi, a Japanese air force base just outside Tokyo. MacArthur, mindful of the ways of the emperor he sought both to emulate and supplant, had refused to meet with them, sending General Willoughby to greet the plane and General Sutherland to conduct the negotiations.

We had worked through the night in the war-scarred city hall. The Japanese turned over detailed maps and lists of their military units throughout Asia. Sutherland delivered MacArthur's instructions for the mechanics of the formal surrender and the logistics of our arrival at Atsugi. They had discussed the need for full command chronologies of all units during the war, a first step toward the nasty issue of accountability for war crimes. All of this was expected and went smoothly. But when Sutherland handed them the proposed surrender document that would be issued in the emperor's name, General Kawabe, his Japanese counterpart, dropped it onto the table as if it were on fire.

Drafted by the State Department in Washington, the document required that the emperor refer to himself as *Watakushi*, the ordinary and humble Japanese term for "I." The emperor, as with his predecessors before him, had always used *Chin*, an ancient word taken from the Chinese and reserved only for the royal family, meaning, roughly, "the moon that speaks to heaven." For the emperor to speak of himself as *Watakushi* would be to announce to the world, and to his own people, that he was now little more than a commoner.

This thought did not exactly displease the acidic, fury-ridden Sutherland, who was having the time of his life humiliating the Japanese delegation. But Katsuo Kasaki, the senior Japanese foreign affairs representative at the table, pleaded with Sutherland that the issue was "of the utmost importance. It is impossible for me to explain how important it really is!"

Sutherland had called a break in the meeting, and I had taken the matter to General MacArthur, who was following the course of the meetings in his own office, along with the ever-present Willoughby and Court Whitney. The General had understood instantly.

"We will not debase him in the eyes of his own people," MacArthur had said. "We will be attempting to govern a nation of eighty million people with a few hundred thousand soldiers. A few weeks ago every man, woman, and child in Japan was preparing to fight us, even if it meant dying with a pitchfork in their hands. This whole thing will be impossible without the help of the emperor."

He had nodded to me, his form of a grand compliment. "Good work, Jay. And make certain that you tell General Kawabe that I personally insisted that the emperor receive the respect of the royal *Chin*."

Isabela Ramirez had smiled softly as I told her this story. Her lined face held a map of knowing memories. And once I finished, she laughed softly, waving an arm into the air as if the whole thing were predictable.

"So this is Douglas MacArthur. Just as I told you! Now that he's going to Japan, maybe he will worship the emperor, too!"

Again I remained silent. Finally, Isabela squinted at me as if this tale had affirmed her own disbelief. "So you are going to Japan with MacArthur? How can you live with us if he's taking you to Japan?"

"I'm not staying in the army," I said. "MacArthur is bringing me to

Japan because I speak Japanese. He needs me at the beginning of the occupation. But I'm a reserve officer. The war's over. They can't keep me forever. I should be released within the next six months."

I reached over and took Divina Clara's hand, deciding it was time to boldly face Isabela. "I want to come back here and to be with Divina Clara. Mrs. Ramirez, I'm speaking to you from my heart. This is what will make us happy."

"What do you know about happiness, Mr. Marsh?" I saw her glance toward the *batalan*, giving the cook a subtle nod. "You're a very nice young man, and you should know this—I trust Divina Clara's judgment! But life has taught me some things. It has taught me that we rarely know when we are making a mistake. Only when we look back, perhaps years later, and see that we did."

Divina Clara leaned over the small table, taking Isabela's hand. "I love him, Grandma! It is something I have thought about."

"You're always thinking," smiled Isabela, patting Divina Clara's hand. "Sometimes you think yourself to death."

"Yes, it's my curse isn't it?" Divina Clara laughed lightly. "But I can feel its truth, Grandma. Sometimes it's like the wind—truth, I mean. You can't see it but you know it's there! And I feel that way about Jay."

Isabela let go of Divina Clara's hand. She grew silent, as if she were a judge mulling over the evidence. The cook brought in a tray of steaming food and set it on a nearby table. The food smelled delicious, a mix of rice and meat with vegetables and gravies. I was starving from the long trip. Divina Clara shifted in her chair, sneaking me a smile as she pretended to look over at the dining table. I could tell she was very happy from the way the conversation had turned. Her breasts pressed against her satin blouse and her hips tightened into her skirt as she twisted in the chair. In this intense, compressed moment I ached for her. She was five feet away, but as distant as forever.

"Shall we eat?"

Isabela rose from her chair and walked slowly toward the table. We followed her. The doting, flat-faced cook served us our food, smiling and nodding to me as she urged me to take an ever-larger portion. Isabela had become serene and did not lecture me again. As we ate we talked of her husband, Fidel, and of his genius for business, and how he had died in a summary reprisal taken by Japanese soldiers who had lost a friend killed by a guerrilla just down the street from their house. Isabela then spoke proudly of her son Carlos, Divina Clara's father, retelling the stories I had already heard about how he had expanded the business into Manila, then left for the jungles and fought the Japanese with a special ferocity after his father's death. But she was not really talking about the Japanese. Hidden in her words was an even stronger message.

We are proud. We are capable. We have survived, not only the Japanese but the Spanish and, yes, the Americans. And we will prosper. So what is it that you are bringing to us once your uniform is in the closet and the war is in the past?

And she was right. Who was I but an interloper who like my father and his fathers before him for the last two thousand years was willing to fall into a new unknown, bringing nothing but the brain between my ears and asking everything—to take her granddaughter into my genetic chaos as if she were the prize that might somehow belay all this Celtic wandering? I had no answers, and so I said nothing.

After dinner she walked us out into the courtyard and to the jeep. She embraced Divina Clara deeply, almost as if apologizing. I stood sheepishly by, finally reaching out to shake her hand. She looked me over from toes to top and then took my hand in both of hers and held it tightly for several seconds. And then she surprised me by reaching up and embracing me also.

"You are a very fine man, Jay Marsh. Are you really coming back?"

I was so elated that I accidentally picked her up off the ground, causing Divina Clara to laugh delightedly.

"As soon as I can," I said. "As soon as MacArthur lets me."

I eased her back to the ground. She smiled as we climbed into the jeep, still holding back a piece of her approval. "When I see that you have come back," she said, "we'll talk."

I had never seen Divina Clara so happy as when we drove back to Manila. In the jeep she sang me all the songs her grandmother had taught her when she was a young child. I recited for her the turgid poetry and proverbs that had traveled with my father and sustained him even in the bleak remoteness of our dead-end swamp. We shared a packet of bundled food that the little hunchbacked cook had prepared for us. And I knew that we belonged together.

At the wide river the bridge had already been repaired. We reached Manila just after dark. Back at the villa where I roomed we swam together in the pool, chasing each other and embracing underwater, our limbs sliding against each other and our hands teasingly touching secret, sacred parts. In my room she came to me, long-limbed and high-breasted from the shadows beyond my bed, and I devoured her as if this were the first and last time I would ever know her.

Afterward I ran my hands lightly all over her golden body and her slim legs and then up to her beautiful, rounded breasts, finally covering my face with a veil of her thick and silky hair. I was committing every part of her to my memory. We dozed and then she began again, touching me and pressing against me as if she wanted to take all of me inside her so that only my apparition would escape on the flight to Japan.

We slept again and when we awakened it was almost dawn. We knew her father would be furious and that her mother would be bent fervently over her rosary beads. But we had a broken bridge to blame and a seeming eternity apart to begin suffering through in a matter of days or maybe even hours. This was the last time we would be together until I somehow made it back from Japan.

It surprised me that she was suddenly sulky and crying as I drove her to her house. She said very little to me as we passed through the somnolent, still-ravaged streets on the way to San Miguel. The perfume of night-blooming jasmine wafted against me and it made me sad, knowing the happiness and romance that its aromas had carried into my life. I really wanted to stay here. Manila had become my home.

She looked over at me as if reading my thoughts and squeezed my arm. "I never thought you'd really leave. I don't know how to say good-bye."

"I hate good-bye. I never say it."

She took her hand from my arm and arched her back, resting her head on the top of the seat. Her eyes were closed as if she were trying to sleep. "When will you be back?"

"I don't know."

She paused, her eyes still closed. I could tell she was working up the courage to ask some great and difficult question. "How will I know when you're coming?"

"I'll find you."

She took a deep breath. "How do I know you're telling the truth?"

It shocked me to hear her say that. I looked over at her. Her eyes were still closed. Tears streaked her smooth and golden cheeks. And I finally understood the harsh things that Isabela had been saying. What certainty could I offer, when I did not even know what my own life would look like in one week?

"I love you, Divina Clara. This is where I want to be."

"How do I know?"

A panic began to seize me, as if my own certainties were being stripped away. "How can you doubt me?"

"You haven't even seen Japan. What if you like it?"

We reached her house. She sat unmoving, looking away from me. I started to say something stronger, but then she turned and kissed me fiercely, briefly clutching me to her, and suddenly broke away from my grasp.

"I believe you, Jay. I will wait for you."

Without warning she bolted from the jeep, running inside. I wanted to chase after her, but the thought of entering her home uninvited at five in the morning and trying to assuage her as her father and mother and brothers gathered to watch and possibly referee was too much. Finally I drove away, promising myself that I would come back that afternoon.

But by that afternoon I was no longer living in my comfortable shared villa. I was at Clark Field, supervising the staging of a mass of equipment and files that would accompany MacArthur on the flight to Atsugi. I thought of Divina Clara constantly as we inventoried and prepared, checking and rechecking, knowing from our leaps to Hollandia and Leyte and Luzon how to make such moves and how unforgiving MacArthur would be if they were not done with precision. There was no way to contact her. I wrote her a note and posted it from Clark, telling her I loved her and that I would write her as soon as I reached Japan.

And by the next morning I was gone.

CHAPTER 6

★ ★ ★ ★ ★

Winston Churchill would term the General's unprotected landing at Atsugi and the first days at Yokohama to have been "the bravest single act of World War Two." Beyond doubt, the supreme commander's bold touchdown inside the heart of Japan ranks as a great moment in modern history. But Churchill knew nothing of the royal *Chin*. And in truth we were far from the first American occupiers to step onto Japanese soil.

On August 28, 1945, a contingent of forty-five C-47s arrived at Atsugi, formally putting into motion the occupation. Once on the runway the first flight of Americans had deliberately taxied away from the operations buildings to the far end of the airfield, then disembarked from their planes with rifles at the ready. But hostilities were not what the Japanese military commander had in mind. He raced up to them in a truck and greeted them warmly, indeed with an almost arcane patience. He had brought along a Russian naval attaché to help break through the racial nervousness. And after the normal courtesies, he served the American officers a full lunch on white tablecloths, complete with fruit and wine.

The Americans quickly finished their lunches, and then set to work with a precision and speed that astonished the Japanese. By that evening more than five thousand ragged and starving Allied prisoners of war had been liberated and evacuated to U.S. warships off the nearby coast, and one particularly sadistic doctor at the Shinagawa POW hospital north of Yokohama had already been taken into custody for the murderous experiments he had performed.

All through the next day a continuous stream of C-54s poured into Atsugi, landing and taking off at two-minute intervals as the Eleventh Airborne Division took its defensive positions, which were in place by nightfall. That same afternoon the Fourth Marine Regiment, once disgraced by having lost its colors at Corregidor, had come ashore at Yokohama. Its first wave of landing craft consisted of, in the words of a grizzled and sarcastic Marine sergeant, "admirals trying to beat MacArthur ashore." And most stunning to our former enemy, by the morning of the thirtieth a new fifteen-mile oil pipeline had already been put into place between Atsugi and the port of Yokohama.

But this was all little more than a warm-up. The lingering stares of the Japanese and of the world would be on MacArthur. And no one knew better how to stage a main event.

On August 30 we flew from Manila on board MacArthur's personal C-54, on the side of which, just underneath the pilot's window, he had predictably emblazoned "BATAAN." As the hours went by and the engines droned, the sterile sameness of the military aircraft put my spirits into an odd limbo. A part of me could not believe I was really leaving the Philippines, and a part of me could not believe I'd ever even been there. I could hardly fathom that it had now been three years since I had left my own country, perhaps never to permanently return. Who had I been then, as I boarded a transport ship for Australia? I could not even remember. And it seemed equally inconceivable that in a few hours I would be landing in the ancient kingdom of Nippon, alongside the man who would be responsible for harnessing its energies and changing its directions. For who was I now, up in a cold drab space capsule, eating a box lunch sandwich and drinking rotgut coffee while the most powerful military man in the world paced up and down the aisle, near enough to touch, pointing with his corncob pipe and yelling out last-minute thoughts to his lawyer and political adviser General Courtney Whitney?

Who was I? Jay Marsh, chopper of cotton, picker of strawberries and poke greens, raiser of banty hens, whose father's greatest gift had been the liberation inherent in his death, setting a family free by the grace of its poverty. What would you think of me now, Dad, seeing the fruits of an athletic grace that would have gone unnoticed in Arkansas except for the strength of my hoe, and yet got me into college in California? And knowing that a war which took your other son has so rewarded me?

Not a fair trade. But in the incessant drone of the engines, I thought I heard both my father and brother singing just the same.

And who had MacArthur become? A subtle change had occurred in the past few days. We all had stopped publicly referring to MacArthur as the General and instead had begun calling him the supreme commander, the short version of his new official title, supreme commander of the Allied powers. MacArthur clearly loved the nuance of his new moniker, sensing that it would set him apart from other military men, especially in the eyes of the Japanese. There were many generals, just as there were many government ministers. But there was only one supreme commander, just as there was only one Supreme Being. And only one emperor.

We stopped briefly in Okinawa. General Eichelberger, who had just landed at Atsugi, radioed MacArthur that he was establishing a perimeter defense around the New Grand Hotel in Yokohama. Then he warned the General of fresh rumors that an ultranationalist rebel faction might try to assassinate him. Eichelberger recommended that we delay our flight for two more days to ensure complete security.

Willoughby, the intelligence chief, joined the argument. "We have a report that someone tried to assassinate the emperor," said Willoughby. "What kind of a target does that make you?"

"Nonsense," laughed MacArthur, ordering everyone back onto the plane. "They would never try to kill the emperor. And they will not try to kill me. A disappointed or rebellious Japanese would only make a scene and then kill himself. Trust me, gentlemen. I know the Orient."

On the flight from Okinawa it was the others who began pacing nervously, while MacArthur himself fell into a relaxed sleep. Over the Kanto Plain we approached Mount Fuji, all of us gaping at its beauty, and finally General Whitney nudged MacArthur awake. Seeing it, the supreme commander smiled as if he had found a long-lost friend.

"Good old Fuji," he said, his eyes going soft with memories. "It makes me miss my father, so very much. How I wish he were here for this moment! I first climbed it with him more than forty years ago, right after I finished West Point."

And so we had that in common, I thought when I heard his words. That this momentous journey made us both wish for dead fathers.

MacArthur stretched, looking around him, and saw that General Whitney and several others had strapped on their pistols. He immediately frowned, pointing to the weapons. "Take them off, boys! If they were going to kill us, do you think a pistol would make any difference?" They sheepishly began unstrapping their shoulder holsters. MacArthur rose from his seat, newly agitated, pacing and pointing as he lectured them.

"Don't ever forget this! There will be no second chances! Everything I say, and everything I do, will be scrutinized in intricate detail by millions of Japanese. They will be searching for clues, analyzing and discussing me as if even the way that I hold my pipe might give them a clue to the future. And in the Orient, the man who shows no fear is king. Nothing will impress them like absolute fearlessness! Nothing! Fearlessness on the outside! Serenity on the inside! And certainty when you act! That is the Asian way! And the first time you or I blink, even for a second, it will be a new ball game."

He sat back down, pulling out his old leather tobacco pouch, and began refilling his favorite corncob pipe.

"So, relax, boys. No one who rides with me carries a gun, because in peacetime a gun on a senior officer is a sign of fear." He winked over at Whitney. "It's been a long road from Melbourne, Court. But it's over! This is the payoff."

The aircraft began its descent. In the fields below us I could see the red markers laid out by the advance party, marking the Atsugi runway's landing approach. The C-54 hit the runway smoothly but soon bounced and yawed as it braked on top of huge cracks and recently patched bomb craters. We taxied past a hangar that already flew the American flag. In the hangar, American soldiers and airmen waved delightedly at our plane. On the ramps outside were hundreds of silvery little kamikaze aircraft, lined up in neat rows, their propellers now removed.

The C-54 stopped near the operations terminal and began shutting down its engines. In front of the operations terminal I could see perhaps a thousand people waiting. Eichelberger had even flown in a military band, which stood at the ready, near our aircraft. The last propeller did its last turn and in the eerie silence that overcame us we could hear the ground crew yelling to one another as they chocked the wheels and called to the pilot.

At the rear of the plane the loadmaster now unlocked the side door. A metal ramp was quickly wheeled out by the ground crew and he grabbed it, affixing it to the doorway. And then he cheerily called to MacArthur. "All set, General! Welcome to Japan."

At the door MacArthur paused for a moment, smiling serenely and lighting his pipe. He touched the saluting, pimply faced young airman on the chest.

"Remember this moment, son. We're making history here."

And then he stepped outside.

As MacArthur walked onto the ramp a mob of journalists rushed forward, surrounding the airplane's tail area. Cameras clicked and flashed. The army band began to play a spirited march. He paused dramatically a few steps down the ramp, clearly enthused by this welcoming. The cameras clicked in greater earnest as he puffed away on his trademark pipe, wearing those famous sunglasses, turning this way and that as if surveying the conquered landscape. MacArthur knew a good photo opportunity as well as any seasoned politician. This was indeed the payoff, a moment far greater than he might ever have anticipated when he escaped in humiliation on a PT boat little more than three years before as the Japanese guns pounded Corregidor and the soldiers he abandoned on Bataan prepared to surrender.

General Eichelberger waited for him at the bottom of the ramp. They grinned widely to each other as they exchanged salutes and handshakes. Then he and Eichelberger went over to thank the band and to shake hands with the crowd of clamoring American soldiers and airmen.

One of General Eichelberger's aides had recognized me as I followed MacArthur down the ramp. As soon as MacArthur and Eichelberger walked away, the young major began pulling me toward the terminal building.

"You're General MacArthur's interpreter, right?"

"One of them," I answered.

"We've got a little problem over here."

Forty of the ugliest cars I had ever seen awaited us in a long line just outside the terminal building. An ancient red fire truck was parked at their front. Behind the fire truck sat a battered American Lincoln that was at least ten years old. The rest of the cars, most of them charcoal-burners, made the Lincoln look absolutely elegant. Uniformed chauffeurs sat dutifully inside each car, staring straight ahead.

A dozen formally dressed Japanese waited somberly near the cars, lined up in two ranks, nervously watching MacArthur as he waded through a crowd of reporters and well-wishers. A small man dressed in full morning dress and top hat stood in front of them at a rigid, near-military attention. He was obviously acting as their leader. As I approached him it occurred to me that even though he was motionless, he was probably the most animated person I had ever seen. He simply emanated energy. He looked to be in his sixties. He had wide, shocked eyes that were accentuated by full grey eyebrows. Underneath his long curving nose was a thick, Hitler-esque mustache, trimmed and shot with grey. He seemed to be taking in everything at once, peering from behind round, wire-framed glasses as though he were looking through binoculars at a new and confusing battle-field.

As I neared him the Japanese dignitary smiled brightly, intuitively knowing that I was his man. Without waiting for the formality of an introduction he nodded to General Eichelberger's aide as if dismissing him, and then began speaking to me in Japanese.

"So," he said, "you speak Japanese."

"Yes," I answered. "I'm Captain Jay Marsh. I work with General Mac-Arthur."

"Ah, so." He took off his top hat, revealing a pate of sparse, greying hair, and bowed ever so slightly, a gesture of moderate respect. "Yes, you speak our language very well! I am Koichi Kido. Lord privy seal to Emperor Hirohito. The emperor asked me to meet General MacArthur, and to welcome him to our country."

I returned his bow, restraining my astonishment. This dapper little man now standing in near anonymity amid all the celebration and confusion happened to be the chief civilian adviser to the emperor himself. I already knew from Willoughby's intelligence briefings that Kido, a marquis in the royal family and the son of the emperor's foster father, had been a close confidant and friend to the emperor for more than twenty years. Since childhood the emperor had called Kido the first of his Big Brothers, a special term of endearment. And Kido had served inside the Imperial Palace as lord privy seal since 1940, spending the entire war literally at the right hand of the throne. Prime ministers and generals had risen and fallen from the words of advice Kido had whispered inside the impenetra-ble palace walls. There could have been no greater signal, other than the emperor himself driving out to Atsugi, that the emperor was in a coopera-tive mood.

But cooperative hardly meant humiliated. Having in his own mind dismissed Eichelberger's aide, Kido began taking charge of me as if I worked directly for him. He cocked his head, giving him a look of great confusion, and pointed toward the army band, where MacArthur was still working his way through the crowd like a campaigning politician.

"They have taken our interpreter!" said the lord privy seal, as the men behind him solemnly nodded. "I don't know what for. To talk to the press, I think. We have prepared a formal welcome for General MacArthur, and so it is necessary to ask for your assistance."

MacArthur and Eichelberger were slowly heading in our direction. I moved as if to retrieve them, but Kido grabbed my arm.

"First," said Kido, as if it were natural to be giving me instructions, "let me tell you about the cars. Your superiors asked for fifty. It is perhaps a compliment to your General LeMay and his bombers that we could not find fifty. We have forty-one. Yokohama is not far, fifteen miles away. If forty-one are not enough, they can come back and make two trips."

"I will tell the supreme commander."

"Yes," said Kido, his eyebrows arching as he instinctively caught on to the manner in which we were now addressing MacArthur. "And tell him that according to the wishes of the emperor, we have made all necessary arrangements for security along the way." He gave me a small, almost conspiratorial smile. "I think the supreme commander will be satisfied with the emperor's welcome."

MacArthur had seen me standing with the Japanese delegation and now was approaching us. Seeing this, Kido's eyes went even wider. He gave off another confused look that I began to understand was his normal call to action and then grunted a quick command as he pointed to one of his fustily dressed subalterns. The middle-aged deputy ran quickly inside the terminal building. And by the time MacArthur and Eichelberger reached us, the assistant was standing at Kido's side, smiling expectantly as he held a tray with a dozen glasses of freshly squeezed orange juice just underneath MacArthur's chin.

"What have we got here, Jay?"

MacArthur stood facing me, his face lit almost dreamily from his enjoyment of the moment. Except for the tray-holder, the entire Japanese delegation had leaned forward in identical deep bows, their faces below their waists. The deeper the bow, the greater the respect, and their bows could not have been deeper unless they had prostrated themselves on the tarmac.

"It looks like orange juice, sir."

He shot me an irritated glance. "Are you trying to be funny, Jay?"

"No, sir," I protested, quickly recovering. "I thought that was what you were talking about. This is Lord Privy Seal Marquis Koichi Kido, the emperor's closest personal adviser. The emperor sent him here to personally greet you."

MacArthur watched the deeply bowing Kido for a moment, then gave him a polite nod. "That was kind of the emperor."

"Yes, sir. But I was getting a little worried about the juice."

"What about it?"

"I don't know what it is."

"Then why don't you ask him?"

"I mean—what it really might be."

MacArthur gave me an impatient look. "Ask him."

"Yes, sir," I answered rather sheepishly. "I was just getting ready to do that."

I tapped the bowing Kido on the shoulder, causing him to rise up. It would have been easy to mistake the lord privy seal's too-glad smile and hyperactive eyes for foolishness and his deep bow for sycophancy, and I wondered at that moment if MacArthur or even I was making that mistake.

I switched to Japanese. "The supreme commander is very thankful to the emperor for having sent his regards. And he was wondering what the orange liquid was."

Kido uttered a quick command and the entire delegation ceased its bowing. He pushed the subaltern forward, urging the tray again on MacArthur. "General Kawabe informed us that when he boarded the American plane in Okinawa on his way to Manila, he was served orange juice. And when he reached the meetings with General Sutherland they served orange juice. And when they had breakfast after the meetings they gave them—"

"—orange juice," I said, repressing a smile. "I understand." I turned back to MacArthur. "He says General Kawabe told him that all Americans like orange juice."

"Well, I can't speak for all Americans, but I do," smiled MacArthur, looking at Kido with a condescension he had formerly reserved for native Papuan chieftains. "Tell him thank you very much."

As MacArthur reached for a glass, General Willoughby stepped forward. "Be careful, General!"

"What are you talking about?" said MacArthur.

"It could be poison," said Willoughby.

Court Whitney, who had just joined them, pointed suspiciously toward Kido. "There's plenty on that tray. Make them drink one first."

MacArthur shook his head, belittling them. "Gentlemen, what did I tell you on the plane?" He raised the glass, silently toasting the delighted Kido, and drained it. "Come on, boys," he now said. "Have some orange juice." Willoughby, Eichelberger, and Whitney looked abashedly at one another and reached for glasses on the tray.

"They've only been able to find forty-one cars," I continued, as the generals obediently drank their juice. "But he says that they can make two trips. And that the emperor has arranged for your security."

"We don't need the emperor's security," scolded Willoughby. "What kind of signal would that be sending? And how can we trust it?"

"If it's genuine, we'll take all the help we can get," answered General Eichelberger, checking his watch and peering at the antiquated cars.

"It will be genuine," said MacArthur. "Make no mistake about that." MacArthur placed his glass back on the tray, causing the subaltern to bow deeply. The General grinned delightedly at the little man. He was enjoying himself beyond all expectations. "Well, gentlemen, let's head to the hotel, shall we? Jay, thank Mr. Kido for me, will you? And tell him to give my regards to the emperor, whom I hope to meet very soon."

I turned to Kido. "The supreme commander is very appreciative of your thoughtfulness and thanks the emperor for all of his courtesies. He now wishes to go to the hotel."

"Good," said Kido, still sounding as though he were somehow in charge. "It is time for that."

MacArthur and Eichelberger were now walking toward the old Lincoln that was parked just behind the thoroughly ancient fire truck. General Willoughby had caught up with them and was earnestly discussing something with MacArthur. Kido made a move as if to join them. "We will ride with the supreme commander, if that is considered permissible?"

I watched MacArthur, Eichelberger, and Willoughby climb into the car, clearly savoring this moment of absolute triumph. I had instinctively picked up on where MacArthur was placing Kido, and it was not with them. The emperor's chief adviser might properly welcome the supreme commander to Atsugi, but he surely was not going to deliver Douglas MacArthur to Yokohama. Only the emperor might have been permissible, and on this journey I wasn't sure that even Hirohito would have made the lead car.

"I am very sorry," I said as I began leading the lord privy seal toward a car further back in the column. "But that will not be permissible." And so we boarded a sputtering charcoal-burner, and settled into its musty, just-brushed rear seat.

Off to Yokohama went our ludicrous convoy of battered cars, led by the hopeless old red fire truck. The truck's siren wailed mournfully. It turned off only when the truck broke down, which seemed to be every few minutes. Behind it our column of charcoal-burners sizzled and popped and roared, backfiring through worn gaskets. And yet these were the best that had survived the war's final bombings. Never in history, except perhaps at Carthage, had a great and aspiring nation been so reduced to junk.

But once outside the airport we came upon a sight so chilling and yet so magnificent that even now I can only recall it with a breathless awe. Before us on both sides of the road, under the searing summer sun for as far as the eye could see, two interminable lines of Japanese infantrymen stood side by side, spaced only a few feet apart, their lines stretched endlessly over nearby hills and around far turns. This trail of identical leather and khaki uniforms, of seemingly changeless bronzed skin and coal black hair underneath khaki caps, of glinting bayonets fixed onto rifles and rifles pushed forward at the ready, was peering out with the forlorn emptiness of Ozymandias toward a desert of dry fields and the dusty ruins of what once were cities.

For mile after mile we drove between the two rows of rigid, sweating, unsmiling infantrymen. I did not see one of them so much as twitch. Their eyes remained averted, as if the emperor himself were driving past. Kido informed me that we had passed thirty thousand of them by the time we reached Yokohama, a steadfast honor guard that at the same time both welcomed and protected the new supreme commander. Watching them, I knew what MacArthur would be thinking as he peered out from his car behind the stuttering, whining fire truck: our century's Caesar was now entering the latest Gaul.

Next to me in the old car, Lord Privy Seal Kido caught my amazed stare. He smiled proudly, as if he had personally conjured up this commanding scene. And looking at him, I realized at once that he had.

"Before, only for the emperor," said Kido. "But now for the supreme commander, too. This is the emperor's gift. You will please tell General MacArthur that?"

"The emperor's gift?"

"Yes," said Kido matter-of-factly. "The emperor is expressing his thanks to the supreme commander."

"I will tell him," I said, somewhat uncertainly.

"We received very good reports about the American point of view from General Kawabe," said Kido, as if explaining. "I am glad that attitudes are positive, as I have been working on this for some time."

"On what, Lord Privy Seal?"

"On an honorable peace," said Kido, as if my question were ludicrous. "A way to end the war and still preserve the dignity of our emperor. I have been working on this every day for more than a year. General Kawabe reports that MacArthur understands this." He gestured grandly toward the long line of soldiers outside the car window. "And we especially thank him for preserving the royal *Chin.*"

The royal *Chin.* Yes, I thought, remembering the intense discussion in the General's office in Manila. If it were not for MacArthur's intervention, the emperor would have been forced to refer to himself in public by the humiliating word *Watakushi*, forever diminishing his position and shaming not only himself but his ancestors. MacArthur had protected the emperor's royal prerogative. And this honored welcome, which was certain both to please and flatter the supreme commander, was not so much an act of obeisance as a gesture of thanks.

MacArthur was no doubt in ecstasy as we drove past the long lines of conquered soldiers, congratulating himself on his mastery of the Oriental mind. But it was not simply MacArthur's arrival that had brought the lord privy seal to the airport and conjured up the thousands of soldiers along the roadway. The emperor's edict had ordered it. And so long as the supreme commander continued to protect the emperor from shame, he would never be in true danger in Japan. MacArthur might never admit it, but at that moment I comprehended that he had known this all along.

Nearing Yokohama the desolation from our bombings seemed almost total. I looked out at the dusty, crumbling ruins, at the boarded windows of little shops, at ragged people of all ages who stared curiously toward us over the heads of the rigidly solemn lines of soldiers. Piles of rubbish overflowed into the streets. Electricity and water service were still knocked out. Since the fire bombings began in March, hundreds of thousands had died between this road and downtown Tokyo, perhaps twenty miles away. And I could not help but think in my own mind that the terrible debt for the rape of Manila had in some way already been paid.

Kido nodded sagely, catching every innuendo in my absorbing stare. "It has been very bad for our people. And it is wise that the supreme commander chose first to stay in Yokohama rather than entering Tokyo at once. The supreme commander has a very profound understanding. We are impressed with him. He is an immensely wise man. Maybe in one week he can come to Tokyo. It will be better after the official ceremonies ending the war. We will ease into this new situation. There are still many preparations to be made. Many people who need to be worked with and reassured."

Listening to the lord privy seal as I continued to absorb the enormous destruction that surrounded us, I could not help but marvel at his unbreakable self-assurance. We had entered a beaten and ravaged nation, but this was not a beaten man. His crisp words and certain judgments would have been more fitting if MacArthur had been a visiting dignitary rather than a conquering proconsul. Then it occurred to me. He hadn't even used the word "surrender." He spoke of "ceremonies ending the war," Of this "new situation." In their language the Japanese did not even have a word for surrender. In their minds they did not understand the concept of surrender. To discuss what westerners termed surrender, Kido would have been required to mention shame. So he did not broach it. And despite all the bowing and the laying down of arms and the spiking of the guns and even the coming pomp and ceremony where Allied military leaders would be profusely congratulating themselves, I knew that somehow in their own minds the Japanese were not actually surrendering.

And then I remembered the text of the emperor's radio message of two weeks before. In his stilted broadcast, given in the odd idiom used by the imperial court, the emperor had been strangely unrepentant about the war. He told his subjects that Japan "had declared war on America and Great Britain out of Our sincere desire to ensure Japan's self-preservation and the stabilization of East Asia, it being far from Our thought to infringe upon the sovereignty of other nations or to embark upon territorial aggrandizement." He lamented that "the war situation has developed not necessarily to Our advantage" and criticized "the enemy" for its "new and most cruel bomb." He thanked "Our Allied nations of East Asia, who have consistently cooperated with the Empire toward the emancipation of East Asia." And then he warned the Japanese people about their conduct in the coming occupation, saying that they should "beware most strictly of any outbursts of emotion which may engender needless complications," that would take away from his ultimate goal: "We have resolved to pave the way for a grand peace for all the generations to come, by enduring the unendurable and suffering that which is insufferable."

In plain words, as history's most gruesome war was ending, the emperor had denied that Japan had erred and told his people to prepare again for the future. Watching and listening to his lord privy seal as we drove toward Yokohama, those words took on a fresh meaning. The Japanese people may have been in shock, but their leaders, with their fierce loyalties and incredible minds, were not stumbling blindly into these new days of peace. MacArthur and Willoughby had their plan, which was to harness the emperor in order to rule Japan through his offices. But there could be no doubt that Kido and the emperor had their strategy as well. In his radio message the emperor had embarked on a sacred mission: to deliver Japan and the imperial system intact to future generations. Were they planning to do so by harnessing MacArthur? If so, this appeal to his vanity was a proper beginning.

We had reached Yokohama's waterfront park area. Soon the comical little convoy halted before the old, Edwardian New Grand Hotel. A tuxedoed, elderly man whom Kido pointed out to me as Yozo Namura, the hotel's longtime owner, greeted MacArthur with a deep bow as the supreme commander stepped out of the ancient Lincoln. I began to hurry out of the car, knowing that MacArthur and his generals would need me to help arrange their accommodations. But the lord privy seal tugged insistently at my arm.

"Captain Jay Marsh!" said Kido, his eyebrows raised and his face as always looking shocked and alert. "I am very happy that you speak such good Japanese and that you have such a strong understanding of what needs to be done. We must work together! Please let me know if there is anything the supreme commander would like to pass on to the emperor."

I shook Kido's hand. "I will tell the General. You should call on me anytime, Lord Privy Seal."

"We can talk freely, yes? You and I? Without pretense?"

I searched into his eyes, unsure why he would seek to share any intimacies with a young and lowly officer such as myself. I knew that my position on MacArthur's staff meant something to him. And perhaps it was essential that Kido return to the emperor with at least one American who could be dealt with directly.

I shrugged in agreement, mildly flattered by his invitation. Behind me, General Whitney was calling my name, demanding that I help the senior officers check into the hotel. Kido noticed this and smiled with obvious pleasure. That a senior general was calling urgently to me seemed to be elevating my status even more.

"If you want to talk freely to me, Lord Privy Seal, I will talk freely with you."

"Without pretense?"

"Yes," I said. "Openly."

"Excellent!" His bright, active eyes were now everywhere at once, as if recording all the events and assimilating them for his report to the emperor. "So. Now I will go. And I will talk to you very soon!"

The charcoal-fired car stumbled off into the almost-empty street. From the backseat, Kido waved at me as if we were now old friends. And then I hurried into the hotel.

The lobby was a madhouse as senior generals and their aides began to fight for the best rooms. In the midst of all this chaos, MacArthur stood next to General Court Whitney, talking quietly. Nearby, Mr. Namura and four bowing maids were waiting to show him to the hotel's finest suite.

Always autocratic, MacArthur had taken on a regal air during the motorcade from Atsugi. As I neared them, he was glowing euphorically, his eyes glazed with satisfaction. He tapped General Whitney on the chest.

"Did you ever have a dream that came true, Court?"

"What a day," said Court Whitney. "Never in my wildest imagination did I think I'd see anything like that."

I cleared my throat, trying to get MacArthur's attention. "Sir—" I began. "Excuse me, sir?"

"Yes, Jay?"

"Sir, Lord Privy Seal Kido asked me to tell you that the soldiers along the road were the emperor's gift, and that—"

He froze me with a glare, as if I had been insubordinate. "Captain Marsh, how many Americans in this hotel can speak Japanese?"

I swallowed, looking at him with embarrassment. "Yes, sir. I'll go take care of them. I thought you'd like some feedback from the lord privy seal, sir. He's a very powerful man."

"Not anymore, he's not."

"I spent a good bit of time with him, sir. He talks directly with the emperor every day."

The reminder of Kido's direct connection to the emperor penetrated MacArthur's ebullience, causing him to glance shrewdly at Court Whitney. "Did he speak openly with you, Jay?"

"Yes, sir. He was impressed that I knew Japanese. He wants to—

continue a dialogue, I guess. He said that if you wanted to pass anything on to the emperor, I should contact him."

"We'll have our own ways of doing that," shrugged MacArthur. "But stay in touch with him. We'll need every piece of intelligence we can get our hands on."

"Just keep us posted," reminded Court Whitney. "There will be only one policy coming out of this command."

"Sir," I hurriedly agreed, feeling young, clumsy, and outclassed. "I know when I'm in over my head. I'm not a policy-level officer."

MacArthur fixed me with a piercing stare. "Well said, Captain Marsh. I know this is an exciting time for you, but I have two senior generals advising me on policy, and I will remind you that I have more than forty years' experience in the Orient myself. We don't want to offend the emperor, but we don't want young captains thinking they know how to operate in Japan, either." He now glanced around at the discord that had invaded the lobby, then smiled benignly to me as if I were an overeager child. "In the meantime, help these people check in, will you?"

"Yes, sir. Right away, sir."

I walked quickly toward the front desk, making myself available to the long line of loud and eager officers, fierce conquerors all, as they fought for rooms equal to their real and imagined statures. MacArthur had every right to dismiss my advice. It did not faze me. I was no one, really. I knew and accepted that. But at that moment I somehow knew that General Douglas MacArthur had changed, even from the brilliant and undeniably egotistical leader I had served on the journey from New Guinea to Manila.

It was as if the final defeat of Japan had been his own liberation. He had at last climbed the high wall that marked the edges of mortal behavior and was alone and free on the other side. He was the supreme commander, off in the virgin wilderness, beyond where anyone else had ever traveled, running toward his own eternity. An eternity that he himself would define and bring to fruition. Who would dare to make the rules for such a probing pioneer? No one, from me all the way up to President Truman, was going to tell him who to listen to or how to run Japan.

I did not like this feeling. I did not want to see him this way, or to know him so well. I began to long for the simplicity of Manila, where the world on the far side of the war was something to be dreamed about rather than lived in.

CHAPTER 7

★ ★ ★ ★ ★

For two days the front desk of the New Grand Hotel became my full-time post as I helped the hotel manager sort out American and Allied military ranks and create priorities regarding who would get the better rooms. There were plenty of squabbles. All day, all night, and into the next day the dignitaries flooded in, preparing for the surrender ceremony that would take place aboard the USS *Missouri* in Tokyo Bay on September 2. And on the evening of August 31 I presented MacArthur with a ghost that would not die, no matter how hard he tried to dress it up with praise, or disassociate himself by pushing it back into the cobwebbed closet.

Wainwright.

The three-star general whom MacArthur had left in command when he fled Corregidor made his way into the hotel lobby, hobbling horribly as he leaned on a brown walnut cane. His hair had become snow-white and feathery. He was gaunt-faced and wispy-thin. His eyes protruded from scarred and sunken cheeks, carrying a beaten opaqueness as they searched the unfamiliar openness of the lobby. After the humiliating surrender at Corregidor, Wainwright had spent the remainder of the war at Japanese prisoner of war camps in the Philippines, Taiwan, and finally Manchuria. He had been freed by Soviet troops only four days before. Our pilots had flown him briefly to Manila, where he had received a medical checkup and a haircut. A khaki uniform had been specially tailored to fit his emaciated frame. He and General Arthur Percival, the British commander who had surrendered to Yamashita at Singapore, would be special guests aboard the *Missouri*.

I did not recognize the ill-fated general as he walked slowly to the front desk, a half dozen photographers following in his wake. At first I thought he was an old World War One commander, perhaps brought in to receive some special honor for past glories. I left my post near the desk and met him at the center of the lobby.

"Good evening, General," I said, noting the three stars on his collar. "Are you checking in, sir?"

His voice was throaty, a near-whisper. "I'm looking for General MacArthur."

"Yes, sir," I answered. "And who shall I say wishes to see the supreme commander?"

"Wainwright," he said, searching my face as if silently asking whether I recognized his name. "Jonathan M. Wainwright."

"*General Wainwright?*" My stare betrayed my utter shock. It seemed incomprehensible that this aged, wasting man now leaning against his cane had graduated from West Point four years after MacArthur and served under him as a subordinate commander.

"Do I know you, son?" He was squinting terribly, trying to place my face. "Were you with us at Bataan?"

"No, sir. But I'm very proud to meet you, General."

"Where is General MacArthur?"

I raised both of my hands, as if to still him. "Don't go away, sir. I'll be right back."

MacArthur was in the hotel dining room, starting his second dinner of the evening. I approached his table quietly, uncertain not only about intruding but of the reaction I would receive. For it was well known that despite MacArthur's passion for erasing the stain of Bataan, he had not been kind to the abandoned Wainwright after his own escape to Australia. In truth, it had been Wainwright all along, rather than MacArthur, who had led the actual defense of Bataan. During the entire siege, MacArthur had left the relative safety of the dark, cool tunnels of Corregidor to visit his soldiers on the Bataan Peninsula only once. It was Wainwright who had directed the artillery, and walked the lines, and suffered the mosquitoes and pellagra and dysentery, and looked into the hopeless faces of dying American and Filipino soldiers as they withstood an unremitting Japanese advance. And it was Wainwright who in the end had been left behind to face the grim reality of defeat.

Then from the safety of Australia as the Japanese sledgehammer pounded the trapped and abandoned Bataan defenders and their rations dwindled toward an inevitable starvation, it had been MacArthur who had humiliated Wainwright by radioing Washington, "it is of course possible that with my departure the vigor of application of conservation may have been relaxed." And as the Japanese swarmed through the Bataan Peninsula and began the direct invasion of Corregidor, which was now cut off from all resupplies, it had been MacArthur who had fantastically urged that Wainwright "prepare and execute an attack upon the enemy," arguing that he was "utterly opposed under any circumstances to the ultimate capitulation of this command."

And as the Japanese began dropping sixteen thousand artillery rounds a day on the overwhelmed Corregidor defenses, and then assaulted, forcing their surrender, it had been MacArthur who had radioed Washington that "Wainwright has temporarily become unbalanced, and susceptible of enemy use." And MacArthur, whose Medal of Honor after his flight from Corregidor was proposed by General George Catlett Marshall as a propaganda measure to erase the stain of his having fled, had for years been the main obstacle to Wainwright's receiving the same award for having remained and fought. Wainwright's actions, according to MacArthur, did not warrant this great distinction, and his having surrendered would have brought injustice to the hallowed medal.

I approached the supreme commander quietly, watching him slice into a steak. "Sir," I said, "you have a visitor outside." He looked up from his plate, chewing his meat, quietly rebuking me for having interrupted his dining. "General Wainwright, sir."

A kaleidoscope of emotions swirled inside MacArthur's eyes as he finished chewing. Swallowing, he peered toward the dining room's entrance and then took a slow drink from his water glass. Finally he rose quickly from his chair and began to stride in the direction of the lobby.

Wainwright had been walking slowly toward us from the lobby, and the two generals met just inside the dining room. Without hesitation MacArthur embraced his former subordinate, smiling dotingly into his wounded eyes, summoning up all his charm as the cameras flashed in their faces.

Wainwright was trying mightily to smile, but the weight of more than three years of uncertainty was too much.

"The last time I saw you," said MacArthur lightly, "I was giving you a box of my best cigars and two cans of shaving cream."

"You said you'd return," said Wainwright. "And you damn well did." He paused, shaking his head. "General," he said, "I'm—I'm sorry. We did the best we could."

"Why, Jim," said MacArthur, using Wainwright's old nickname, "I know that. I always knew that."

Wainwright began choking up. His mind was still in the mud and drek of 1942, having had to relive the degradation of his surrender a million times as he wallowed in taunt-filled shame from one Japanese prison cell to another. He could not discern that MacArthur's was now in 1946 or maybe 1964, far on the other side of war. He tried again.

"I don't suppose they'll ever let me have another command."

"Jim," said MacArthur, "mark my words. Your old corps is yours whenever you want it."

"General—" said Wainwright. And then he could say no more, for he began weeping uncontrollably.

Watching Wainwright cry as MacArthur stood with an almost fatherly arm around his bony shoulder, I found myself awash with a sense of injustice that I could not define. Or perhaps it was merely that I was young. I had never before seen with such clarity that great triumphs and disasters can be spawned unexplainably by the same moment, that courage could destroy one man while flight could make another man king. I did not wish to be unfair to MacArthur, but Wainwright had carried the load, fought the impossible fight, suffered the insufferable, borne the unbearable. And here he was, begging for forgiveness from the very man who had left him and the others behind to suffer death, starvation, and captivity.

It could have been the other way around. These were not dissimilar men. Wainwright, less intellectual but a better soldier, shared MacArthur's pedigree. His grandfather, a Union naval officer, had been killed in action at the battle for Galveston Harbor in 1863 during the Civil War. His uncle had been killed fighting Mexican pirates in 1870. His father, a West Point graduate, had fought in the Indian Wars and in the Spanish-American War, and then died on active duty in Manila in 1902, just as Wainwright was entering West Point. Like MacArthur, Wainwright had been chosen First Captain at West Point, had seen action in the Philippines immediately after graduating, and had been in heavy combat during World War One. Among Wainwright's high decorations for heroism was a Distinguished Service Cross for maneuvering his forces from northern Luzon onto the Bataan Peninsula in a hard-fought retrograde just after the Japanese landed at Lingayen Gulf in 1942.

Unlike MacArthur, Wainwright was utterly guileless. And unlike Mac-Arthur he was loyal to a fault. Wainwright at that very moment could have been arguing that had MacArthur listened to him in 1942 and moved sooner onto the Bataan Peninsula, they could have brought along tons of food and ammunition, and there would never have been an admonition from MacArthur in Australia, much less a surrender or a death march. But Wainwright was a true soldier. He would never in the rest of his life speak a word against his old commander.

In MacArthur's smiling face I saw relief, because with his instinctive cunning he had quickly realized that Wainwright would never do so. But I also saw something else. As his gaze lingered on Wainwright's frail fea-tures and white hair, then met the eyes that seemed at that moment only half back from the near dead, MacArthur was staring into an uncomfort-able mirror. There but for an escape stood he himself, had he been strong enough at his age to survive what Wainwright had endured. Wainwright was the living reminder not only of the ignominy of his earlier failure but of the fate that had befallen the very luckiest of those who had been left behind.

Where would MacArthur have been at this moment, and what would he have looked like, if he, like Skinny Wainwright and even Tomoyuki Yamashita, had stayed behind with his men? This was not an idle or unfair question. Even Eisenhower had proposed to General Marshall in 1942 that MacArthur stay and fight. But instead of standing white-haired and broken before the world in crimped khakis, begging for some fresh under-standing of an ever more distant plight, MacArthur was the new Caesar. During the siege of Corregidor MacArthur's dreams were so narrow that he had shamelessly inveigled a promise from Philippines president Quezon to rehire him as grand marshal once the war ended, with the same salary and benefits as before. Now he was preparing to take the Japanese surrender and to run the entire government of an ancient and mighty nation.

"The cane," said MacArthur, pointing to Wainwright's side. "Didn't I give you that? In Manila?"

"Yes, General," said Wainwright, flattered that MacArthur would remember, his eyes now going far away into a past that could never be recaptured. "Before the war. You said I needed a swagger stick."

Manila. Like a song it held a special romance for all of us, leading even me to stutter in my thoughts. The memory of life before the war hung like a heavy weight between them, causing both of their heads to sag. For several seconds, neither man could speak. Finally MacArthur gestured toward his table.

"I'm having dinner. Could you join me?"

A grateful smile grew on Wainwright's face, and he shook his head. "No, General, I wouldn't do that to you." Wainwright seemed suddenly exhausted, as if MacArthur's blessing had taken away an enormous load. "I believe I'd like to take a rest if you don't mind."

MacArthur pointed at me. "Make sure General Wainwright is given a superior room, Jay. A suite."

"I don't need a suite," chuckled Wainwright.

"A suite, Jay," insisted MacArthur. "Even if you have to evict a current occupant."

"Yes, sir," I said.

MacArthur gave Wainwright another fatherly hug. "We'll have a special place for you on the battleship. I want the Japanese to be staring right into your eyes when they sign the surrender document."

"I'm pleased to be invited, General," answered Wainwright. "The last time I went through one of these the shoe was on the other foot."

MacArthur visibly winced as he released Wainwright. Then he headed slowly back toward his dining table.

I turned to Wainwright, gesturing toward the lobby. "General?"

We crept carefully, paced by Wainwright's cane. "We're not going to evict anybody, Captain," he said as we exited the restaurant. "I've lived in a box for three years. I'd go stir-crazy in a suite."

"We'll get you a good room, sir."

"So you work directly for General MacArthur?" asked Wainwright as he hobbled toward the desk.

"Yes, sir."

"You're a lucky man," he said, staring back toward the restaurant. "I'd follow MacArthur to hell and back. In fact, I guess I just did."

I found a handsome suite for Wainwright and had the hotel staff bring him a full meal. An hour passed. A cable arrived, posted from our military headquarters in Manila. The cable was marked "URGENT—PERSONAL ATTENTION—SUPREME COMMANDER ALLIED POWERS." And reading it I knew instinctively that another, far more dangerous ghost had emerged to confront MacArthur's pleasant leap toward deification.

General Tomoyuki Yamashita, still commanding the Japanese defenses from a fortified redoubt high in the mountains of northern Luzon near Baguio, had radioed Manila that he would formally surrender on September 2, once he was certain that the Japanese government had signed the surrender documents aboard the *Missouri*.

It was well after dinner. I found MacArthur in his suite, pacing exuberantly before Generals Willoughby and Whitney. The three had been meeting around the clock for days, analyzing the gargantuan Willoughby's carefully prepared, if spotty, intelligence reports and preparing the positions Court Whitney would take on behalf of MacArthur in his meetings with Japanese government officials. The supreme commander had spent most of the day working on what would become a masterpiece performance aboard the *Missouri*. Watching him as I entered the room, I could tell he was sensing for the first time that he was assured of a special place in history.

I stepped hesitantly into his suite, stopping just inside the doorway. He gave me a fatherly wink. "Isn't it past your bedtime, Jay?"

I flushed, smiling back, content as ever to play the jester to his royal court. "The forces of freedom are never asleep, sir."

"Spoken like a true liberator," joked Court Whitney, looking up from his yellow legal pad.

Willoughby spoke gruffly in his thick Teutonic accent. "Captain Marsh. Is this important?"

"Yes, sir," I answered, holding out the cable. "It's marked urgent, for the supreme commander's personal attention."

I handed the cable to Willoughby, who read it quickly and then gave it to MacArthur.

"You won't like this, General."

The General stared at the cable for a long time. It was almost as if he were trying to see beyond the words, perhaps all the way across the ocean to the jungled retreat where his greatest adversary was now preparing to surrender, so that he might fully comprehend the moment. Finally he handed the paper to General Whitney and began pacing again.

"I felt certain he would commit *seppuku*." MacArthur mumbled it bitterly, his face reeking with disappointment.

"In his case," agreed Willoughby, "it would have been an honorable gesture. An acceptance of responsibility."

"I warned him," said MacArthur, pacing, his voice tightening with a new and raw emotion. "I warned him as soon as we landed at Leyte. Radio messages. Published documents. He knew beyond doubt that he would be held accountable for any acts of harm that befell prisoners of war or innocent civilians." Suddenly he waved a finger into the air, raising his chin. "It is an ancient precept that the soldier, be he friend or foe, is charged with the protection of the weak. Of the unarmed."

MacArthur was speechifying now, as if justifying himself before the world for the actions he was certain to take. "And what happened? The grand city of Manila, sacked, its rare monuments in ruins. A hundred thousand innocents—*Christians*—many of them women and children, slaughtered. Rarely has so wanton an act been exposed to public gaze!" He looked over at his two generals, as if for support. "That he would now decide to hand over his sword in full dress uniform, wearing his soldiers' medals, is an unspeakable disgrace."

"The Potsdam Declaration covers Yamashita's conduct," said the lawyer Whitney in his matter-of-fact tone. "It's on the list, General. One of our first responsibilities. To round up the war criminals. I'll take care of this situation, beginning the moment we set up shop in Tokyo."

"*I don't want him back in this country.*"

The way MacArthur spoke lent a ferocity to his words. When he said "this country" there was a note of ownership, as if Japan were now his very own fiefdom and Yamashita had become a dangerous enemy subversive.

"We can try him in the Philippines," shrugged Whitney, giving MacArthur a curious glance. "We'll have to do some creative lawyering, but we'll find a way. The offenses were committed there. The witnesses are there. In fact, Manila would be better, all things considered. It should be a catharsis for the people of the Philippines to see a major perpetrator brought to justice before their eyes."

"—*Ever*," continued MacArthur. He had stopped pacing, and was now looking at his two key generals with a measured stare which told them beyond cavil that this was an irreversible order.

"*Ever* is OK. A part of the equation." Whitney nodded, looking down to his legal pad and writing as if making a note of it. "I'll start talking to the legal people. We can set that up."

Willoughby scrutinized MacArthur's scowl as if trying to determine the General's mood. Then he agreed. "I see no reason for you to worry about General Yamashita coming back to Japan," said Willoughby. "Certainly he will be convicted, and our legal staff can arrange for the trial to be in the Philippines. And then he will be put to death."

"The return of his remains will be *permissible*," said MacArthur with a cold finality. The two generals nodded, taking him seriously.

He turned to me now, watching me silently, pondering unspoken options. I grew uncomfortable under his meditative stare. And finally he spoke again. "Jay. Go back to the Philippines. Tomorrow morning. Waste no time. Go to Baguio. I want to know what he's planning before I decide what to do."

He had confused me. "What he's planning, sir?"

MacArthur's mind was working furiously, off in a complicated region of power, politics, and reputation that was beyond my ken even to imagine. He began speaking of Yamashita as if the Japanese general held great authority and unseen sway. I had no idea what he meant. "Yes, Jay, what he's planning. There will be a surrender—a *ceremony* of some sort—and there will be a trial. He will have the opportunity to speak, and he will be heard. So why is he surrendering? What is it that he wants to say? He knows he's going to die. An honorable Japanese in his situation would accept that and take his own life, unless there is a reason to prolong his death. *So what is it?* Does he want to prolong his death so that he can make a statement about the war? About the future of Japan?"

MacArthur hesitated, and in the shadows of his eyes I recalled all his moments of frustration over the past year in never having fully defeated the great Tiger of Malaya, despite his constant public utterances to the contrary. "About me? What?"

Douglas MacArthur seemed to me at that moment a very worried man, although I still could not fathom his concerns. With all the war's great players swirling about, and with all the millions of words now being spoken, why did it even matter what General Tomoyuki Yamashita wanted to say?

"I don't want a word of this in our message traffic," he continued. "I don't want General Yamashita to become a topic of conversation for half the American soldiers in Asia, and I don't want the media to start debating his fate. But I do want to know what's going on."

The General stared fiercely at me. "I want you there when Yamashita walks out of the jungle. I want you to talk to Yamashita on my behalf. Privately. Speaking in Japanese. Then I want to know his intentions."

I still had no idea what MacArthur was talking about. "Why he didn't kill himself, you mean, sir?"

"Why he remains alive." The supreme commander said it as if there were somehow a difference in interpretation.

"Right, sir. I'll let you know."

I left it at that. After all, Willoughby and Court Whitney were nodding their silent agreement, fully understanding the supreme commander's intonations. I decided that the rest of it would somehow clarify itself once I confronted Yamashita.

The General turned away, abruptly dismissing me. "Don't dally in Manila, Jay. We have plans to make. After you meet with Yamashita I want you back here immediately to give me a personal briefing."

PART TWO

SEPTEMBER 1945–FEBRUARY 1946

CHAPTER 8

★　★　★　★　★

T oday the guns are silent. A great tragedy has ended. A great victory has
been won. The skies no longer rain death—the seas bear only commerce—men everywhere walk upright in the sunlight. The entire world
is quietly at peace. The holy mission has been completed. And in reporting
this to you the people, I speak for the thousands of silent lips, forever stilled
among the jungles and the beaches and in the deep waters of the Pacific
which marked the way. I speak for the unnamed brave millions homeward
bound to take up the challenge of that future which they did so much to
salvage from the brink of disaster . . .."

MacArthur's poetic cadence sounded flat and hollow, echoing like
ricochets off the sharp rocks and barren peaks of the central Cordillera
Mountains. We were in northern Luzon's Asin Valley, a mile high and a
world away from Tokyo Bay, where Japan's formal surrender was taking
place on the main deck of the USS *Missouri*. But the surrender ceremony
was being broadcast live across the world, even reaching this last remote
outpost through radio speakers mounted on a nearby truck.

Behind me a few American and Filipino soldiers faintly cheered the

General's rhetoric, but as with the rest of us the object of their greatest attention had yet to appear. All eyes remained nervously focused on a sharp break in the mountains to our front. We were standing at the infamous Bessang Pass, a deep cleavage in the raw, clifflike slopes through which General Tomoyuki Yamashita had withdrawn several months before to form his final defensive perimeter. There had been a few attacks and an attempted encirclement, but the Japanese had shut the Americans and Filipinos down at Bessang Pass. Narrow and long, it was Yamashita's impenetrable Thermopylae.

Near me, mulling about anxiously, were a half dozen senior officers sent up from Manila by Lieutenant General Wilhelm Styer, commanding general of army forces, western Pacific. General Yamashita had agreed to walk through the pass and give himself over to General Styer's staff members. It would then be their duty to escort the Japanese commander by truck and aircraft to the city of Baguio, where he would formally surrender at Camp John Hay to General Styer himself.

Colonel Brute Petrulakis stood anxiously at my side as we waited for Yamashita to appear. A lanky, grey-haired veteran of two wars, Petrulakis commanded one of the regiments in the Thirty-second Infantry Division. Since I was General MacArthur's personal representative to the surrender, he had been assigned to escort me during my visit to the division's front lines. His regiment had been pursuing the Japanese general for months. In the process the colonel had become both leery and admiring of the general's battlefield skills.

Petrulakis checked his watch, peering toward the pass. "It wouldn't be like him to come out here and quit," he said.

"He'll come, sir," I answered. "He's probably listening to the ceremony on his own radio. His message indicated that he wouldn't surrender until his government actually signed the documents. The war isn't officially over until then."

MacArthur's historic speech continued to echo through the mountains. This was the General's greatest moment, and a part of me lamented that I was not there to witness it. I tried to imagine him standing on the deck of the battleship in the midst of perhaps the foremost assemblage of military legends that had ever gathered—Americans, British, French, Australians, Chinese, Dutch, and even the Russians. These were the men who had led the soldiers, sailors, airmen, and marines of all the Allied nations back from the dark days of 1942. They would be in raucous spirits as they milled about, calling to one another across the ship's deck and renewing old acquaintances that for some spanned several decades.

And in front of the General as he spoke would be the eleven-man Japanese delegation, led by the tiny, dour-faced Foreign Minister Mimoru Shigemitsu. The announcement that Shigemitsu would head the delegation had surprised the supreme commander. The proper signatory should have been the prime minister, Prince Naruhiko Higashikuni. But Prince Higashikuni was the emperor's uncle, and the emperor had remained adamant that no member of the royal family should sign the humiliating surrender document. Foreign Minister Shigemitsu was old, one-legged, and in poor health. In Japanese eyes this made him the proper candidate to absorb this unprecedented shame on behalf of the royal family. At the right time, he could then be discarded from government as the new peace took hold, taking the shame with him to his retirement home, moving it quickly into the nation's past.

MacArthur's words took on an unusual resonance here in the hard-fought Cordillera Mountains. *"The issues, involving divergent ideals and ideologies, have been determined on the battlefields of the world and hence are not for our discussion or our debate. Nor is it for us here to meet, representing as we do a majority of the peoples of the earth, in a spirit of distrust, malice, or hatred. But rather it is for us, both victors and vanquished, to rise to that higher dignity which alone benefits the sacred purposes we are about to serve, committing all our people unreservedly to faithful compliance with the understanding they are here formally to assume.*

"It is my earnest hope and indeed the hope of all mankind that from this solemn occasion a better world shall emerge out of the blood and carnage of the past—a world founded upon faith and understanding—a world dedicated to the dignity of man and the fulfillment of his most cherished wish—for freedom, tolerance, and justice.

"As Supreme Commander for the Allied Powers I announce it my firm purpose to proceed in the discharge of my responsibilities with justice and tolerance, while taking all necessary dispositions to insure that the terms of the surrender are fully, promptly, and faithfully complied with."

Tolerance, he was now promising. *Justice. A higher dignity. . . .* And I could not help but wonder again what all these words had to do with the personal motivations that led to my present mission. Was it tolerance, justice, and a higher dignity that had caused the supreme commander to send me here to discover why General Yamashita wished to surrender rather than kill himself? Or was it a clever and unspoken fear?

"It's been like fighting a ghost," said Petrulakis warily, still searching to his front. "A ghost with guns."

"MacArthur's speech is over," I said. "The documents are being signed. Then the war will be officially ended, and he'll start walking out from his command post. He'll be here soon."

"I just want to get a look at him," continued Petrulakis. "I hear he's big. He's definitely smart. We chased the son of a bitch all over Luzon with eight infantry divisions, plus the First Cav, the Eleventh Airborne, three separate regimental combat teams, and a bunch of organized Filipino regiments. We killed a lot of soldiers, but I'll tell you something. I've been in the army nearly thirty years and I've never seen anything like him. He ran our asses ragged. And we never caught him. What did he have to throw back at us? Soldiers, that was it. Bullets and grenades. No air force, no navy, no reinforcements, and no resupply."

Watching the Brute's hard brown eyes squinting toward the pass, I empathized with him and his men. Though Japanese losses had been high, Yamashita's gritty defense in the last nine months alone had caused nearly 40 percent of all the U.S. army's battle casualties in the Pacific for all of World War Two, including the killed and wounded of the Army Air Corps. The long months of combat in the jungled mountains had taken another toll as well: our nonbattle losses—from battle fatigue, disease, and accidents—were twice as high as the combat injuries, an unusual occurrence.

The Tiger had worn our soldiers out.

On July 5, MacArthur had declared the Philippines "entirely liberated," claiming that his battle against Yamashita "was one of the rare instances when in a long campaign a ground force superior in numbers was entirely destroyed by a numerically inferior opponent." In his desire to outdo Yamashita, MacArthur had taken to dissembling, talking cleverly of "long campaigns," and comparing only "ground forces" so that his numbers would not acknowledge a total superiority in the air and on the sea. He knew that the greatest example in the entire war of a numerically inferior ground force conquering a larger foe was the brutally short campaign waged by Yamashita himself, in his lightning conquest of Singapore.

In early 1942 the brilliant Tiger of Malaya had taken the supposedly unconquerable British colony from behind, landing four hundred miles up the coast on the Malaya Peninsula and driving relentlessly past outpost after outpost, his troops sometimes even on bicycles in a strangely Japanese version of *blitzkrieg*. Outnumbered three to one by the British defenders, Yamashita had bluffed and scrapped his way to the very edges of the central city, forcing a quick and startling surrender that echoed throughout the world, and particularly in Asia. British and Australian prisoners of war from the Singapore battle were paraded by the Japanese through city streets as far away as Hanoi and Seoul as evidence that the West, and particularly the Caucasian soldiers, were inferior to the Japanese. Throughout Japan, and particularly among the common soldiers of the imperial army, Yamashita had become a true folk hero.

The radio loudspeakers went silent behind us. Near them, from a higher bluff and on the truck beds themselves, dozens of soldiers began talking excitedly to each other, pointing toward the Bessang Pass. There was movement along the valley's floor, an antlike string of uniformed men passing through the narrow break in the cliffs, heading in our direction.

Brute Petrulakis lifted his field glasses to his eyes, scanning the rocks and crags of the pass for several seconds. "Here he comes," Petrulakis finally said. A grin crossed his face. "I know that's him. The guy's got a big potato head, just like the pictures. And I'll be damned. He's the first one through the pass. He's marching at the front of his men!"

A small column of jeeps and trucks headed out toward the Japanese from the Thirty-second Division's lines. Petrulakis and I stood in one truck bed along with a squad of soldiers, bouncing slowly along a rock-strewn road toward the pass. The war was now officially over but the soldiers were taking no chances, still looking nervously ahead as the truck lurched and groaned.

Petrulakis joked with one of his sergeants as we neared the approaching Japanese. "Keep your eyes peeled, Chambers. Nobody wants to be the army's first peacetime casualty, huh?"

"Not on your life, Colonel," answered the leathery-faced, battle-hardened squad leader. His M1 rifle was at the ready, pointed upward toward the rocky cliffs behind the Japanese. A finger rested uneasily on the trigger. "I didn't last this long to end up in a box."

But there were no surprises. The string of American vehicles slowly pushed forward along the broken road, ever further from the safety of the Thirty-second Division's front lines. The group of Japanese soldiers cleared the pass and soon were in a narrow valley at the far end of the road, trudging toward the Americans. And finally the two groups neared each other in the artillery pocked no-man's-land that had separated their positions for more than two months.

Our little convoy halted. Infantry soldiers jumped from the trucks and moved quickly off the road, setting up a perimeter around the place where the two groups would link up. Dozens of dud artillery shells and unexploded rocket rounds littered the rocky soil near where the soldiers walked. General Styer's emissaries disembarked and gathered nervously on the road itself. Colonel Petrulakis and I stood somewhere in between, watching with fascination as the Japanese continued to approach.

Petrulakis whistled softly, watching the hulking Yamashita march resolutely toward us. He broke into an excited grin. "Get a load of that!"

Standing next to him, my own heart was racing. Not unlike Petrulakis, as I watched General Yamashita approach I was overcome with an odd thrill of recognition. Accustomed as I was to being near the aura of Mac-Arthur, this was my first vision of the very embodiment of all that we had viewed for so long simply as the enemy. Marching solemnly toward us, without fanfare or even a point man, was the force behind the stunning conquest of Singapore, the man who had pushed our own army through the long months of frustrating, never-resolved, cave-by-cave, ridge-by-ridge battles of Luzon.

The burly, imposing general was wearing a brown service-dress uniform, complete with a full-length jacket, medals, knee-high leather boots, and a cloth campaign hat. In his left hand as he marched along the rough, rocky road he gingerly carried his officer's sword, the symbol of his power. He was bull-necked, thick-shouldered, and at least six foot two, the first Japanese I had ever seen who was taller than I myself. His huge head was shaved to the scalp. His face was a mask that showed absolutely no emotion—neither fear nor arrogance, neither anticipation nor regret. The dozen senior Japanese officers who followed him seemed like lost midgets as they stumbled bravely in his wake.

He stopped near us, catching his breath. Then he began peering intently at the Americans who stood on the road waiting to take him prisoner, as if inspecting them. *Yes,* I thought, watching him calmly search the faces and uniforms among the group, *this is a great soldier.*

Finally Yamashita found what he was looking for. An American one-star general, the senior emissary from General Styer's staff, had begun walking toward him. The Tiger met him halfway. Coming to attention in front of the American, Yamashita saluted, gave him a slight bow, then handed over his sword. He spoke in Japanese, but his words were quickly interpreted by a soft-voiced, bespectacled officer who had stepped up to a position just behind him.

"The general says, 'In accordance with the imperial rescript, I am surrendering command of my army and placing myself under your control. My soldiers have been ordered to lay down their weapons and subject themselves to your decisions. The war is over. They will fight no more.' "

Taking the sword from Yamashita, the American general turned to the interpreter, giving him a shocked gaze. "You speak perfect English," he said. "Not even an accent!"

"I am Colonel Masakatsu Hamamoto," said the interpreter, bowing as he grinned with a shy embarrassment at the attention that had been drawn to him. "Harvard, class of twenty-nine."

"Does General Yamashita wish to say anything else?"

Hamamoto shook his head, not even bothering to ask the general. "Not here. It's over. He has given you his sword. He would ask that you treat his soldiers well. But there is nothing left to say."

We quickly reboarded the trucks and jeeps. The dozen surrendering Japanese were divided into groups and ordered onto different trucks, except for Yamashita, who rode in the brigadier general's jeep. Then our little convoy set off again, following fifteen miles of treacherous mountain roads as we retraced our earlier route to a tiny airstrip in a valley at Bagabag, where those of us who had come up from Manila had arrived just after dawn. Yamashita rode next to the driver in the jeep just in front of our truck. The American brigadier general sat just behind him. An armed guard sat next to the general. After watching Yamashita surrender, the guard seemed a gratuitous and unnecessary gesture. The Tiger did not so much as turn his head during the hourlong journey.

At Bagabag we boarded two C-47 aircraft and took off within minutes, heading for Baguio and the official surrender that would take place at the high commissioner's old residence at Camp John Hay. Canvas jump seats ran the length of the aircraft's narrow fuselage on both sides. Aboard the workhorse cargo plane I found a place directly across from Yamashita, so that we sat facing each other, our knees almost touching. The hourlong flight to Baguio would be my best chance to talk with him privately, as I had been ordered to do by MacArthur.

The aircraft lifted slowly above the endless mountains. We nodded slightly to each other. Then I leaned forward, speaking to him in Japanese. "General, I am Captain Jay Marsh. I work on General MacArthur's staff. He sent me down from Yokohama to—give you his regards."

Yamashita gave me an immediate, knowing smile. "That was very kind of the General. And you honor us by speaking our language." He gestured easily toward his interpreter, as if we were exchanging pleasantries at a cocktail reception. "Perhaps you and Colonel Hamamoto knew each other at Harvard?"

Hamamoto and I both exchanged tight smiles. Neither of us were as relaxed as the general seemed to be. "I don't think so," I answered.

Yamashita continued to look deep into my eyes, as if openly examining my subconscious. "I assume you are an intelligence officer, Captain Marsh?"

"No," I said, taken slightly aback. "I am a member of the supreme commander's personal staff."

"It is a long journey from Yokohama, just to say hello to a battlefield adversary. Don't you think?" The Tiger's twinkling eyes were still breaking my mind apart.

"The supreme commander is a very thorough man."

"I have studied MacArthur," said Yamashita. "He has made many statements about me since the battles on Leyte. It is fair to say that he does not like me. Personally, I mean. Not to mention militarily."

His bluntness surprised me. And then I remembered that such forthrightness had been his forte throughout the war. Indeed, he had forced the surrender at Singapore by uttering only three words to General Percival: *Yes or no.* No negotiations, no debate. Surrender or fight. And the beleaguered British commander had folded on the spot.

"I am only a captain," I finally demurred, watching Yamashita's face again break into a knowing smile. "The supreme commander does not share his personal feelings with me."

"He does not share them with me, either," said Yamashita. "But on this issue it is not difficult to know what they are."

"It's not my business to speak for the supreme commander in the area of his personal views. That is, as we say in the American army, above my pay-grade."

"You're a very smart man. Very careful with your words. Perhaps you should become a politician." He had not lost his smile. "It is a short plane ride, so we should speak honestly, don't you think? Why did MacArthur send you? What does he want to know, Captain Marsh? Go ahead! Ask me! Go ahead! You've traveled a long way!"

Sitting so near the Tiger, I felt swept along by the force of his physical presence, as well as his easy candor. He had no fear. He refused even at this moment of utter humiliation to descend into the obsequious double-talk I had expected, or the flattery toward MacArthur that I had witnessed from the sly, calculating Lord Privy Seal Kido. I felt a warmth for him grow inside me, one that I had neither expected nor desired.

"He asked that I inquire about your—frame of mind," I finally answered.

"I predict that he will find me sane."

Yamashita laughed softly, eyeing me with an amused certainty. "I have been a soldier for a long time, Captain. I served close to the imperial court in the years of palace intrigue before the war. I myself have played the messenger before, sounding out rival factions on behalf of the emperor and others. I even went to Germany in 1940 on behalf of the emperor, spending seven months—*listening*, as we say, and reporting back to him on our options. So you should relax. And don't worry about pretending!"

"I don't know what you're talking about, General."

He shrugged. "Then let me make this easier for you. General MacArthur sent you to listen to me, did he not? He wants to know something about me that he doesn't want to put into his standard message traffic, where it will be read by subordinates or perhaps competitors. Something he might not even want his intelligence officers to discuss. Something personal, perhaps?"

I gathered my thoughts, peering out the window for a moment at the thickly canopied mountains we were traversing. Naively, I had expected to maneuver Yamashita, but he had completely stripped away the facade. So there was no need to put the question subtly.

Still, I attempted an indirectness. "The supreme commander is aware that certain other Japanese commanders found it honorable to commit *seppuku* rather than surrender once they lost their battles. This happened all across the Pacific."

Yamashita knew at once where I was heading. He seemed amused. "But they had no recourse in their honor, Captain. They lost."

"Excuse me, General?"

He looked out the window of the C-47 for a long moment, his gaze lingering on the raw mountains into which he had withdrawn six months before. Soon we would be at Baguio, where he had once kept a headquarters before being pushed further and further into the pocks and caves by our overwhelming forces, until he had formed his final defensive perimeter on the far side of the Bessang Pass.

"My orders were to delay the Allied advance on the Japanese mainland.

To tie up as many American soldiers as possible. To continue to fight as long as possible. I carried out those orders. And I would still be carrying them out, except that the emperor ordered me to stop."

His answer startled me, coming as it did from a man who had just given over his sword and was now on his way to prison. His face remained calm, supremely self-confident. And I knew that he wanted me to say those words to MacArthur.

"You're saying that you were not defeated?"

"How do we define defeat? I'm saying that I had not lost. I turned over my sword only after the war was officially ended. After the last assault was made, and the final shot was fired. I did not desert my soldiers, and I did not surrender under fire. And so I still have my honor."

There was an arcane patience in the way Yamashita continued to smile at me, and I began to understand MacArthur's concerns. His comment about not deserting his soldiers under fire was a deliberate tweak at Douglas MacArthur himself. His refusal to surrender until the war was officially over would indeed preserve his integrity and his stature. An enormous power emanated from his simple, inarguably precise code, one that the Japanese people would have no trouble comprehending.

MacArthur was entering Japan as a conquering regent, the Blue-Eyed Shogun, his credibility riding on the strength of his military prowess. He was fond of pointing out that the Japanese were an ingenious but barbaric and superstitious race. Under this notion, the very basis of his power depended on this nation-family's viewing him as an all-powerful demigod, a peer of the emperor himself, or even an alternative to him. Yamashita had conquered the British cleanly and swiftly at Singapore. He had held off MacArthur's armies in the mountains of Luzon until the moment the war was ended. If he returned alive on Japanese soil, his fiercely simple self-assurance could provide a visible counterpoint and even a rallying point for those who wished to oppose the supreme commander's powers.

"You wish me to say this to MacArthur?"

Yamashita shrugged as if unconcerned. "I would never tell you what to say to General MacArthur. The war is over. MacArthur will have his way with me. But I carried out my orders, Captain Marsh. And so there is no loss of honor in obeying the emperor's edict to cease fighting."

"I will tell MacArthur."

"If you wish."

He gave me a small wave, then turned and began talking quietly to Colonel Hamamoto. There was really nothing left to say. The C-47 began its quick descent into Baguio. A heavily armed convoy awaited us on the ground to take the Tiger to Camp John Hay, where he would officially surrender. And within two days he would be imprisoned at the Muntinglupa Bilibid, near Manila.

He did not kill himself, sir, because he does not believe he was defeated. And so he never lost his honor."

The simple truth of those words was like a slap in Douglas MacArthur's face. He bit into his pipe as he paced before me, then took it out of his mouth and began jabbing it into the air like a pointer as he talked. "His forces were demolished at Leyte! His troop transports were sunk as they tried to reinforce! He was driven off the beaches at Lingayen Gulf and into the north. He was driven out of Baguio and even further north, into the mountains! And there he hid, until the war was over!"

Like MacArthur in the tunnels of Corregidor, before he was able to escape? I was unable to shake that thought as the supreme commander paced and fretted. "He said that was his mission, sir. Not to defeat us but to tie up our forces and prolong the war. And that he carried out that mission."

"He surrendered, Captain Marsh! He turned over his sword."

"Only after the emperor ordered him to, sir. And only after the war officially ended."

MacArthur seemed to lose his normal composure for a moment, eyeing me bitterly with a gaze that froze my heart. And then he spoke calmly, almost as if taunting me. "Are you now his advocate, Jay?"

I shrugged helplessly under the supreme commander's stare. "I'm only stating his views, sir. You asked me to find out what his intentions are. That was the best I could do."

"Did you ask him about the rape of Manila?"

I swallowed hard now, feeling that I had failed him and stifling my embarrassment. "No, sir. We didn't have much time. I didn't know you wanted—"

"That's enough." MacArthur had regained his bearing. "It's what I wanted to know. Good work, Jay. You did indeed find out what I asked you to." He turned and began looking expectantly at Court Whitney.

"We're working to set up a military commission," said Whitney, as if on cue. "We can arrange for an early trial."

"Soon," said MacArthur, pacing again. "The world must learn of the terrible transgressions that took place, before the war fades in its memory." His mind shifted gears in midstride, as if he needed no more from me. My simple report had clearly verified his preconceptions. Now he pointed at Willoughby. "Tell Jay about the meeting we want him to cover."

"Captain Marsh," began Willoughby, holding up a thick, meaty hand. "The Japanese diet is meeting tomorrow. They've labeled it an emergency session. The emperor is going to speak. We've been invited, but the supreme commander isn't making his formal entrance to Tokyo for another five days. I don't think it's a good idea for any of our senior people to precede him into the city, even for an afternoon."

"An excellent point," interjected MacArthur, "on which I absolutely agree. There must be a ceremonial majesty, a feeling of absolute change, when I move into the city."

"But it would be very helpful to our preparations if we have an unvarnished report on the proceedings," continued Willoughby. "From someone who carries no—*weight,* in the official sense. We would not want the Japanese to consider his presence as *prima facie* the supreme commander's. It would give them too much face too early, as if we were condoning whatever it is that will be said. But it would be good to have someone there who understands the culture and the language and can be trusted to report to us with some insight on what they are saying."

"Jay, you're well suited for that task," agreed Whitney, no doubt repeating an earlier recommendation he had made to MacArthur. "You had some damn good insights after the ride in from the airport with the emperor's adviser, that—"

"Kido," I said. "Marquis Kido. The lord privy seal."

"Exactly," said Whitney, looking at MacArthur as if to verify their earlier discussion. "In fact, when we floated your name to the Japanese, Kido jumped on it. I think he believes he can use you."

"Use me, sir?"

"To communicate unofficially to me," announced MacArthur. "An excellent diplomatic device if done properly, by the way."

"Yes, sir." As I watched MacArthur's doting nod I was remembering Tomoyuki Yamashita's comments of the day before. And I suddenly realized that I had gained a new and enormous power that transcended both my age and rank. I had become a trusted listener.

"We'll need a full report," continued Willoughby, his piercing eyes peeling me back like an onion. "What is the emperor's mood? How about the rest of the parliament? What are they thinking? What do we need to be thinking?"

Whitney gave me a small smile. "Let him think he's using you, Jay. Are you up to it?"

"I'm flattered, sir."

"No notes," said Willoughby.

"Sir?"

"Don't take notes. It weakens our position if someone from our staff seems so concerned that he's transcribing the proceedings."

"*Attend*, Captain," smiled MacArthur, having regained a lighter mood. "Show your face. Nod and smile. Express good wishes to those who greet you, on behalf of the supreme commander. Above all, make no political statements and give no judgments on my behalf."

"Can you play the game?" asked General Whitney.

"The game, sir?"

"*Listen*," said Willoughby, confirming my earlier intuition. "There is no substitute for human intelligence. Watch what is going on, and listen to what they want you to communicate back to us. That's it. And then report to us on what you've heard."

"Like a duck, sir."

"What?"

I smiled gamely. "You look at a duck on a pond and he's calm and serene, floating along on top of the water. But if you check underneath the waterline, he's paddling like hell."

Whitney laughed indulgently. "OK, Jay. Like a duck."

As I walked out of the hotel room MacArthur called to me one last time. "Jay!"

I stopped, turning toward him. "Yes, sir?"

"Did you see your young lady in Manila?"

My heart sank a little, thinking of the opportunity I had missed. "No, sir. There wasn't any time, sir."

MacArthur smiled indulgently. I could not tell whether it was from satisfaction or empathy, but I could sense that he felt even closer to me.

"That's the price one pays when he assumes a larger role in the tapestry of world affairs, you know. Another lesson. Because there always is a price, Jay."

CHAPTER 9

★ ★ ★ ★ ★

I know what it might have been like to drive a chariot through the just-plowed and salted soil of defeated Carthage, or to make an accidental turn at the edge of a jungle and end up alone in the ruins of what once had been a thriving ancient culture. Except for the thousands of silent, ragged Japanese who stopped momentarily to stare at my passing as they pulled their homes back out of the dust and rubble, I could have been in either place as my jeep made its way from Yokohama to Tokyo. And driving through this wasteland I became overwhelmed with emotion. Merely to see Tokyo had been one of my greatest dreams before the war. Passing through its devastation on my way to be Douglas MacArthur's untitled emissary at an emergency meeting of the Japanese diet seemed like an odd and twisted fantasy.

We were early. I asked my driver to make a loop past the Imperial Palace grounds before I went to the diet. Approaching the center of the city we reached the district of Chiyoda, and the rubble suddenly abated. As we moved closer still to the center of the city, it stopped altogether.

Rickshaws appeared on tranquil streets. Now and then a bus passed. Here and there I could even make out a charcoal-burner car. Lord Privy Seal Kido had not brought all the charcoal-burners to Yokohama, after all. More importantly, it was clear that our bombers had been careful here.

Suddenly the Imperial Palace grounds revealed themselves, high and remote across a series of moats and bridges. Within a few miles, hundreds of thousands of people had been killed by the firebombs that had begun in March. Across the country, more than two million homes had been destroyed. But as we drove past the emperor's home, I saw that not even a brick on the palace moat was charred.

The grounds covered a vast, roughly circular area about a mile across. There was no grand palace in the European sense but rather a series of low buildings and sprawling gardens mixed among thick stands of bamboo and lines of tall, old hardwood trees. Stone watchtowers loomed above the far side of the moat, at the edges of the grounds, their curving roofs speaking of an ancient past.

Here on this veritable island in the middle of the city the emperor lived, untouched by the bombings that had so completely devastated his loyal people. Hidden beyond the towers and the walls were an inner palace, an outer, ceremonial palace, a chamberlain's abode, a concubines' pavilion, a villa for the crown prince, a library and biological research lab where the emperor liked to putter, and a large barracks complex for the Imperial Guards. Among the villas, just adjacent to the Fukiage Gardens, was a pond where the emperor was fond of taking his afternoon walks. Near the pond stood a special palace shrine where he prayed daily to his ancestors.

A few minutes later I reached my destination. The national diet building was less than half a mile from the palace grounds, at their southern edge, where the Akasaka district began. In addition to the national diet, Akasaka was the home of the most important government ministries, as well as the prime minister's office and the national theater. It was Tokyo's version of what Washington, D.C., calls Capitol Hill.

I felt a small triumph as I jumped out of the jeep and headed for the diet building. I had beaten MacArthur to Tokyo!

Other than four journalists who did not speak Japanese, I was the only American who entered the diet building for this special session. More than thirty correspondents mulled suspiciously outside, having declined to enter when asked to check their weapons at the door. I laughed quietly to myself, listening to their suspicions. What did they think the Japanese would do, round them up and send them to a prisoner of war camp? They had violated MacArthur's cardinal precept: *In the Orient, the man who shows no fear is king.*

I walked alone into the building, entering the assembly floor area and proceeding to a control desk, where I gave a nervously smiling clerk my name. When I wrote my name into the guest book the old man's face suddenly lit up, recognizing it immediately. He spoke to me without hesitation in Japanese.

"*Marsh-San,* you will please wait here," he said, rising quickly from his chair. "Only for one moment."

Before I could answer he hurried off to an office down a shadowed corridor. And within a minute he returned, jogging just ahead of the beaming, electric-eyed Marquis Koichi Kido. The lord privy seal was dressed in an elegant grey wool suit. He gave me a covetous look, as if he had chosen wisely on that recent afternoon when we had met next to the bomb-pocked runway of Atsugi. Reaching me he bowed slightly.

"Captain Marsh! Foreign Minister Shigemitsu told us you would be coming. We are so pleased that the supreme commander has sent you as his representative."

And I knew The Game had begun.

For MacArthur it had begun yesterday, when Shigemitsu had paid him a cranky, contentious visit at the hotel in Yokohama. The supreme commander had hinted that he was going to give women the vote, and was intent on rewriting the Japanese Constitution. He had also announced that he would be happy to allow the Japanese to disarm their own soldiers and even to make the actual arrests of those charged with war crimes if they so desired. Then he had added, with an obliqueness that would have made a mandarin proud, that so long as they performed such duties properly he would continue to bring in food to feed the near-starving population.

In truth, MacArthur had always believed that disarmament would take place successfully only if the Japanese authorities performed the task. And he had already sent a secret, desperate message to Washington: *Send me food or send me bullets.* But MacArthur and the Japanese both were madly posturing, as if they were now chained together in the same cage, dependent on each other for survival while at the same time probing one another with falsely polite diplomatic sticks.

The emperor's welcoming gesture to MacArthur at Atsugi had been, *preserve my dignity and I will continue to cooperate.* MacArthur's subtle message to the foreign minister, part of a series of emerging threats, was, *continue to cooperate or your people will blame you when they starve.* To a point, they both were right. Beyond that, both were bluffing. Both sides knew this, but neither knew the precise edge where the other side's reality ended and its bluffing had begun.

I returned Kido's bow. "Lord Privy Seal, I am honored to be with you. As you know, the supreme commander is very busy. But even though we are not a part of these proceedings, he believes that such an important occasion as today should not be ignored by our office."

"Of course!" answered Kido. As he spoke, Kido's hands and head seemed to be in constant movement. Behind the thick, wire-framed glasses his eyes glanced in all directions, as if helping to expend the energy he kept so tightly bound inside. "Then you must come and sit with me."

I had known he would invite me, but it was necessary first to decline. "Thank you for your kindness, Lord Privy Seal, but I will be fine in the visitor's gallery."

"Oh, no!" he protested. "You will be my guest. And I can help you understand our proceedings."

"I understand your language quite well," I replied.

"Oh, I know that," said Kido. "And I do not wish to insult your obvious expertise. But it is not the language. It is the proceedings."

Having not appeared too eager, it was now proper to agree. "All right, then. I am very thankful for your courtesies, and I would be happy to sit with you."

"It is for the best," Kido said, his eyebrows arched and his face giving off a conspiratorial smile. "You must know that in our culture, and particularly among politicians, words can hold different meanings. Even very specific words. So I would like to be with you when they are being spoken."

"Now I truly understand," I said, beginning to follow the lord privy seal to a separate sitting area near the floor.

Kido was warning me that there would be much "belly talking" going on that morning. Words would be uttered, some filled with false bravado, that might have an entirely different intent than their literal interpretation. It would take an expert observer to sort out posturing from reality. The lord privy seal wished to guide me through these interpretations. I did not fully trust him, but Kido and perhaps the emperor himself wanted to blunt the impact of the posturings before the supreme commander decided to act on them.

"Have you ever read the writings of Goethe?" I asked him as we neared our seats.

"Goethe? The German philosopher. Of course." Kido grinned ironically, gesturing for me to sit down. "As you know, we had a certain relationship with the Germans for some time. It became my duty to read Goethe."

"Goethe was quite perceptive," I said.

"Ah, yes. A brilliant man."

"He once wrote, 'whenever one is polite in German, one lies.' "

For a second, a stunned look accompanied Kido's normal wide-eyed expression, as if I were rebuking him. And then he began laughing. "That is very good, Captain Jay Marsh. Goethe, from your own memory. You are young, but you are obviously a well-schooled man. Now I understand why you are so valuable to General MacArthur."

"Oh, I am nothing to MacArthur," I protested. And I saw from Kido's seemingly knowing smile that with every denial my closeness to MacArthur became greatly exaggerated in his eyes. To Kido, my simple statement was itself a form of belly talk, false modesty to accentuate my very importance.

The members of the diet began somberly filing in, walking toward their assigned places on the floor. Many of these elders, clansmen, and members of the imperial family were clad in traditional kimonos. Others wore military uniforms. A few were dressed in Western suits. This was the aristocracy of Japan, still reeking with humiliation from the surrender of two days before. All but a few were unspeaking. They stared numbly toward the front of the room at the rostrum where the emperor would soon appear. The rostrum was decorated on its front with a large chrysanthemum that symbolized the imperial family. Those who did speak held their voices to a whisper, giving the room a breathless, anticipatory sibilance.

Kido leaned over and touched my shoulder, an act of camaraderie, whispering also. "We are very pleased with MacArthur's understanding of our situation," he said. "His speech during the ceremonies to end the war was inspiring to all of us. The emperor ordered that the speech be printed in its full entirety in every newspaper in the country. MacArthur is becoming very popular in Japan! Our people love him!"

Kido raised a finger in the air, testing my reaction as he quoted from MacArthur's speech. "Justice! Tolerance! We must reach to a higher dignity. Many bad things happen in war. We cannot live in the past."

"It was a great speech," I finally managed to mumble, trying very hard to obey Court Whitney's instructions. "And I am happy to be with you today, Lord Privy Seal. I have always admired the Japanese culture."

"Then you know that this is not an easy moment for the Japanese people," continued Kido. "We have been preparing them for some time."

"How have you been preparing them?" I asked.

"You must understand the nature of suffering," answered Kido. He hesitated for a moment, as if he were going too far. "We did agree that we could speak openly, did we not?"

"Absolutely, Lord Privy Seal."

"Yes," said Kido. "We are more alike than others might think. The elites of our governments, I mean. We are more cosmopolitan. We have read Goethe and Tolstoy. We have seen the world. But our native cultures? Not so similar! For instance, what do you think about the bombing of Tokyo? Not the areas that were destroyed, but the areas that were not destroyed?"

"It was a conscious decision of our government that we would not destroy Japanese national treasures," I answered, for despite the carnage and obliteration it had been a firm policy. "Just as we did not bomb the ancient capital of Kyoto."

"Exactly!" Kido was animated in his excitement. "You see, your royalty and ours understand that no matter how ferociously a war is fought, in the end the royalty must respect each other. If we do not, there is no civilization."

"We have no royalty in America, Lord Privy Seal."

"Now you're playing with semantics," shrugged Kido. "But I am sure you and the supreme commander both get the point. And then I must ask you, what does an ordinary Japanese think when all the bombs come down for months at a time but none of them touch the emperor's palace or the holy shrines?"

"I don't know, Lord Privy Seal. What does he think?"

"He thinks nothing, Captain Jay Marsh. Nothing. Because he expects this to happen. Do you understand? He might die, and the entire population of commoners might be incinerated. But no harm can ever come to the emperor."

Kido's words amazed me. I had never thought of it, but in an odd way his logic was unassailable. Our decision not to bomb the Imperial Palace became, in the minds of many Japanese, either an act of magic or a divine intervention, as if the power of the emperor had been strong enough to deflect the bombs.

"So, we had to work with the people to prepare them for the end of the war. It could not come too early, or they would feel betrayed in their sacrifices. It could come only when they were secretly begging for it. They would have to feel not only that they had sacrificed but that they could sacrifice no more. And so the time came when their suffering was so great that the emperor, through his decision to accept personal shame even though he was not at risk, was relieving them of their own suffering. Deciding to end the war finally became an act of imperial benevolence. Do you agree, Captain Jay Marsh?"

Agree? I thought to myself. Kido's logic was so powerful and profound, and yet so foreign to the way that Americans were taught to think and believe, that I was not even certain he was being serious.

"An interesting thought, Lord Privy Seal."

"Yes, interesting! And important." He became earnest. "I personally have been working on this for more than a year!"

"More than a year?"

"Yes," he said. "Since the fall of Saipan. We knew then that although we might lose the war, we could not lose our way of life. The Russians were going to help us but they continually betrayed us. The less help we had from the outside, the more important it became to the future that our sacrifices be complete. That no one could look back and say that we did not do enough. But once the sacrifices were complete, it would be time for the emperor to relieve the people of their suffering. I am a man of peace, Captain Jay Marsh. And so is the emperor."

Kido had now dumbfounded me. After Saipan had come Guam, Tinian, Peleliu, the entire Philippines campaign, Iwo Jima, Okinawa. And the firebombs that had leveled most of the cities in the Kanto Plain. And Hiroshima. And Nagasaki. Ensuring that the sacrifices would be complete? Waiting for the right moment?

Kido had caught my look and anticipated my unspoken question. "We worked very hard for peace. But the people could not be betrayed. If their sacrifice was not complete, would they be so easily welcoming MacArthur, or would they wish to continue the fight? So you see," shrugged the lord privy seal, "by having the struggle run its course, the emperor has delivered the people to MacArthur. Because in the end we must maintain order, and work together."

Kido was confusing me even further. Who, in his mind, was *we?*

I did not have a chance to ask, for a hush fell over the diet floor. In moments the emperor himself began to walk slowly toward the rostrum at its front. Watching him walk, I remembered reading years before that Hirohito had inherited a slight motor malfunction from his grandfather, the emperor Meiji, causing him to move with what some prewar Western correspondents had irreverently called the "imperial shuffle." Most Japanese by contrast had seen his odd gait as an attribute, giving the emperor a direct connection to his revered grandfather.

The entire diet, in their mix of kimonos, military uniforms, and tuxedoes, was now bowing deeply, as did Kido, who had stood up as soon as the emperor appeared. The emperor reached the rostrum and returned their bows, standing still for several seconds before finishing his own bow and moving to the microphone. He was wearing a dark, high-necked naval uniform, modified with royal embroidery at its front. The uniform was stripped of all badges of rank except for his Order of Merit, First Class, a bright, swirling badge sewn onto his left chest. After having heard years of wartime propaganda I noted with surprise when he stood ready to speak that he was an erect, handsome man with a narrow face and a thin, neatly trimmed mustache.

The diet took its seats. Hirohito began speaking in the slow, rather high-pitched singsong reserved for imperial pronouncements. "It is important that we should discuss our coming responsibilities under the new situation that has arisen," he began. "Last night I brought my closest advisers to the palace shrine. We announced the end of the war to the ancestors, and to the Sun Goddess. The new era has begun, but it does not end the old. And we must conduct ourselves in a manner that will bring credit to the sacrifices of those who went before us."

The diet sat rapt and attentive, for the quiet singsong of the emperor carried with it an immense strength. It instantly struck me that despite the Western news reports that were portraying him as weak and out of touch this was no puppet king or ceremonial figurehead such as the incidental and irrelevant monarchs of Europe. Emperor Hirohito was back from the palace shrine, bringing to Japan's ruling class a modern equivalent of the tablets that Moses carried down from the Mount.

"We must remember that our country accepted a termination of hostilities based on certain understandings," continued Hirohito. "We expect that all sides, including the Japanese people, will live up to those understandings. We have faith in our people and know that they should abide peacefully by the terms of the Potsdam Declaration, just as the other side will be careful in its enforcement. Then it will be possible for us to rebuild in all areas, and to keep our national structure."

The emperor paused, gazing out at the diet as if to look into the face of each of his subalterns. I marveled at the indirect power of the message he was sending. Again, he had not mentioned the word "surrender." And by tasking the Japanese people to respect the Potsdam Declaration, he was also reminding the Americans that they had guaranteed that the imperial system would remain intact. In effect, he was giving MacArthur a warning: if the Americans did not live up to their guarantee, he had the power to ensure that the Japanese people might not act so peacefully in the future.

Now he continued. "We stand by the people. We wish always to share with them in their moments of joy and sorrow. The ties between us and our people have always stood upon mutual trust and affection. They do not depend on mere legends and myths. They are not predicated on the false conception that the emperor is divine and that the Japanese people are superior to other races and fated to rule the world."

I did not know what to make of this statement. Was the emperor telling them that they had fought for a lie? I doubted it. Was he telling them that the bond between rulers and subjects was greater than any false debate over divinity and superiority that outsiders might wish to pursue? Probably. Was he tossing out these words about legend and myth and false conceptions to secretly mock the foreign media attacks that seemed continually to ridicule the Japanese system? Maybe. Or was there something else at work here, a kind of "belly talk" that few westerners would ever comprehend?

I could not tell. But I did notice that his comment brought nods of quiet agreement, even from Kido sitting next to me.

The emperor now held a piece of paper in front of him. "I have written a poem for our people," he announced. The diet whispered with an excited anticipation, for here would come the emperor's true message. It was common practice for members of the aristocracy to communicate their sincerest emotions through such thirty-one syllable tanka. And then the emperor began to read.

"Courageous the pine/that does not change in color/under winter snow./ Truly the men of Japan/should be a forest of pines."

The well-schooled members of the diet murmured their admiration, and as a group stood from their chairs and bowed deeply to the emperor. They knew exactly what he meant. They were the forest of pines. We the Western occupiers were the winter snow, bringing a temporary whiteness upon their branches. But spring would come, and after that the summer. The snow would melt away. And the forest of pines, stronger and more eternal, would still remain.

The emperor returned their bows, then without further comment shuffled slowly out of the room. Only after he had departed did the members of the diet cease their farewell bows.

"And now the prime minister," said Lord Privy Seal Kido after the emperor had gone. "We must discuss later what he says, yes?"

"If you wish, Lord Privy Seal."

"Yes," said the lord privy seal earnestly. "We must."

Prince Higashikuni, the emperor's uncle, now walked to the podium and bowed. He had been prime minister only since Japan's surrender. I knew from Willoughby that Higashikuni was an army general with thirty-one years experience, including seven years as an intelligence officer in Europe. In many ways the opposite of Hirohito, the sybaritic prince was known for fast cars, French mistresses, and an addiction to intrigue. In the 1930s he had been involved in numerous assassinations, religious hoaxes, and threats of blackmail or murder as a part of a campaign of terror against moderates who were opposed to Japan's continued expansionism. In 1937 he had commanded Japan's initial bombing campaign against key Chinese cities. It was believed that Hirohito had convinced his reluctant uncle to become the first peace government prime minister because of Higashikuni's influence, as a member of the royal family, over those who had still been opposed to surrender. Without Higashikuni, the extremist factions might have begun a palace intrigue designed to subvert the emperor's decision to end the war.

Not that Higashikuni seemed in the mood to cooperate. He was wearing a single-breasted khaki uniform, from which he had stripped his many personal decorations. Now nearing sixty, he was a small, balding, hard-looking, flat-faced man. He brought with him to the podium an air of boldness that bordered on arrogance. Preparing to speak, he surveyed the seated members of the diet with an expression that did not conceal his great bitterness. And the prince wasted no time in venting that emotion.

"And so it has come to this," began Prince Higashikuni. As he looked out toward the diet I felt him staring directly at me. "Today, one hundred thousand foreign soldiers are occupying our sacred soil. More will come. Throughout the world, commentators are now saying that Japan was wrong to have taken territory in other countries. *Morally wrong,* they are saying! Evil! That such acts of aggression are contrary to the way nations should conduct their affairs."

The prime minister surveyed his fellow aristocrats with an expression that told them he believed this was all absurd. "But what of the conduct of these same nations who now celebrate our defeat? Yes, we seized territory in a ruined China, but did not Great Britain and even Portugal precede us? After all, who was it that ruined China, with their opium trade and forced concessions? Yes, we took Singapore and Malaya, but from whom? Not the Singaporeans, not the Malayans, but the British. Yes, we took Indochina, but did we take it from the Vietnamese, Cambodians, or Laotians? No, we took it from the French! We did not take the Philippines from Filipinos but from the Americans, who themselves less than fifty years ago took the Philippines from the Spanish! And from whom did we conquer Borneo, Java, and Sumatra? Not their own people but the Dutch! And what of New Guinea, split in half like a sausage between the Dutch and the British? When we ousted these European regimes, did the people of Papua and Hollandia feel violated?"

The unrepentant Higashikuni raised an angry fist into the air and pounded it onto the podium. "No, they did not! It was our sacred mission to retake Asian territory in the name of Asia. To free it from the white man's rule!" Several in the diet squirmed in their seats, cringing as the prince remembered their old objective so baldly. Seeing this, he scoffed.

"What? Why do you look down at the floor as I speak? Am I wrong? Are we now ashamed even to say it? And should we not remember that in time these territories would have been returned? Liberation was our goal! Co-operation was our aim!"

A great emotion pulsed back and forth through the seated diet. Many of its members were struggling mightily to repress the grand ambitions of a very recent past. Others were visibly wondering where the prime minister was heading with these openly defiant comments. Only two days before, MacArthur had spoken eloquently aboard the USS *Missouri* in the name of tolerance, justice, and dignity. On this very day, the emperor had ordered the supreme commander's *Missouri* speech to be published throughout Japan. What was the prime minister trying to accomplish?

Higashikuni had stopped to take a few deep breaths, staring defiantly into the faces of his fellow aristocrats. And finally he continued.

"We lost this war, yes. But it was conducted under historic principles of international conduct. Where did we learn these principles? They were first dictated to us by the European and American powers nearly a century ago. I am here to accept responsibility on behalf of the imperial family for this loss. But we are serving notice, too. The new rules of accountability that are the result of the Potsdam Declaration and other Allied proclamations are dangerous revisionism! We must demand that they be very carefully applied."

A murmur washed across the diet floor, for the prince's public uttering of this warning could only be interpreted as having come at least indirectly from the emperor himself. Higashikuni seemed to seethe with resentment as he went on.

"A new and unfair concept is upon us. It threatens to label our honored leaders with the term 'war criminal' simply because they carried out policies that have been a part of international behavior throughout history. Is it an international crime to take territory by force? If so, who convicted the British, French, Dutch, and American leaders after they took the territories we recently liberated? No one! They congratulated each other, and competed to take even more territory! And what is different with Japan? Nothing! We do not accept that our leaders have conducted themselves as criminals. We will never accept this concept."

The members of the diet nodded slowly, but many of their faces were addled and confused. The war was lost. Shame was upon them. The Allies had landed. MacArthur had been given unilateral powers. Japan had signed the document. What more was there to accept or reject? As I stared out at them, I could feel Kido slyly watching me. He touched my arm, as if reassuring me.

"I will explain later," said Kido.

Prime Minister Higashikuni had wound down, the emotion of his speech seemingly exhausting him. Now he waved a hand toward the diet, as if reassuring them. "We will cooperate at every level with the occupation forces, so long as they are involved in activities to which we agreed. But the war was ended under very clear conditions. And we will not allow anyone to dishonor the leaders who conducted themselves according to the historic conduct of international affairs."

Murmurs and whispers coursed across the diet floor as Prince Higashikuni stepped away from the podium. He had inspired some, confused others, and left the majority nodding to one another with what appeared to be a knowing acceptance, as if the speech had been expected.

Kido tapped my shoulder once again, his face bright with a smiling intensity that masked an obvious concern.

"We should speak now," said the lord privy seal. "Would you come with me?"

He rose from his seat. I hesitated, thinking of the report I would be required to give upon my return to Yokohama. "What about the other speeches?"

He waved dismissively toward the floor. "They will be nothing. Water projects, road construction, and power plants. Governments!" laughed the lord privy seal. "After the rhetoric, they are all the same."

I followed him back down the dark hallway to the small room where he had been waiting before my arrival. Inside was a round wooden conference table surrounded by four chairs. At the middle of the table were a plain grey ceramic teapot and two ceramic cups. The walls were grey and bare, except for a large, ornate chrysanthemum symbol just across from the doorway where we entered. A second, closed door on the right-hand wall led to an unseen inner office.

Kido took a chair. I automatically sat across from him. He carefully poured us both some tea. The tea was steaming hot. Some unseen hand had known the exact moment we were leaving the diet floor and had placed the teapot onto the table just before we entered the room.

"You should please tell the supreme commander not to worry about this speech," urged the lord privy seal. "It was necessary, but he should not make too much of it."

"I will inform General MacArthur," I replied, sipping my tea and trying to remain diplomatic. "But there will be questions. After all, the speech was given by the prime minister, and there were a lot of reporters."

"Oh, we can take care of the Japanese reporters. They understand such things. And our interpreters were working with yours. And do not worry about the rest of it. The prince will not be prime minister for long."

Kido continued to force his smile, looking at me as if he were my tutor. "You see, we are playing many roles here. A great deal of preparation has gone into this! The prince became prime minister only so that the imperial family could accept responsibility to the people for the war. When it comes time to move into the future, he will go."

"We are moving into the future already, Lord Privy Seal. That was the basis of General MacArthur's speech two days ago."

"Yes, yes," said the lord privy seal with the wave of a hand. "But you must understand, these moments are necessary. We are reminding—our people—of certain things. As the emperor said, the new era should not ignore the old."

Kido picked up on the confusion in my stare. "We are in a transition, Captain Jay Marsh. The prince must have his say, or there would be trouble. But then he will be gone. It is the same as with the foreign minister! Shigemitsu will be gone soon. He is old. He signed the papers ending the war. He will leave government soon, and he will take the shame away with him. Others—"

Kido seemed to catch himself now, as if he were assuming too much from my own background and revealing himself too clearly. "Others are tasked with different roles. Each has a role to play. It is very important."

A giddiness coursed through me, for I was loving my own new role as a listener for the supreme commander. And I could not restrain my curiosity. "And what is your role, Lord Privy Seal?"

"Me?" Kido laughed lightly, as if he thought I already should have known. "My *duty* is to advise and protect the emperor from those who might use or shame him. My *role*? My role is to assign the roles."

We stared at each other for several seconds, then Kido shrugged. "Our culture is very exact, Captain Jay Marsh. For instance, it would have been—destabilizing—for Prince Higashikuni to have signed the documents onboard the *Missouri*, even though he was prime minister. This is why the foreign minister signed. We know that MacArthur understands these things. Just as he understood the importance of the royal *Chin*."

My mind began to crystallize as I watched Kido's smiling face, as if I were looking through binoculars that were finally focusing on a distant object. Of course, I thought. The prime minister's remarks were meant as a signal to MacArthur, particularly with regard to any charges for war crimes that might affect Japan's top leaders. And it was Kido who had picked Higashikuni over other members of the imperial family to be prime minister. The prince was playing out an assigned role even as Kido tried to convince me that his remarks had been harmless.

I sat my teacup onto the table. "There will be charges for war crimes, Lord Privy Seal. We all know that."

"Yes, we know that. But not to the royal family."

His bluntless stunned me. "The royal family?"

"The emperor. His cousins and uncles. They committed no crimes. To charge them would be nothing but an attack on the throne."

Kido's gaze was now clear and commanding. I did not know what else to say. It was time to go.

I rose from my chair. "Lord Privy Seal, I would like to thank you for your precious advice."

"Oh, you are most welcome." Kido rose, giving me a small bow, knowing the message was received and switching back to his diplomatic posturing. "You are moving to Tokyo soon?"

"Four days," I said.

"Yes! As soon as you are living in Tokyo, you must be my guest for dinner, Captain Jay Marsh. It is so helpful to be able to discuss issues in my own language. And it is very important that the supreme commander is able to hear of our concerns in other than official meetings. Don't you agree?"

I gave him a small bow in return. Without open discussion, our new relationship had been cemented. "I would be most honored. So long as General MacArthur approves."

"Yes!" he said, brightening, for to him General MacArthur's approval would also mean that MacArthur was agreeing to this unofficial channel of communication. "The perfect answer. General MacArthur is lucky to have you as his adviser."

"I'm not his adviser, Lord Privy Seal. I'm—"

"Yes," said Kido with a smiling impatience, as if we both were sharing the secret of my unspoken role. He led me toward the door as if dismissing me. "I know, I know."

The historic impact of this day settled over me on the ride back to Yokohama. As the sun began to disappear behind Tokyo's vast rubble its rays filtered through the dust, giving the city a beautiful pastel pink aura, like a dawning mist. It made me think of the teachings of Buddha, whose sway mixed among most of East Asia's cultures, leavening them without replacing their native distinctness. *Out of the muck grows the beauty of the lotus.* So Buddha had observed. And out of the hazy dust of Tokyo's ruins would soon come the pink and glowing nimbus of resurgence.

The prime minister's angry speech reverberated through my subconscious. How could I not be troubled by its boldness? Indeed, what would the reaction have been in Europe if a German leader had made such recalcitrant claims less than a week after the Third Reich's surrender?

And just as important, I had watched with my own eyes the majesty of Emperor Hirohito and the seamless movement of the symbols that propelled Japanese society far more powerfully than law or edict. He and Lord Privy Seal Kido had arranged through his simple speech, and Prince Higashikuni's diatribe, to lay down strong markers for postwar relations, including their view of the limits of war crimes prosecutions. As we sipped tea, Kido had reinforced the message so smoothly and yet so bluntly that I was still shaking my head in amazement as we reached the New Grand Hotel.

A fight was brewing. MacArthur was intent on changing Japan's Constitution, and with it their way of life. The Japanese would resist and at the same time would never agree to what the Allies were viewing as full accountability in the area of war crimes. And it occurred to me that as this battle brewed, I was becoming the only person who fully understood the weapons that both sides were quietly deploying. MacArthur brought with him an innate respect for the throne, but he did not yet comprehend the emperor's full power. Nor did the emperor and his lord privy seal have a true sense of the wiliness and intellect of Douglas MacArthur.

And me? Court Whitney had been right to trust me. I had found a new calling. I loved the subtleties and pretense of diplomacy. I was a natural smiler, double-speaker, and half-truther. I was addicted.

I loved it.

CHAPTER 10

★　★　★　★　★

Father Garvey sat alone and pensive at a center table in the Grand Hotel's dining room. It was after nine o'clock, and he was the only patron left in the restaurant. More interestingly, he was still sober.

I walked in and took a chair just across from him.

"You're looking weary, Jay," he said.

"Yes, Father. And you are ugly."

I waved across the room, summoning a tuxedoed little waiter. When he reached the table I told the old man in Japanese that I wanted a bottle of beer. A very large bottle. He smiled with appreciation at my fluency in his language, then bowed deeply before running off to fetch me my brew.

"I know women who would dispute that," Father Garvey said mysteriously. "But anyway, what's your point?"

"Well, tomorrow I will be rested. And you, Father, will still be ugly."

"I would dispute that as well," he said, now breaking out into a smile. "The part about you being rested. They're wearing you out, Jay!"

I felt myself come alive. "No! Do you realize what I've seen? Where I've been in just the last ten days? I was there when MacArthur landed on

Japan! I rode in the car with the emperor's number-one adviser, and now I'm, sort of, his—back-door messenger! I watched Yamashita walk out of the jungle, and I interviewed him when he surrendered! The Tiger of Malaya, personally, face to face! And today I watched the emperor speak to the Japanese parliament! *The fucking emperor of Japan!* Me! Jay Marsh, strawberry picker and chopper of cotton, from fucking Kensett, Arkansas!"

"It does not endear you to me to hear you swear like that," murmured Father Garvey, fully unimpressed. He eyed me almost accusingly. "And how is Divina Clara?"

"I don't know," I answered, coming back to earth.

"What do you mean you don't know? You were in Manila. Do you mean to tell me that you didn't even see her?"

"MacArthur wouldn't let me."

Father Garvey spat over his shoulder, an ancient Irish gesture meant to insult royalty. "Was MacArthur there, driving your jeep and watching your every move?"

The beer came. I took the bottle from the waiter's hand and drank straight from it as he left the glass on the table. "Father. I had to take a jeep to Atsugi, a C-54 to Okinawa and then to Manila, a C-47 to Bagabag, a truck to the Bessang Pass, wait for Yamashita to come out of the mountains, take the truck back to Bagabag, the C-47 to Baguio to drop off Yamashita and then fly back to Manila, then catch another C-54 back to Okinawa and up to Atsugi, and then another jeep back to Yokohama. Not to mention trying to sleep every now and then. All in three days!"

"Don't tell me you couldn't have gotten a message to her when you first landed at Manila and then managed to see her when you returned from Baguio, even if it was just for an hour?" Father Garvey's eyes went far away. "It's what I would have done, you know."

"And what does that mean, Father?"

He stared at me for a moment, seeming almost embarrassed. Then he looked away again. "It means I wonder if you love her. Or if you've just decided to end your—fling and ruin her little life."

I searched his face, looking for more. These were serious words, and it seemed something deeper was impelling them. But they were not wrong. "OK, Father, I'll admit I was scared. She was so emotional when I left. Do you know what would have happened if I'd only been able to see her for an hour? What she'd put me through—the guilt and the tears, when I don't have any answers for her yet, or any promises that I can make? I can't take that right now. There's too much else—"

"Oh, and he can't take what the lady would put him through," said Father Garvey. He turned his eyes on me again, rubbing his chin as if making a judicial pronouncement. "And have you thought at all about what you're putting her through?"

"I'm not putting her through anything. MacArthur is putting us both through something."

"Well, now there's a loyal statement. Be a brave man and put it all on MacArthur! As if that excuses your decision to ignore her?"

"What's gotten into you, Father?"

"No, what's gotten into you? You're going cold, Jay. Too caught up in your—flirtation with greatness and history. You'd better cut that out."

I watched him as I took another pull from my beer. Then I shrugged, forcing a smile. "I'm sorry, Father. You're right. I do miss her."

"When you die," said Father Garvey, pulling wisdom from a place I did not know he knew, "you are not going to be remembering that you saw the emperor give a speech."

"MacArthur will."

"You're not MacArthur. And what does that say about him, anyway? You'll be remembering who loved you. And how you dealt with it."

I finally raised my hands in surrender. "I was wrong, OK? But give me a break, Father! I hardly slept for three days. Can we talk about something else?"

"Of course," said Father Garvey. He had made his point and now offered me a forgiving smile. "I think it's time for us to debate whether Ted Williams will bat .400 next year."

The waiter reappeared, wanting to take my order. I looked at Father Garvey's plate. "What's for dinner?"

"So it's beef and noodles. Unless you're MacArthur. Or perhaps you'd like some Spam?" Father Garvey stopped, waiting for me to make a face, but I wasn't in the mood. "Did you know they found him an egg?" he finally said.

"I heard the story," I answered, sending the waiter off to fetch me some dinner. On his first morning in Japan, the supreme commander had asked for eggs for breakfast. After an exhaustive search, he was told that only one egg could be found in all of Yokohama. "But I refuse to believe that in the entire city of Yokohama there was only one egg."

"Well, they brought it to him, on a satin pillow."

"I grew up raising hens, Father. If there's one hen, there's two, and usually a rooster. And if there's two there's four. And one scared hen living by itself isn't likely to lay any eggs at all. Are you getting my point?"

"All right," shrugged Father Garvey, "let's for the sake of argument say there were ten. No, let's say there were a hundred. And how many million people live in Yokohama? That's still not very many eggs."

"No, let's just say that the General, for all his intelligence, is known at times to be quite impressionable. He's a romantic, Father. Like you."

"You're being very hard, all of a sudden. Have you lost your compassion? The war is over, Jay."

"Maybe. You didn't see what I did at the diet today." We sat quietly for a while. "Did you know that it's an honorable tradition in Japan for a loser to take the low position, to show himself as humble and helpless? It allows him to play the fool while he's waiting for revenge."

"Oh, it's revenge now, is it?" Father Garvey shook his head, waving a hand toward the sky as if talking directly to the Lord. "The former enemy is preparing for *revenge!*" He leaned across the table. "Have you taken a walk through Yokohama? Our bombs have destroyed everything. These people are destitute and impoverished."

"I don't dispute that."

"So what's your point?"

"I never said they weren't hungry. I just don't believe the egg story." I waved him off. "Never mind. Have a drink, Father."

Father Garvey grinned almost sheepishly. "Well, it's an unusual feeling, Jay, but since I've been here in Japan I don't care for one."

"Too bad. I like you better when you're drunk."

He laughed lightly, enjoying my irreverence. "My drinking is a long-lamented weakness. It's not something you should respect me for."

"I never said I respected you. I said I liked you."

"I suppose I could find a sin in making that kind of remark to one of God's servants."

"Not here," I joked. "There is no sin in Japan. Remember that, Father. I wouldn't want you to be confused."

"No *sin?* Then we've ended up in heaven."

"Hardly. They just don't believe in it. Get used to it."

Father Garvey's thick eyebrows furrowed, as if I were worrying him greatly. "You're sounding rather hateful today, Jay. I didn't hear you saying these things about the Filipinos, and they are Asian as well."

"They're Christians, Father. Christians accept the notion of sin. Sin goes to individual conscience. It's between you and God, and you will be held accountable when you die. The Japanese are motivated by shame, not conscience. Conscience is inward. Shame is outward. It goes to whether or not you will remain a respected member of the group. You're accountable here, and again later to the ancestors who are also a part of the group. On the one hand, sin compels a clearer set of actions, doesn't it? There are rules. But on the other, shame is more permanent. You can be forgiven for your sins, but how do you lose your shame? Shame is eternal! So you tell me—which do you think is a more powerful force?"

Father Garvey looked at me with a deepened respect. "That was quite profound, Jay. Where did you learn it?"

"From a girl named Kozuko. In California, five years ago."

"Then you're an old hand at this, aren't you?" He was only half teasing now. "But what does it have to do with hens and eggs?"

"Everything," I said, remembering my recent dealings with Lord Privy Seal Kido. "If there's no such thing as a sin, there's no such thing as a lie, is there? Not in absolute terms. What we condemn as a lie can be a noble act to the Japanese, if they're lying for the good of the group. The only shame comes if you fail in your obligations to the group. And here the group is the nation-family. And it will reject you for disloyalty."

Father Garvey pondered that, picking at his food. "The single egg indeed had a great impact on the *supreme commander.*" He sarcastically rolled the General's new title on his tongue as if he were pronouncing MacArthur to be a Pomeranian prince. "He brought in twenty-one truck-loads of food for the Yokohama government yesterday."

"So the lonely little egg served its purpose, didn't it?"

"And any American soldier caught eating Japanese food will be court-martialed."

"Exactly," I said. "Another victory for Yokohama."

Father Garvey scrutinized me as if I were ruining his romantic tale. "You should work to control your cynicism."

"But did the General eat the egg, Father? Or did he send it back to the starving Yokohamans. That's what I want to know."

"Of course he ate the egg. He's MacArthur. Why?"

"He's an American soldier. He ate Japanese food. When is *his* court-martial?"

Father Garvey regarded me with a grin that slowly widened, until he began laughing. "Have a hard day, did you, Jay? Up there in Tokyo with all the bigwigs?"

"Actually it was fascinating, Father. I loved it, all the intrigue and double-meanings. I feel like this is what I was born to do."

"Oh," he said, with false indulgence. "Lying, cheating, and stealing appeals to you, then?"

I laughed. "You know I wouldn't steal."

The waiter brought me a plate of beef and noodles. It was my first food since early morning. I ate ravenously. A few minutes later the waiter brought me another beer and I took a long pull, right out of the bottle. Father Garvey watched me drink, somehow pristine and noble in his newfound sobriety. Finally he shrugged.

"There are some very weird things going on, Jay. Don't you think?"

"I will admit to you, Father, that it's even weirder than you might think. Sometimes I feel like I'm in the middle of a play where all the lines have already been written, only I don't have the script. It's like no matter what we decide to do, they've already thought about it and prepared for it and know where to take it."

"Just because they lost doesn't make them stupid, Jay. And we're playing on their home court."

"We have our first point of full agreement," I said. "They are definitely not stupid."

Father Garvey watched me with a brooding seriousness as I finished the noodles and drank my beer. Then he gestured toward the hotel lobby. "Would you go with me for a walk?"

I shook my head, uninterested. "Not tonight, Father, I'm beat. I had the drive to and from Tokyo, the meetings at the diet, then an hour upstairs being interrogated by Generals MacArthur, Willoughby, and Whitney. And now two beers."

He persisted. "It would be most helpful to my understanding if you would let me show you something. It might—amaze you."

I could tell he was struggling mightily with some deep, intellectual thought. "What is it, Father?"

"A whorehouse," he said, without particular emotion. He saw my surprised laugh and waved an arm almost angrily at me, jumping out of his chair. "I have not indulged, Jay Marsh, and I will not tolerate the evil insinuations inherent in your silly laughing!"

"Well, I'm not interested, Father."

"Of course you're not," said Father Garvey, pacing next to the table. "You're in love with a beautiful woman and you're engaged to be married. But I think you need to see it."

"Father, it embarrasses me to admit this, but I've been inside a few whorehouses before."

"Not like this one, you haven't."

It was late. The dark streets around the port were nearly empty of people or traffic, save for the occasional American jeep or truck that rumbled past. Father Garvey and I strolled along the unlit, broken sidewalks, squinching our noses from the harsh sewage that ran in narrow canals just below the concrete. All around us the crickets were chirping; winter would come early this year. Along the roads and in front of the small houses, paper lanterns glowed like fireflies for as far as we could see. Above us hung a large and lustrous moon.

The laughing repartee of American soldiers wafted to us from the passing vehicles and from the two-man sentry posts that had been set up on street corners throughout the city. Gentle smoke curled out of nearby open windows. Inside the quiet, darkened homes we could see small charcoal fires glowing, making rice and tea. Somewhere in the shadows of every broken room were silent, watching faces. They were hungry and whispering and waiting. They had yet to know their full fate at the hands of these oafish foreigners who now camped on their previously unconquered streets. And it struck me again, as it had so often in the waning days of wartime Manila, that these odd combinations of American troops and vehicles on dazed and waiting foreign roadways had become one of my life's most natural rhythms.

After several blocks, the sidewalks began to fill with American soldiers moving in small groups. They walked jauntily, passing us in both directions with the cocky, electrified strides of victors on the prowl. Their heads were back. Their hands were in their pockets. Their voices were filled with a sibilant excitement. They paid us no attention as they passed us.

Finally Father Garvey pointed toward a huge, semidarkened building that sat just on the harbor's edge.

"Over there," he said.

We crossed the street, heading toward the building. "Does MacArthur know about this?" I asked.

"I informed him," shrugged Father Garvey. Then he became suddenly defensive. "It was, after all, my duty."

"What did he say?"

"A bunch of gobbledygoop. He told me that his men had been in the jungles for a long time, and that sex is a natural human function. That there was no way to stop it. And that the greatest lesson he'd ever learned from his father was never to give an order that could not be enforced."

We finished crossing the street and were now near the building. "Sorry, Father, but you can't argue with that logic."

"That was not my intention!" said Father Garvey, his face intense. "This isn't fully a religious question! It isn't even a military question. Just take a look, and tell me what you think, Jay!"

A steady stream of American soldiers was pouring into and out of the building. Above its entrance, in English, was a large, precisely lettered sign:

YOKOHAMA

RECREATION AND AMUSEMENT

ASSOCIATION

The door opened into a vast, dimly lit lobby with an uncarpeted concrete floor. A chest-high wooden front desk had been placed just inside the doorway. The reception desk was very likely a portable bar that had been taken from a real hotel to this makeshift building, which looked as though it had recently served as a factory. On the other side of the desk, two stairways led up to four floors of honeycombed rooms. I could see several of the rooms from where I stood. They seemed to have been recently partitioned with lightweight bamboo and paper walls.

An air of happy chaos reigned on the far side of the reception desk. Giggling, plain-faced Japanese girls waited near the desk as dozens of American soldiers walked among them. The girls were wearing simple cotton kimonos that amply revealed their smooth skin and rounded soft-ness behind the clinging fabric.

The enchanted soldiers were joking and poking and teasing as they decided on their choices. Other smiling girls were returning from the stairway with clearly satisfied soldiers, some of whom were holding hands as if they had just fallen in love. Soldiers were leaving. Soldiers were coming, some of them yelling loudly with surprised delight when they walked inside and saw this treasure trove of Asian femininity. Girls were waiting. Girls were walking. Girls were waving hello and good-bye.

Yes, here it was: peace had come to Japan. No booze, no fights, no jealousy, at least not yet. The Yokohama Recreation and Amusement

Association was a very happy place, much more so than had been the surrender deck of the USS *Missouri* a few mornings before.

A small, fortyish Japanese man wearing a grey wool suit stood behind the desk, alongside an older female assistant. The woman was wearing a full brown kimono and was keeping meticulous records in a large note-book. The man smiled brightly when he saw us. He waved an inviting hand toward the teeming pool of girls and spoke to us in English. "Yes, good evening, gentlemens. We have very good time for you. You choose one girl, sucky-fucky, no problem. She want to know American way of love! Five dollars one half hour. OK? OK?"

"Are you understanding yet?" asked Father Garvey.

"Why'd you bring me here?" I answered. "How did this happen?"

I stood stunned and gaping on the other side of the desk. The Japanese had surrendered less than three weeks before. We had been in Yokohama less than a week. Before our landing at Atsugi we had heard reports that the more proper classes were sending their wives and daughters to the hills, some carrying cyanide capsules to swallow in case they were faced with a rapacious Allied soldier. And yet here before us were a seeming legion of knock-kneed, coarse-featured girls from slums and farmlands and ordinary brothels, collected and organized to render a conduit for the Red-haired Barbarians' lust.

Organized. That was the difference. Collected, by the ever-unseen hand, and put into service. A phenomenon wholly distinct from the ran-dom, sultry turmoil of Subic, which at bottom had represented nothing more than a crude form of opportunism and false hope. There was design to this, and strenuous effort. This whorehouse was not born of opportu-nity. Rather, it had been created by government effort. The converted building, the immaculate English-language sign, even the smiling, record-keeping host who now tugged at my arm and gestured toward his lovelies. Up from the ashes, compliments of—who?

"You like which girl? Tell me. Five dollars, no problem."

"You speak very good English," I said. As we spoke a soldier walked to the desk with the girl he had chosen and paid the man's assistant. Taking the money, the older woman wrote neatly into a ledger, cataloguing the amount and crediting the girl's account. Then she casually waved the girl upstairs with the back of her hand.

"You are surprise I speak your language?" he asked. "I went to school at Boston College, two years."

"*Boston?*" said an amazed Father Garvey.

"You know Boston College?"

"It's my alma mater!"

"Hey, then we are maybe classmates!" The host gestured again toward the girls. "For you, only four dollars. No problem! Classmate discount."

"I'm a priest, you idiot!"

Another soldier, another girl, another credit to another account, another trip upstairs. Several other soldiers filed past us, finished with their visit, heading back to their bivouac area. One of them reached out and touched me on the shoulder.

"Hey," said the soldier. "It's an officer! I thought this was an enlisted club!" And now a dozen soldiers laughed and pointed, as if Father Garvey and I were there to join in the fun.

The Japanese man looked at us with fresh clarity, for the first time seeing that we both were officers and also noting the cross on Father Garvey's collar. A quick confusion seemed to freeze the expression on his face. I began speaking to him in Japanese.

"We work for General MacArthur," I said. "Don't worry. We are only here to inquire about the success of your obviously well-run establishment."

"Ohhhh," he answered, immediately bowing deeply. "Ah so, ah so."

"How long has this building been a hotel?" I asked.

He smiled proudly. "Only ten days. We had to work very hastily! Before this, it was a munitions factory."

"You should be congratulated," I said. "To have been able to convert a building so quickly, and then recruit your ladies, at a time of such great shortage and hardship."

"Yes," he answered proudly. "We had remarkable cooperation. We needed girls with the right—background and experience. It became an important project."

"And how many employees do you have here?"

"More than three hundred," he answered. "But not all of them at the same time. And not all of them—entertainers. We clean up. Wash towels, wash sheets, bring fresh water. We are working very hard to manage a clean and respectable recreation association."

The line before his assistant was now five deep. Hands that had carried rifles against Yamashita's soldiers in the northern Luzon jungles now were gaining fresh experience as they squeezed the softness of golden skin hidden casually beneath cotton robes.

"And your business is going well?"

"Oh, yes!" He checked his register, finding the bottom row of two separate columns. "Today we have had 2,195 customers. Five dollars per customer. This makes—10,975 dollars."

Father Garvey gave the man an amazed stare. Behind his bushy eyebrows I could see him trying to calculate the magnitude of 2,195 acts of copulation, in a world where he was not allowed to play.

"And where does the money go?" I asked.

"To the association." Now the man seemed uncomfortable, as if I had finally probed too far.

"And who owns the association?"

His eyes moved quickly to his female assistant and then back to me. "The—association owns the association. I am sorry. I don't understand your question." More soldiers, in and out of the busy door. He gave me a deep bow, then switched back to English.

"We are very busy here, sir. You will please tell General MacArthur that everything is A-OK?"

We were quiet on the way back to the hotel, but as we neared it Father Garvey suddenly elbowed me, shaking his head with amazement. "And now thanks to your keen insight I finally understand the dilemma, Jay! For us, 2,195 acts of fornication. Sins to be forgiven, if you would. To them, 2,195 contributions to the well-being of the larger group. Blessings, shall we call them? Do I have it correctly?"

"And some pretty heavy cash," I added.

"Right," said Father Garvey. "And cash. And this is only Yokohama."

"What do you mean, Father?"

"Well, in a few days we'll be in Tokyo."

"Yes."

"Led by the famous First Cavalry Division. A grand parade, I'm told."

"That's what the supreme commander is planning."

"And I don't exactly expect the soldiers to be met by enemy fire."

"No, in fact the Japanese army will be totally withdrawn from the city, probably tomorrow."

"Tokyo is a very large city. As populous as New York, they say."

"More or less. I mean, with all the bombing it's hard to count."

"We can expect a great deal of—how did the gentleman, my fellow alumnus, put it? Friendship and cooperation?"

"No, Father, I believe the precise words were, 'recreation and amusement.'"

"Yes," said Father Garvey. "Recreation and amusement." He walked silently for a while. "So give me some advice."

"Me, Father?"

"Yes." He looked dubiously up into my face. "As a priest, what should I do about all this?"

I laughed. It was midnight. We had reached the hotel.

"Pray, Father."

" 'Pray,' he says," said Father Garvey. "Is that it?"

"Pray," I answered. "To the patron saint of lost causes."

On September 6, General Courtney Whitney arranged for the American reporters who had beaten MacArthur into Tokyo to be removed from the city, explaining that it was "not American military policy for correspondents to spearhead an occupation." On September 7, all Japanese regular army soldiers were withdrawn northward out of Tokyo, leaving behind only one division of imperial guards.

The guards were instructed to dress in civilian clothes. They had been "secretly" kept in the city by the Japanese, with the acquiescence of MacArthur, in order to protect the Imperial Palace. From whom the palace was being protected neither side acknowledged, but MacArthur's gesture did allow both him and the emperor some quiet saving of face. For MacArthur, despite all his assigned powers, could never have stopped the Japanese from keeping selected soldiers in civilian clothes from remaining, anyway. And what would it have said about the emperor if even the seat of the throne were left naked to anyone who wished simply to cross that sacred moat, subject only to the discretion of some pink-cheeked twenty-year-old MP from Ohio?

By dawn on September 8, MacArthur's longtime favorite division, the First Cavalry, had massed at the edge of the giant city, along the road that the supreme commander would take from Yokohama. We joined them at midmorning, then rode behind them in our cavalcade of broken-down cars, marking the General's formal entry into the capital.

The drums beat. The old cars popped and backfired as they chugged forward. The soldiers marched smartly through the pink haze and the sea of unremitting rubble. The ragged Japanese gathered near the road to stare and even cautiously wave. And the unspoken but intense preliminaries between MacArthur and the emperor continued.

Mindful of the quiet but awesome display of imperial power shown by the thirty thousand soldiers the emperor had sent to greet him at Atsugi, MacArthur had instructed the Japanese government that this would be an all-American procession. The entry into the city, watched by hundreds of thousands of bystanders, was the supreme commander's first show of symbolic force in Tokyo itself. The General had an Asian's grasp of the impact of ceremony. In this maiden exhibition of his authority he did not want to create any impression that he was being delivered to his quarters through the benevolence of Japanese security.

But still the hand of the imperial government was never far from us, however hidden in the quiet crowds and broken buildings. At the outskirts of the city the General's car stuttered, coughed, and finally broke down. As the driver climbed out to check the engine, a dozen hard-eyed plainclothes policemen immediately emerged from the nearby crowd and formed a ring around the car. Silent, stoic, unmovable, and always staring outward, they protected the fuming supreme commander until a different car was brought up from the rear of the column.

The high-walled American embassy stood on Renanzaka Hill in Akasaka district, not far from the government buildings and only a few minutes from the grounds of the Imperial Palace itself. Reaching it, the First Cavalry continued forward to take up positions throughout the nearby area, including the diet building and the cold, grey-moated walls of the palace grounds. An honor guard from the Seventh Cavalry, remembered since the Indian Wars for having lost its flag with General Custer at Little Big Horn, stayed behind and moved inside the embassy grounds. Our command group moved with them, led by MacArthur and General Eichelberger.

We assembled around the empty flagpole in the embassy yard. Across from us the yard filled up with an ever more deeply cynical media, still angry at having been temporarily ejected from Tokyo by Court Whitney. The bugles played. The ubiquitous photographers clicked their cameras. And finally MacArthur marched to the flagpole, where he turned to the saluting Eichelberger. The cant and tone of his words themselves seemed to come out of an era gone just as cold and dead as Custer.

"Have our country's flag unfurled, and in the Tokyo sun let it wave in its full glory, as a symbol for the hope of the oppressed and as a harbinger of victory for the right."

The Imperial Palace being unavailable, MacArthur took the second-nicest villa in Tokyo for his home, moving into the American embassy. The embassy had been closed for nearly four years, but there was no difficulty in recruiting and training qualified employees. He had no need even to ask about them. One by one, without command or advertisement, those who had served in the building before the war crept into its familiar rear entrance, reporting back to work. Nor was there any need to clothe them. They had stored their brown staff kimonos in airtight trunks and left them in the embassy's attic.

The dishes were in the cupboards. The linens were in the closets. The cleaning materials were in the storage rooms. Without so much as a stutter the embassy was again vibrant and polished, in the capable hands of its smiling, bowing Japanese staff. It was almost as if there had never been this unpleasant interruption called a war.

For his headquarters the supreme commander chose the Dai Ichi Insurance building. Six stories high, it was one of the tallest buildings in Tokyo, since after the great Kanto earthquake of 1923 restrictions had been placed against erecting buildings any higher. More important, the white-columned, marble-and-granite structure was just across the street from the southern edge of the Imperial Palace grounds. MacArthur and the emperor would now go about their daily tasks within easy eyesight of each other.

And emanating as it did from the Dai Ichi, the ordinary Japanese would understand the power of MacArthur's office. Inside this same building, Japanese political cabals had festered and brewed for decades. Only a few weeks before, the Dai Ichi had been home to a contrived and symbolic political movement called the Peace Faction, and it had also been the headquarters for the Tokyo Area army. Its security facilities were un-equaled elsewhere in Japan and included tubelike slides for escaping to the ground floor in the event of fire or earthquake, or—not that MacArthur seemed worried—an attempted assassination.

I and several lesser members of the command group were given quarters in a nearby *ryokan*, a small, traditional Japanese travelers' hotel that was now being converted into a bachelor officers' quarters. A raw thrill rippled through me as I hauled my seabag up two flights of steep stairs and walked the dark hallway to the small room that would become my Japanese equivalent of home. MacArthur was finally settling into his latest and perhaps last mansion. The other generals would soon find their villas. Father Garvey had been given quarters more than a mile away. My isolation in the *ryokan* was a ticket to freedom. Already I was savoring my first true moment of privacy since I had left Manila. I was really in Japan, and I was finally alone.

My little room had already been fitted with a Western-style bed, a portable wooden closet, and a small mahogany desk. Our ever-anticipating hosts had adorned the desk with a reading lamp and had left me five sheets of writing paper as well as an old quill pen. The pen was set into a sunken inkwell. The inkwell was filled with black India ink. For so long as I stayed in the *ryokan* the inkwell would be neatly refilled every morning, and my writing papers would be replenished up to exactly five sheets.

The bathroom area had two tiny rooms. In one was a toilet that consisted of a faucet next to a hole in the concrete floor, over which one was expected to squat and then rinse. In the other stood a small sink, above which the *ryokan*'s staff had recently hung a little circular mirror, and next to the sink was a chest-deep sunken bath.

Not much, according to MacArthurian standards. But it was far better lodging than had been the corn-shuck mattresses, nighttime chamber pots, and outdoor wells and pumps of Kensett, Arkansas.

I wearily took off my cap, dropped my seabag onto the floor, then laid back on the bed. The welcome sense of aloneness washed over me like a warm and comforting breeze. I suddenly felt drugged, as though I could fall asleep and not wake up for weeks. The incredible tensions of the past several days had finally abated, if only for an evening, making me realize for the first time how much pressure I really had been under.

It was as if the past few days had all been an odd dream, and in falling asleep I somehow would finally be awakening to reality. It seemed like decades since I had hugged my mother and brother good-bye and climbed up the ramp of the transport ship on my way to Australia. And it seemed like years since I had last seen Divina Clara run from my arms down the jasmine-cluttered path and disappear inside her darkened home. How long had that really been? Less than two weeks?

I had mail. I slapped open the upper pocket of my uniform blouse and pulled out the two letters I had been given before departing Yokohama that morning. Still lying on the bed, I examined and then opened the envelopes. One was from my mother, having been written on the day Japan announced its surrender, telling me how happy she was that I would not die, *"provided you are still alive, that is."* With the war winding down, she had lost her job at the defense plant. But she hoped that I would be happy because she was marrying the Italian. I resolved to write her the next morning with my quill pen and Japanese paper, to let her know that I was indeed still alive but would not be coming home anytime soon.

The second was from Divina Clara, written only four days before, its quick delivery helped no doubt by my address as a member of the supreme commander's immediate staff. *I have been thinking about this*, she wrote. *And I am believing you will come back. Because what did you have to gain if you did not really love me, but only told me that you did? You already had all of me as well as the memories, and that would not change even if you did not return, except that the memories would be cheapened if you had lied. And if you wanted to leave me it would have been simple for you to decide that at Subic. You could have just told me that my grandmother was too forbidding, and that we would have to part. But you did not, and so you do love me. I am sure of this. And I will never stop loving you.*

I smiled fondly. *She has been thinking about this.* Indeed, she was always thinking. I held the letter to my heart, wishing it somehow were Divina Clara's face and that I was now running my hands along her cheek and through the silky length of her wonderful, thick black hair. She was the most unusual and intuitive person I had ever met. She had built herself a logic, divined my feelings not from what I had told her so much as from what I did not say.

Father Garvey had been right. I felt traitorous for not having tried to see her while I was in Manila. I pressed her letter to my face as if I could find her fingers in the writing on the page. And then I fell asleep.

CHAPTER 11

★　★　★　★　★

It was unlike MacArthur, but he had indeed given the larger, grander corner offices of the Dai Ichi building's sixth floor to lesser-ranking generals and had selected for himself an interior room with a less sweeping view of Tokyo's landscape. Many on the staff were puzzled by this gesture, but from the first moment I walked into the phoneless, walnut-paneled office I understood why he had chosen it. Pacing in front of its one wide window, he could tamp his pipe each morning and stare past the palace plaza just across the street, where Tokyo Rose had once claimed he would be hanged, over the top of the sacred double bridge called Sakurada that led into the palace grounds, and look directly at the emperor's home in the Fukiage Gardens, less than half a mile away.

He was doing just that as I quietly entered his office. His firm, surprisingly youthful face was lost in some mystical quandary as he paced. His slender hands and neatly manicured fingers perfunctorily tamped tobacco into a favorite corncob, taken as always from a nearby rack that held more than a dozen pipes. Outside it was raining. Underneath a lamppost just below us, two rickshaw drivers were sitting knees-up below the bonnets of their little pedicabs, trading cigarettes and stories. The splashing streets were filled with a mix of horse-drawn wagons, rickshaws pulled by tiny men, ancient charcoal-burning Japanese cars, and a host of American and British military vehicles. On the sidewalk below, I saw an American soldier walking with his arm around a young Japanese woman, sharing her pink umbrella. We had entered the city only ten days ago, but Recreation and Amusement had already come to Tokyo.

The palace grounds were covered with a small forest of carefully cultured trees, in all a gorgeous mix of reaching, heavy-branched pines, sycamore, bamboo, and cypress. As MacArthur continued to stare, the rain filtered through their branches, giving the grounds a steamy, cobwebbed haze. Near us, just in front of the Sakurada Gate, an old bus pulled up. Its dozen or so darkly bundled occupants climbed quickly out. As the rain soaked them they bowed deeply in one collective motion toward the gate and to the unseen emperor on its other side. Then all together they turned and faced the Dai Ichi building, bowing a second time, not quite so deeply, toward the unseen supreme commander. Drenched, they quickly reentered the bus, which continued on its journey.

MacArthur noticed this. I could see him struggling to fight back a thin, appreciative smile. He was becoming an immensely popular figure throughout Japan. Every public word he spoke was published verbatim in Japanese newspapers. Virtually every Japanese now knew his name and associated it with hope for the future. Women were already naming babies after him, and some were even writing to him asking that he might sire their next child. Groups of schoolchildren sometimes appeared magically on nearby street corners, waving the American and Japanese flags together in one hand.

It was September 18, 1945. It was hard for me to believe, but it had been only one month to the day since we had hosted General Kawabe and his haggard, shamefaced delegation in Manila, where the cameras had clicked like a million crickets, the rocks had pelted the limousines like hailstones, and MacArthur had preserved the dignity of the royal *Chin*.

Only two days before, President Truman had sent a cable inviting the supreme commander home to the United States for a ticker-tape victory parade down Broadway, of the sort already given General Dwight Eisenhower. MacArthur had declined, even though he had not been on the North American continent since his honeymoon in 1937. The reason he gave had frosted the president: "If I were to return from Asia only for a few weeks," MacArthur had written, "word would spread throughout the Pacific that the United States is abandoning the Orient."

The true reasons were less grand but equally pompous. The war was gone, vanished, mere prologue. Who needed the temporary, confetti-filled adulation of New York when he had the full idolatry of Tokyo? Why follow in his former aide Eisenhower's footsteps, becoming simply another war-hero general, when he stood on the cusp of true historical greatness? Who needed to defer for days in speech and ceremony to this bumpkin Truman, the former haberdasher and political-machine crony from Kansas City who had by the accident of death replaced his urbane friend-enemy and fellow aristocrat Roosevelt, when MacArthur himself was now the semi-sovereign ruler of his very own country?

And there was another reason. How long would it take to remake Asia? Maybe, just maybe, there would be a run for the presidency in 1948 and MacArthur would want his own grand return to America. Why share the newsreel with Truman?

I crept slowly forward as MacArthur continued to stare through the window. His eyes were now fixed longingly on the inner palace at the edge of the gardens, where he knew the emperor walked each day to pray at the palace shrine. I wondered again what it was that the General thought of and wished for as he stared out toward the palace and whether the emperor himself was awakening each morning and secretly peering from a palace window, trying to see MacArthur. Had there ever been a moment like this in all of history, where two supreme rulers were perched within easy view of each other, each with undeniable but different kinds of power, each carrying the uncertain fate of the same country in his hands, and neither trying to kill the other? I did not think so.

At such moments I had learned not to speak lest I incur the supreme commander's wrath by breaking his train of thought. Stepping ever further into the room, I nodded to Generals Whitney and Willoughby, who sat waiting patiently in two identical worn brown leather chairs. The chairs faced each other from opposite ends of a long, equally scarred leather divan. Between them was a low mahogany end table. Across the room, in front of a bookcase that held an onyx clock and the General's pipe rack, his personal swivel chair was pushed neatly into a table-desk.

The desktop was immaculately cleared, save for a fountain pen and a letter opener. Its in-box and out-box were both empty. It was not quite nine in the morning, but the General, a frenetic yet meticulous worker, had already gone through more than a hundred letters, as well as a stack of official cables. As was the case every morning, the paperwork had already been fanned out to key staff assistants for action.

I remained standing. A seat in MacArthur's office was taken only when offered. Finally he seemed to notice me, and spoke.

"What is it, Jay?"

"Sir, the lawyers are here."

MacArthur turned to Whitney, as if he had just been rudely awakened in the middle of a pleasurable dream. "I must tell you, Court, I find this whole process odious and counterproductive."

Whitney shot the hulking Willoughby a quick glance, then shook his head, standing up to the supreme commander. "I know how you feel, General, but these are matters of the utmost importance. We can't put them off, not even for a day."

"There are a lot of things we can't put off!" fumed MacArthur, pacing again before the window. Without looking, he reached into his pocket and took out a box of matches to light his pipe. "It's going to be a long and bitter winter. I need three and a half million tons of food, that's what I need! Three and a half million tons, that's *seven billion pounds* of food! And if I'm going to implement my reforms, it must happen quickly. You know what Sherman said to Grant before his march toward Atlanta, don't you? 'Celerity is the key to success.' "

He stopped pacing. As he lit his pipe I empathized with the enormity of both his assigned chores and his grander desires. He was disarming an entire nation, even as he tried to feed it. He was negotiating a relationship with its government at the same time he was creating a mammoth second bureaucracy designed to oversee its actions. He had publicly pledged that he would rewrite Japan's Constitution in a way that would cause the country to renounce war and at the same time emancipate its women, press, labor unions, and religions. He had announced that he would institute land reform. Most controversially, he had guaranteed that he would dismantle the *zaibatsu*, the longtime corporate oligarchy dominated by eleven historically powerful families, most notably the Sumitomos, the two branches of the Iwasakis, who controlled Mitsubishi, and the eleven branches of the Mitsuis.

And what was it that the Allies wished to see on top of his agenda? War crimes. The one issue that in MacArthur's eyes would mire these emerging improvements in the vitriol of the past.

The pipe was lit. He began pacing again. "This is going to be messy. And what I need right now is simplicity."

"Yes, sir," sighed Court Whitney. The General's chief political adviser looked again at General Willoughby, wordlessly asking for support.

Finally Willoughby cleared his throat, speaking slowly in his deep, heavily Teutonic accent. "Our War Crimes Board is receiving a great deal of pressure from the other Allies," said the General's intelligence specialist. "The entire world is waiting for us to assign accountability. The Australians and the Chinese are especially serious in their demands that the emperor himself be tried."

MacArthur waved his pipe angrily into the air. The corncob had already gone out and he was reaching for another match. "It would serve no purpose. In fact, it would defeat our purpose."

"We have to address these issues, sir," said Willoughby. "If we do not, they will grow."

"Have I ever said otherwise?" He faced Willoughby as if now speaking before a tribunal or a press conference. "Have we not been addressing them? Did we not create the War Crimes Board as one of our first orders of business? Is Field Marshal Sugiyama not dead, he and his wife both killing themselves when we tried to arrest him? Is not General Tojo in the hospital with a bullet in his stomach after having attempted suicide, the direct result of our decision to make such arrests?"

"A lousy shot," panned the irreverent General Whitney. Catching MacArthur's quick glare, the lawyer gracefully retreated. "It's the joke on the street among the Japanese, Boss. Tojo shot himself with an American pistol taken from a downed pilot. As far as they're concerned, if he'd been a real man he'd have slit his stomach with a samurai sword."

"A lousy *joke*, Court."

Generals Willoughby and Whitney both looked down, knowing when it was better to remain silent. Finally MacArthur nodded to me.

"All right, Jay. Bring them in. Let's get this over with."

I stepped outside and returned with the three senior lawyers from the General's judge advocate staff. They were led by a craggy, balding colonel named, oddly enough, Samuel Genius. I continued to stand as the three nervously sat next to one another on the wrinkled leather divan. Colonel Genius opened up a legal-sized folder. His two assistants, both majors, held legal notepads on their laps and looked attentively at the colonel as he began to speak.

"Actually, I have some good news, sir," began Colonel Genius. "The Japanese are just as shaken as we were about Field Marshal Sugiyama and General Tojo. They've agreed that if we consult with the Cabinet in advance on war crimes arrests, the suspects we name will turn themselves in."

"How would that take place?" asked MacArthur, puffing on his pipe and still standing before the window.

"We would designate what we call 'Allied detention points.' The suspects would turn themselves in to Japanese police, and the police will deliver them to the detention points."

"And just what do they mean when they demand that the office of the supreme commander *consult* with the Cabinet?"

Court Whitney interjected. "That's not a problem, General. We'll tell them. Period. I think their wording is just a matter of face."

"Delete 'consult'," decided MacArthur. "You consult someone who has greater power than yourself. We will 'inform.' We will 'coordinate.' And if they so desire, they can 'consult' with us." He shrugged. "In truth, we probably should have been doing that already."

Colonel Genius nodded, relaxing a bit as his majors scribbled notes onto their legal pads. "Yes, sir. Excellent point." He flipped a page inside his folder. "And we have some more good news. When we searched Field Marshal Sugiyama's home we found his diary. It's being translated even as I speak. We're getting some fascinating information from it, I must say."

MacArthur seemed guarded. "Regarding what?"

"Meetings at the highest level, throughout the war," said Colonel Genius. "Who was at them. Who recommended certain actions. Sugiyama was army chief of staff from well before Pearl Harbor to after the battle of Saipan. We're picking up notes on who knew what and when, from the emperor on down."

The General had begun his inveterate pacing again, but now he stopped and walked slowly to the swivel chair at his desk. He pulled it out and sat down. It was the first time I had seen MacArthur sit during a meeting since I had been on his staff. It was clear to me that he had been caught completely off guard.

"I will tell you, personally," began MacArthur, "that for some reason it would unsettle me to be reading through a dead man's diary."

The mention of the emperor had jolted the supreme commander, and the very earnestness of his face told me that this comment was classic MacArthurian misdirection. It would unsettle him not at all if the contents of Field Marshal Sugiyama's diary were likely to suit his own desires rather than enlarge the debate over the emperor. "Of what possible use can a diary be in a court of law?"

"These aren't ordinary diaries, General." Genius looked to his left and right, drawing convinced nods from his assistants. "High-level Japanese officials apparently have always used their diaries to record in great detail what actually went on in these meetings. Who said what and why. Who objected and why. It seems they have a constant need to protect themselves from blackmail and political assassination. Intrigues and betrayals are a part of the inner workings of the Japanese system." Colonel Genius took on an animated look, like a dog on the hunt. "So what we are finding is, in many cases, a day-by-day accounting of how decisions were made throughout the war."

"I am of course not an attorney," said MacArthur, "but as I recall a diary is not admissible in court as evidence. It would be hearsay. People exaggerate when writing to themselves. They fail to remember all the details. They slander their enemies. How do we know that any diary contains the truth?"

"We find other diaries, and cross-reference," answered Genius immediately. The lawyer took a slow breath and held it, then threw his hands up into the air, venting his frustration. "General, when the war ended in Germany our people were able to capture voluminous amounts of evidence, and we had people fluent in German who knew how to read it and analyze it. Here, just about the only information we have are the papers the Japanese themselves decided to turn over to us. Can you imagine how bizarre that is? And we're working overtime trying to find Americans sophisticated enough to be able to read through all the nuance and subtleties of Japanese *kanji*."

"Why haven't you simply moved in and taken over the files?" asked the supreme commander.

"What files?" Colonel Genius seemed incredulous. "They claim the war ministry's records office was hit by firebombs, destroying all the files. They say the navy ministry was burnt out, too. Anything we really need— command chronologies, minutes of key meetings—they're burnt."

"By our firebombs."

"That's what they maintain," said Colonel Genius cynically. "Very convenient. By our firebombs. Amazingly accurate bombing, with the ministries right across the street from the emperor's palace, isn't it? In fact, last May a building on the palace grounds caught fire *three hours* after one of our fire bombings ended. The fire was started by cinders blown across the street from the war ministry building. The cinders came from—you guessed it, sir—burning military records. And the records they are turning over? I have no way of knowing if they're accurate. To be frank, they've known they were going to lose for some time. Without the minutes of the meetings themselves, any materials that they turn over to us can easily have been changed. So, ironic as it might sound, a diary, cross-referenced with another source, becomes very good evidence."

MacArthur rose from his chair and began pacing again. "We should have expected this. It's one reason why I have been opposed to this form of sweeping damnation from the beginning. What good will it do? How much of our energies will be expended in cat-and-mouse games that cause both sides to lose face?" He glanced at Genius. "How far does this go, Colonel? How much of this does justice require us to do?"

Colonel Genius flipped through his legal folder. He had completely relaxed. His voice took on an academic tone. "We're dealing with three different categories of war crimes, General, and our lists are reflecting these distinctions. The first, and as you might imagine the easiest both to deplore and prosecute, are the individual cases. Individual atrocities, if you would. For instance, we have reports of doctors conducting savage and inhumane experiments on our prisoners of war. Deliberately injecting soybean milk and even urine into their veins. Deliberately bleeding to death healthy men in order to capture their plasma. We have reports of Japanese officers in the island campaigns having cooked American airmen and then eaten their organs. I have a report that certain members of the Japanese secret police kept pens of naked Western men and women underneath the torture chambers of Bridge House in Shanghai. These kinds of things."

"Yes," said MacArthur, clearly repulsed. "Those are without question crimes for which individuals should be held accountable. And bringing them to court will provide a valuable education for the Japanese people. Go on."

"Yes, sir." Colonel Genius wiped a hand over his balding pate and frowningly flipped past a few pages. "The second category is a little harder but is of equal concern. It involves accountability for what we might call mass atrocities. Situations where Japanese soldiers went out of control for days or weeks at a time, resulting in the large-scale slaughter of innocents."

"Like the rape of Manila," interjected MacArthur, his face suddenly a map of vivid, angry memories.

"Exactly, sir," said the colonel. "And Nanking, which was actually twice as savage as Manila. Over a period of a month, more than two hundred thousand innocents were slaughtered in Nanking. Thousands of women were raped. Babies were hoisted on bayonets. These acts were witnessed by large numbers of westerners who had been living in the city and were then interned by the Japanese. The key question in both Manila and Nanking is the extent to which the commanders must be held accountable for the actions of their subordinates. No matter how much we might condemn the acts themselves, in the law the issue of command responsibility is not a simple matter. If they ordered such actions, we have one standard, which is murder. If they openly or brazenly allowed them, we have another, which is probably reckless homicide. If they were negligent and did not know but should have known, we have a third standard, which is more likely manslaughter. The extent of the killing also affects the gravity of the crimes we prosecute. It will be difficult to sort all this out."

"Not for Manila, it won't," said MacArthur.

"In one sense that is correct," said Colonel Genius, impervious to the personal vitriol in the supreme commander's voice. "I must say, from the first day he surrendered, General Yamashita has been cooperating fully in the interrogations, as have the members of his staff. We're developing a reliable day-by-day account of his command. It seems more difficult to do that for Nanking. As of now we don't even have a list of the division commanders at Nanking."

"Develop a day-by-day account of the sacking of the ancient Christian city of Manila, and the rape of its innocent women and children," countered MacArthur. A heavy sarcasm was ringing in his voice. "And there will be little left for the supposedly cooperative General Yamashita to add."

Genius gave the supreme commander a quick but somewhat startled glance, then returned to his notes. "Yes, sir. We'll do that."

The supreme commander seemed unusually energized, intent on pushing his point. "And there is another distinction with reference to Nanking. We should not lose sight of it." He had returned to his swivel chair and was grasping the back of it with one hand as he spoke. "These actions took place eight years ago. At that time, World War Two as we came to know it had not yet begun. Two ancient Asian peoples were throwing themselves against each other in a way that westerners might not fully comprehend, but filled with symbolic signals that each Asian side understood full well."

Colonel Genius and his two majors looked uncomprehendingly at the supreme commander, then at one another. Finally Genius shrugged, fully mystified. "I'm sorry, General, but I don't understand the significance of what you're saying, sir."

"Do you know what it means to kill the chicken in order to scare the monkey?"

Genius paused again, then shook his head. "No, sir."

"The Chinese and the Japanese do." MacArthur walked back to his window, looking again across the rain-swept palace grounds. "China is a vast nation, with nearly a billion inhabitants. How does a foreign army conquer it? I am not condoning it, but the Japanese may have been sending a message at Nanking to break the Chinese spirit, not much different in concept than our firebombing of Tokyo. I'm not comparing the two, mind you. Only the concept. But Manila? That was different. Manila was gratuitous and wholly evil."

"A message sent by whom, sir? From what level of government? The theater commander? The prime minister? Or perhaps the *emperor?*" Colonel Genius looked steadily at the General. "Two hundred thousand innocent Chinese were raped, bayoneted, used for target practice, buried alive, and otherwise grotesquely done away with." Genius spoke quietly, but his livid face betrayed the calmness of his voice. "That's a pretty big chicken. And in all due respect, General, I would call it wholly evil as well."

"We are *prosecuting*, Colonel Genius!" MacArthur's flat statement was filled with the full power of his office, and an unspoken warning that his words had better not be used elsewhere as evidence that he was seeking anything other than full accountability. But the exchange had clearly chilled all three lawyers. "Have I said anything to the contrary?"

"No, sir."

"Very well, then."

Genius wiped his face with a hand, turning back to the pages inside his file folder. "Yes, sir. We are prosecuting."

"Yes," said MacArthur. "Proceed."

"Yes, sir." Genius referred to his notes. "The third type of war crime we have been charged to investigate is the vaguest while at the same time it is the most far-reaching. Consequently, it is also the most controversial. We are calling these suspects our 'Class A' war criminals. The offenses relate to, shall we say, national-level atrocity—prosecuting the war itself. They include categories such as 'conspiring to wage aggressive war,' and 'crimes against peace.' General Tojo is an example, since he was the wartime prime minister. Another is Field Marshal Sugiyama, obviously. There will be others."

The unspoken names of the "others" hung in the room like a damping cloud. The General turned his head away and stared through his window, out into the rain-drenched mini-forest of the palace grounds. Generals Willoughby and Whitney sat motionless, disciplined to MacArthur's sudden retreats into contemplative thought. Colonel Genius and his twin majors squirmed on the divan, writing notes and pointing to one another's legal pads. And I, never having been invited to find a chair, shifted absently from foot to foot as if I were in ranks, standing at parade.

"We must be extremely careful," MacArthur finally said, staring out toward the emperor's inner palace. "I do not wish for you to misunderstand me, Colonel, but all this relates to the past. The day-to-day decisions of high government officials regarding the conduct of a war are not in my view criminal acts. I know what the Potsdam Declarations say, but we cannot live in a world of small-minded recrimination. I'm dealing with the future every day. The future, do you understand? I am working to secure the well-being and security of a region that holds more than half the world's people."

"Yes, sir," said Colonel Genius. "I do understand."

A silence followed. Colonel Genius rose from the divan, joined by his two assistants. He closed his folder. General MacArthur had turned away from him, as if he were no longer present. Then I saw something flash in the colonel's eyes, a quick, unvanquished pulsing that seems to be intrinsic in so many lawyers that I can only surmise that the very study of American and British justice permanently embeds it, no matter how powerful their opponent, no matter how intimidating the instructions of their superiors. Colonel Genius understood. And the flashing of his eyes was telling me that, in the colonel's mind, perhaps MacArthur was the one who did not.

"But what if some of these 'Class A' suspects *directly ordered* the army to kill the chicken in order to scare the monkey? What do we call that, General MacArthur?"

MacArthur turned quickly around to face the colonel again, his movement itself an imposing warning. The colonel smiled, raising both his hands and his eyebrows as if there were nothing further he could do.

"So," said Genius, as if himself closing the meeting, "I thank you for your time, General, and we will continue to carry out our instructions here. We have twenty-three suspects already approved for arrest, most of whom are in the first category I mentioned. Now that you've approved the"—he referred to his notes, and chose the word carefully—"*coordination* of the arrests with the Japanese Cabinet, we'll get right on the new policy."

Genius took a deep breath. I could tell from the brightness in his eyes and the near smile he was suppressing that he was enjoying this little moment. "As for the rest of it, I don't know for certain how many more Japanese officials will be on this 'Class A' list, or whether it will include the emperor, but I'll keep you fully posted."

"*It will not include the emperor!*" MacArthur's voice roared as he spoke. "And you will consult with me before you publish any list. Do you understand me, Colonel?"

"I take it that this is a direct order, sir?" Colonel Genius asked calmly, holding MacArthur's stare.

"Beyond question. You are not empowered to make international policy, Colonel."

"No, sir," said Colonel Genius. "But I am obligated to carry out my duties as a member of the bar."

"Your obligations are to carry out your duties as a member of my staff."

"This is a very complicated situation, sir," answered Genius, yielding nothing to the General. "But I am of necessity wearing two hats here. I can assure you that as I fulfill my ethical responsibilities as a lawyer, I will also carry out your orders and consult with you when I go forward."

MacArthur watched imperiously as I shuffled the lawyers out of his office. I knew that once I closed the door behind me the supreme commander would fly into a livid fit. But what I was not prepared for was the equally angry reaction of Colonel Sam Genius.

The dumpy lawyer took my arm as we stood in the darkened corridor, leaving his assistants in the hallway and pulling me into my small cubicle of an office so that we would not be overheard. Then he put a finger into my chest.

"What the hell was that all about, Captain? I'm trying to do my job, here. Don't tell me I've got to fight MacArthur as well as the Japanese."

I suppressed a smile, for I had come to admire the colonel's feisty style. "I think what he was saying, Colonel, is that if we charge the emperor with war crimes the entire country is going to come at us with pitchforks and kitchen knives and cut us up into little bitty pieces and throw us into the sea."

"Oh, *that*," joked Genius, grinning cynically. "And I suppose that's going to slow us down in Germany, too?"

"This is a different system. It's been in place, in one form or another, for thousands of years. There was no cabal at the top directing all the evil. Everything the Japanese did was worked out in a form of national consensus. The whole nation did it."

Genius shook his head in amazement. "Boy, they've gotten to you, too, haven't they? Look, I don't need an anthropologist here, OK? I'll tell you the real difference. It's not that complicated. We don't have anybody— *anybody*—who is good enough at Japanese to break apart all the codes in these diaries and other documents. Not to mention that we don't have very many documents. That's it. I think they're just smarter than the Germans."

"Maybe," I said. "But if so, the reality is that you're going to have to live with it, sir. Because the supreme commander is the only guy who can decide on prosecution."

Genius watched me unflinchingly, and I knew that MacArthur was facing yet another determined and capable adversary. Except in this case his opponent was supposed to be under his command. "I have my weapons, as do the other Allies," said Genius. "We're not working in a vacuum here. He doesn't want to be embarrassed, does he? Or accused of betrayal?" He snorted with disgust. "I can't believe he tried to minimize the Nanking atrocities!"

I casually checked the hallway, to be sure we were not being overheard. "Can I give you a piece of advice, Colonel?"

He grinned mischievously. "The General's flunky wishes to speak."

"Only in confidence."

"Fine," said Genius. "He's not only a flunky, he's a coward."

"I like my job."

"An understandable hesitation. And I, sir, am a suborner, anyway, fully used to informants. So you are now a client, fully protected by ancient precepts of legal ethics."

"Now, there's a scary thought." We both chuckled, having reached a point of amicable understanding. "First," I continued, "don't go directly after the emperor. It only sets MacArthur off. You might not like it, but that's not going to change."

Genius raised his eyebrows sarcastically. "Is there a 'second'?"

I grinned. "Yes, sir. A very interesting second. Second, if you're looking for diaries, why don't you confiscate the lord privy seal's?"

"Who's that?" Genius was so lit up that he seemed to glow.

"Marquis Koichi Kido," I answered in a near whisper. "He's been the closest adviser to the emperor for years. If the others kept diaries, you can be sure he has, too. He was in on every single decision of the war."

"Right next to the emperor?"

"At his very elbow, Colonel. Forever."

"The lord privy seal, huh? I'll put my people on that." Genius slapped me on the shoulder, then waved good-bye. "See you around the campus, Captain. And I take back what I said about the 'flunky' thing."

"That's perfectly OK, sir," I protested, grinning a good-bye. "I'm just the General's monkey boy."

As he left I congratulated myself. Manipulating world affairs was turning out to be great fun.

O ver the next five days the remaining twenty-three war criminal suspects on Colonel Genius's initial list turned themselves in, and were delivered alive and well by the Japanese police. Prince Higashikuni, still hanging on as prime minister until the emperor decided it was time for Japan, in Lord Privy Seal Kido's words, to "move into the future," provoked an outrage back in the States when during an interview he opined, "People of America, won't you forget Pearl Harbor? We Japanese are ready to forget the devastation brought on by the atomic bomb!" The emperor's uncle claimed that Japan had already been prosecuting its war criminals but could not come up with even one example when asked by the interviewer. Hanson Baldwin of the *New York Times*, arguably the most influential military commentator in the country, angrily accused MacArthur of "accepting the emperor as a sort of junior partner in the occupation." And on September 20 Senator Richard Russell of Georgia asked the U.S. Senate to resolve that the emperor be tried as a war criminal along with former prime minister Tojo.

But that was just high-level noise. The greatest news was that Colonel Sam Genius had listened to my quiet advice. On September 23 a group of MPs and lawyers showed up at the lord privy seal's home and seized his diaries. And two days after that Kido called, reminding me of his earlier invitation, and asked if I might like to join him for dinner at his favorite restaurant. The next evening, with the concurrence of General Court Whitney, I set off to dine with Koichi Kido.

And, of course, to listen.

CHAPTER 12

★　★　★　★　★

I strode young and easy along the jammed, dusty streets of downtown Tokyo. Low masonry buildings hugged the street, mixed among endless pine shanties and a sea of rubble from the Allied bombings. The main roads that once marked Tokyo's origins as a fort had all but vanished years before, inside a maze of smaller streets and even narrower alleyways. Telegraph and electric wires crisscrossed like dark Jacob's ladders just above my head.

It was warm and windy, like Indian summer. Night was coming. Beyond the pink nimbus that blanketed the city I could see the moon's half-empty crescent lingering low and beautiful above the southern skyline. I walked amid an unending stream of dusty, mask-faced people. They were dressed in dull-colored kimonos, army uniforms, and bundles of rags. Dust, that was Tokyo in 1945 when the rain stopped and the sun came out. It was in their hair. It was on their clothes. It caked their nostrils and coated their lungs. They looked straight ahead and down, as if careful to respect one another's privacy. I had come to marvel at their acute sense of order as they walked. So accustomed were they to the close quarters of their overpopulated city that it was rare in all this bustle when two bodies so much as touched.

To my right, in the ruins of a firebombed building, a just-returned soldier was playing a slow, sad song on a bamboo flute. He was still in uniform, sitting in the dirt against his military rucksack. The khaki uniform was faded and worn, but he still wore it with the precision of a proud veteran. His large eyes followed me as I passed him. I nodded to him. He nodded back, still playing. Where had he served? I wondered as I watched him play. And what has vanished from his life, that brings out such a melody of lament?

I had found it necessary to stop frequently and ask for directions as I searched for the address Lord Privy Seal Kido had given me. Even without the wartime damage, Tokyo's smaller streets frequently changed names, and the street numbers were rarely posted. I finally reached the building, which several helpful, giggling young women had assured me was the correct address, but it did not appear that the place was actually a restaurant. Its nondescript front facade was no different than the buildings that abutted it on both sides. There were no windows, no advertising signs, no hanging lanterns. And curiously, no line of patrons waiting for seats.

This was the place? I stared hesitantly at the narrow wooden door. Inside the building, according to Kido, was one of Tokyo's best and most exclusive dining places. Finally I opened the door and entered, still wondering if somehow I had made a mistake.

On the other side was a dank cement landing. Nothing else, not even a lightbulb. I stood for a moment, my eyes adjusting to the darkness, then began following a strangely odorless corridor toward the rear of the building. It was almost sterile in the hallway. I could not imagine that anyone had lived, cooked, breathed, smoked, sweated, or even walked along it for a very long time. I began to feel eerie, looking for rats and spiders, as if I were in the dungeon of an old castle. The corridor turned right and then left. Finally at the end of the hallway I saw dim lights and another door. I reached the door, standing motionless in front of it. I could hear nothing on the other side. Hesitating, I opened it.

And the world changed.

I might have been Alice, falling through the Looking Glass. On the other side was a wide, low room that seemed to reach forever in front of me. The room was crisscrossed with bamboo screens, filled with rich colors, lit by warm lights, and resonating with soft, welcoming music from a hidden, harplike *loto*. I could smell meat cooking, candles burning, and the delicate aroma of an entrancing perfume.

The source of the perfume now stood before me. She was a long-limbed, firm-bodied woman of about fifty who had been waiting just inside the door, off to the side next to a little fountain that splashed into a guttered, artificial stream. The stream, which wound its way across the entrance area behind her, was lit by floor lights. At the far end of the stream I could see another entranceway, where several Japanese seemed to be waiting for tables. And then I understood. The front door, like so much else when it came to the elites of this intricate society, was indeed a facade. One had to know the secret path, just as he had to know the secret code word, the secret handshake, the secret society, so that he might conceal his advantages from the dust-covered commoners, entering and departing comfortably out of the public's view.

The woman was wearing a gold-colored silk kimono. Her hair was pulled tightly back behind her ears, accentuating her smooth skin and high cheekbones. She watched me with flirtatious almond eyes from behind the mask of her official face. She seemed to recognize me, and began smiling and bowing deeply as I entered.

The lights glowed low and warm throughout the large room. Simple but beautiful paintings emanated like welcoming embraces from tall, lacquered screens that defined the entranceway. Three young and very beautiful geisha stood just behind the bowing woman, matching her bows and smiles, their eyes telling me that they also knew who I was, and had been expecting me.

I gave them a slight bow in return, and spoke to them in Japanese. "I am here to meet Marquis Koichi Kido, the keeper of the emperor's lord privy seal."

Listening to me speak their language, the older woman smiled graciously, as if I had just uttered a personal compliment. The three geisha giggled with delight, covering their mouths with their hands.

"You speak beautiful Japanese, sir," the older woman said. She bowed a second time, more deeply, and despite my usual cynicism I felt flattered by their thanks.

"I am only a simple beginner," I answered, for it would have been rude to agree.

One of the geisha knelt and slipped off my shoes. Another fitted slippers onto my feet. They were beautiful. They were trained. This was their profession, passed down for hundreds of years inside the lanterned, red-lacquered archways of officially approved cantonments: to learn and practice the very definition of femininity, and to deepen the enticements of hedonism by hiding them behind a mask of propriety, self-respect, and careful flattery. And I did feel both hedonistic and flattered as they knelt before me, giggling and fretting over the largeness of my feet and the strength of my calf muscles as they finally fit me with my slippers.

The older woman gestured inside, and I followed her toward the private dining room where Lord Privy Seal Kido awaited me. There were no open tables in the restaurant. I caught fleeting glimpses of other customers, all Japanese except for me. They seemed happy and well dressed, even content, dining in small groups as they sat on the floor around square tables on the other side of bamboo and paper screens. Few acknowledged my presence, even with so much as a glance. They spoke in hushed tones to one another, as if the world ended at their screens. They were sharing memories and secrets, their whispers occasionally interrupted with brisk little bows and stifled barks of laughs.

As we walked I felt the eyes of one table staring harshly at me. Turning, I saw four well-dressed men of about Lord Kido's age. Their flushed faces and watery eyes told me they were well into their evening's ration of sake. Their gazes could not conceal a deep and angry hostility. One of them spoke gruffly, unaware that I understood Japanese.

"It is not over. It will never be over. We will defeat them, even if it takes a hundred years."

"What is a hundred years?" said the man next to him. "For us, a heartbeat. For them, more than half the life of their barbarian civilization."

A man across from him grunted, staring directly at me. "*Warui osoroshii kaibutsu gaijin . . .*"

Evil, horrible monster foreigner . . .

My hostess blanched, noticing that I had heard the exchange. Seeing that I had slowed down, she gestured forward, regaining her smile as if the words had not been spoken.

"Please, sir, this way—"

I stopped and stared directly at them. Come to think of it, I did feel slightly monsterish, not to mention offended. Who were the people in this plush restaurant, dining in comfortable extravagance with their talk of eventually prevailing over the evil monster foreigners as the supreme commander sent cable after cable to Washington, urgently requesting his seven billion pounds of food?

I stood before their table and bowed slightly, speaking to them in Japanese. "Good evening, gentlemen. I am here on behalf of General MacArthur. He will be most pleased when I report to him that you have eaten so well this evening. He sends his best wishes to all of you for a happy and prosperous future."

They stared at one another for a shocked and inebriated moment, then concealed their embarrassment and anger with wide smiles. Suddenly they were nodding their heads toward me as if I were a friend.

"Ah, so. Ah, so desuka."

"Please, sir," said my perfumed, smooth-skinned hostess, gesturing again toward the restaurant's rear. "It is only a game they were playing with each other. You should not misunderstand Japanese word games!"

"Then I am sorry for my misunderstanding," I said. I smiled and bowed to the drunken men. We all were lying, and we all knew we all were lying. "I am a simple barbarian, still unfamiliar with your customs."

And resuming my pace, I decided that I did not like the patrons of this fairy-tale wonderland very much at all.

At the very rear of the partitioned restaurant, in its most private dining area, Lord Privy Seal Kido waited alone. He was pacing away with a nervous energy that reminded me of MacArthur himself. I had been warned that Kido could be something of a poodle and he was indeed groomed impeccably, wearing a light waistcoat, wool trousers, and a red silk tie. When he saw me his face took on his customary look of practiced astonishment behind the binocular-thick round wire glasses. After our past meetings I was now used to this startled gaze, recognizing it as a shrewd way of disarming me by pretending my presence made him unsure of himself.

He raced to greet me, bowing before me. "Captain Marsh, you are very good to join me! Please, sit down! Sit down!"

A pot of steaming green tea had already been placed on the low hard-wood table, above a small charcoal-fired hibachi. Kido eased himself onto a set of silk-covered cushions and immediately poured me and himself a cup. As he sipped his tea a sense of calm and even strength seemed to visit him. He stretched easily onto his cushions, at once becoming happy and magnanimous. In this little room, it mattered not that I was with the conquering army, or even that he had invited me for reasons that had not yet been fully revealed. I was inside his culture, and he was both older than I and my host.

"I consider myself fortunate to have met an influential American who speaks Japanese with such fluency," he said, waving with his hand toward the cushions where I was to sit. "You are certainly a much smarter man than I, for I cannot speak a word of your own language."

I eased quickly into my cushions, taking a sip of tea. "I am lucky only to have had some training, Lord Privy Seal. I can struggle through another language, but you, sir, have advised emperors."

"Oh, you are very kind," he replied, giving me a scrutinizing smile. "But even at your young age you are serving General MacArthur, who has more power even than the emperor."

With our smiles and flattery, Kido and I both knew we were playing out a careful ritual. We were "belly talking," saying one thing while meaning something else entirely. In Japan, any meeting between two men of power, the precursor even to a game of Go, the national equivalent of chess, required that each man attempt to convince the other that he himself was less powerful. To pretend you were less powerful in this excruciatingly indirect culture was to call attention from others to your very power. And if the other side did somehow believe your protestations, to be actually seen as less powerful might lull the opponent into an exaggerated self-confidence, causing him to lose. And it also saved face if one did eventually lose, making one's loss more palatable by calling intricate attention to the strength of the adversary.

Kido sipped his tea and relaxed into his cushions, visibly delighted that I knew his game. And so I continued.

"General MacArthur is a great and powerful man," I said. "But I am nothing to his power. At times his ears, perhaps. But you, Lord Privy Seal! You are the source of great wisdom to the emperor."

"Oh, no!" protested Kido. "The emperor is a very wise man without me. It has been my duty only to protect him at times by preventing unscrupulous schemers from harming him. But for you to be the General's ears is in many ways to be his brain and his voice. It is the ultimate form of power, Captain Jay Marsh."

I sipped some more tea, smiling and waving him off. "As you know, General MacArthur allows no one to be either his brain or his voice. I am more like—a reference book that he might choose to read from time to time. But to be the emperor's gatekeeper, Lord Privy Seal—to decide who might spend a few precious moments with him, and who should not—that is the ultimate power."

The lord privy seal grinned and serenely nodded his head as if in great deference. "But I am sure your book is filled with wisdom, even for so young a man."

I shook my own head, declining the compliment. "I am a simple tome, Lord Privy Seal, very quickly read."

"Not so!" Kido answered. And then he frowned, as if carrying a great burden. "Besides, holding a gate when scheming men wish to see the emperor gives me no power. No! Instead it gives me fresh enemies every time one unsuccessfully wishes to abuse the kindness and good graces of the emperor." The lord privy seal gave off a false sigh. "But even that does not matter. Those were other days."

I smiled, as if giving encouragement to a longtime friend. "You are too modest, Lord Privy Seal. I see that your influence has not waned. Just think of our discussions while I was observing the proceedings of the diet! The emperor seems to treasure you greatly."

Kido breathed more easily, now satisfied with our relative positions. He smiled indulgently. "Do I detect a flavor of, perhaps, Osaka in your dialect?"

"Perhaps," I answered.

I hid my amazement as I relaxed further into my own cushions. Kozuko's family had indeed emigrated from Osaka, and it was from her and her mother that I learned my first Japanese. But that had been so long ago. Since those lazy, playful college conversations I had spent a year in an army language school and another two interrogating Japanese prisoners, thoroughly homogenizing my diction. Kido had either a finely attuned ear or a remarkable intelligence apparatus still in place that had delivered him a background file on me, replete with Kozuko's family history. Either was possible, and either possibility was both impressive and disarming.

"Osaka is a wonderful city for merchants, but unfortunately they do not make very good soldiers." He seemed to take delight in confessing this tidbit of inside information to me, as if it made us conspirators. "Not like, say, Hokkaido, where they are farmers and it is cold and they grow up tough and strong. Oh, yes, I am speaking openly to you, Captain! The Osaka regiments fought without great heart, even against the Chinese. See? There are no secrets anymore."

The three beautiful geisha soundlessly reentered our room, shedding their lacquered geta at the doorway, their stockinged feet sliding along the floor. They knelt near us, replenishing our tea and laying out bowls of dried fish and seaweed appetizers. The woman closest to me was the one who had commented on the strength of my calf muscles as she fitted my slippers. She was wearing a sea blue silk kimono. She was slightly younger than I, beautiful and slender, almost delicate. Her long fingers worked the pointed ebony chopsticks without conscious effort. Her dark, laughing eyes were as warm as a memory. My own eyes sought to swallow up her averted stare just for a moment as she leaned toward me, and Kido intercepted my secret wish as if I had suddenly announced it.

"She is from Kyoto," he announced without prompting. "Very well schooled. A practiced musician, trained carefully in the martial arts, and an expert at Ikebana! Only the very best geisha are allowed to work here! Her name is Yoshiko. I think you like her very much, yes?"

Yoshiko had risen as he spoke, and I watched her with appreciation as she glided back toward the bamboo door. "She is very beautiful," I said. She heard me and turned and smiled to me as she departed. "But I don't wish to embarrass her by saying that in front of her. And I am engaged to be married."

"You do not embarrass her, Captain Marsh! You make her very happy! In these times, when General MacArthur's ears find you beautiful, there is no greater compliment. Especially when he is a young and handsome man."

Kido was seizing on my moment of vulnerability and now was taking on an air of command. "All powerful Japanese men have women other than their wives. It is expected. If you have more talent and more responsibility, you will need more women also. As long as a Japanese man takes care of his wife, there is no shame. We understand these things."

"She is very beautiful," I repeated, surprised and yet suddenly uncomfortable with the open encouragement Kido was giving me. "But I already told you that I am not a powerful man."

Kido brushed off my truthful disavowal as simply more belly talk. He dabbled in his appetizers. "You must be from a very fine family, to have studied Japanese and then to be with General MacArthur. Maybe your father has served with the diplomatic corps, and you have spent much time in Asia? Or maybe your father knows the General?"

"My father is dead."

"I'm very sorry. Did he die in the war?"

"No, he died in a cotton field."

Kido smiled with embarrassment, stifling his own confusion, not knowing how to respond. "Cotton field?" he said, rolling the words as if they contained a hidden mystery. It was clear that he thought I was making a joke, or that I was perhaps being too intellectual, even too subtle for him to understand.

"My father was in fact a genius," I continued, not wanting Kido to feel he had lost face. "And actually, he did serve with General MacArthur. In France, in World War One."

This seemed to satisfy the lord privy seal immensely, enabling him finally to place me in an understandable Japanese hierarchy. And I had not totally lied, since my father, then known as Private Aloysius D. Marsh, had indeed served as an infantryman in France, certainly at times within a hundred miles or so of the General.

"Ah, so," said Kido. "So you are from the warrior class. Just like the General."

"More than that," I answered, beginning to enjoy this new version of my family history, "we are both born in Arkansas. Many great warriors are born in Arkansas. Like maybe in Hokkaido."

"Strong and tough," announced Kido, giving me a warm, encouraging grin. "I see. And highly intelligent. Yes, I see that in both of you."

"And what about you, Lord Privy Seal? It is said that you are first among the emperor's Big Brothers."

Kido seemed enormously pleased that I knew this. His face swam in memories. Behind the thick glasses his eyes went far away. "My mother was an imperial princess. Yes! A very beautiful woman. My father, who I must confess to you adopted me, was named Takamasa Kido. He was the son of a samurai who died in the emperor's service in 1862. This gave us favor in the imperial court. I have taken care of the emperor since he was four. Served him, you understand."

"Since he was four, Lord Privy Seal?"

"Yes," said Kido. "My father was placed in charge of the Imperial Grandson's Abode. It was specially erected for Hirohito in the Aoyama-Akasaka compound when the emperor's first foster father, Admiral Sumiyoshi Kawamura, suddenly died."

"He didn't live with his parents?"

"Not then. Admiral Kawamura lived very simply in Azabu, a more traditional district several miles away. The emperor was sent to live with him after his first birthday. A very conservative household. It is our tradition that the heir apparent spend much of his childhood in simpler surroundings, away from the throne."

In all my years of study I had never heard this. The details of the emperor's early life were almost completely unknown in the West, even by scholars. Listening to the lord privy seal, I felt my heart race. I sensed that in telling me his own life story, he was deliberately opening up this door for me, perhaps to help sensitize MacArthur.

"So," continued Kido, intuitively knowing his story was fascinating me, "I was fifteen when the emperor came to live under our care. He would see his mother once or twice a week. His father, who then was crown prince, would sometimes visit him and take him back to the Akasaka Palace for the night. The rest of the time was with us, under the direction of my father. I was known as his First Big Brother. There were other Big Brothers. We all played with him, looked out for him, helped to teach him. Prince Higashikuni—"

"The prime minister?"

"Yes, of course," said Kido absently. "His uncle, but still a Big Brother. Prince Asaka—"

The name leaped at me from a war crimes briefing Colonel Genius had provided Willoughby only that afternoon. We were hearing bad things about Prince Asaka. "Asaka. Wasn't he an army general?"

"Yes," said Kido, now becoming more wary. "Another uncle."

"He served in China."

"Yes. He was a division commander."

"At *Nanking?*"

"Yes. And other places." Kido watched me carefully now, seeking to move away from the obvious next question. "And among us also was Prince Konoye." Kido laughed nostalgically. "Younger than the rest of us, an impudent teenager! We teased him constantly! But older than the emperor. A Fujiwaran prince. Very intelligent and loyal."

"Konoye!" I said, unable to restrain my amazement. "He was prime minister when Japan went to war in China!"

"Yes," said Kido. "The Fujiwara family has served as the emperor's Inner Companions for more than two thousand years."

"All these—*key people*—were the emperor's Big Brothers?"

"Yes! And a few others." The lord privy seal seemed almost insulted, unaccustomed to such directness, working to control his emotions. "And is there something unusual about that? We are all members of the imperial family. We grew up together. It was our duty to study our history and to consider the future. We had just defeated Russia! Do you remember the battle for Port Arthur in 1904? There were many discussions about Japan's role in the world, and the Western colonization of Asia. And it has been our duty to look after the emperor as he governs. You should have some more appetizers, Captain Jay Marsh."

Kido fell silent, cutting off my questions and ignoring me as he pretended to sample several kinds of appetizers. His mind was working furiously, churning his eyes and causing his hands to flit about the tabletop. He was on a mission, there was no doubt, probably on his own behalf, though possibly for the emperor himself. And I could tell that he was silently cursing himself for having given me too much, too soon.

The three geisha reappeared, bringing us miso soup, more tea, and two grey pottery decanters of warm sake. They knelt next to us, smiling and indulgent, and poured us sake in small pottery thimbles. In moments, Kido regained his cheerful demeanor. He and I toasted each other, tossing down the sake as the smiling geisha refilled the thimbles.

"To your health," announced Kido.

"To the future," I replied once my glass was refilled.

"To General MacArthur, a man of greatness," praised Kido.

"And to the emperor, who has shown continuing wisdom."

"I will give you a small lesson," said Kido after our fourth toast. "Never pour your own sake in Japan. If there are no geisha, pour the sake for your dinner partner, and he will pour yours for you." He eyed me shrewdly. "You must never look too eager, not about anything, not in Japan. But I think you already knew that?"

"Lord Privy Seal," I answered, raising my fifth thimble of sake, "I am deeply honored to receive your precious advice and to have this opportunity to be able to speak so directly with you. And so now I would like to toast you, for having had the courtesy and the thoughtfulness to invite me to this special place tonight."

He raised his thimble, looking at me with a careful appreciation, as if he knew I had penetrated the facade of his kindness and was myself proceeding to the next level of our offstage diplomacy. "Yes, yes, and also to you, for having the kindness and courage to come here, where you are surrounded only by Japanese!"

"That is no concern." I laughed. "Everywhere I go in Tokyo I am surrounded only by Japanese!"

The sake was as smooth as warm water and as deadly as a drug. My senses were already dulled from it, and I found myself fighting to keep my concentration. Kido studied me with faintly controlled amusement as he set his thimble down. I was primed for the kill, whatever that would be, and he had decided that his moment had arrived. "They are doing this together, you know. And that is as it should be."

"Who? Doing what?"

"The emperor and the General, of course. Implementing the occupation. Ruling the country. Moving into the future."

I watched him carefully, for despite our informalities, it was a bold stroke to state those words so bluntly. The war had ended hardly a month before. And they were being uttered by the emperor's most trusted adviser. "I think you should be careful when you say such things, Lord Privy Seal."

He smiled, his face electric as usual but unperturbed. "Oh, please don't take offense! We know you won the war and we know that General MacArthur holds almighty power. And most of all we know that the world outside Japan is angry, filled with vengeance. So we can do nothing without you. But inside Japan you should understand that you can do very little without us, either, Captain Jay Marsh."

"I personally know that General MacArthur appreciates the emperor's courtesies. But he has absolute power, and he takes this very seriously! You should not consider testing him on it. He would be forced to take dramatic measures in his own defense."

Kido spoke calmly. "We know that, and we do not dispute it. And please don't misunderstand me. I am speaking to you only as a friend." He giggled softly, waving a hand as if catching himself. "Or maybe it is the sake, no? But this is my personal observation. If the emperor pulls away his support and the people follow him, what will MacArthur do? Bring in a million more soldiers? Who will they attack? Drop another bomb? Where? On whom?"

I was amazed to hear these words, but Kido obviously felt comfortable enough to lay down a frank and daring marker. The imperial government had spent a month dragging the bait of cooperation. Now, it seemed, they were prepared to set the hook. Kido was telling me that without shared power, the cooperation might disappear. "It's not the same anymore, Lord Privy Seal. The old ways are gone. He has even told the people himself. I was at the diet when he said it. He admitted he is not a god."

"If the new ways come, in Japan that does not mean that the old ways are gone. You must understand that. Think about this, Captain Marsh. If they believe the emperor is not a god because he told them so, don't you think they would again believe he is godlike if he tells them his earlier announcement was made only to spare them more suffering? Did not your Christ accept a human death in order to show that he could rise again?"

The lines on his face as Kido smiled told me he was somehow playing with me, toying with my intellect as if I were a child. And now he raised his hands again, as if to protest his own words. "That was not fair. I did not mean it! But the emperor is not the same thing as your Western God, anyway. We checked this carefully before the emperor made his speech. It was important that he say exactly the right words."

He eyed me as if presenting some sort of evidence. "The imperial court is very fortunate to have an American-born friend, William Merrell Vories. Do you know Vories?"

"No," I said. "I can't place that name."

"A very fine man, Vories," said Kido. "He was born in Kansas, which is very near your Arkansas, is it not? He came to Japan in 1905. He became very rich here. He is famous for selling the ointment Mentholatum. Oh, yes, a very popular product. He married the daughter of Viscount Yanagi Hitotsu and became a Japanese citizen. He is a Christian, the founder of the Omni Brotherhood Christian movement."

"Vories. Yes," I answered, finally remembering. "He asked to see the supreme commander when we were in Yokohama."

"Yes," said Kido, impressed that I both knew and remembered that Vories had approached MacArthur. "The supreme commander was very busy at that time."

"Very busy," I said, nodding in false agreement. For MacArthur's refusal to meet with Japan's most eminent native-born American had nothing to do with his schedule. Rather, it was adamant and permanent. The kindest word the General had used was "collaborator."

"Yes," continued Kido. "So we asked Vories why the Americans objected so strongly to the emperor's godliness. He showed us the Western dictionary definition of 'God.' We studied this definition. All of us, and especially the emperor, agreed that he is not that kind of god. His godliness is *kami*, do you understand? All things Japanese possess *kami*, even rocks and trees. But the emperor possesses the largest and most powerful share. Our people understand this, and nothing will change it, no matter how he had to belly talk to MacArthur in order to make peace."

"Then those Americans who heard of the emperor's remarks might decide that the emperor lied, Lord Privy Seal."

Kido seemed impatient, as if I had not understood. "It has nothing to do with lying."

I started to answer him, then I remembered my own long speech to Father Garvey a few weeks before. "You are right. It is only my simple observation."

"It is irrelevant anyway," said Kido. "We lost the war, and we will accept your terms. But what happens tomorrow, and next year, and ten years from now? Nothing the emperor says about a Western god will change his godliness to the Japanese people! They will follow him. I am not trying to argue, Captain Marsh. This is only my observation. But do you really think our people are able to throw away two thousand years of beliefs in one month? Are you willing to take that chance?"

My head was buzzing, and my very bones felt numb from the sake, but I knew that Kido was throwing down a gauntlet, not only to me but to the General. It had become my responsibility to respond to him.

"Lord Privy Seal, my only advice to you is that the emperor should never think of publicly confronting General MacArthur. It will gain him nothing. Is he willing to take the chance of losing everything?"

This answer seemed to bring Kido an immense satisfaction, as if I had somehow closed a loop in his reasoning. "So you see, Captain, it is like I said. We are in this together. Neither side should take that chance. Neither side should speak of losing. What would be the point? We should work together in harmony, that is the Japanese way. You have now embraced us, and we have embraced you. That is the future! We are inseparable, from this moment forward."

The beautiful geisha in the blue kimono had returned and knelt next to me, serving me rice, vegetables, and a plate of wood-skewered yakitori. Kido caught my lingering eyes again and smiled with quiet delight. "Yes, you see! Yoshiko can help you understand! It is like that—you and she together. We are intertwined. Wedded to each other."

He retreated into silence again as we ate. The food was wonderful and again I marveled at its availability in a city so recently sundered by the bonfires our bombers had left behind. But Lord Kido and the others of the aristocracy had not starved. He was rumored to have kept enough red meat throughout the war to feed not only himself but the pack of guard dogs that roamed the narrow yards of his private villa.

The thought of him feeding his guard dogs as Tokyo starved shook me from my sake-filled complacency. Gracious as he was, I had no delusions that Kido sought to be my friend.

"Lord Privy Seal, there is a list of people who might be tried as war criminals. You are on that list."

"Yes, I know," he answered, outwardly unperturbed. "There will be vengeance. They have even confiscated my personal diary—an extremely unthoughtful act, although in the end meaningless, would you not agree? I have done nothing wrong. I began working for peace more than a year ago. And yet I am comfortable in the thought that if it is necessary for the future, I will accept my fate."

"The emperor may soon be on it, too."

"I told you before, that would be a very bad mistake," he said. "The emperor and his immediate family must not be shamed." His face had grown taut, and for the first time I sensed that I had reached the epicenter of our dinner.

"It is not my decision."

"I know that, Captain. But it is as we discussed. Read my diaries, that is fine! Check the records of our meetings! The emperor personally led the peace campaign, from the time Saipan fell, more than a year ago!"

"Our allies are demanding that he be tried."

"We have heard that. And I know of the pressures in your own government. I told you that we understand the need for revenge, Captain Marsh. But I must strongly warn you that the country may revolt if the emperor or his immediate family is put on trial. I am serious! Our people can be very emotional!"

The almost brazenly defiant look on Kido's face told me that he was not bluffing. "I cannot speak for General MacArthur, but I believe he is sympathetic to your logic, at least with respect to the emperor."

Kido became coy, toying with his food and studying me. "General MacArthur has—very strong feelings about our General Yamashita. I assume he is also on the list."

"High on the list. I saw what happened in Manila, Lord Privy Seal. It is my most disgusting memory of the entire war."

"Yes," said Kido, lowering his eyes respectfully for a moment. He had become curiously melodramatic. "At times our army disgraced us, taking things into their own hands." He offered me a small, conspiratorial smile. "Yamashita was not popular here, you know. We do not like Yamashita. He had bad tendencies."

Kido's comment amazed me, catching me completely off guard. I leaned forward, trying to read his face. "I thought he was the most popular general in Japan?"

"With the common people. Not at the imperial court."

Kido avoided my eyes, squirming on his cushions. His hands worked furiously, playing with his chopsticks. He was giving the impression that he had slipped up and now was trying to concentrate, to measure his response. But it suddenly occurred to me that he was actually making an offer, masked in drunkenness so that it could be quickly negated if I took offense.

He cleared his throat, searching for just the right words. "After Singapore, Yamashita was very popular. But he had always been too independent, and now the adulation went to his head. He took issue constantly with our war planners. He had spent time with the Germans in 1940, and was a strong supporter of mechanized warfare. Before Pearl Harbor he argued that Japan should not make war on the United States unless we built up our mechanized forces."

"Yamashita opposed Pearl Harbor?"

"Yes," said Kido. He stared curiously at me, as if it were common knowledge. "He predicted that we would lose. And after the victory at Singapore he said the only chance of winning the war was to invade Australia, quickly, rather than fight in the jungles."

"Australia?"

"Yes," said Kido, his face drawn with sudden agitation and shame. "Strike suddenly, force a quick negotiated surrender, as in Singapore. The Australian army was scattered all over the world! We did not wish to do this, but many commoners agreed with him. After our army became bogged down in the jungle battles throughout the islands, he became a problem."

Kido looked at me as if we shared a common bond in our elite responsibilities. "He himself is a commoner, you know. He had a wide following that was harmful. That is why he was posted to China after Singapore."

I was still lost in his logic. "Why?"

"I told you, Captain. He had become too popular. And he was against the policies of our war planners." Kido shrugged casually. "The difficulty is not that he opposed the policies, now that they have failed. It was with his arrogance. His—independence. As I said, Yamashita had bad tendencies. He still does. He could be a problem again if he returns to Japan and speaks about how the war was fought."

"A problem? For whom?"

"For *everyone*."

I now knew precisely what he meant, but I wanted him to say it. "I am very sorry, Lord Privy Seal. Perhaps my Japanese is not as proficient as I thought. Could you please explain?"

Kido watched me carefully for a moment. The offer was on the table, and both he and I understood it: the imperial court had no great stakes in General Yamashita's situation and no objection to his execution. He was not going to take my own bait by belaboring the obvious. Finally he deflected the question. "I was only attempting to agree with you that General MacArthur is a very wise man. As always, he sees the larger picture! And he should know that the Japanese people deeply regret the atrocities that occurred in Manila under General Yamashita's command. I am only trying to agree with you, Captain."

Dealing away a great general's life as I drank sake and chewed on yakitori was, to say the least, a new concept for me. I had no idea what to do or say, but I felt obligated to signal to him that the offer, as it were, had been received and would be communicated. "General MacArthur has great emotion when he thinks of what happened in Manila. He deeply loves the city and its people. It was one of the immense tragedies of his life to see so many of them deliberately killed, raped, and shot."

"The debt should be repaid." Kido was finished eating. "I am only telling you that we understand and will support General MacArthur on this matter. The Japanese people will benefit if the General and the emperor work together."

The meal was over. As we both rose to leave, Kido raised a hand as if to stop me. He had saved the most important news for last. "The emperor wishes to pay a call on the supreme commander. It is time for them to meet, Captain Jay Marsh, and to begin working directly together."

"I will tell MacArthur," I announced as we bowed to each other.

"Soon," said the lord privy seal. "Too many people are trying to drive a wedge between them."

"I will tell him that as well," I said. "And thank you again for all your precious advice."

Kido smiled, pretending embarrassment. "It was only my sake talking, Captain! We will work hard for the General. There is no other way. The emperor is committed to this."

An hour later I was back in my hotel room, still unsteady from Lord Kido's moonshine-strength sake. As I began brushing my teeth I heard the clicking of geta shoes on the stairway outside my room, and then a hesitant scratching on the door. My heart raced with a confused, denying excitement as I quickly rinsed out my mouth, for I knew immediately what was waiting on the other side.

I walked to the door and opened it. Yoshiko stood expectantly on the landing. She smiled shyly to me and then looked down at the floor, as if not wanting to watch my face while I registered her presence. She was still in her kimono. Her long hair was pulled back and up, on top of her head. In front of her, with both of her hands, she was holding a small white-pine box. She was indeed beautiful, long and smooth, with tight, unblemished skin, pink petals of lips, and a muscular firmness in her hips and legs. Her studied passivity transcended into an inner power that somehow made her even more attractive.

The box was wrapped with a wide pink ribbon. Finally she bowed, extending the box. Her voice was soft and velvety, carrying the high-pitched, whispery intonations that Japanese women frequently use when speaking to powerful men.

"I am here to express my deep apology, Captain Jay Marsh! The lord privy seal scolded me greatly for not serving you dessert! He asked that I bring you some sweets."

She finished her bow but kept her head slightly downturned, smiling coyly and peeking up at me to see if I understood her full intent. She smelled wonderful. An honest warmth emanated from her eyes. I was lonely and slightly drunk. She was near enough that I would not even have had to extend an arm to touch her, and beautiful enough that every part of me wanted to.

I stared at her for a long moment, stunned not so much by her presence as by my reaction to it. Why could I not control these feelings? I was overwhelmingly in love with another woman. And yet I was in free fall, losing the innocent purity of that relationship as I stepped aside and welcomed Yoshiko into my room.

She stepped inside, slipping off her geta and socks just inside the door, and continued to smile sweetly as she passed me. Her left hip and shoulder brushed against me when she walked into the room. I wanted simply to grab her at that moment, but I sensed there was a ritual in this seduction, indeed another script that should be followed. Was this real, or was this not? Or for that matter, what did reality have to do with it? We both knew what was about to happen. And is there any feeling more exhilarating than when two people admit to each other for the first time, however silently, that they will soon be lovers?

Oh, yes, the war was truly over. Yokohama be damned. Recreation and Amusement had descended upon Captain Jay Marsh, bearing sweets and dressed in a splendid blue kimono.

The kimono did not last long. She set the gift box on my little desk, then went into the bathroom and carefully took it off, hanging it neatly over the door. She was now wearing a sleeveless, sheathlike cotton shirt that went down to her mid-thighs. Ignoring me for the moment, she knelt at the sunken tub and opened the taps, running mostly hot water. As the tub began to fill, she stood and walked back to me. Her smile was slightly devilish but still coy. She bowed, then dared to stare openly and directly into my eyes.

"The lord privy seal was very concerned that you learn the custom of a properly scalding bath."

For the first time that entire evening, I lost my restraint and started to genuinely laugh. Perhaps it was the *sake*, but it seemed so utterly Japanese that a bath was proper only if it was scalding, as if every movement and emotion was fully acceptable only if taken to its inner or outer extreme.

"So a warm bath isn't proper?"

"No!" She started laughing too, her eyebrows raising and her hand automatically covering her mouth.

"How about just a—*hot* bath?"

"No," she laughed. "It is only proper if it's *too hot!*"

As we laughed together, for the first time we both relaxed. She was not a geisha, and I was not a captain. She was not Japanese, and I was not American. A threshold had been crossed. She was a woman, one who had dropped her pretense and decided that she liked me. And I was a man who found her captivating, at least for this moment. She was no longer merely on assignment. And I was no longer simply—what? The recipient of a human gift? A target of Kido's intelligence apparatus? A betrayer of the woman I had promised to marry?

Whatever. It was too late. It didn't matter. The rest of the world was no longer out there. The water was running, steaming up my little room. She was standing only inches away from me in a simple but sensuous cotton shift. It clung to her hard, protruding nipples. It stopped high enough for me to admire her long and sinewy legs. And we were laughing in a way that told each other that there was more to this than simple duty. How much more, who knew? It was going to happen. And if nothing else, it was becoming fun.

The tub was three-quarters filled. She turned off the taps, kneeling on the tiles that surrounded it, and pointed at the steaming water.

"So, now you must get into the tub."

I was still wearing my khaki trousers and a white T-shirt. I grinned at her, looking dubiously at the tub. "It's too hot."

"It's never too hot!" She eyed me flirtatiously. "It is very late, Captain Jay Marsh, and it could be that you are unsteady from having so much sake? So maybe I should help you undress."

"Oh, no," I said, grinning wildly at the thought. My self-control was shattered. I knew that if she had touched me at that moment I never would have reached the tub. "Is the bath important?"

"Yes!" She began laughing again, her hand once more held daintily over her mouth. "You're a funny man, Captain Jay Marsh."

"You should please call me Jay."

She seemed almost to blush. She lowered her head for a moment as she knelt on the tiles, accepting my gesture as a deep compliment. And in her eyes I saw that she was starting very much to like me. "Thank you very much. As you wish. It will be my honor to call you Jay."

"And I should call you Yoshiko?"

"Of course." She experimented with my name, as if it were itself a sweet to be rolled upon her tongue. "Jay. What does it mean?"

"It means 'lover of beautiful women.' "

She giggled. I undressed quickly. Surprisingly, she averted her eyes as I walked naked and aroused toward her. She pointed, insisting once again that I climb into the tub. I put a foot into the water and then backed away—it was indeed scalding.

"Ahhh! It's too hot!"

Her eyes still averted, she laughed again, softly chiding me. "It's never too hot!"

Suddenly she stood and in one smooth motion slid out of her cotton shift, placing it carefully with the kimono on top of the bathroom door. She was hardly two feet away, but still she would not look at me. Standing next to her, I could not keep my eyes off of her slender body with its round, surprisingly full breasts and the small triangle of pubic hair where her thighs joined together.

She turned and without flinching slid into the steaming tub. She held a bar of soap in one hand. Tilting her head back, she began slowly washing, first her neck and shoulders, then underneath her arms, and finally her breasts, one at a time. Her eyes still averted, she called again to me.

"So, Jay. You must get into the tub!"

I moved behind her, starting to kneel, and suddenly she began splashing me with hot water. She laughed as I howled, splashing me again and again until finally I sank into the tub behind her. My hands quickly went around her, sliding along her waist and then up to her breasts. I pulled her to me, kissing her cheek and then her lips. She kissed me back for a very long time.

Finally she pulled away. She looked into my eyes for a moment and then looked down, as if this were becoming too personal. "You have the softest mouth I have ever kissed," she said. Her voice was low and relaxed, as if she were taken completely by surprise. And then she firmly removed my arms from her breasts. "But you must get in front of me."

"What?"

"Get in front of me!"

Adeptly, she moved behind me in the small, deep tub, bending her legs a bit as if putting me on her lap, and began soaping me. We sat like that for fifteen minutes. She slowly washed my hair, and then every part of my body. Then she drained the tub and refilled it, sitting with me as the hot, clean water rinsed us. She said nothing as her long fingers massaged me expertly. The intense heat seemed to penetrate the marrow of my bones, leaving me weak and floating. Her kneading fingers removed the tension from every muscle in my back, neck, arms, and legs. By the time she pulled me from the tub I was wrung out like a dishrag. My mind felt drugged from the heat, floating in some stupefied nirvana.

I do not know how long we made love. Looking back, all I remember is that it was like slow string music, a Tchaikovsky serenade. She was in full control, touching and kissing and smiling, guiding my hands and body and in the end moaning and croaking with pleasure. She had come to perform a duty, but by the time she again dressed in her kimono and leaned over to gently kiss me good-bye, something in Yoshiko had visibly changed. Anyone might feign their enjoyment, but she could neither hide nor pretend the worried tenderness that had crept into the very set of her lips and eyes.

"Thank you, Jay. I hope I see you again."

I had been dozing. After she kissed me, she pulled a sheet up to my chin and crept soundlessly out of my room. Lying in bed I heard her geta clicking on the staircase as she made her way back to Kido or whomever. And I knew also that something had happened to me.

Something powerful. And probably something wrong.

CHAPTER 13

★ ★ ★ ★ ★

Well, well, well," said Colonel Sam Genius as I walked into his cluttered office. "The master spy approaches."

"I told you, Colonel, I'm not a spy."

"You smile a lot, you live comfortably, and you perform no clearly identifiable functions during daylight hours. That makes you either a spy or a whore."

Behind Genius, the two majors who worked with him looked up from their desks for a moment, registering my presence, and after chuckling to each other decided to ignore me. Whatever my own duties might have been, in their minds there were war criminals to catch and prosecute. And they were hard at it.

I sat easily in the wooden chair just across from his desk. "So, do you know how to save a drowning lawyer, Colonel?"

"No," grinned Genius. "How?"

"You don't."

"A totally transparent attempt to shift the focus, that." He snorted. "If you're not a spy, how did you, a mere junior captain, arrange for the emperor to make a pilgrimage to MacArthur?"

The word had traveled quickly through the General's staff, and I had become moderately famous. The morning after our dinner, I had told General Court Whitney of Lord Privy Seal Kido's suggestion that MacArthur and the emperor meet. Within an hour, Whitney indicated that MacArthur was interested, and I placed an "unofficial" call to Kido. By late afternoon, Prime Minister Higashikuni and Shigeru Yoshida, who had just replaced the aged and ailing one-legged Shigemitsu as foreign minister, had presented a formal request to the General himself. And so today, September 27, the emperor would call on the supreme commander at his residence in the American embassy.

MacArthur was thrilled by this. Throughout East Asian history, the notion of face dictated that the supplicant travel to the throne of the ascendant. And now, due in some small part to my sake-filled diplomacy, the emperor would come to him.

"I told you, Colonel, I'm just the monkey boy. Or maybe think of me as a two-hundred-pound carrier pigeon."

" 'Spy' sounds better," teased the balding, frazzled-looking Genius. "Anyway, I've got something for you." He dropped a manila folder on my lap. "Look through this, will you? It's got me so pissed off I don't know whether to shit or go blind."

His two silent assistants raised their heads again, watching me alertly as I opened the folder. Genius spoke solicitously, not attempting to hide his sarcasm. "Let me help you out, monkey boy. While you and the great lord privy seal were downing yakitori and toasting the emperor's health, your boss was approving a directive that creates a military council to address the issue of war crimes committed in the Philippines. What this means is that he's carving away General Yamashita's case from the war crimes trials that we'll be holding here in Tokyo."

"He said he wanted Yamashita tried in the Philippines," I murmured, leafing through the hundred-page file that Genius had handed me.

"Yeah, but down there it's not even going to be a court," said Genius. "We're putting together an elaborate international tribunal up here for the war crimes trials. I'm talking historic. It'll take another six months to arrange all of this. It'll be headed up by a group of distinguished civilian judges from eleven different nations." He tapped my shoulder, as if to get my full attention. " 'Judges' is the operative word, Captain. As in, your basic law-school graduates who have had careers and then been selected to impart their wisdom by sitting on a bench and running trials."

"I understand the concept," I answered dryly. "It may surprise you, Colonel, but even in Arkansas there are such people."

"Yes," grinned Genius. "But not in the Philippines! At least not in the case of General Yamashita! MacArthur has created what he calls the Philippines War Crimes Commission. Note the choice of words, now— 'commission,' as in nonjudicial."

"But the word 'crimes' somehow reminds me of the law," I said, stifling my own sarcastic smile. "As in, the violation of a statute? You can't try somebody for a war crime without a court." I hesitated. "I mean, I'm not a lawyer but it sounds kind of—illegal?"

"Well, just wait," said Genius. "He's going to put a bunch of army generals in a room and tell them to hang the son of a bitch."

"Not that he doesn't have the evidence to hang him anyway," I said, thinking of the slaughter I witnessed in the aftermath of Manila.

"So, if he's got the necessary evidence, why is he doing *this*?"

Genius flipped through the materials he had put on my lap, then pointed at a page that contained MacArthur's directive creating the Philippines War Crimes Commission. He glanced for a moment at his assistants. "Some lawyer—not one of us, I can assure you—has found a presidential proclamation from 1942. Right here, read it. Actually, let me." He pulled it out and read it for me. " 'Enemy belligerents who during time of war enter the United States, or any territory or possession thereof, and who violate the law of war, should be subject to the law of war and to the jurisdiction of military tribunals.' "

"Yeah, but the war's over," I said.

"You noticed that, did you? Over there sampling Mister Kido's—delicacies?" Genius grinned meanly, as if seeing a reflection of Yoshiko's firm body in the guilt on my face. "But here's what they're saying. Yamashita, of course, was a 'belligerent' who 'entered' the Philippines—a possession of the United States—during 'time of war.' And since the formal treaty hasn't been signed yet, technically we're still at war. So in their clever reading of it, the proclamation still applies."

"Oh, yes, Colonel. Very clever. Now you have a small idea why the rest of us hate lawyers."

He grunted. "This only begins to be clever. Someday remind me to tell you about the case I studied in law school, where an appellant proved conclusively that a horse was a bird, at least for the purposes of commerce. But it's clever enough."

"Another reason why, Colonel."

"OK, OK." Genius flipped the page. "Look here. MacArthur has appointed himself the sole convening authority of the commission. This means that only he has the power to supervise the makeup of the court, to determine the procedures for presenting and rebutting evidence, and to decide the standards of proof. In other words, he's rigged the front end completely."

He flipped the page again. "He's also assigned himself the role of sole reviewing authority of its findings. This means that he has the exclusive discretion—read it right there, monkey boy—to 'approve, mitigate, remit, commute, suspend, reduce, or alter the sentence imposed.' You get that last part? He can actually alter the sentence if he doesn't like it! Which means he's rigged the back end, too. And as its first order of business, Lieutenant General Styer is directed to instruct the commission to proceed with charges against General Yamashita." Genius caught himself. "Actually, they charged him two days ago."

"He doesn't like General Yamashita," I muttered weakly. "Personally, I mean."

"It's fair to say that he's pathological on the subject." Genius glanced at his two assistants, sharing a private laugh. Then he looked back at me. His face was lit with the same challenge that I had seen in MacArthur's office at the end of his first briefing. "But I have what we might call a—*broader* theory on the whole matter."

I thought for a moment. "The emperor," I said.

"Intuitive, but not so fast," answered Genius. "Your boss hates Yamashita. He's obsessed with the rape of Manila. But I'll tell you what he really despises—the very *thought* of going after the rape of Nanking. It repels him. It makes him want to barf. Why? First, he doesn't believe it's his problem, since it happened before we came into the war. Second, he looks at it as two Asian cultures kind of, settling scores."

"The chicken and the monkey," I said helpfully.

"Right," said Genius. "You ought to be fully sympathetic with the monkey thing. And third, there's a blood trail in it that just might point toward the imperial family."

"He hates that," I said.

"Yeah," said Genius. "He hates that. And fourth—I'm almost done—he's getting yelled at by the press and our allies to do something about war crimes, when we're not going to have the international tribunal up and running here in Tokyo until next spring. So what does he do?" Genius pointed at the folder on my lap. "He throws them some raw meat. And in his view it couldn't happen to a nicer guy."

I held the folder gingerly, flipping through the pages without reading them. Finally I looked up at Sam Genius. "So why are you telling me?"

"Because it seems to me that MacArthur listens to you, or he wouldn't have made you a spy. Maybe you can let him know that I'm on to this."

"He doesn't listen *to* me. I listen *for* him. There's a difference, Colonel. And it wouldn't do any good, anyway. You think he's afraid of you?"

Genius watched me for a moment, then nodded his agreement. "OK, you're right. I'm a peon. So what is he afraid of, Captain?"

I thought about that. Douglas MacArthur, afraid? "I don't think he's afraid of anything."

"The emperor," said Genius flatly.

"No," I said. "I don't think so. I mean, he might want to use the emperor. He might even want the emperor for his friend. But not afraid." I thought about it some more. "What's he afraid of? Failure, maybe."

"I still say the emperor," said Genius. "They're meeting in less than an hour."

I checked my watch. "You're right. I have to go."

Genius teased me one last time as I left his office. "I changed my mind, Marsh. You're not a spy. You're just a moderately low-class whore."

J ust as he did every morning, MacArthur had commuted to work in his highly polished black 1941 Cadillac, recently shipped to him by an old and very rich friend in Manila who had heard of the comical, Chaplinesque convoy from Atsugi to Yokohama. His morning ritual had already become famous in downtown Tokyo. Two white-hatted MPs on motorcycles drove slowly in front of the General's limousine, which bore five-star fender flags and license plates. As the limousine approached the bottom of Renanzaka Hill, Japanese policemen immediately halted all other traffic along the short route to the Dai Ichi offices. Usually the General would reverse the route in the early afternoon, going home to the embassy for lunch and a siesta, and then return to the Dai Ichi in midafternoon, working late into the night. But on this day, the General returned from the Dai Ichi building after only two hours.

I and a dozen other staff members were waiting for him on the driveway near the embassy's front entranceway when he returned. The Cadillac halted just inside the gate. He stepped out from the right rear door and slammed it behind him. He was electric, visibly eager, ramrod-straight as he walked briskly away from the Cadillac. When MacArthur was energized he seemed taller, more physically powerful, even young. Hardly looking at us, he began striding toward the steps that led up to the embassy's front doorway.

We saluted him as he neared us. "We'll have a half hour, Jay," he suddenly called to me, all business as he returned my salute. "One official photograph, at the end of the session. You'll be in with me. Keep everyone else out of the meeting."

He had taken me by surprise. "In with you, General?"

"Colonel Mashbir has strep throat. You're my only interpreter today."

As was his practice in Japan, MacArthur was wearing only a starched working khaki uniform, devoid of military decorations. I began to panic, realizing that I myself was wearing only working khakis, and did not have time to return to my hotel if the General wanted me to change into a more formal uniform.

I called after him. "General, excuse me! What's the uniform, sir?"

"You're wearing it."

"You're not going to change, sir?"

"Which are you questioning? My word, or my judgment, Captain?"

I flinched, embarrassed, as the other officers began to laugh. "Neither, sir. Working khakis."

"Working khakis." MacArthur now jogged up the steps and went into the embassy.

General Court Whitney laughed loudly after the supreme commander disappeared inside. "What backwoods Arkansas swamp did you say you crawled out of, Jay?"

"He changes uniforms three times a day!" I protested. "For all I know he could come out in dress whites."

"Read my lips," said General Whitney. "He's wearing working khakis for a reason."

I nodded, suddenly appreciating the innate shrewdity in MacArthur's decision. Working khakis, to meet the emperor. It told me that MacArthur knew what he wanted, both from the meeting and from the all-important photograph that would follow. I sensed that, not unlike my initial conversation with Lord Privy Seal Kido in the restaurant, the supreme commander and the emperor would be engaging in their own belly talking before getting down to any serious discussions. And I knew that MacArthur would order that the photograph be displayed in every newspaper in Japan. Dressed as he was it would show MacArthur raw and simple, without adornment, emphasizing his forbidding presence and imperious personality. Stripping away his soldierly embellishments would make clear that his present powers did not emanate merely from military accomplishments or accoutrements but from the force of his personal wisdom and intellect.

Thinking of this, I recalled Divina Clara's grandmother joking slyly about MacArthur in his gaudy uniform when he was serving field marshal of the Philippines, a mess of black pants and white tunic, with splashy medals and gold cord draping his chest, even a gold braid on his officer's cap. Then, many in the war-frightened Philippines had delighted in Mac-Arthur the flamboyant warrior-soldier. Today, with equally meticulous thought and attention, he would stand serenely before the emperor and the world, all-powerful in a simple khaki shirt.

A new role had been born: MacArthur, like Mao Tse-tung and Ho Chi Minh, the all-wise, quasi-pajamaed, hybrid-Confucian leader.

I eyed Whitney. "I'm the only one in there with him, sir?"

"You heard him. No witnesses. We each get one interpreter, Captain Marsh. That's it."

I found myself chuckling. "The lord privy seal is going to have a heart attack over that."

"Excellent," jibed Colonel Sam Genius from just behind Whitney. "Then we won't have to put him on trial."

"The Boss wants this to be absolutely private," emphasized Whitney, giving me a warning look. "The more people in the room, the more pressure on the emperor. The more pressure, the greater the chance of some kind of diplomatic foul-up." He shrugged. "The meeting is the message, anyway."

" 'The meeting is the message!' " panned the grinning Colonel Genius. "Well said, General Whitney! Have you considered a career in politics?"

Whitney smiled thinly, not to be outdone. "How do you think I've spent the last three years?"

Genius rubbed a bulbous, bright red nose, feigning confusion. "For the rest of us, I seem to recall there was a war in there somewhere."

It was one minute after ten o'clock. A young sergeant ran outside from the embassy's main door and called to General Whitney. "General, we just got a phone message from headquarters. The emperor's motorcade has crossed the palace moat at the Sakurada Bridge! They're heading toward the embassy."

Whistles began to shriek not far away. The Japanese police were halting traffic at the bottom of Renanzaka Hill, just below the embassy. Now we heard car engines snorting and gears downshifting as a small convoy made its way up the steep hill on the other side of the compound's high white masonry walls. And then the embassy's gates cranked slowly open, revealing a line of old plum-colored Daimlers.

The World War One–vintage German autos chugged and jerked their way inside the embassy grounds. Surprisingly, the emperor was in the first car, sitting stoically in the backseat next to the ever-stunned and wildly staring Lord Privy Seal Kido. His car and the four others that trailed it moved slowly along the driveway as if in formation, then seemed to halt all at the same time. Immediately a swarm of chamberlains, bodyguards, and household staff poured from the other cars. They raced with an almost comical adoration to the emperor's limousine, forming two quick welcoming lines. The doors were opened for him and then for Kido. The imperial household staff members bowed deeply, looking to the dirt as the emperor slowly emerged from the car and walked between their two rows.

In contrast to his commanding and quietly powerful performance before the diet three weeks before, the emperor now seemed smaller, shyer, and somewhat dazed. He stood for a long moment between the two rows of bowing subalterns, staring blankly at the embassy building as if lost and unsure of what to do next. Appearing at the same time cowed and agitated, the emperor's very demeanor seemed to me a conscious taking of what the Japanese termed the "low position" that was customarily used in order to gain an adversary's sympathy. He had worn a simple but elegantly tailored naval uniform to speak before the diet, but now he was dressed in baggy prewar morning clothes that seemed more appropriate for one of his lowly chamberlains. He carried a silk top hat and wore a shabby claw-hammer coat over an old pair of striped trousers.

Kido and an interpreter joined him where he stood. The lord privy seal whispered into his ear, taking an elbow and pointing toward the embassy. Finally the emperor nodded and moved forward, shuffling toward the embassy's entrance. He seemed to tremble as he walked. At the bottom of the embassy steps Brigadier General Bonnie Fellers, one of MacArthur's chief assistants, stood waiting. Reaching Fellers, the emperor surprised him with a self-conscious Western-style handshake.

The handshake seemed to break the ice. Members of our staff began approaching the emperor and his household staff. Handshakes and nervous bows mixed together, as did smiles and guttural laughs. Few knew the relative ranks of the people they were greeting, or even what the other side was saying, but everyone understood that history was being made in the privacy of this small courtyard.

I rushed quickly forward, reaching the lord privy seal, who was standing near the emperor. Kido was smiling with the satisfied look of a parent watching his only child graduate from school. He gave me the slightest of bows.

"Captain Jay Marsh! Good morning!"

"Lord Privy Seal, I need to talk to you. I'm very sorry, but the meeting will be closed, except for—"

"Yes, I know," said Kido, cutting me off with an unconcerned wave of his hand. "It was the emperor's wish. A sound decision. We discussed this for many hours yesterday!"

His answer surprised me. We had been told that the emperor never spoke directly for himself during open-ended policy deliberations, preferring only to weigh in at the end of a meeting with his imperial judgment. I had believed he would want the lord privy seal in the meeting as a foil, to explain his views during preliminary questions, and to insulate him from having to answer any serious questions that might lead to confrontation.

"You don't wish to be with the emperor?"

"He is well rehearsed," said Kido. He gave me a careful look. "There will be no surprises?"

"I will be the only other person in the meeting," I said.

"Excellent!" said the lord privy seal, beaming warmly. I could see that once again he was congratulating himself on his judgment as he continued to misread the strength of my relationship with the supreme commander.

The emperor began slowly walking up the steps. Kido took me by an elbow as we walked, speaking furtively in low, hushed tones. "We decided that if it were a large meeting, unnecessary policy matters might be discussed. And many people would report, perhaps incorrectly, on the details of the conversation! It was too great a risk. It is better that the two rulers meet alone."

The two rulers. Something in the way Kido said it irritated me, as if I were automatically expected to agree with its inference of equality.

Knowing I was needed to help interpret, I broke away and moved toward the front of the entourage. Kido called softly after me. "You are enjoying Yoshiko?" His eyes were leeringly round, and his face carried a conspiratorial grin.

His question startled and embarrassed me. There was an implied ownership in it, an assumed fealty, that left me feeling soiled and angry. I raced away from him, not answering.

The emperor had reached the top of the steps. I joined him and introduced myself to his interpreter, a short, bullnecked young man about my age. The interpreter gave me a snaggletoothed smile, and announced in practiced English that he had studied at UCLA.

"You played football for Southern Cal." He grinned. "Our old crosstown rivals! Yes, I remember you! Jay Marsh, tailback! You had a Nisei girlfriend. Very daring! We used to talk about it. You were very famous among the Japanese students!"

"Then I'm surprised I never met any of them," I answered.

"Perhaps we were too shy," he said, smiling again.

I smiled back, uncertain of his true educational origins, thinking again of Marquis Kido's comments about my supposed Osaka accent during our dinner. Maybe this was all innocent coincidence. Or maybe they did indeed have a file on me. Maybe it did not matter. And then again, maybe it mattered a lot.

Our two delegations shuffled about in the embassy's foyer for a few minutes, making small conversation. And then General Whitney nudged me, nodding toward the doorway that led into the embassy's reception room.

"*The supreme commander,*" announced Whitney, speaking with a loud, formal officiousness that I knew was meant for the emperor's ears.

Everyone fell silent. As if on cue MacArthur suddenly appeared in the doorway, halting for a moment to gaze with a deliberately noble pose into the foyer. As promised, he was dressed in his working khakis. The emperor seemed overpowered. He stared humbly at MacArthur, then moved slowly toward him. Hirohito hesitated again, appearing confused. Fumbling, he turned back and gave Kido his top hat. And finally he walked forward, until he stood small and mute before the supreme commander.

It was a vintage MacArthur moment. The supreme commander smiled grandly, savoring it. Few Americans would understand, but I knew exactly what the supreme commander was thinking, for with this simple imperial gesture, history had thrice been made. The emperor had been the first to request a meeting. The emperor had brought his entourage to the seat of

MacArthur's throne. And now the emperor had made the first move to greet the supreme commander.

"*Your Majesty!*" said MacArthur in his best and warmest baritone. There was a victorious gladness in his voice, but the General emanated a deep and sincere respect as he took the emperor's hand and gestured toward the drawing room. And I saw that the emperor had immediately relaxed.

Hirohito's interpreter and I fell in behind the two leaders, following them into the large, high-ceilinged drawing room. It was cool and dank inside and eerily quiet. Tall pillars seemed built into the walls. Dark red, heavy curtains hung over the high arched windows and covered one entire wall. A huge glass chandelier dangled overhead. A half dozen potted plants that reminded me of bamboo lined the room's outer edges.

MacArthur's leather heels echoed off the parquet floor as he led the emperor toward a stiff-looking, cloth colonial couch in the center of the drawing room. I heard the doors click as the staff closed them behind us, locking us in. MacArthur gestured toward the couch, easing into one corner of it. The emperor joined him, sitting at the other end of the couch. I and the emperor's interpreter took wooden colonial chairs, each at the elbow of our respective rulers.

The supreme commander offered the emperor an American cigarette, then held a lighter for him as the emperor put it to his lips. Hirohito's fingers were trembling as he lit the cigarette. Puffing tentatively on it, he did not appear to be a regular smoker. He sat stiffly on the couch, smoking the cigarette and attentively watching MacArthur, who now leaned back casually, smiling at the emperor with an almost fatherly indulgence. And then for what I was later informed was exactly thirty-eight minutes they talked, as I and the emperor's young interpreter translated for them.

"I had the great pleasure of meeting your grandfather in 1905," began MacArthur. "It was just after the Russo-Japanese War, and I was privileged to be touring the Far East as my father's temporary military aide. He was a most impressive man, Emperor Meiji. I'm sorry I did not meet you then. But that was long ago. You were a very small boy!"

"Yes," said the emperor, smiling with appreciation at the mention of his revered grandfather. "A long time ago. But even then we knew of the great warrior family of MacArthurs."

And I knew that the belly talk had begun.

"Thank you," answered MacArthur, not concealing his own pleasure at the emperor's compliment. "My father was indeed a great warrior and a great man. And with Your Majesty's indulgence, it is true that we are the only father-and-son Medal of Honor recipients in our nation's history. I learned so very much from him! But we can make no pretense of having held the long and age-old responsibilities of your own grand imperial family."

"You are very kind," said the emperor. Already I could see a change in his demeanor, a relieved, knowing delight. "But to be trusted by all the nations of the world to come to Japan and work with our people toward a new and better future—that is the ultimate responsibility."

"A great responsibility, but under these circumstances not an over-whelming task at all," replied MacArthur in his stiff, stentorian tone. "I have always spoken of the strength of the Japanese race. The cooperation of your subjects has been most heartening, Your Majesty. My warmest surprise in undertaking these duties has been to see the wonderful, inspiring attitude of the Japanese people as they begin to rebuild their nation."

"Oh, no," protested the emperor, by now smiling with appreciation and pleasure. "Our people have been proud to work with the occupation forces. Certainly the greatest example of exemplary conduct over the past month has been the friendliness and good behavior of your soldiers."

"Yes," said MacArthur. His eyes flashed suddenly with a pulsing of the jealous paranoia that seemed never to be far below the surface of his brilliance. "Despite the predictions of our adversaries, we are all getting along very well, are we not?"

He began dramatically frowning, sharing a concern with the emperor that would draw the two of them closer together. "You may know that I have been so impressed with the cooperation of your subjects that I de-cided to decrease the number of soldiers in the occupation forces. I informed my State Department that my needs should be reduced from a half million to only two hundred thousand soldiers. I had thought that such good news would be greeted with celebration. But no! I am under heavy criticism in the American press, and from my own Acting Secretary of State Dean Acheson for having taken this judgment!"

The emperor nodded several times, indicating his deep appreciation and understanding. "Ah, so. Ah, so, desuka."

MacArthur eyed the emperor shrewdly. "Frequently I am accused of being too soft, you know."

"Ah, so," sighed the emperor again. As he empathized with the General, I wondered if his mind was not on more personal examples, such as the continuing calls for him to be tried as a war criminal. "I speak for all my people when I say that we are very fortunate that you, with your wisdom and understanding, have been sent to work with us, General MacArthur. There are so many issues that could cause larger trouble!"

Back and forth they went for several minutes. Watching MacArthur and the emperor both basking in such mutually reciprocated praise, I could not help but think that these two natural aristocrats might have been cousins or comrades-in-arms, rather than tentatively circling adversaries. With each exchange, both men relaxed further, until it seemed they were indeed friends.

Finally, ineluctably, MacArthur turned to the war. But he did so with the only positive comments available to him. "Your Majesty, I have heard of the important, decisive role you played in ending the war. I am very grateful to you for having done so."

The emperor grew serious. His lips pursed tightly underneath his trimmed mustache. He shuffled in his seat, as if bracing himself. His small hands clenched into secret fists on his lap. The belly talking was abruptly finished. There was no way to speak of the war without some form of direct confrontation.

"Many people worked for the end of the war!" Hirohito said modestly. His voice had lightened, but with a quiet resolve. "And I must sincerely tell you that I took no pleasure in a war with the Western powers. I thought my heart would break when I approved the declaration of war against the British royal family. They were enormously kind to me when I visited Europe twenty years ago as Crown Prince."

MacArthur paused for a moment, trying to find the words that would raise the issue of accountability without causing the emperor to lose great face. When he spoke, I could tell he was giving the emperor room to blame others, particularly former prime minister Tojo, for the war's conduct.

"Sometimes it is difficult, even for a monarch, to withstand the pressure of bad advice."

Surprisingly, the emperor shook his head, disagreeing. "It was not clear to me that our course was unjustified." Hirohito raised his chin, staring directly and seriously into the General's eyes. "I must speak to you honestly, General MacArthur. Even now, I am not sure how historians will view our decision to go to war."

MacArthur was stunned into silence. For the first time in the more than two years I had worked with him, he seemed unsure of how to respond. The emperor shifted his gaze, watching me for a moment as if expecting me to divine the General's thoughts and speak obliquely on his behalf, as some courtesan might have done for Hirohito himself in such circumstances.

Finally noting by my silence that I held no such powers, the emperor continued. His words were precise and rehearsed. This was the moment for which Lord Privy Seal Kido had prepared him, and he spoke for the first time with the quiet power and certainty he had shown when I had seen him address the extraordinary session of the diet.

"General MacArthur, I have asked for this meeting in order to offer myself to the judgment of the powers you represent. I personally am the one to bear sole responsibility for every political and military decision made by my people. Every action taken in the conduct of the war."

MacArthur remained speechless. What forces silenced him, I did not know. His face held the same look that I had so often observed when watching him stare out of his Dai Ichi office window toward the emperor's inner palace. There was a longing in his eyes, and an undeniable respect. I knew that he was both a royalist and a romantic. Was he perhaps also intimidated? He had spoken with deep nostalgia of having met Hirohito's grandfather forty years before—aeons to an American, but a mere heart-beat in Japan. Did he now feel the power and hear the voices of the emperor's ancestors as he looked into this seemingly bland and unassuming face? Did he feel burdened and even afraid, perhaps just like the emperor himself, realizing that with his acts he was jeopardizing a continuous ruling bloodline, father to son, that in its lore reached back 124 generations to Jimmu, six hundred years before the birth of Christ?

The emperor continued, speaking simply and quietly. "I have no fear of being put to death. But I will not shame my ancestors by participating in the taking of vengeance against my own loyal advisers."

MacArthur recovered, nodding sagely as if agreeing with the emperor. "I want you to know that I share many of your views on this issue. The punishment of war crimes for those who made political decisions on behalf of their government during a time of war is repugnant to me. I have argued vociferously against it. But you do understand that I am dealing with a great deal of pressure from the outside."

"It is also my duty to protect the throne," the emperor answered obliquely. "Last week I sent Prince Konoye to Kyoto on my behalf. His family has provided inner counsel to the imperial family for more than two thousand years. I asked him to explore arrangements if I decided to retire. It was Konoye's advice that I might find happiness as an abbot in the great Zen temple of Ninna-ji."

"You would abdicate?" asked MacArthur, stunned by the thought.

"There would be a home for me at the Omura imperial villa," said the emperor, as if the matter were close to being settled. "It is a beautiful and worthy place. My son could ascend to the throne."

Having been present in dozens of planning sessions even as the war continued in Manila, I knew that a thousand questions were exploding like starbursts in MacArthur's mind. His and Willoughby's entire strategy had been built on the notion of keeping the emperor in power in order to govern through him, and of occasionally using him as a hostage, threatening to remove him from power if issues became irresolvable. And now the emperor had completely turned the tables, announcing that he was thinking of removing himself from power in order to protect his honor and to ensure the continuity of the throne.

I knew there was precedent for this, and also that it was a serious warning. In old Japan if a powerful shogun failed to respect the imperial wishes, an emperor might simply abdicate in favor of one of his children, retire to Kyoto, and then work full-time at intrigues and cabals designed to embarrass and undermine the shogun. With his vast political and military authority, MacArthur had in effect become an American shogun. If the emperor were to renounce his formal power and cease cooperating, for so long as he lived the nation would be at best divided in its loyalties.

A thought came to me. Perhaps, just perhaps, MacArthur needed the emperor more than the emperor needed MacArthur.

And it seemed this thought had also occurred to the emperor and his key advisers. So Hirohito had dressed like a beggar, showing only a bland, befuddled countenance to the world outside this drawing room. Then when the doors had closed behind us he had shuffled up to the roulette table, put all his holdings in one pile, and coolly spun the wheel. Watching him stare calmly and unbudgingly at MacArthur, I knew that my first judgment of him, when I saw him speak before the diet, had been correct. This was an iron fist in a velvet glove, a man whose quiet demeanor emanated not from timidity but from an awesome self-confidence.

MacArthur blinked. On this issue, the emperor had won. "That would be unnecessary. You will never be personally charged, you have my word on this."

The supreme commander now waved an arm magnanimously, his face overcome with admiration. "Your Majesty, such a sincere assumption of responsibility, implicit as it is with the risk of your own death, has moved me to the marrow of my bones! You are an emperor by birth, and you will remain the emperor through the force of my own office. But even more— I know you are a true leader, whose first concern is for the welfare of his people. Today I have met not only the emperor but the First Gentleman of Japan in his own right!"

"You are very kind to say this," said Hirohito. He seemed almost distracted by such praise. His face was an indecipherable mask as he looked at the supreme commander. "But as I said, I am very concerned about those who were loyal to me."

"Each case will be treated with respect and care," assured MacArthur. "But you also should agree that there is no harm in punishing those who gave the throne evil advice, for their own personal gain?"

The emperor continued to stare almost blankly at MacArthur. The very emptiness of his gaze was unsettling. "I do not recall receiving any such evil advice," he answered carefully.

I decided that this was not a game of roulette after all. Rather, with these two manipulative geniuses, it was becoming the world championship of liar's poker. Both were coolly throwing huge bets into the pot, while neither of them knew all the cards the other was actually holding.

"That question will be a matter for the legal system to examine," said the supreme commander, quickly extracting this small concession from the emperor by trumping it with a moment of flattery. "But I do believe that you as emperor know best about important men in the Japanese political system. So from time to time, I would like to receive your views on this, and other items as well."

"I would be pleased to advise you in any way I am able," said the emperor, finally allowing MacArthur a small smile. "And the lord privy seal, as well as my grand chamberlain, are available to you at any time."

"I wish to give you an unbreakable pledge," said MacArthur. He rose from the couch as he spoke, nodding to me to go outside and fetch the waiting photographer, and then turned back to Hirohito. "You are the emperor of Japan. That will never change. Every honor due a sovereign shall continue to be yours."

The photographer took one picture, which ran the next morning in every newspaper in Japan. It showed MacArthur, his hands slouched casually in his rear pockets, towering above the diminutive, Western-clothed emperor as they stood next to each other in front of the couch with the white-columned walls and heavy drapes of the large drawing room behind them. Looking at the photograph, one might have thought the emperor out of place in his own country, adrift and lost in the face of a reverse kamikaze, Douglas MacArthur's own, undivine wind.

But late that evening, the supreme commander cabled a carefully worded summation of the meeting to the Joint Chiefs of Staff in Washington. It was filled with his usual self-flattery, but at the end of his message was a recommendation that might have been written by the emperor himself. Since the emperor had accepted full blame for the conduct of the war, argued MacArthur, there remained no strong reasons in favor of proceeding with the prosecution of political figures who had been responsible for its day-to-day implementation.

It did not take long for the Joint Chiefs to respond. Their message was terse. In fact, it might have been written by Colonel Sam Genius.

"Proceed at once with the prosecution of war criminals."

CHAPTER 14

★ ★ ★ ★ ★

"The facts, General MacArthur, are these."

Colonel Sam Genius watched MacArthur pace in front of him as he stood beside a tall easel on which a two-foot by three-foot plain-paper tablet had been mounted. He held a long wooden pointer in his right hand. One of his ever-present majors sat in a small chair on the other side of the easel, ready to flip the pages of the tablet at Genius's command.

The rumpled, craggy lawyer tapped the paper tablet with the pointer, and the major flipped a page. Genius began lecturing, his voice strong and intense, as if he were delivering the opening argument in a trial. "In the summer of 1937 the Japanese army came to a standstill at the gates of the important port city of Shanghai. It was outnumbered ten to one by Chinese forces that Chiang Kai-shek had sent down from North China in an attempt to stop the Japanese advance to the Chinese capital of Nanking, 170 miles up the Yangtze River."

MacArthur abruptly interrupted him. "Colonel, I was in Asia during all of this. I most emphatically do not require a history lesson regarding the late war."

Genius's face reddened, all the way to the top of his balding head. His jaw clenched. He took a deep breath, and let it out slowly. Sitting near him on the supreme commander's scarred old leather couch, I could tell that he had mentally prepared himself for such interference and was determined that it would not stop him.

"This is not simply about the military conduct of the war," answered Genius. "There is a political context to these actions that must be addressed, General. It is all of a piece, and it is important that you see them described to you within that context. I am telling you as one of your legal advisers that you need to listen to every word of this presentation, sir."

MacArthur slowed his pacing. He looked over for a moment at General Court Whitney, sitting near me on the couch, and then at the ever-present General Charles Willoughby, who sat near Whitney in his favorite nest of a leather chair. Whitney and Willoughby both nodded back to the supreme commander, quiet signals borne through years of association. In this momentary exchange of glances I saw MacArthur acknowledge that in the delicate area of accountability for political, "Class A" war crimes he did not fully control this lawyer Colonel Samuel Genius, Judge Advocates General Corps, United States Army, or for that matter any lawyer.

Nor did he desire any further attacks in the press for his supposed softness on the issue. If the supreme commander ignored his adamant warnings, would a disgruntled Colonel Genius vent his anger to the press or even the Congress, either quietly through leaks or openly as a matter of perceived duty? MacArthur was too shrewd a political infighter to take that risk based on a simple briefing on legal alternatives.

"An excellent point, Colonel. Particularly since others in this room may not comprehend the picture in its entirety. You may proceed."

"Yes, sir," answered Colonel Genius cavalierly, not in the least bit mollified by the supreme commander's intended flattery. "I shall be pleased to proceed."

He tapped the page again with his pointer. A crude map had been drawn on the page, emphasizing the port city of Shanghai in central China, and the Yangtze River leading inland to the capital of Nanking. "The Japanese government believed that it could maximize its impact in China if it made a major push up the Yangtze, inflicting heavy damage on the Chinese countryside along the way, and then took the capital itself."

"The Japanese *military*, you mean," corrected MacArthur.

"The Japanese *government*," emphasized Genius, holding the supreme commander's prolonged stare. The distinction between political and military motivation was vital, the very key to the whole "Class A" war crimes issue. "Their strategy was to convince the Chinese people through cruelty and intimidation that they should abandon Chiang Kai-shek, stop their so-called 'anti-Japanese conduct,' and come over to the Japanese side as it established its own government in China."

MacArthur glanced quickly again at Whitney and Willoughby, then nodded to Genius. "We'll hold that point for now, Colonel. Proceed."

"Yes, sir," answered Genius. "Proceeding on, here." He could not resist a tweak as he turned back to the easel. "Rather like your statement not long ago about killing the chicken to scare the monkey, although I didn't realize it at the time. A very large country, right, General? And a relatively small army with which to conquer it?"

"Proceed, Colonel," insisted MacArthur.

"Yes, sir," said Genius. "Just agreeing with you. Proceeding right along." He tapped the tablet and his assistant flipped the page. On the new page was a series of boxes with names written inside them, showing an intricate table of Japanese government organizations.

Genius tapped a box on the page. "In June 1937 Prince Konoye, who was the highest-ranking of the emperor's hereditary counselors and a key personal adviser for more than fifteen years, was chosen to be prime minister." He quietly teased MacArthur. "Chosen by—who? By Hiro-hito."

He tapped another box. "On August thirteenth, the emperor's uncle, Prince Higashikuni, was appointed to the key position of chief of the Japanese air force. Appointed by—who? By Hirohito. On the very next day, the Japanese formally abandoned the international agreement they had signed, where they had pledged to avoid the deliberate killing of civilian noncombatants, and began bombing civilian targets in and around the crowded slums of Shanghai."

Another box. "On August fifteenth, General Iwane Matsui, long known as a proponent of friendship with China, was called out of retirement by the emperor and given a cover assignment as commander in chief of the Japanese forces in central China. By the order of—who?"

MacArthur was working to repress his anger. He pointed at the cocky, irascible lawyer, knowing instinctively where Genius was heading and not liking it at all. "He was not given a cover assignment, Colonel, he was given a military command."

"He was old, tubercular, and retired, General," answered Colonel Ge-nius. "I believe the most sympathetic statement that can be made is that they decided to let the old man have a go at it before they turned to other people and other means. I do not wish to exculpate the general from his own responsibility for war crimes, but when I am finished you might see the logic of what I am saying."

"Then finish," ordered MacArthur.

"Yes, sir," answered Genius. "Finishing is exactly what I'm trying to do." He slapped the pad with his pointer, causing the assistant to flip it over to a new page, then pointed to various boxes that surrounded a map of Shanghai as he spoke. "On August twenty-third—only eight days after he had been called out of retirement, hardly enough time to have developed a plan of his own—Matsui landed at Shanghai with thirty-five thousand fresh troops and immediately became bogged down. Part of the reason was that there were English, American, and French forces nearby, and he had to maneuver carefully because he did not want to end up fighting them. But the biggest reason was that he was not ruthless enough as he pushed through these populated areas, over here."

" 'Ruthless' is a subjective choice of words," interrupted MacArthur. "There may have been other reasons he was not successful. What you are really speaking of is a question of fire and maneuver. And of judgment. A command failure. And a command failure is not in and of itself a failure of government politicians."

"You are indeed correct on that last point, sir," answered Colonel Genius, obviously wearying of the relentless attempts to sidetrack his presentation. "But it was a failure that frustrated these same government politicians immensely. In early September, Hirohito authorized a Grand Imperial Headquarters to be created inside the emperor's palace, in order to monitor the day-to-day movements of the China campaign. In October he issued an imperial rescript explaining to the people that Japan would soon unleash its military power 'to urge grave self-reflection upon China, and to establish peace in the East without delay.' An imperial rescript, General MacArthur. 'Grave self-reflection.' What could those words mean? Think of that."

MacArthur went silent. Genius nodded to his assistant. Another page flipped over. Turning to the easel, the colonel moved his pointer around the edges of a hand-drawn map showing the Yangtze River Delta, from Shanghai to Nanking. Heavy black arrows indicating troop movements dominated the map, all of them ending up around Nanking. "In early November the Japanese launched two massive amphibious operations, one to the north and one to the south of Shanghai, bypassing the city and pushing forward to Nanking. These were masterfully executed invasions that totally fooled the Chinese army, which itself had become bogged down in its resistance of the doddering old General Matsui. Quality troops. Shock troops, if you would. Slash-and-burn types, you know what I mean. Their landings were followed by a trail of deliberate pillage. It is estimated that the two elements of this pincers displaced eighteen million people, and took nearly four hundred thousand Chinese lives in the advance from Shanghai to Nanking."

"Estimated by whom?" asked MacArthur stubbornly.

"By the Chinese, sir," said Genius dryly. "I think they were in the best position to do the counting."

"This part rather reminds me of the viciousness in Manila," said MacArthur, altering his tactics. "And in Manila we are holding the military commander accountable. So where was General Matsui while his troops were committing these despicable acts?"

"Oh, we haven't even gotten to the despicable acts, sir." Genius's soft brown eyes twinkled victoriously. "But the answer to your question is most interesting. General Matsui, as I said, was a sick old man, honored to have been called out of retirement to serve the emperor."

The lawyer's wooden pointer slapped the tablet at a place near Shanghai. "While his troops marched up the Yangtze, Matsui was lying in bed with a tubercular fever at his field headquarters in Süchow. He did have the opportunity to visit Nanking after it was conquered, and so he should be held culpable for not having stopped the rapes and the massacres. But he didn't order them, and he wasn't in charge of the actual grotesquery himself. Because on November twenty-seventh, the emperor relieved General Matsui of direct responsibility for combat operations, supposedly promoting him by giving him another title—command of the so-called central Chinese theater."

Genius tweaked MacArthur yet again. "Rather similar in removed scope to your former Southwest Asian Command, sir."

"Throughout the war I accepted full responsibility for the performance of my soldiers, Colonel. I always have. The record is clear on this point."

"I'm sure it would do wonders for General Wainwright's spirit if you informed him of that, sir."

The supreme commander stopped pacing and fixed Genius with a prevolcanic stare. The feisty lawyer had stepped closer to insubordination than any military underling I had ever watched, save possibly Admiral "Bull" Halsey, who had actually won an argument with MacArthur two years before. But Genius had taken a very careful shot. MacArthur could not argue his abandonment and then his condemnation of Skinny Wainwright, who only days before had finally received the Congressional Medal of Honor that MacArthur himself had worked for years to deprive him of, without opening himself up to some seriously damaging replies. Nor could he follow his usual course of summarily relieving an unpleasant or unproductive officer of his duties. There was no doubt that Genius possessed both the intellect and the information to publicly embarrass MacArthur, thus feeding the anger among the media and the other allies regarding the supreme commander's lack of enthusiasm for prosecuting political war crimes.

But in truth, the stare itself was enough. It froze Colonel Genius for a full five seconds. Finally the frumpy lawyer shrugged uncomfortably, giving off one of his disarming, helpless grins. "Sorry, sir. I withdraw the comment on the grounds of lack of relevance. Maybe even poor taste. Anyway, the truly important point here is that the emperor relieved Matsui of direct battlefield supervision. And the commander in chief of the army that now surrounded Nanking became—the emperor's uncle, Prince Asaka. Appointed by—guess who?"

MacArthur resisted yet again. "But General Matsui remained the overall commander. We cannot lose sight of that, Colonel."

Genius picked up a sheaf of papers and thumbed through them as he spoke. "This isn't a question of General Matsui's guilt, General, although his own culpability probably is more from negligence than criminal intent. By this time, sir, it's pretty clear that General Matsui was out of it. It's more about who actually ordered the activities. A higher level of guilt. That's the focus. That's what 'Class A' war crimes are all about. A higher level of guilt. And why, in this instance, must we look higher?"

Genius had found the paper he was looking for. He glanced up to MacArthur, then read from the paper. "Matsui did in fact issue an edict from his sickbed, ordering his troops to pull up outside the Nanking city walls and to enter the city only after careful negotiations. He said that the occupation of Nanking should be carried out in a way that would—and I'm quoting here, sir—'sparkle before the eyes of the Chinese and make them place confidence in Japan.' He reminded them that by entering the Chinese capital they would be 'attracting the attention of the world.' Nanking was, after all, an international city. Large numbers of American, German, and British residents had remained behind as Chiang Kai-shek and his government evacuated to Hankow, 350 miles further upriver.

Matsui ordered in writing that the occupation be—another quote here—
'absolutely free from plunder.' "

Genius flipped through the papers some more, finding another document. "Prince Asaka—the emperor's uncle—had other ideas. As his troops closed around Nanking, he sent out his own orders, under his personal seal, marked 'secret, to be destroyed.' The orders were very simple. They said: '*kill all captives.*' "

The colonel's pointer slammed the pad again. His assistant flipped it to another page. Now on the easel was a series of columns, with dates and then statistics broken down into categories.

"What happened after that," said Genius, "is extremely well documented. The rape of Nanking began on December fourteenth. It continued unabated for six weeks, despite worldwide protest. It was systematic and deliberate. At least twenty thousand women were raped, some of them repeatedly until they died. More than two hundred thousand unarmed people were murdered. Not just killed but obscenely murdered, General. Shot for fun. Used for bayonet practice and for instructions on how to behead someone with a samurai sword. Buried neck-deep, alive, so that their heads could be kicked like soccer balls. Lined up in front of trenches and machine-gunned. It was so bad that a German diplomat, Mr. John Rosen, wrote a long, angry report to Hitler condemning the barbarism of the Japanese army. Imagine that! It even turned the *Nazis'* stomachs! And it did not stop until Prince Konoye admitted to the emperor that it was having no effect on the Japanese government's objectives of unseating Chiang Kai-shek."

"I have always been told that it was an army run amok," insisted MacArthur, adamantly steering the incident away from the imperial family. "A drunken orgy."

"For six weeks?" asked Genius. "It would take a lot of booze for them to remain drunk that long. And it's pretty hard to imagine one hundred thousand men killing two hundred thousand people through spontaneous disorderly conduct, is it not, sir?"

"They did it in Manila."

"They may have, General. We're looking into that. But in Manila the Japanese were surrounded. They knew it was all over, that they were all going to die, anyway. By contrast, it was a proud, conquering army in Nanking, sir. They'd just kicked Chiang Kai-shek up the river. Have you ever known of a case where a *victorious* Japanese army lost control of its soldiers for a full six weeks?"

MacArthur had finally had enough. "I've listened patiently, Colonel Genius. It's nearly lunchtime. Make your point."

"All right, sir. Lunch is waiting. Stomachs are growling. Proceeding at once to the point, here." Genius slapped the pointer onto the chart. His assistant flipped it over to the last page. On it were a list of names. Now his pointer hit the names themselves.

"You're not going to like this, sir, but it must be addressed."

They were the very names that MacArthur dreaded most, the names that would put the rest of his occupation goals into an irreversible tailspin.

HIROHITO

KONOYE

HIGASHIKUNI

ASAKA

"Let's deal with Matsui first," said Genius, "since I know you're going to ask me why his name isn't up there. It's not up there because it's foregone that he should and will be charged. On December seventeenth, during the worst part of the carnage, he made a ceremonial entry into Nanking, riding a chestnut horse ahead of Prince Asaka's entourage. At the center of the city he stopped and led the Japanese soldiers in a series of three grand 'Banzais' for the emperor. He returned to his headquarters in Shanghai that night, but he was in fact present at the scene. Perhaps they hid it all from him, or perhaps he saw it and knew that he was powerless to do anything about it. But as a military commander he knew or should have known. He had certain duties and did not exercise those duties."

"Precisely," agreed MacArthur. "The protection of the weak and the innocent are the most holy responsibilities of a battlefield commander."

"I actually feel a little sorry for Matsui," admitted Genius. "I can tell from reading his messages that he had no such intentions. He had always been a supporter of a Chinese-Japanese alliance. Can you imagine this sick, doddering man riding on his horse through the streets of Nanking with Prince Asaka right behind him, passing the mausoleum of his old friend Sun Yat-sen, who had actually founded the Chinese Republic, while Japanese soldiers raped and plundered the entire city?"

"I feel no such sympathy," intoned MacArthur. "He should have honored his old friend's memory and stopped the carnage."

"Indeed he should have, sir. But this is what he was facing." Genius slapped the tablet paper with his pointer again and again as he spoke.

"The emperor, setting up an imperial military headquarters in his palace and issuing a damning imperial rescript. The longtime hereditary adviser to the throne, selected as prime minister just before the punitive invasion. One of the emperor's uncles—the same man who would serve as prime minister when the war ended—picked to be chief of the air corps the day before the policy toward bombing innocent civilians changed. Another uncle selected to command the ground forces that took Nanking and razed it, riding on a horse right behind him."

Genius stopped for a moment, letting his words sink in. Then he began again, as if providing the closing summary in a legal argument. "The question, sir, is not whether the rape of Nanking is a war crime that demands international justice. There is no doubt about that. Rather, the question, for you and for us, is whether the Japanese political process, at its highest level, should be held accountable for deliberately and consciously planning and conducting acts of mass terrorism and extermination. As an instrument of national policy. That, sir, is the question."

The room became quiet. Genius wiped a sweating forehead with a white handkerchief, then shifted from foot to foot, waiting for a response. MacArthur looked at the lawyer with an unbending frown, as if he were processing the allegations and weighing them against an invisible standard. Finally he spoke.

"What you say is emotional, Colonel, and persuasive, so far as it goes. But it hardly scratches the surface of how the imperial government actually worked! Of course those three princes would be involved. It is a historical maxim that during a period of war the emperor would trust his closest associates with key positions. That we know. And the end result in Nanking we know. But that, really, is all we know. Did these proclamations and appointments in and of themselves translate into an obligatory savagery on the part of Japanese soldiers? Or was there something else at work here, something that we in our culture do not understand, that nonetheless sprang from events at the battlefield level? We don't know."

"We know a lot, sir," said Genius quietly. "And in all due respect, I also know this: If you're going to try General Tojo for planning and directing the war from the attack on Pearl Harbor and beyond while he was prime minister, certainly there is enough hard evidence to bring charges against these people."

MacArthur did not hesitate in his response. "Pearl Harbor was the beginning of a new war, an uncalled-for series of aggressions against Western nations who had not in any way directly provoked Japan. To me—and

I don't mind saying this—Pearl Harbor was the beginning of World War Two in the Pacific. The Japanese had been operating in China, and even expanding their holdings, for decades. Nanking was principally an ongoing matter between Asians that occurred before our entry into the war. So when did this war actually begin, for our purposes? Shall we also examine the conduct of the British during the Opium Wars? That happened in China, too."

Colonel Genius was fighting back an incredulous scowl. "The rape of Nanking was conducted by the same system, and in large part the same people, who brought us Pearl Harbor, General. It was committed against our ally, the Chinese. The perpetrators should not be allowed to escape justice."

"We will pursue justice, Colonel. But there is a distinction here."

The supreme commander paused, measuring Genius for a moment and then looking out his window at the Imperial Palace grounds. "And there is another point. Do you, or I, dare even to imagine that we can lay out before a court of law the intricate, historically driven circumstances under which the emperor of Japan received advice and participated in the making of policy decisions? I don't think so."

Genius stared quietly at the supreme commander, unanswering. Finally MacArthur turned back to him and continued. "The emperor will never be charged. We will not make fools of him or of ourselves through such a process. As for the rest of it, on the other political issues there may be some question. I'll await your further analysis, Colonel. On the military issues, there are none."

Genius held MacArthur's gaze, then nodded to his assistant, who began taking notes. "The military issues meaning General Matsui, I assume?"

"Precisely."

Genius nodded, understanding exactly what MacArthur meant. He now seemed tired, as if all the adrenaline had suddenly drained out of his system. "Very well, sir. We'll charge him and let the matter be tested in court." He waited for a moment, as if looking for more, then deliberately tweaked the supreme commander one more time. He was going to make MacArthur say it. "None of the others?"

"I told you about the others," frowned MacArthur, glancing over to the impassive Willoughby and then to Court Whitney, who merely returned a mirror of his own frown. "At present, we're lacking sufficient information to proceed in a court of law."

"Yes, sir," said Colonel Genius. He now nodded to his assistant. The major stood, removing the notepad from the easel and beginning to take apart the easel itself. "Well, we thank you for your time, General MacArthur."

"Not at all," answered the General. "Excellent work, gentlemen."

"And we'll be back to you when we come up with the additional information you requested."

"Excuse me, Colonel?" MacArthur had started to turn away from Genius. Now he was facing him again.

"You said you didn't have enough information. Well, I'm going to get it for you."

Colonel Genius was standing with his feet slightly apart, facing the supreme commander like a worn-out, pudgy old boxer who was taking a severe beating but nonetheless was electrifying the crowd by answering the bell for yet another brain-crushing round. His eyebrows were slightly raised. His lips were pressed tight into a thin line, almost as if suppressing a smile. He was breathing in shallow but rapid breaths, making his chest heave quickly in and out.

The colonel's adrenaline was back. The burning in his eyes was telling me yet again that MacArthur had a problem, and it was not simply Nanking. It was a fire that the supreme commander's pomposity and intellectual dissembling had created in Colonel Sam Genius's sense of—what? Fairness? Equity? Or perhaps merely in his competitive spirit?

It didn't matter. It was fire, sure enough. Sam Genius had put a lot of work and thought into this. He believed in the truth of what he had found. He wanted Asaka. And Higashikuni. And Konoye. And, more than likely, he wanted Hirohito, too.

MacArthur nodded slowly to him. "Good day, Colonel."

"Good day, General. Enjoy your lunch, sir."

The door closed quietly behind Colonel Genius as he departed. MacArthur continued to stare toward it for several seconds, almost as if he were waiting for the acidic lawyer to reenter the room and deliver one final riposte. He was standing stiffly, with his hands in his back pockets, as he had stood when the photographer snapped the now-famous picture of him and Emperor Hirohito. But his face was tight and angry, and his own eyes were aflame.

Finally he turned to Court Whitney. "I don't imagine it would be difficult to find something important for Colonel Genius to be doing in another venue? Like, perhaps, evaluating war damage claims in New Guinea?"

Whitney chucked softly, knowing instinctively when to humor the General rather than indulge him. "Bad idea, Boss. Do you really want him outside the tent, pissing in, instead of inside the tent, pissing out?"

"He wouldn't dare."

"And why not? If you send him to New Guinea he knows his career is over. And I'm sure he'd find a wide and receptive audience for his frustrations. People who feel they've been wronged will seek vengeance. I know you don't like it when I point this out, but you're being criticized extensively for being too soft on the Japanese. Not only in the States, Boss. The Filipinos, the Dutch, the French, the Australians, the British, all are rather loudly expressing their disappointment. Most are wondering whether you'll act strongly on the war crimes issue. If your own former judge advocate says he was relieved from his duties because he agrees with that feeling, how can there not be controversy? Controversy sells newspapers. It's how they make their money."

"You're right."

MacArthur began his inveterate pacing, walking back and forth in front of his window. We waited silently and patiently, knowing that for the moment we did not exist to the General. The onyx clock above the pipe rack on his bookcase ticked over to one o'clock. MacArthur was late for lunch. Soon I began to notice that he was glancing over at me after every few turns. Shortly after that I watched a small, grim smile creep onto his face.

"What do we control?" he asked, somewhat rhetorically.

We all looked blankly at him, unsure of where he was heading. Finally General Court Whitney shrugged, grinning ironically. "Just about everything, from what I can tell. What do you want?"

MacArthur put his hands in his pockets, stopping to stare at his key political adviser. "Yamashita. Or at least a—*resolution*—in his case. Soon."

Whitney turned facetious. "It would be a good idea if we tried him first, General."

"By all means," said MacArthur, ignoring Whitney's sarcasm. "A trial is exactly what I have always had in mind. But unlike in Tokyo, this will be *my* idea of a trial. It is my commission, I convened it. It is my court, I am appointing it. It will be my proceedings, my findings, my review, and my—*resolution*. A very public trial."

His mind was clearly racing. He began walking again, slowly now, staring outside the window toward the palace gardens and buildings across the street, those tranquil, eternal acres that seemed always both to haunt and inspire him. Finally he looked over at Willoughby. "One that will demonstrate to the world the horrors that occurred in Manila, and will allow the Filipino people their full measure of catharsis and emotional retribution. One that will cause the Japanese people to comprehend with finality that this so-called Tiger of Malaya, this falsely heroic figure that they once revered, was in fact a butcher of innocents in an ancient Christian city. One that will put the scale of this carnage fully into the minds of all our allies and to the American people at home, and demonstrate to them clearly my own personal commitment to bringing the actual perpetrators of war crimes to justice. I've asked for it. I've ordered it. When will this trial take place?"

Willoughby was examining his notes. I found myself wondering absently what, with his unquestioning loyalty, he could possibly have written on his paper from the General's impassioned rambling, other than doodles or perhaps rhetorical generalities.

I knew what I had written on mine: four words. *Nanking . . . Hirohito . . . Sam Genius . . .*

Finally, Willoughby looked up at MacArthur. "He has already been charged, sir. They are preparing the case even as we speak."

"The trial. When will it happen?" repeated MacArthur.

"I'll have to find out," answered Willoughby, giving the supreme commander a beleaguered and apologetic look.

"It's only been a month since General Yamashita surrendered," interjected Court Whitney. "It takes time to build a case, Boss. They have to interrogate him, collect outside evidence, formalize the charges, prepare the witnesses—"

"It's my court," said MacArthur, cutting off Whitney's analysis. "We know what happened, and we know who was in command."

"Let me check on it," said Whitney, sighing as he began writing a note on his legal pad.

"No, that's OK," said Willoughby. "I'll send a message."

"No," interrupted MacArthur. "This is too important to be left to simple message traffic. Too subtle. Too urgent." He turned to me. "Captain Marsh, I want you to prepare a report for me on the scope and timing of this matter. Go to Manila, immediately. Talk to the lawyers there. Find out what impediments, if any, are in the way of a speedy trial, of the sort I am envisioning. Say nothing specific on my behalf, but make my presence felt. You have become quite good at that. Generals Whitney and

Willoughby can arrange for message traffic that will convey my thoughts about the trial itself. But reinforce my expectations. Leave them with the—firm knowledge—of what we are expecting. And what we are expecting is *speed*."

A sudden and overwhelming thrill had swept through me as the General gave me my instructions. It had nothing to do with MacArthur or the emperor or even Yamashita. *He was sending me back to Manila.*

Court Whitney had nodded again and again as MacArthur went on, agreeing with his judgment. Now he spoke. "Great idea, Boss. If you sent a lawyer, you'd get one of those tedious legal reports filled with caveats and whereases and thuses and therefores, but they'd be afraid to actually touch on the—urgency of the timing, and those—other things. If you sent me, somebody down there, probably the press, would start screaming that you were engaging in command interference of the trial itself."

"It's my trial," said MacArthur. "I have a right to interfere."

Whitney was laughing. "Not so loud, General."

MacArthur ignored that. "I wouldn't send a lawyer because they always end up talking to other lawyers and coming back like Colonel Genius, convinced and trenchant with his briefing charts and his larger accusations. I wouldn't send you, Court, because what you're doing for me here in Tokyo is too important."

All three of them were looking at me now. I tried mightily to repress my smile. "My bags are packed, sir."

Whitney shook his head, grinning. "I imagine it will be permissible this time for you to make a call on my friend Carlos Ramirez? And even to dally for an evening with his young daughter?"

"So she's still waiting for you?" asked MacArthur, having suddenly become indulgent.

"From my mail I'd say so, General. I certainly hope so."

"You mean you haven't fallen in love in Tokyo yet?"

"No, sir. I'm still waiting to get married."

"I'd give him a couple more weeks," chuckled the usually silent Willoughby. "Some sweet little geisha will knock our boy off his feet."

"You should be so lucky," joked MacArthur.

They were laughing at me, but it did not bother me. Their forced humor was a way of reminding me that I was an acceptable little rug rat, useful and of some small importance, but that I was not one of them and would never truly be a member of the royal court. I was glad to play their game, for in truth I did not want to be one of them. I smiled back, secretly laughing at them as well. Their game had two sides. It had already brought me rewards far greater than I might ever have dreamed.

"I'll leave first thing in the morning, sir."

"Tonight," insisted MacArthur. "There's an evening courier flight that runs out of Atsugi. We'll make sure you're on the manifest."

He began pacing again, lightened by his little chuckle over my romantic affairs, his mind swept up in his newfound inspiration. As he walked I watched an uncharacteristic sneer creep across his face.

"I want you to do something else, Jay. I want you to go by and see General Yamashita, in whatever prison cell he is now rotting. I have nothing particular in mind for you there. Just pay him a visit. Have a little fun. Tell him General Douglas MacArthur, who is busily working with the *emperor* in Tokyo to rebuild Japan, asked you to check on his well-being."

"Yes, sir."

For some unexplainable reason the General gave a fatherly, doting smile. "You've been remarkably reliable, considering your age and experience. I am completely pleased with the work you have done for me."

"Thank you, General. It's good of you to say that, sir."

"I'm late for lunch," said the supreme commander suddenly. "Good day, gentlemen."

And with a startling abruptness he strode out of the room.

CHAPTER 15

★　★　★　★　★

I was late, too. But not for lunch.

I walked quickly through the dust and autumn leaves. The smell of rain was in the wind, dank and foreboding. And before me in the grey afternoon sky I could see, even from a block away, the goalpostlike forty-foot bronze torii that marked one of the entrances to the Yasakuni Shrine.

The wind lifted the branches of the trees that bordered the Yasakuni grounds, showering me with freshly falling leaves and carrying in its breezes the aroma of constantly burning incense. I passed under the torii and followed a row of stone *toro* lanterns toward the main area of the shrine, a wooden temple with a steep roof and ancient, curving borders. Soon I was walking through a sea of fluttering white doves. The doves lived at the shrine, raised and fed by Yasakuni's attendants.

Another key landmark that had been left untouched by the Allied bombings, Yasakuni was the resting place for the souls of all the Japanese soldiers who had died in battle since the Meiji Restoration. Inside the shrine's main temple, the name of every soldier who had fallen was kept on a special parchment scroll, along with the place and date of his passing.

The scroll was considered sacred and holy. World War Two alone had added nearly two million names.

It was midday in a workweek, but hundreds of Japanese were in the park. As I walked I became lost among them, towering over them like a gawking Gulliver. Many were soldiers on their way home from the war, stopping to pay their respects to relatives and fallen comrades. Still in uniform, the soldiers hunched forward in their long brown coats as they struggled under the load of bulky rucksacks that carried all their belongings. Women of all ages, some in kimonos and others in the bundled rags of the farmlands, bowed fervently toward the temple even before they reached it, their faces filled with reverence. My presence brought no reaction from the Japanese. It was as if I were not among them at all.

A mammoth seventy-foot torii guarded the entrance to the temple. It was the largest bronze torii in all of Japan. I stopped when I reached it, standing awkwardly. I was supposed to meet her there. And finally I saw her walking toward me, having entered the park through one of its three other gateways.

In stark contrast to the others in the park, she was dressed in a beautiful white kimono. A red obi pulled it into her slender waist. Her long black hair was pulled back and up, twisted tightly above her head. She was wearing bright red lipstick, giving her smooth face a doll's appearance. She walked purposefully toward me. Her elbows were into her sides and her hands were in front of her waist. Her chin was slightly down, as if she knew in advance that the two of us would soon be under an avalanche of disapproving stares.

Reaching me she bowed slightly. Her lips now curled into a secret smile. Her eyes remained merrily on my own. "Good afternoon, Jay-*san*. I am so happy that you could meet me here."

I nodded back to her, then looked toward the earnest Japanese who were milling about nearby. "Will they be offended?"

"Oh, no! They will be honored. And anyway, what does it matter? The lord privy seal wishes greatly that I might bring you here."

Careful not to touch each other in such a public place, we moved together onto the white gravel courtyard that led to the temple steps. *Yes*, I thought again. *The lord privy seal wishes . . .*

I felt a special tenderness for Yoshiko, and I knew she had grown to care for me. But I did not delude myself. After "capturing" me through this lovely gift, Kido undoubtedly viewed me to be a major "asset." As I played my role of eavesdropper on behalf of General MacArthur, I was also now considered a tendril in the Japanese government's own sophisticated intelligence network. The Japanese had always been masters at what was called source-level intelligence gathering. And in these crucial days of transition, there could be little doubt that they would seize every opportunity, from bar girls and taxi drivers to high-level emissaries, to gather information and exploit it for the good of the nation-family.

And so, I knew, with me.

Nearing the temple, I stopped. Before me, the silent, unspeaking worshipers patiently waited in line at the wide steps for their moment at the temple's altar. It was not fear that halted me but rather a sense of propriety, and respect. The war was over. They had lost. But I now was standing in the aisle of a national church. Again I recalled the emperor's broadcast to the nation announcing the end of the war. *Let the entire nation continue as one family, from generation to generation . . .* More than any country on earth, Japan was a nation-family, and this was where its honored uncles and siblings dwelt.

"It's OK," she said earnestly, taking my arm and tugging as she fell in line. "They will be honored."

Seeing Yoshiko's refined clothing, and noticing that she was speaking to me in Japanese, those in line looked at me with a mix of confusion and faint amusement that finally settled in as full understanding. This was not some ordinary American soldier, hanging on to his bar girl from a nearby recreation and amusement association. This was a Japanese-speaking officer, being escorted by one of Kyoto's most refined geishas. They knew instinctively that Yoshiko was on a mission. And the puzzled looks melted into slight but welcoming smiles.

Just before we reached the altar the others watched curiously as she took a ladle from a rectangular vat and poured holy water over my hands. Then we faced the temple together. I clapped three times with her, to awaken the spirits of the dead. I felt no shame as I bowed deeply alongside her and prayed for the respect and blessings of those who had perished in the war. For a moment I thought of my own lost brother, and wished that there were a way that he too could be so solemnly remembered. For what is a soldier's fate but to pour his energy into the soul of his nation, at the behest of leaders who give him the reasons and then order him to die?

At the altar after we finished a sunburned older woman in a formal dark kimono held a bundled infant in front of her, so that it was looking at the altar. The old woman trembled with anticipation as she pulled smoke toward the baby's face, clapped its unknowing hands together, then pushed on its back, moving the body forward to make it bow. The infant had thus been christened. And I knew that nothing from the outside, not even the increasingly exalted regime of Supreme Commander, General of the Army Douglas MacArthur would ever be powerful enough to break the meaning of that bow.

Ever-attuned to subtleties, Yoshiko picked up on my lingering gaze as we walked away from the temple. "The lord privy seal advises that you can learn to fully understand our country here," she said quietly.

"And who did you pray to?" I asked.

She secretly touched my arm for a moment. "My father. And two of my brothers."

"Dead?"

"Yes. My father died in China. One brother in the Solomon Islands. The other—" She looked at me hesitantly. "He was a kamikaze pilot. Off the coast of Okinawa. Only this year."

I watched her face as we walked. She was a professional, rigorously trained since late childhood to control her emotions. But her visit to the shrine had shaken her deeply.

"My brother, too," I said. "Last year."

"I am sorry," said Yoshiko.

As we walked she dared to touch my arm again, drawing stares from a nearby group of returning soldiers. Feeling the weight of their disapproving eyes it occurred to me that Yoshiko was at some level on her own kamikaze mission. For despite Kido's assurances that she was being honored by my affections, what Japanese man would ever want to marry a woman who had spent the first days of the occupation in the bed of an American officer?

"I'm sorry, too, Yoshiko."

We reached the edge of the park. I stopped walking, and we stood silently watching each other under the cold bronze torii.

In her eyes I saw more than duty. "Will I see you tonight?"

"No," I said. "I'm leaving for the Philippines."

"When will you be back?"

Such a simple question, normal for any two lovers, was fraught with complications. Was she asking me as a woman who cared for me, or was she making certain she had a complete report for the lord privy seal? The answer, as it had always become, was probably both.

"I don't know," I said.

The very mention of the Philippines had splashed me with a reality that was as cold as the coming rain. I felt myself withdraw from her, until even my body had stiffened with its own disapproval.

"I will miss you, Jay-*san*," she said.

And as she turned to walk away I knew she meant it.

My flight, a C-54 courier that delivered important mail, messages, and personnel, would leave at midnight. It would stop to refuel at Kadena Air Base on Okinawa, then land in Manila in time to begin the workday. A similar courier ran from Manila at midnight, reversing the course to Atsugi. The couriers flew at night so that officers on important assignments could catnap on the aircraft, work a full day in Manila or Tokyo, then if necessary return to their own headquarters by the following morning. Such tight turnarounds were really no longer necessary in October 1945, but the system, devised elsewhere in the Southwest theater during the exigencies of wartime, had not yet slowed down to keep pace with peace.

I returned to my hotel, packing quickly and racing back downstairs. It was only a two-hour drive to Atsugi, but I had business to take care of before I left. I was afraid to face Divina Clara. And I needed Father Garvey to help me.

The First Cavalry Division had taken over a large Japanese military cantonment not far from the embassy. The cantonment, a collection of low, flat-roofed barracks and administration buildings that surrounded a parade ground, had for years served as the headquarters of the Tokyo district's ground defense forces. One of the smaller buildings, formerly used as a classroom, had been turned into a chapel. My driver stopped in front of it and I jumped quickly from the jeep, trotting inside.

A lanky, longhaired chaplain's assistant sat at a field desk in the chapel's outer office, absently scratching pimples on his pink face with one long finger. A Japanese *kanji* sign was still nailed above the doorway, giving instructions to a now-dead army. An American military field phone sat on the desk. Incongruously for this holy venue, the Chaplain's assistant was reading a Superman comic book.

"Father Garvey?" I asked.

He pointed toward the converted classroom that was being used as the chapel itself. "You'll have to wait in line," the young soldier drawled.

More than a dozen soldiers were standing quietly just outside the classroom. I walked past them toward the room itself, anxious to see Father Garvey. They watched me with caustic glares as I passed, noticing my captain's bars and thinking only that I was pulling rank.

"Sorry," I said, entering the auditorium. "I have a plane to catch."

"Right," muttered one of them. "And my name's Hirohito."

Another soldier was more direct. "God doesn't recognize your rank, Captain. Add this to your list when you see the priest."

"As you were, Sergeant," I barked fiercely, my false authority covering my embarrassment. "I'm under orders."

In a far, darkened corner of the auditorium Father Garvey had erected a heavy cloth curtain as a floor-to-ceiling partition. On its near side sat a young soldier. The solider looked lonely and confused. He was leaning forward with his head down and his hands dangling between his legs. Now and then he would tilt his head toward the curtain, whispering urgently into it. Then he would nod, again and again, as the priest answered him. On the other side of the curtain, Father Garvey was hearing his confession.

Finally the soldier finished. He stood up, seeming somewhat relieved but no happier, and began to leave. I walked quickly across the room, nodding to him as we passed each other, then took my seat on the other side of Father Garvey's curtain.

For a moment I merely stared at the curtain. I didn't know quite what to do. I had never been to confession before. But I had to do something, soon. I was in the chair. At the auditorium's entrance I could see several of the waiting soldiers staring at me. Their arms were folded across their chests. Their eyes held a deep resentment at my having pulled rank and jumped to the front of the waiting line. They clearly had decided that I was a pompous ass.

The clock was ticking. Atsugi was waiting. As I regarded the folds of the curtain a thought occurred to me. I hadn't really seen the priest on the other side. What if it wasn't Father Garvey after all?

"Father Garvey," I said. "Is that you?"

"My son," said Father Garvey, heavily into his priestly duties, "we are meeting under the sanctity of God. That is a question you are not supposed to be asking."

I grinned happily, recognizing his voice. "Father, it's me! Jay!"

There was a moment of empty silence on the other side of the curtain. I began to wonder if in the eyes of Father Garvey I had committed some papal fraud that would cause him to rise from his chair and pull back the curtain and then banish me to my own Protestant hell, or at a minimum endanger our friendship. Then I could hear him chuckling.

"And didn't I always know you were a clandestine Catholic, Jay?"

"Father, I've got a big problem. I need your help."

On the other side of the curtain, I could hear him sigh. "How big a problem? This is confession, Jay. There are many people waiting."

"I'm leaving for Manila at midnight. From Atsugi. I have to clear it up before I go."

"And what does it involve?"

I gulped, taking a breath. "Fornication, Father."

He fell into silence, then I heard a sound. It was either a groan or a stifled guffaw. "Did they get to you, too, lad?"

"It's very complicated, Father. It's personal but it—also involves my duties."

"And doesn't it always?"

"My professional duties."

"And aren't we in Japan, then?"

"You've grown cynical, Father, and it's hardly been a month."

"And what a month it's been, though." He paused for a moment. I could hear him shifting in his chair. "Can you wait thirty minutes?"

"For what?"

"They're expecting to talk with me, burdened as they are with sin. I cannot let them down, can I? Let me finish with confession. Then I'll go with you to Atsugi. We can talk better that way."

I blanched. "I don't want to talk about this in front of my driver."

"Then I'll drive you. I do have a license, you know."

I felt myself starting to grin. "If you drive like you preach we'll never make it."

"And when is the last time you heard me preach, you simple redneck pagan?"

"And when do you ever stop, Father?"

I stood up. The line of waiting confessors had grown, and most of them were glowering at me from the other side of the classroom. They could not hear our conversation, but watching my full, amused grin they seemed collectively confused, as if in addition to having cut to the front of the line I now was violating an obligation by not appearing properly penitent.

"Thirty minutes, Father. Out front."

"Out front where?" he asked.

"In case you don't recognize me, I'll be the guy in a khaki uniform, standing next to a green jeep."

"And what shade of green would that be?" joked Father Garvey.

Thirty-seven minutes later Father Garvey trotted out of the chapel building, holding his cap in one hand and a pack of Camel cigarettes in the other. His eyes twinkled as he neared me. He was trying to be harsh, but even as he shook a disapproving finger in my face he glowed with a blissful smile: he was indeed happy to see me.

"See what happens when I let you out on your own?"

I offered to drive but Father Garvey insisted, as if it were a chance to find a few hours of liberation from his priestly chores. He did drive about as well as he preached. I began to think that it might qualify as a minor miracle if we reached Atsugi at all. Tokyo's streets were filled with rickshaws, horse-drawn carts, military trucks and jeeps, old buses, and everywhere people walking. On all sides of us along the roads the city was flush with construction crews and the dusty, churning chaos that went into the rebirth of thousands of buildings.

Father Garvey wended in and out of the slow traffic, ever at his gearshift and brakes and accelerator as the jeep surged and lurched, yelling and laughing, shaking his fist at some and waving gladly to others. I did not mind his driving. I had never seen him have so much fun.

The canals near Yokohama were filled with squat, unpainted barges that once hauled coal, lumber, and produce. After LeMay's firebombs incinerated tens of thousands of homes throughout the city, the barges had been turned into houseboats. The houseboats were teeming and overcrowded. Their occupants, whom the Japanese simply called the "water livers," seemed to watch us longingly from the portals of the barges and the muddy banks of the canals that neared the road. Under the darkened, rain-ominous afternoon sky scores of bundled women knelt or squatted on the main decks, their hair wrapped in large kerchiefs. Surrounded by dreary pennants of laundry, they were cooking dinners on small outdoor charcoal stoves. The odors of boiling cabbage, roasting fish, and raw, recent sewage embraced us as we passed them.

The rain came in, wet and cold. The road now paralleled a set of train tracks. We passed station after muddy station as we drove through the city that seemed never to end. Relentless throngs of drably dressed Japanese crowded every wooden platform, shivering under the rain. Great rushes of people raced into and out of the old, rounded railroad cars. The commuters seemed focused and intent, like armies. They hurried to and fro in groups, packing the cars to merciless capacity. Those who did not make the doors in time often crawled in and out of windows. Those who did not make the windows sometimes jumped onto the coupling gears that connected the cars.

Raw energy, that was what I was watching. An entire nation boiling, anxious to get on with whatever it was that fate, the emperor, and the supreme commander were at last offering. And as we drove past them I found myself rekindling my respect for General Douglas MacArthur. For all his vanities and frequent paranoia, for all the moments of small-minded vindictiveness and obsequious deference to power, MacArthur did indeed possess a sweeping wisdom that was fueling and even helping to direct this energy. A lesser man might have been consciously stifling it and sending it deep underground, where it would later erupt in national resentment and possible rebellion.

"So," said Father Garvey finally as the traffic thinned. "You have committed fornication. And now you must face the woman that you love."

"You do have a way with words, Father."

"I told you, words are my profession. And I've been hearing this story rather frequently of late." He glanced at me for a moment, then looked back at the road. "More than once?"

"More than once."

"Are you done with it?"

"I don't think so."

"Do you love her?"

"Not really."

"What's gotten into you, you idiot?"

"I don't know."

"What do you mean, you don't know?"

"Well, why do you think I asked to talk to you?"

"To tantalize me, Jay!" I could see his fleshy cheeks working to suppress a smile. "To tease me! To show me that you are capable of winning a lover in whichever country you happen to land. Well, you're a regular Tennessee stud now, aren't you?"

"Father, I'm from Arkansas. And besides this isn't funny."

"Well, he has a conscience. That's a start." He glanced over at me again. "What are you going to do about it?"

"She was sent to me by the lord privy seal. He saw me looking at her. At first I couldn't turn her away without shaming her."

"Ah," said Father Garvey. "He couldn't turn her away. Poor lad! He took her into his bed for the cause. The old conundrum, the Jay Marsh view of the universe. A tale of Asian shame versus Christian sin, is that what I'm hearing?"

"Kind of," I said. "It would have disgraced her if I'd just sent her back. She would have failed." I shrugged wearily. "I don't expect you to understand that." He didn't answer me. "There's something else," I said. "I have to keep seeing her. We each have a duty, here. We've become messengers to the other side."

"Oh, I see," said Father Garvey, mocking me with false understanding. "She brings you messages from this fellow, the lord whatever—"

"The lord privy seal."

"Yes," said Father Garvey sarcastically. "And you pass on messages to him through her."

"Mostly I just listen," I said. "And I pass on the information to General Willoughby and General Whitney."

"The Bobbsey twins of the occupation," grunted Father Garvey.

"Now you're being disrespectful, Father."

"I'm a priest, Jay! I don't even have to salute them!"

"You criticize me, but you're the one who's lacked humility. You haven't been the same since we've been in Japan."

"You're trying to throw me off," said Father Garvey. "To sidetrack the very road to your salvation."

I smiled sheepishly. He knew me too well. "Sorry. I'm embarrassed, Father! Anyway, I'm expected to continue. It's become quite useful."

"No doubt!" Father Garvey glanced over at me again. "And the only way these messages can be transmitted is if you and she—"

"Fornicate?" I said, trying to be helpful.

"Fornicate. Of course."

"No. I mean, not really."

We were on the same road that we had taken from Atsugi on that first historic day after MacArthur's grand entrance to Japan. As we drove I remembered it all, the Keystone Cops convoy and the lord privy seal in his morning coat and the tens of thousands of rigid, sweating infantrymen that the emperor had sent to MacArthur as his welcoming gift. So much had happened in those five short weeks that it seemed almost to have taken place during my childhood. Suddenly I felt very sad.

"It just happens when I see her, Father. And I'm not strong enough to stop it. She's so—pretty, and so sweet. And I can't decide on my own to stop seeing her. It's part of my job."

"Oh, a regular gigolo now, are we?"

"Father, I'm not proud of this. That's why I came to see you."

"Perhaps you don't really love Divina Clara. Have you ever thought of that?"

"But I do."

Just the mention of her name snapped me back into a different world, the place of harmony and happiness where I longed to be. Within a day I would be with her again. How could I keep this from her, and if I could not, how could I explain it?

"It was a magical time, Manila," said Father Garvey with a sudden, quiet passion. "The electricity of war. The loneliness and fear. The way that the trees and flowers and the very earth smelled each morning when the sun cooked out the rain of the night before. The joy of falling in love."

Watching his face, I could see that his lament was personal as well as instructive, coming up from someplace deep inside him that he had never shown to me before. Had Father Garvey himself fallen in love in Manila? Were those booze-filled evenings of denial brought on not by an attempt to drown out his attractions but by the terrible, sweet confusion of having yielded to them? Suddenly I realized that he probably had indeed fallen in love and that his advice to me was wiser and even sadder than I had expected.

"Yes. It was a wonderful time, Father."

"But it's gone, Jay. It will never be the same. You can't recapture it. So perhaps your future is elsewhere."

The jeep bounced and surged on the rough, potholed road. Dusk had settled over us like a hovering blanket. The rain was cold. Winter was coming, I could feel it in the icy air. For the first time in years I felt my face begin to numb, and it reminded me suddenly of fetching winter firewood for my father. Peasant poet that he was, he had even invented a phrase for it: *the bleak rainwinter air.* And here it was, upon us, in Japan.

Father Garvey turned on the headlights. Just in front of us was the side road that led to the Atsugi airfield. As he made the turn I could see the air terminal just ahead. In a few hours I would lift off and reverse course, and by dawn I would once again step into the hot, perfumed, welcoming air of Manila. That moment would be my homecoming, far more so than breathing in the crisp salt air at the pier in Santa Monica or standing lonely in the cemetery just above the bleak rainswept cow pasture where my father still lay in an unmarked grave.

"No, Father," I said. "My future is in Manila."

"I understand that. In fact, I envy it."

He looked over at me and in his eyes for the first time I saw the truth, that Father Garvey's past held a burning glory that was also in Manila, but that unlike me he could never reclaim it without abandoning his God. And now his words took on a different meaning. In a way, he was speaking them for both of us.

"But if that's where you want to be, then you'd best be tending to your future, Jay. Stay pure in your love for this woman. Have the courage to give her all your heart. Or you'll end up a very lonely man."

CHAPTER 16

As in the case of so many true people of action, the man who was to become my father-in-law had a deceptively mild appearance. The top of Carlos Ramirez's head did not even reach my shoulders. The tight, gnarly muscles on his arms and legs seemed actually to have bunched and wizened as he aged. He wore too much jewelry for a man. He dyed his hair so deeply black that it was clearly unnatural. His perpetual smile seemed alternately mischievous and ingratiating. Sometimes when I looked at him I imagined that the offhand smile, the gaudy rings and neck chains and gold bracelets, and even the soft, irreverent voice were all a deliberate camouflage, Carlos's own form of belly talk. Certainly they caused many, and particularly Americans with little experience in Asia, to underestimate both his tenacity and his shrewd intellect.

He fixed this disarming smile on me as we stood on the old round bricks of his back terrace. It was just after dusk. An hour before, a warm but heavy rain had washed over the city, cleansing the air and leaving behind a cool and windless calm. I stood blissfully next to him, at peace with the rhythms and the natural beauty of this country I had come to love. Gone for now was the dust and yearning struggle of Tokyo. On the dark waters of the small pond just across the yard, clumps of water lilies and lotus floated with a gorgeous serenity. All around us the *kalachuchi* bloomed, their perfume lingering in the still air like the scent of a departed lover. Lovely orchids hung open from their perches on a nearby tree. Heavy vines filled with white-flowered *sampaguita* made an arch above the nearby gate. I was at peace. Manila was a soothing and addictive drug.

Carlos handed me a tumbler of warm scotch. He was wearing a loose-fitting white barong. The long-sleeved, hip-length traditional evening shirt made him appear even more diminutive as he stared up into my face. "May I say, welcome home, Jay!"

"Thank you, Mr. Ramirez. After Tokyo, I feel like I'm in heaven."

"Maybe soon you can return for good."

"Very soon, I hope. I'm a reserve officer. General MacArthur can't keep me in Japan forever."

"But Divina Clara tells me you are doing very important things."

I smiled, flattered. "To be honest, it's been amazing. I even sat in on a private meeting with the emperor, just last week!"

"Hirohito himself! And tomorrow, General Yamashita, yet again." He eyed me carefully. "So probably, the thought of coming back to Manila and working in a family business now seems boring?"

I held his eyes, sensing that he was laying down a careful gauntlet, asking for a moment of truth. "I miss Manila. I feel like I belong here. I'm learning a lot. And I think it could be useful."

"You have many talents," said Divina Clara's father. From him, it was a grand and cherished compliment.

Carlos Ramirez was the kind of man you would want walking close beside you if you had to enter a dark, strange alley. More to the point, he was the last person you would want to face in a dark, strange alley if he were waiting in the shadows to fight you. The little Filipino went through life like a fox terrier. He was fiercely loyal, he had no fear, and he did not know how to quit. And even though he was now fifty-five years old, only those with a death wish would have thought it a good idea to challenge Carlos Ramirez's pride, particularly by insulting his family.

In his younger years the boxily built native of Olongapo had often been his father's point man in the scraps and brawls that attended their slowly expanding business ventures at Subic Bay and later in Manila. Unlike many of the Philippines' oligarchy, whose families had made their fortunes by carefully cultivating centuries-old relations with the Spanish, the Ramirez clan had found their success only after the American navy arrived in Subic Bay at the turn of the century. And they had garnered their riches through brains, hustle, and a willingness to fight anyone—criminal gangs, political bosses, business rivals, even rogue American sailors—who stood in their way.

It was often remembered, even in 1945, that while in his late twenties Carlos Ramirez had wielded the fastest and surest banana knife in central Luzon. And he had not been afraid to use it.

He was measuring me carefully. As he spoke he reached up with one hand and absently touched his still-youthful forehead where an old knife scar creased it just above an eyebrow. Intentionally or not, he was pointing to a penciled memory of his own journey to success. "And you would not have a problem working for an Asian man?"

I smiled, sensing where he was heading. "I'm going to marry an Asian woman, and I'm going to have Asian kids. Why should it bother me to work for an Asian man—as long as I respect him, that is?"

His eyes twinkled merrily. I could tell it was the answer he had been hoping for. "A lot of Americans like our women, Jay. But not as many seem to respect our men. When Americans see us they mistake our size for weakness, I think. And because we smile they think we are afraid of them. And because we do not wear ties, they believe we lack sophistication."

He puffed out his chest, grinning proudly. "If I were weak, or afraid, or lacking in sophistication, I would not have made so much money trading with Americans. I would not even be living in this house."

"You're far more successful than anyone in my family," I answered honestly. "And I respect you because you and your father did it on your own."

In the nearby yard, the same young servant boy who had been with Divina Clara in the *caratela* the day I met her now stood in a white coat, methodically turning a large side of beef over an open fire pit. Inside the house, other servants were preparing dinner and setting up the bar. Carlos's youngest son was away at school. The other two, now married, would be coming later. Mrs. Ramirez, Divina Clara, the two aunts, and the other two sisters were all upstairs, dressing and preening. Soon the dinner guests would arrive, more than twenty of the Ramirez family's favorite friends.

They were celebrating my return. Since I had indeed come back, in the mind of Carlos Ramirez it had finally become safe to announce that Divina Clara and I were engaged.

"I would like you to work for me," he abruptly announced. "This is not simply family. Coming from the staff of General MacArthur, I'm sure you can be very valuable to our business. We will be doing a lot of work with the American military. Also I know you could be helpful in negotiating our government construction projects."

"I don't mind saying that I'm becoming a pretty skilled negotiator, sir," I said. "I think I can really help you."

Carlos and I raised the scotch-filled tumblers, toasting each other. His smile now turned friendly and ironic, as if he and I were sharing the same eternal joke.

"It will be a struggle, Jay. You should be prepared for that. If you are not one of the historic landholding families, everything is a fight in the Philippines." He shook his head ironically. "Every day we hear about all the new changes in Tokyo, and sometimes I ask myself why there will be no change here?"

"But there are," I answered hesitantly. "The commonwealth is gone. The Philippines are free. On July fourth you'll be a republic."

"But this is not real change. Who will run this republic?"

I did not get a chance to answer, for his eyes had suddenly shifted behind me. A genuine smile crept across his face. He melted with un-abashed pride. "Ah. She enters. I know I am her father, but have you ever seen anything so beautiful?"

Following his eyes, I turned to see Divina Clara walking slowly toward us. Her sudden, shimmering appearance reminded me somehow of the night when I first saw Consuelo Trani standing underneath the frangipani tree at Tacloban. She was wearing a gold-colored sleeveless dress that caused her caramel skin almost to glow. She held her chin high, seeming self-conscious as she walked. Her thick black hair was pulled up to the top of her head, then cascaded behind her, onto her shoulders. She wore long golden earrings that seemed to frame her smooth, high cheekbones. Her eyes were warm, almost shy. She offered me an unbelieving smile as she reached us, as if it were impossible that I had actually come back so soon.

She was slightly taller than her father. She leaned over and kissed him on a cheek as she reached us. Then she came smoothly to my side, brushing against me and almost covertly taking my hand.

"I was telling Jay he should work with me when he leaves the army," said Carlos.

"No," she said, chiding him, "I heard you. You were going to start in on Roxas again."

"Not only Roxas," said her father abashedly. "The whole bunch of them. If Jay is going to live and work here, he'll have to start studying Filipino politics."

"So, they will remain in power, Father," she said. "And to do business we must learn to live with it."

"A new government," grunted Carlos Ramirez bitterly. "A republic, they say. But it will be the same as before. Only MacArthur could have changed it, and he looked the other way. The stench of corruption still hangs over our islands."

She took my hand and secretly squeezed it. As she spoke I could tell that on such issues her father clearly viewed her as an intellectual equal. "MacArthur, MacArthur! He did not bring corruption to the Philippines, Father! He did not put the great families into power! They are born believing that since their great-grandfather kissed the ring of some Spanish governor they have a natural right to live above the other Filipinos."

"Yes," said Carlos. "But he protected them. They collaborated with the Japanese while I and the others went to the jungles and fought as guerrillas. Now they tell the people that in a war between two foreign countries, their concern was only for the Philippines. So what did I and your brother suffer for? And what did your grandfather die for? The truth is, they will do anything to stay in power themselves. Work with the Spanish? No problem. With the Americans? Of course. With the Japanese? Certainly, if it protects their interests. Join forces with a Filipino government that desires independence? No doubt, because staying in government means they still have the votes to prevent change, and remain rich. So, independence will come, but nothing will change!"

"I'm not saying they're right, Father." She was smiling indulgently at him, almost as if humoring his rampage. "The question is, why do you blame MacArthur?"

"Because he could have stopped it," said Carlos stubbornly. "Don't forget that MacArthur has many years in these islands. So long that in many ways he has become Filipino. He and Roxas might as well be brothers! MacArthur told the people when he returned that he would run to earth and punish every single disloyal Filipino who had aided the enemy! Again and again he said that! But then he found out that most of them were his longtime friends!" He shrugged as if helpless. "That is the Philippines. Different rules for friends."

"Then we must find our own friends. Father. It does no good to hold such bitterness over something you cannot change!"

"Stop arguing with me, Divina Clara." Carlos was pretending irritation, but on one level he was showing off Divina Clara's knowledge, basking in her wisdom. "I'm beginning to think it was a mistake to send you to the Jesuits for all these years of training."

Now he looked at me, feigning complete frustration. "How will you ever be able to live with a woman with such education, who argues so decisively, Jay?"

I smiled. She squeezed my hand again. "I will become her student, sir. She knows far more than I do."

He paused for a moment, then elbowed me playfully. "Do you know General Whitney?"

"I work with him every day."

"He has many, many investments here in the Philippines, and many friends among the old-line families. Whitney has great influence with MacArthur, too. So, think about this. When Quezon and MacArthur escaped from Corregidor to Australia, Roxas took the gold bullion reserves of our country and hid them in a secret place. Many, many millions of dollars. Has anyone seen this gold since? No! But Roxas knows where it is. And Whitney is a big supporter of Roxas. Maybe Roxas and Whitney have made a secret, complicated deal!"

I shook my head, instinctively disagreeing with Carlos. In October 1945 the Philippines were rife with rumors of what had happened to the lost gold. It had come up in almost every conversation since I landed. To some it was MacArthur's gold. To others it was Yamashita's. More than likely it was indeed Roxas's, or it was lost. But Whitney?

"General Whitney doesn't have that power, Mr. Ramirez."

"Your opinion is important to me, but probably uninformed." Divina Clara's father was almost mandarin in his obtuseness. "You are only a small officer on MacArthur's staff. I don't think you understand Whitney's power."

"Father," she interrupted commandingly. "Stop it. It does no good."

"And so Divina Clara is right, as usual!" He raised his tumbler in a mock toast, winking to me conspiratorially. "To Roxas and his rich, spoiled, traitorous *compadres!* We must learn to live with them. Until the moment comes that we can destroy them."

"Father!"

"Just kidding." But the knowing smile on his face told me that deep in his heart he was not kidding. He fixed me with yet another sly look. "We also read that General MacArthur and the emperor have become good friends?"

"They are working together," I said vaguely.

"They will become good friends. After all, that is MacArthur's way," said Carlos vaguely.

"He has great responsibilities," I replied.

Carlos patted me encouragingly on a shoulder, as if my answer had pleased him. "A very wise answer. You are loyal, Jay. I respect that."

We stood quietly for a while, sipping scotch and watching the servant boy laboring over the beef. Divina Clara softly rubbed a hand along my back and then put it around my shoulder. Watching the silent messages that went back and forth between us, Carlos beamed with a possessive happiness. Finally he reached out and took one of our elbows in each of his small, scarred hands, turning us toward each other in a gesture that indicated his full approval.

"I think I will check on your mother," he said.

"She's probably watching from the window," laughed Divina Clara. We all looked up. Mrs. Ramirez was indeed just above us, her arms folded contentedly across her chest, surveying us from one of the upstairs bed-room windows.

"Then I think I will go close the window," panned the smiling Carlos. And he walked slowly into the house.

We were standing very near to each other. She needed no perfume because the air was filled with it. Out in the yard the servant boy grinned widely, trying not to watch us as he slowly turned the side of beef. Holding my hand in both of hers, she pulled me slowly toward her until she had pressed it secretly against the top of her thighs, all the while never taking her eyes off my own.

"What I have been thinking—is that I would live anywhere with you," she finally said.

"We could live anywhere, but I would like to stay in Manila and work with your family," I answered. "If it's all right with you." We were saying a lot of things in a very few words.

She began staring deeply into all the parts of my face and neck, as if reading me. "I forgot what you looked like."

"But it's only been six weeks."

"So you see, Jay, that's the brutality of a soldier's view of things. Six weeks is—fifteen percent of the time we've been together! And how much longer will we have to wait?"

She was partly joking, but I heard an unusual urgency in her voice. I began to wonder if she was noticing some undeniable, telltale glint of shame in my eyes, or feeling some vague, apologetic tension in my body. "Not much longer, Divina Clara. Certainly by Christmas."

"Christmas!" she said. "Three more months?" She thought about that for a moment, then put her head into my chest. "So much can happen in three months."

Something was indeed bothering her, but I could not tell what it was. I pressed her into me, daring to kiss her on the top of her head despite the hidden stares that I knew were coming from the windows behind me. "We're almost halfway there, Divina Clara. See how fast it goes?"

"No, I don't, actually." She looked up into my face again. "What do you like best about Japan?"

Her question made me nervous. "I can't think of anything."

"You have to tell me something."

I teased her, grinning with remembrance. "Is this one of your tests?"

"I told you, tests are never obvious. Tell me something. What is it that you like best about Japan?"

"The thing I like best about Japan is—that being away from you makes me understand how much I really love you."

She punched me playfully. She was happy again, and there was a cleverness in her smile. "That isn't an answer, it's a deflection. Although it was a sweet thought. But you have to tell me. I know you like some part of Japan because I see more power in your face, and in the way you stand. You've become stronger!"

I marveled at her intuitive genius, that she could know me so completely that by looking into my face and frame she could tell how much the past six weeks had changed me. And her probing was neither a guess nor a ploy. Divina Clara simply possessed that certainty. It was a part of who she was, just as some men could read a trail and know where an ambush might occur, and others could anticipate a baseball's trajectory the moment a bat began to swing.

"They've trusted me," I finally said, for the first time having to consider it myself. "MacArthur and the others. They've sent me off on important missions. I watched General Wainwright cry when MacArthur forgave him. I was at the Bessang Pass when Yamashita surrendered. I've met with the emperor of Japan. I've negotiated with his closest advisers. Me, can you believe it? I was on the airplane, in the car, aboard the ship. I've been in the room, Divina Clara. The private room, where only the giants gather. I've seen history, even before it was made!"

She watched my face, studying it again. "Do you want to have children soon?"

I had been in a reverie, surrounded by self-adulation. Her question was like a pin, plucking my balloon. *"Where did that come from?"*

For a moment she seemed startled at my reaction. Her eyes became very round. She threw her hands up into the air. "You've overwhelmed me, so I was just thinking—"

I recovered. "I'm sorry I yelled."

She laughed with surprise as I gave her a reassuring hug. "I can't stop thinking, Jay! But it's clear to me that our little place in Manila is a long way from being in this room you talk of, filled with giants."

Soon the guests began arriving. Divina Clara and I stood together on the terrace as Carlos proudly brought each couple to us, introducing me formally for the first time as his future son-in-law. He seemed to take great pleasure in pointing out again and again that I would soon work for him after completing my special duties with General Douglas MacArthur. As the evening grew longer and the tumblers of scotch passed on one into another, his descriptions of my exploits on behalf of the supreme commander grew. By dinner's end Carlos seemed to have convinced them all that I, Captain Jay Marsh, the brilliantly schooled, multilingual former football All-American, was truly the hand behind MacArthur's throne, and that the future of Japan itself would be put into jeopardy when I returned to Manila to join my blood with the Ramirez family and take my position next to the other sons as an equal partner and joint heir-apparent.

It was great fun. Divina Clara laughed and teased, her eternal eyes flashing messages to me from across the long mahogany table. No one fully believed the exaggerations of the feisty, speech-ridden Carlos, but everyone came away with the comprehension that I had his full affection, and more important his complete loyalty. The word would go out quickly through the business elites of Manila: there would soon be another Ramirez to deal with, one who was Caucasian and had a slightly different surname but on behalf of whom the unbending and redoubtable Carlos Ramirez was prepared to fight and die.

I spent that night in the guest bedroom of their home. Lying on the plushly sheeted double bed, surrounded by delicate porcelain and richly wooded antiques, in my mellow good fortune I thought of the corn-shuck mattresses and chamber pots of my youth. There was an unshakable irony in my having journeyed from a land of wealth to a land of poverty, where I would make my own final break toward wealth by joining an Asian man's family. Had my father even known what was on the other side of Arkansas? Did my little sister ever feel one moment of luxury before disease had stalked and destroyed her? Did my brother have a chance perhaps to glimpse an ancient castle before the machine guns of Normandy stitched him lifeless? Was my mother happy in Santa Monica with her walk-in bungalow and her live-in Italian?

In this undeserved place of contentment on the far side of the sea I dozed. And I will admit I prayed.

The house fell unearthly quiet. Two rooms away I could hear Carlos's peaceful, semidrunken snores. Then, unexpectedly, my door slowly opened. In the dim shaft of light that shone behind it I could see the sure and graceful movements of Divina Clara. She silently clicked the door shut behind her. She was barefoot, wearing a loose-fitting satin robe. Her hair was brushed out, full and long, falling onto her shoulders and down her back. The robe opened as she walked toward me. And when she reached the bed it dropped onto the floor.

"*I love you.*"

She whispered it, then eased naked into my bed. When I pulled her to me I could smell the faint aroma of *sampaguita*. As I began to kiss her I remembered that after dinner her mother had playfully woven a garland of those wondrous blossoms like a tiara into her hair. She kissed me back, eager and unafraid, and I realized that although a veil of propriety would be publicly upheld, now that her father had officially announced we were engaged there was no objection to her visiting me like this in the middle of the night.

"*Don't make a sound!*"

She knelt over me, slowly taking my hands. For a long time she rubbed them in easy circles along her firm stomach, smiling teasingly and staring unspeaking into my eyes. I started to grasp her waist. As I squeezed it she arched her back, sending her breasts dancing in the shadows before my eyes. Then she moved my hands up to them, one at a time. She held them there, moving them slowly, controlling their motion as if holding back my power at the moment of my greatest arousal. Her chin went high into the air. I began softly kneading her nipples with my thumbs, accepting my imprisonment. She moaned, as if all her energy were seeping away. And then she fell on top of me, covering every part of my body with her own.

She was all fullness and warmth and honesty, that is the only way I can describe those moments with Divina Clara. The fullness of her lips, of her breasts, of her flesh at every point it touched me. The warmth not only of her skin but of the energy that emanated from inside her, her arms and legs grasping me and squeezing, her eyes burning into me when they opened and then slowly closed again. The honesty of her emotions, a simple power filled with promises, the depth of which I had never before imagined.

Yoshiko had come to me obsessed by duty, fraught with the desire to please. She had soon begun to care for me, but more in the manner of someone living in a cage, with both the burden and protection of knowing she would never be free and thus also knowing that our moments together would never pass beyond fantasy. Divina Clara had stripped away all her own defenses, leaving her heart just as naked as the rest of her when she dropped her robe and clutched me to her round and luscious breasts. She was there before me, deliberately and unspeakably at my mercy, to be loved or crushed for all the rest of her life.

Finally I rolled on top of her. She whispered with pleasure, almost as if she were singing. In moments I was gasping and shuddering with an intensity that I did not believe was possible. And as I held her to me, falling to sleep, I knew that no one else would ever make me feel so full.

That was why I loved her. Indeed, that is why I love her still.

CHAPTER 17

★ ★ ★ ★ ★

I had been to Muntinglupa's Bilibid before.

In February I had traveled with MacArthur as he made the thirty-mile journey south from Manila to Muntinglupa on the day our soldiers liberated the old prisoner of war camp. It was at this Bilibid—the Filipino word for prison—that he first forced himself to peer into the faces of those he had left behind when he escaped to Australia. Or to be more precise, those from that ever-dwindling pool who survived more combat after his escape, then the death march down the Bataan Peninsula, and finally the harshness of captivity. More than 40 percent of the army that had surrendered after his escape, those who had already fought at Bataan and on Corregidor only to face the terrors of torture and captivity, had died as prisoners of the Japanese.

The faces into which MacArthur stared at Muntinglupa were like haunting mirrors, the dreadful forever after that combat commanders dream of only in their nightmares. Long rows of shocked, bulging eyes had peered curiously back at him, belonging to men who truly were half dead. They limped and shuffled when they walked. Their heads were perched loosely atop wrinkled pencils of necks. Ribs were countable. Clavicles protruded. Uniforms had dissolved into dingy gauze.

These were his once-proud soldiers. After he had greeted them he left the prison camp and forced our driver to take him far into the battle lines, telling us he needed to hear the sound of guns. In what he called an avenging moment he marched past a squad of frontline troops into direct range of Japanese machine-gun fire, daring his fate. But I knew it was not vengeance that impelled him toward those barking guns. Rather, it was guilt. He had left the battlefield three years before, under orders from Washington to be sure, but nonetheless he had deserted his soldiers to those guns, and his only expiation was to face them again and again until he was either forgiven or dead. In this mix of Christian and Asian that had become both his conscience and his spirit, each time he marched so recklessly forward he tested his Asian karma and then decided afterward that his Christian God was still sparing him for some even greater task.

As MacArthur was touring the just-liberated prisoner camp, I met an emaciated wisp of half-ghost who laconically informed me that he once had been a sergeant. He was a tall, teetering man with parched eyes and a voice that had been starved into a whisper. His hair had flecked into grey over the years of his captivity. It was impossible to discern his age, but he seemed somewhere between thirty and fifty. The sergeant wanted to show me a spiritual vision that he said had kept him alive. Despite myself I had recoiled slightly when he pulled on my sleeve, staining my just-cleaned fatigues with the filth of his captivity. And so I followed him, more out of embarrassment than curiosity, as he led me behind the run-down buildings to a place of stench and ruin.

Once in the rear yard, the sergeant pointed to a tree that from a distance reminded me of an oriental julep, rich with pink and orange blossoms. It seemed beautiful and fecund. He called the tree the Joshua tree. I do not know why.

The sergeant told me that for long months he had looked at the tree from the barracks bed where he had been left to die and had gained strength from its beauty. If the tree could thrive in these hateful times, he reasoned, then so could he. Then when he had regained his strength and his resolve, he had visited the tree, only to discover that the tree was dead. Its blossoms were not blossoms, but rather were large jungle-bred insects that clung to its twigs and branches by day and fed like green flies off the ever-increasing piles of nearby American corpses once the darkness fell.

Still, the feathery-voiced sergeant insisted that he had taken meaning from this grotesque anomaly. "Death regenerates into an ugly beauty," he informed me solemnly, as if he had rehearsed these lines in his heart a million times. "But even beauty feeds off of death. Do you understand? When I get home I will paint this tree and keep it in my living room."

I still do not know what he meant, or why he would want to rise every morning in his later years and stare at this haunting reminder of his terror. But this was the old Muntinglupa Bilibid: dead trees whose branches hosted clusters of cockroach-sized flying insects that fed and thrived off the carrion of American flesh, courtesy of a Japanese army that could not understand why any surrendering soldier would even want his family to know he was still alive after having disgraced them into succeeding generations by choosing surrender over an honorable death in battle.

The Muntinglupa Bilibid had been scrubbed, deloused, and sanitized by our army. The army was using the facility as one of the administration points for the repatriation of some fifty thousand Japanese soldiers who had survived the brutal combat that killed off a majority of their ranks. It was at Muntinglupa that I was sent to again meet General Tomoyuki Yamashita. If one chose to believe Sam Genius, the wages of the emperor's relatives at Nanking would soon be paid by this commoner general in Manila. But even if one did not agree with this theory, it was undeniable that the thought of this so-called Tiger of Malaya having a podium of any sort on Japanese soil put fear into both MacArthur and the Japanese imperial court. MacArthur had said it bluntly in the privacy of his office: Yamashita was not going home, other than as a pile of ashes inside a ceramic jar.

Yet at this moment I did not regret that reality, either. I had seen the corpses and the wreckage of Manila, and I had heard other, personal tales of senseless slaughter from Divina Clara's family. The retreating Japanese had gone on an insane rampage of bloodlust and chaotic ruin. These were not the leavings of battle, they were the sediments of mass murder piled on top of deliberate destruction.

Among my other errands, MacArthur had ordered me to meet with General Yamishita's American defense counsel, a courtesy call meant to make the supreme commander's presence felt all the way from Tokyo. MacArthur's outward justification was that I should discuss the convening orders for the special commission and assure that the preparation for trial was proceeding smoothly. The subtler message would be clear to any soldier involved in these proceedings: General MacArthur wanted Yamashita dead, and he was in a hurry.

Since MacArthur had also instructed me to conduct a physical inspection both of General Yamashita and of his living spaces, I arranged to perform both assigned tasks simultaneously. Captain Frank Witherspoon, Yamashita's principal lawyer, had offered to come to the Muntinglupa Bilibid and brief me on the case.

Witherspoon met me in the prison's small chapel, explaining that it was the only building capable through size and privacy to hold such a meeting. He was a spare, hawk-faced man in his early thirties, with red hair and the soft, slender hands of an academe. He was waiting for me as I walked into the chapel, sitting irreverently at the small pulpit just underneath a large cross on the wall. A statuette of Jesus was still nailed to the cross, which told me that I had entered a Catholic chapel, as Protestant churches showed only the cross. We simple Baptists, never able to afford such luxuries as statuettes in our little country churches, rationalized that He shouldn't be up there anyway, since He'd been taken off the Tower and carried inside a cave, where He had risen from the dead, rolled back the rock, and disappeared.

Witherspoon came to his feet when I entered the chapel and walked briskly to meet me. His eyes darted electrically all over me as we shook hands. He was taking everything in, looking for clues. Witherspoon was not a career soldier and had been slated to leave the Philippines before he had been brought into the Yamashita case. I had heard that he was a graduate of Harvard Law and that before the war he had been a top trial lawyer in Boston. He had a clear air of both money and authority about him as he grasped my hand.

"I'll get right to the point," he said, gesturing toward a pew where I took a seat. "This is a fucking mess."

Although he was older than I, we were of equal rank and neither of us were career soldiers. So there was no need for drawn-out formalities. I clutched my briefcase to my chest as I crossed a leg, and then laughed at his abruptness. "Do you know Colonel Sam Genius?"

"Why should I?"

"You've got a lot in common. He's in charge of the war crimes accountability section on the supreme commander's staff, and you just summed up his views on this case."

Witherspoon grunted, unimpressed. "Then he must be a lawyer with at least half a brain."

"He believes Yamashita should be tried in Tokyo next year, with the other major defendants."

"How about simply 'tried,' Captain? In a court of law?"

I carefully demurred. "Isn't that what they asked you to do?"

Witherspoon shot me a withering glare. "I said a court of law." He threw up his hands in exasperation. "Look, I've been ready to go home for a long time. The war is over, I've got a lucrative practice, and up until a week ago all I'd been doing was tracking down war claims for Filipino citizens whose houses were blown up or whose pigs got killed. But then they ask me to defend a man in an extremely complicated murder trial, and how can I say no?"

Witherspoon caught himself, as if he were a machine gunner about to waste a lot of ammunition on an irrelevant target. His eyes swarmed all over me again. "In what capacity are you here, Captain? I mean, will it do any good for me to go through this, or is this just a feel-good little chat?"

I shrugged casually, trying to be candid. "I'm a captain. MacArthur wears five stars. He wanted me to pay you a visit to make sure things are going smoothly, but I can't guarantee he'll listen to a word I say."

"He sent you down here to intimidate me, didn't he?"

Witherspoon was getting hot. I could sense immediately that if MacArthur wanted a quick trial with a doormat for a defense counsel, his legal staff had picked the wrong attorney. His eyes had a way of locking me into his gaze, just as physically as if he were holding me by the shoulders. "If this were even a real *court-martial* that would be undue command influence. It would be illegal."

"Look," I answered, "I'm down here because MacArthur wanted no misunderstandings. He wants General Yamashita tried, and he wants a speedy resolution to the case. If you want to shoot the messenger, fine. I'm just a running back from SC who heard about Pearl Harbor on the radio and went down and signed up for the army because ships make me throw up. OK? That's it. If MacArthur tells me to go, I go. If MacArthur tells me to report, I report. I don't know what's legal or not. And I may be taller than you, but I don't feel particularly intimidating."

"Cute," Witherspoon muttered. "The perfect General's weenie." He may as well have been spitting onto the floor.

I gave off an exaggerated sigh, trying to lighten him up. "Let's not get personal, all right? I could pick you up and break you in two, Witherspoon. But it wouldn't help either of us, would it? If you've got a problem tell me, and I'll bring it back to him."

He had not lost his look of disgust. "What are you to him? He doesn't need to hear from you about what I'm going through. Why the hell do you think he has a legal section? But he sent you for a reason. He's smart. So, why are you here?"

"I'm here because he sent me. That's the way I live these days." I could not fathom this unprovoked anger from a man I had never before met. I stood up from the pew, making to leave. "Look, don't overestimate your importance to Douglas MacArthur. Back home you may be a famous lawyer, but here in the army you're a puky little captain, just like me. Why would MacArthur waste his time wanting to intimidate you when he can scare the pants off of three-star generals? Maybe I'm offering you an avenue to the General, in case you felt you needed one. I'll just assume you feel like you don't need one."

"OK, maybe the asshole actually wants to hear the truth. Tell him this, Captain." Witherspoon's chin was raised defiantly. His eyes were ablaze. "Tell him I may be a puky little captain, but I'm not afraid of him, OK? Tell him I don't need a promotion and I don't need a good assignment when I go home, so there's nothing he can do to me. I've been given a job to defend a man against serious charges and I really don't give a rat's ass if my client is a yellow-skinned Nip general with slanty eyes and a shaved head. I don't care if people back in the States might think I'm a turncoat for trying to keep him from being convicted, either. They all hate lawyers, anyway, so what's new? Tell him that."

Despite myself and my reservations about Yamashita, I found that I was tingling with an odd satisfaction. I admired Douglas MacArthur immensely, but after nearly three years I was perhaps too aware of his obsessive need to be worshiped. And although I had often heard petty bickering, no officer had ever spoken so bluntly about him to my face.

"All right, Captain," I said, smiling ironically. "I'll leave out the 'asshole' part, but I'll tell him that. Anything else?"

Rather than slowing Witherspoon down, I seemed to have encouraged him. "Oh, leave it in. And there's a lot more. Tell him I've represented criminal defendants for nearly ten years and what he's doing is a sham. We're Americans, Captain. We're supposedly bringing an accused man into the American system of justice. This is a capital case. Yamashita's life is at stake. I know a lot of people died in this war, and life was cheap, but the war is over. Tell MacArthur if he wants to kill Yamashita, why hide behind us? Why doesn't he just come down here and shoot him in the fucking head?"

From the trial's convening order I had some idea of what Witherspoon was talking about, but still I did not comprehend the depth of his fury. I felt myself shrugging again. "He's getting a trial. Everything I've heard about you indicates that you're as good a defense lawyer as General Yamashita could ever hope to find. I'm sorry. I'm not a lawyer. I don't understand."

"That's exactly the fucking point." Witherspoon began pacing. "You're not a lawyer, MacArthur's not a lawyer, and this isn't a court! He's convened a military *commission!* It's *not—a—court.* It's his own little creation. A commission composed of five generals, less than a month after this war is over. Do you think any of them want the papers back home to say they were softies when it came to facing down a Nip general? And none of them are lawyers, either! I don't even have a military judge to object to on points of law, like I would in a regular court-martial, for Christ's sake! Do you think any of them are even going to understand the rules of evidence? Admissibility? Relevance? Probity? And MacArthur is the sole reviewing authority for their actions! Do you think they want to ruin their careers by pissing off their supreme commander? He's waived traditional rules of evidence. He's sent the prosecution team all over the countryside for months, gathering information about every Japanese atrocity that was committed during the war. He didn't appoint the defense counsel until *three days ago,* and then they dropped sixty-four sets of charges on Yamashita and expect us to be ready to go to trial within a few weeks! There's no way I'll ever be able to interview witnesses, break down the specifics of the charges, and connect them with the actions of my client. What do you call that? Tell me! What do you call it?"

Witherspoon stopped pacing. He was facing away from me now, looking up toward Jesus on the cross. He was breathing rapidly, genuinely upset. This was not the posturing of some high-priced defense counsel but rather the struggling of a man obviously torn. And yet I was torn, too.

"Did you see Manila, Captain?"

"Yeah, I saw Manila," he said. "But who did it?"

Witherspoon turned back around to face me. "These are complicated charges! They're not accusing him of pulling the trigger, you know. They're charging him with failing to discharge his duty as the commander of the Japanese army, that his actions were tantamount to permitting his soldiers to commit the atrocities. These are extremely intricate issues involving the laws of war. We're into areas that have no precedent. To what extent is a commander responsible for the acts of others?"

"I know something about the Japanese culture, Captain."

"Oh, yes," he said, still pacing agitatedly. "I hear you're quite the little linguist."

"I ought to kick your ass for that."

"Go ahead," he dared. "MacArthur will get you off."

"MacArthur would love it."

"Exactly my point."

"I know this," I said, deciding to ignore his sarcasm. "I know that Manila was at some level a payback, ordered from above. Japanese soldiers would not have gone on such a rampage unless they had at least the go-ahead from their superiors."

"Maybe," said Witherspoon, looking at me with a victorious sneer. "But who said these were Yamashita's soldiers?"

His comment caught me completely by surprise, as he had known it would. He pointed to a chapel window. On the other side, in the gathering darkness, we could see the sparse barracks of the Bilibid. "Yamashita had already pulled his soldiers out of Manila. He had declared it an open city and declined to fight there. He'd issued written orders to his soldiers against any form of atrocity. *Written orders!* When all this happened, he was hauling his ass through the mountains of central Luzon, fighting off twelve American divisions."

"There were soldiers in Manila, Captain. I was there. We killed a lot of them. I saw their bodies."

"I know you consider yourself an expert on the Japanese, Captain, but I'm telling you that you did not see Yamashita's soldiers. You saw sailors, and marines, and a few soldiers from local commands. None of them were under Yamashita's command. *None of them, not one!* They were under some admiral named Iwabuchi. Iwabuchi got a different set of orders from naval headquarters in Tokyo to destroy the port facilities, so they stayed in Manila. When Yamashita heard they'd stayed back in Manila he radioed them, ordering them a second time to get out of the goddamned city! Iwabuchi ignored him, because he had orders from Tokyo. So Yamashita's going to get fried for the acts of soldiers under his command, but the acts were committed by Iwabuchi's fucking degenerates. But Iwabuchi's already dead, so that doesn't satisfy your General's needs, does it?"

I found myself wondering whether Witherspoon had developed a quick case of "clientitis," as happens so often with well-meaning defense lawyers. I watched him with mild cynicism. "You've learned a lot in the past four days."

"Well, that's another thing." I had fired him up again. "The prosecution has been talking to Yamashita for nearly a month, without a defense lawyer present. Yamashita's got a staff member over in the barracks, a guy named Hamamoto, who speaks perfect English. It seems he graduated from Harvard in the class of twenty-nine, a few years ahead of me, then came back to Japan and worked for General Electric before the war. The prosecution has every single fact in this case. And even *they* don't dispute what I just said! They know as well as I do that it's not going to matter! Do you realize what this trial—if you can call it a trial—this *illegal, judgeless commission* is going to look like? It's going to be nothing but a public circus!"

Witherspoon had now stunned me into silence. I was not conversant in the finer points of the law, but still I felt somehow soiled by both his anger and his recitation of the facts. I spoke quietly. "I'll tell MacArthur."

"That'll do a lot of good," said Witherspoon, giving off a cynical, barking laugh. "He's the Svengali of this whole preposterous charade. But you do that. And when you're done, let me know what he said."

There was nothing else left to say. "I'm under orders to visit General Yamashita."

"He's expecting you." Witherspoon pointed out the window toward Yamashita's barracks. "The guard will bring you inside."

He stopped me as I began walking away. "One more thing."

I turned to him. "Yes?"

"A prediction."

Witherspoon's face held a grim look of prophecy. "Sooner or later, some American soldier in Tokyo is going to have too much to drink. And he's going to go out in the town like some big-time conquering hero, and he's going to rape a Japanese woman. Somebody might try to stop him, and maybe he'll fight that guy off and end up killing him. If that happens, the precedent your General wants to set in this case means that he should hang for it. MacArthur, not just the soldier who does it! Oh, yeah, he can say that he issued all the appropriate instructions against it, but if we're going to hold commanders accountable for all the acts of those under their general jurisdiction, MacArthur's a criminal every time one of his soldiers is! What are we doing here, Captain? Of all the bloodsucking criminals who did grotesque things in this war, why are we wasting our credibility as the United States of America on this man? And in God's name, *what is the hurry?*"

I looked at him for a moment. In truth I knew the answer, but as Court

Whitney might have put it, I was on the inside of the tent, pissing out. Clueing in Witherspoon would be to put my own head on the chopping block.

"Ask Sam Genius," I finally said.

"What good would that do?"

"Probably none."

"What are you going to do with Yamashita?" There was a protective tone in Witherspoon's question.

"MacArthur wanted me to pass on his regards."

"Then he is indeed an ass, isn't he?"

"He's my boss, Captain." Addled, my briefcase in tow, I headed out of the chapel toward the gloomy, silent barracks.

An odd mix of aromas that reminded me of battle seemed to surround General Tomoyuki Yamashita as I entered his room. Not cordite, not gunpowder, but the heavy, soldier's mix of sunbaked canvas, bad tobacco, and a nervous perspiration that inundated clothes and cots and the very grains of the barracks' wooden walls.

The prison guard who escorted me to the barracks told me that in Yamashita's first moments in the Philippines the previous October an American aircraft had strafed the general near Clark Field's runway, causing him to seek refuge in an open ditch that turned out to be a sewer, and that Yamashita had taken command while still wearing the same stench-filled uniform. The guard had told me the story as a jokeful boast of American military superiority, but I thought of that moment in a different way as I watched Yamashita rise from a small field desk and walk across the room to greet me.

The story seemed in perfect character with the demeanor of the man who was walking toward me. General Yamashita emanated calmness, an inner peace that would not be shaken by such externalities as physical discomfort or the judgments of others. His uniform had been filthy but he had proceeded to his command before tending to himself. General MacArthur, ever paranoid despite his brilliance, always concerned about his impact on the judgment of others, would surely have washed off and changed even if a battle were raging, not simply from hygiene concerns but because he would never have allowed himself to be photographed or seen by junior officers in such embarrassing garb.

As with the first time I had spoken with him, Yamashita emanated an unflappable serenity when he greeted me. He bowed slightly, then gestured toward the field desk, offering me his only chair. As I sat, he gave me a teasing smile.

"So, Captain Marsh, we meet again. Perhaps General MacArthur remains disappointed that I'm still alive?"

The general sat on the edge of his army cot, watching me expectantly. With one quick greeting he had again penetrated any facade that I might have brought to our meeting. Rather than setting me back, his unflappable sense of humor had quickly relaxed me, as if he were my host. Indeed, why posture? What would have been the point of double-talk and innuendo, anyway?

"He has accepted that reality, General." I looked around the room, and then back at him. "You're looking well."

He shrugged. "I am being treated with great courtesy, considering the circumstances. Although I must tell you, I am terribly disturbed by the circumstances."

"Captain Witherspoon told me about the charges."

"They are outrageous." His eyes locked into mine. His whole body seemed to twitch with a vast, unconquerable annoyance. "I had no knowledge of these events. I issued orders, you know."

"There will be a trial. You will have the chance to say that."

"Captain Witherspoon has been clear on that," he answered, regaining his full composure. "Although he is not optimistic."

I grew serious. "General MacArthur wants to make sure you understand the seriousness of the charges that have been brought against you. He also wants you to know that you can have other legal advice if you wish. You can even ask for a Japanese lawyer. We could bring you one from Tokyo."

An ironic gleam filled Yamashita's eyes, and he smiled again. "Captain Marsh, I am very fortunate to be represented by Captain Witherspoon. And you can imagine how well your military court would react to a lawyer we flew in from Tokyo?"

The ludicrous vision filled my mind. I pictured the absurdity of some bowing but argumentative Tokyo lawyer in his ill-fitting Western suit trying to argue through translators with five American generals about the rampant slaughter of Manila in the aftermath of this brutal war as the whole nation of Japan knelt with its nose on the ground to General

Douglas MacArthur. We suddenly found ourselves laughing together at the very thought. And I could not help but like this unpretentious man.

And then Yamashita himself became solemn. "But the charges, I do not understand. I have asked to hear more specifics. Captain Witherspoon has made a petition. I am being charged with failing to perform my duties as a military commander. I have asked them to tell me when? And where? I have never failed to perform my duties. You should please check the records. After the fall of Singapore I made certain that General Percival's soldiers who surrendered received good treatment. The policy changed when I was transferred back to Manchuria. But it was my policy. I was even reported to the imperial court with disfavor on these issues."

"For what?" I asked, my senses suddenly awakening with interest.

"For disciplining officers in my command who permitted battlefield atrocities," answered Yamashita. "Colonel Masanobu Tsuji, who ran a special operations unit in my command, was very close to the imperial family. He once tutored the emperor's youngest brother, Prince Mikasa. He lodged a formal protest against me to the imperial government. Many officials, including Prime Minister Tojo, claimed that I was betraying my own officers. But I have trained with the European armies, Captain, and I understand the Western view on these issues. You should please ask the American prisoners of war and internees who were held under my authority near Baguio. They will tell you. Last December I expended precious gasoline to take them all out of the area where I planned to make my final stand, so that they would not be killed in the fighting."

A memory lit my brain, from my sake-filled evening with Lord Privy Seal Kido. I could not restrain my curiosity. "Did you really propose an invasion of Australia?"

The general's ugly, furrowed face broke out into a nostalgic smile. Watching me with fresh respect, he took out a cigarette and lit it, tossing the match into an ashtray made from the casing of an old American tank round. "And may I ask, who told you this?"

"Koichi Kido."

"You've met the lord privy seal?"

"Many times," I answered.

Yamashita grunted cynically. "How is the old bastard?"

"Cunning," I said. We both laughed. It was clear to me that now we did have something in common. "For some reason he seems afraid of you."

"I would never embarrass the emperor," said Yamashita carefully. "But there are many who gave him bad advice."

We fell silent. He dragged slowly on his cigarette. His gaze was far away, lost in old memories. I could not restrain my curiosity. "Do you really think you could have taken Australia?"

The Tiger's eyes lit up. I could tell that in his mind he was not at that moment in an odorous, sweltering jail cell at Muntinglupa but instead was in Singapore at the moment of his greatest victory, the victory that forever reversed the notion that the Western fighting man could not be out-thought in a major battle. He peered at me with a quiet certainty.

"You should understand first that in July 1941 I returned from seven months in Germany and advised a two-year moratorium on any war plans. I had watched the European war. It was clear to me that our army was seriously deficient if Japan began a long campaign against Western forces. We had no paratroops, no good tanks, no long-range bombers, no radar. But I was told that an immediate war was inevitable. Many of our planners argued persuasively that the Americans and British empire forces were very weak in Asia and that Asia was not important to the Western powers. When the emperor made his decision, I carried out my orders. That was my duty, as a soldier. And I did not look back."

He hesitated, a careful, scrutinizing smile growing on his face. "Why did Kido mention Australia to you?"

"He said you were too independent," I answered. "Dangerous. And I think he believes it makes Tojo seem reasonable for not having done it."

The general chuckled ironically, obviously not one of Tojo's admirers. "And was it reasonable to send whole armies of Japanese soldiers out into the island jungles to die of disease and starvation while waiting to be either attacked or bypassed? We are a hygienic people, you know. We do not fare well in jungles."

He ground out his cigarette inside the tank casing, then shrugged. "After Singapore it was possible to take Australia. We had taken Bali and Timor. Our navy was perched on the northern coast of Australia. In February 1942 they had raided Darwin with impunity, sinking ten ships in the harbor and destroying nearly two dozen Allied aircraft. Only seven thousand regular Australian soldiers remained in the entire country. The rest were off fighting for the British empire in Europe, Africa, India, or in prisoner of war camps. The Americans had not yet arrived. Later that month I volunteered to lead an invasion. It was not an idle plan. We could have quickly landed a large force at Darwin, then used railroad and highway links to press all the way to Adelaide and Melbourne. Very soon thereafter, we could have landed a second force on the eastern coast and linked up in Sydney. Admiral Yamamoto agreed with this approach. Either we would have won quickly, forcing a settlement of the war, or we would have lost far fewer soldiers than we did in the island jungles later on. Tojo and his elders did not like this idea. So I was posted directly to Manchuria, without home leave in Tokyo. I remained there until they sent me here to the Philippines."

Watching his face, and hearing the almost mathematical certitude of his approach, I was left with an eerie certainty. Win or lose, this was a man whose vision and strategic grasp was on the scale of MacArthur's. And for the first time I comprehended the powerful effect that Tomoyuki Yamashita's moral leadership and simply put examples of lost strategic opportunities might have on the emotions of most Japanese if he were allowed to return to Tokyo for a proper trial.

We sat quietly for another moment, digesting the possibilities that Yamashita had laid out. I really had nothing else to say. MacArthur had told me to inspect him, and I had done that. I felt awkward, oddly overpowered by his contemplative presence, and still stung by Frank Witherspoon's angry tirade.

Near me on the desk was a fresh-clipped pile of fingernails. Yamashita noticed that I had glanced at them. He smiled whimsically, as if sharing a joke.

"I am facing a soldier's dilemma. Perhaps you would have some advice. It is our custom when we are cremated to send fingernail clippings and locks of hair to the family. But as you see, I shave my head every day. If I keep shaving my head, I will have no hair to send to my wife. But if I stop shaving my head, or leave one spot growing, my soldiers might think I have lost my self-respect."

He continued to smile, and I found myself smiling with him. The issue had increased our sense of camaraderie. It was a riddle that we might solve together. "You should wait until the trial is over," I finally decided. "Perhaps there will be no need."

"We should speak honestly about these things, Captain." He had not lost his smile. "But perhaps it would be better to wait, anyway. I would look foolish in the courtroom if I were growing hair."

"I must go," I finally said.

"You will please tell General MacArthur?"

"Tell him what, General?"

"That I do not understand these charges against my honor." His eyes continued to hold mine, as if he could peer through the retinas and read the message traffic in my brain.

"I will tell MacArthur," I said, reeling inside from my own dissembling.

"I thank you for that, Captain. If nothing else, General MacArthur is a fellow soldier. I know he dislikes me, and perhaps—may I say this?—he is somehow jealous of me. But I am certain he appreciates the place that honor holds in a true soldier's heart."

"Yes, he does," I said. "And now it is time for me to go."

I rose from his little chair, and he stood up from the cot and bowed again. "I hope you understand that it is not dying that worries me. In Japan we have a saying, 'life is a generation, but one's honor is forever.' I will die. I have now accepted that. But it is important to me that I not be remembered as one who failed in his honor."

"I understand," I said, waving good-bye to him as I left the dim-lit room. "I will tell MacArthur."

I was gloomy in the car on the way back to Manila. I tried to console myself with the knowledge that in a few hours I would again be in Divina Clara's arms, but that usual consolation did little to stifle a growing uneasiness. For I had decided that I did indeed understand it all, and especially Douglas MacArthur's true motivations, far too clearly.

Sam Genius was not wrong—shifting attention from the rape of Nanking, with Sam Genius's hit list of royal conspirators, was important, both to MacArthur and to the emperor. But the possible impact of Tomoyuki Yamashita's return to Japan, where he might state his case before the same international tribunal that General Tojo and the others would face in a few months, was more than the supreme commander or the emperor either one could bear. Dead or alive, the stoic, patient Yamashita would survive that forum as a national hero, one whose vision, dignity, and exploits might overshadow every other figure in the Pacific war.

Every other figure. The imperial government might never live down Yamashita's clear-eyed predictions that the course they had chosen for the war was doomed from the beginning. And more important, Douglas MacArthur could never destroy Yamashita's reputation as a principled and brilliant battlefield general. So instead, Yamashita would be kept in the Philippines, to be tried before a panel of nonlawyer military careerists, whose very purpose would be to destroy his honor.

CHAPTER 18

★ ★ ★ ★ ★

Marquis Koichi Kido was struggling, climbing up the steps. Many, many steps, carved into the mountainside. A thousand steps, at least. They curved slalomlike as they terraced up the steep, rocky slope, swaying back and forth past ancient pines and through the shade of endless, big-leafed hardwood trees. Stone *toro* lanterns bordered the walkway, like miniature street lamps. Shinto prayer sticks lettered with *kanji* blessings mixed among the rocks. We were not the first to make this silent pilgrimage.

We were near the top. The sky was cloudless, as blue as robin's eggs. The air was crisp and cool, the freshest I could ever remember breathing. Far below us I could see the sparkling beaches of the famed resort town of Atami and after that the endless and inviting sea. Looking south, in my fresh nostalgia I could imagine the sea growing warmer and more turquoise, filling with flying fish and giant eels, then rubbing up against the edges of Luzon, where at this time of year the rain-laden rice fields seemed to melt back into it as if the island were tilting, water meeting water. But from this hallowed point of origin, the sea in Kido's mind went further west, not south. He had brought me here to talk about Nanking.

Kido would climb perhaps twenty steps at a time and then stop, sucking in the cool mountain air with deep gulps as he caught his breath. Ever the peacock, he was wearing puffy-thighed, tight-ankled English riding pants and a rich brown woolen sweater. He had tucked the bottom of the pants into well-polished, knee-high leather boots. When he had arrived at my hotel to pick me up that morning, I had not been able to suppress a laugh as he stepped out of the emperor's plum-colored Daimler limousine, dressed in such fanciful garb. But my laugh seemed actually to have pleased the lord privy seal, causing his shocked eyes to widen and a smile to crease his own face. He clearly did not mind seeming to be almost a caricature of Western aristocratic taste.

Now Kido gulped in more air. His skin was going ashen. The nearer we came to the top of the mountain, the more ghostlike he had become. I was beginning to realize that only a part of this hesitation was physical. A surprise awaited me around the next few turns, something powerful and even monumental, and the lord privy seal had bet an emotional bundle on the impact it would have on me.

"Are you feeling all right, Lord Privy Seal?"

"Of course I am," he answered. He stiffened his back, raising his chin into the air as he breathed. "I am stopping only for my health, Captain Jay Marsh. The air is so clean here that I am washing out my lungs."

"I have noticed that," I answered. "It is a great feeling after the constant dust of the city."

"A worthwhile journey, yes?" said Kido. He pointed upward. "And now we are almost there."

Resolutely, he put his head down and marched forward, and again I followed in his trace. Kido had told me nothing of our destination. In a curious mix of flattery and cunning, he had said only that it would allow me to "understand." Up the endless steps we went, heading for the mountaintop. The mountain narrowed near its crest. On the far side I began to hear faint music, the low, melancholy plunking of hands against a hollow bamboo tube, accompanied by a sad, high-pitched female voice. In the lonely isolation of the mountain, the music and the woman's voice seemed to be emanating from the trees and rocks themselves, fluttering inside the gentle wind.

The steps ended. We had reached a level, graveled terrace. Kido stopped for a moment, catching his breath again, and then bowed slightly to me. He gestured invitingly toward the other side of a rocky knoll, from which the music was coming.

"So," he said. "We are here. And now you will see. Go ahead!"

Hesitantly, I began walking through a thick stand of young pines, in the direction he had waved. The music and singing grew louder, as if some unseen hand were turning up the volume. On the far side of the pines I reached a clearing, where an open, houselike shrine revealed itself. The shrine fit naturally into the mountain. It had been built low and wide out of dark, hard wood. A polished wooden prayer rail ran across its entrance, flanked by two large, smoking pots of incense. On the far end of the rail from where I walked was a lectern, and on the lectern sat a thick, well-signed guest book. Strands of brightly colored paper dangled like kite tails from the roof's wide and curving eaves. The dancing strands were sending messages of comfort to the spirits of the dead.

The shrine's entrance was open, without windows or doors. On the walls inside were countless mementos of Japan's war in China—photographs of towns and camps and long-dead soldiers, pieces of uniforms, maps that clearly showed the imperial army's invasion route from the port of Shanghai up the Yangtze River to Nanking. And in the center of the room, cradling the bamboo tube as she knelt in the *seiza* position on a white cushion before the altar itself, was the singing, chanting woman.

Her long face remained perfectly still as her eyes followed my approach to the altar. She seemed leery and yet unbending, as if she were a she-wolf protecting her den. She wore a flowing white kimono, which covered her traditional red *hakama* slacks. Her grey-streaked hair was very long, pulled away from her face and down until it ended in one large, gathered curl at the base of her hips. I sensed immediately that she was the priestess of this shrine.

Even in this isolated place I knew that it would be shameful to fail to respect the dead. Nearing the prayer rail, I stopped first at one of the smoke pots. As Yoshiko had taught me on other journeys, I leaned into the pot, curving my arms around the smoke, waving my hands and pulling it toward my face to cleanse my presence. Then I stood solemnly at the prayer rail, clapping my hands three times to awaken the spirits of the dead, and bowed to the priestess.

Watching this foreigner present himself, the old woman's face lit with a flash of surprise and even fear. But her hesitance quickly abated when she recognized the lord privy seal, who had finally reached the top of the mountain and was now standing in my wake. She smiled, ceasing her music, and bowed nose-down on the shrine's wooden floor.

"Marquis Koichi Kido, adviser to the emperor, keeper of the lord privy seal," she sang with the same chant she had been using in her singing, "I welcome you once more to the Shrine of Remorse. On behalf of all our ancestors and the family of Iwane Matsui, we are deeply honored that you are again visiting us."

Kido had also embraced the smoke. Now he returned the slightest of bows, not much more than a nod, indicating his high position. "I have brought my American friend," he said simply. "He is the only man on General MacArthur's staff who truly understands our culture. It is important that he comprehend the measures we have already taken to atone for the suffering of Nanking."

Raising her face, she now looked fully at me, moving her head this way and that as if peeking around the corners of my body into my soul. Her aged, opaque eyes twinkled for a moment. "I have never met an American before! He is so big! And look, he does have red hair! But I think this boy is too young to understand our enlightenment, Lord Privy Seal."

"To start with, he understands every word we are saying," said Kido, bringing an embarrassed shock to her face. "And he is much older than he looks. Did you see him present himself to the altar? Wait until you hear him speak! No foreign accent, only a slight Osaka dialect! May I explain to you that he has already sat in the presence of the emperor himself?"

At the mention of my meeting with the emperor the priestess again bowed deeply, looking to the floor for several seconds. When she raised her head, she was watching me with new respect as Kido continued.

"The divine spirits work in mysterious ways," said Kido. "I believe he has been Japanese for two thousand years, and American for only twenty-four. I believe he has been sent to us by the emperor's ancestors to help us explain ourselves to the supreme commander."

Watching Kido's stern face as he made this comment, I struggled to discern whether he was belly talking to me or pandering to the priestess. And then it occurred to me with a chill that he actually believed what he was saying.

And so did she. She scrutinized me for a few more seconds, then bowed deeply once again, this time to me.

"Ah, so. It is in our teachings. Such miracles do occur. I welcome you also, sir. And tonight I will pray for a blessing from the spirits who showed you to us."

Standing with them in the temple on top of the mountain overlooking Atami, I felt suddenly vested with enormous power. A part of me wanted to believe that this fantasy which Kido had mentioned and the priestess had accepted might actually be true. It had its logic. After all, what do we really know about spirits? At that moment the mountain wind pressed against me, unseen but real, a force of energy that brought heat and cold, that carried dust and pollen from one village to the next. Could not the invisible journeys of the soul do the same thing, carrying forward the energy and memories from generations past? And if the Japanese had believed sincerely in the kamikaze, the divine winds that had repelled the massive Chinese invading fleets from their shores—not once, but twice, in 1274 and 1281—could they not also conclude that a divinely sent spirit might now inhabit the body of a young American?

Perhaps so, perhaps not. As for me, I could not help but think that if the spirits had planned to inject themselves into an American body to help save Japan, they could have started in a better place than the wilds of eastern Arkansas. But it did not matter. I had gained new, real power, just from the reality that Kido might even pretend to think it. Either way—if the lord privy seal was sincere or if he was merely maneuvering me with such awesome flattery—he also was deliberately putting himself into a position of attaching some great, symbolic importance to my presence. I had been chosen, and an odd drama was about to play itself out.

I returned the old woman's bow. "In truth, gentle priestess, I am here only as the lord privy seal's guest. But I am deeply moved by the confidence he has shown in me, and awed to be in your presence at this shrine."

"Indeed," she said, peering at Kido, "he speaks with no accent."

"I speak your language poorly," I demurred. "But I am flattered that you so fully understand."

"Ah, so." She smiled broadly, nodding again to Kido, a recognition that I knew how to accept a compliment properly.

I waved toward the emptiness that surrounded us. "What is it that you do here, all alone on top of this mountain?"

"I weep," she said simply.

"For whom?" I asked.

"For the dead of Nanking."

"How long have you been doing this?"

"Since 1938," she answered, looking west toward Nanking on the far end of the distant sea. "More than seven years. Every day, from dawn to dusk. This is my temple."

"Why do you weep?" I asked.

"Because it is my duty." She glanced at the mementos that lined the shrine's inside walls. "And the duty of my family."

I remembered the way she had greeted the lord privy seal. Her welcome had been made on behalf of the family of Iwane Matsui. "You are of the family of General Matsui, who was the commanding general in central China."

"Yes," she answered quietly. "I weep on his behalf, for he is in truth a most honorable man. A great man, who has been misunderstood. A friend of the Chinese people. I weep to remove the shame and to purify the future." She slowly turned away from me, beginning a hymnal chant.

I felt a moment of confusion. I had heard Sam Genius speak of Matsui's having been pulled out of retirement and posted to China, of his tubercular illnesses that had hospitalized him once he arrived, and of the "promotion" that had actually removed him from any direct authority. And of Prince Asaka, the emperor's uncle, having commanded the troops inside Nanking itself.

"But General Matsui was not the commander at Nanking?"

She continued the chant, not answering.

Kido stepped forward. "Yes he was!" he interjected quickly. "Yes, also at Nanking!"

She finished the chant and began singing again, completely ignoring us as she slapped low tones out of her hollow bamboo instrument. Kido took me by the arm, pulling me toward the far side of the shrine.

"There is more. You must see it," he demanded.

We left the terrace, walking for a few hundred feet along a dirt path that had been worn through the underbrush. To our left the mountain dropped sharply down. A thousand feet below us the vista opened up, showing the pristine beaches and bustling seaside of Atami. Kido pointed earnestly in front of us as we walked toward some object that I could not see. We made a tight turn past a column of large boulders. And then with an abruptness we were standing at the feet of a large, glazed statue.

"Kanon," said Kido as we reached it. "Do you recognize her? The goddess of mercy."

I stared at the statue for a long time, trying to appreciate its power. It lacked the intricate detail that informed so much Japanese art. The ugly, mustard-colored clay that was its base showed crudely through the glaze. Nonetheless, its place on the hillside, with the mountains surrounding it and the sea-swept vista below it, gave it a grand, breathtaking aura. From her promontory the robed Buddhist goddess was gazing off into the distance, far to the west. Just as the singing priestess of the shrine wept only for atonement, here Kanon, the goddess of mercy, stared eternally out to sea, forever focused on Nanking.

"It was made in 1938," announced the lord privy seal. "At the same time the shrine was built. We are on General Matsui's family grounds. This is his personal expression of apology, to the Japanese people and to the people of China as well. Half of the statue is made from Japanese clay. The other half is made from mud taken out of the banks of the Yangtze River. The mud was carried back to Japan in sacks, after the unfortunate incident at Nanking. The mud of China was mixed in with the mud of Japan until the two soils were undistinguishable, just as our two countries will always be different but intertwined. From this clay was carved the goddess of mercy. They are baked together, inside the same glaze. It is our way. Do you understand, Captain Jay Marsh? Do you recognize the importance of what I am saying?"

"I think so." I was too overwhelmed to say any more.

"Then let me ask you this," said Kido, his shocked eyes staring bluntly into my face. "We are not a shameful people. We do not lack honor. What is it that your war crimes trials would accomplish that we have not already done for ourselves?"

I suspected that there was an answer, but I did not have it. Finally he nudged me, pointing down the well-worn path to a place on the other side of the statue.

"Over here."

I followed him along the winding, rock-strewn path for another twenty yards. We turned inland, away from the sea, and came upon a second white-graveled pavilion. At the center of the pavilion a tiny woman, shriveled with age, was sitting on a bench underneath a simple wooden canopy. Seeing us, she rose and bowed deeply, pressing her hands prayerfully together at the bottom of her chin. From her shaved head and flowing blue robes I could tell that she was a Buddhist nun. She had no doubt been sent to the top of this mountain to tend to the well-being of the goddess Kanon.

I pressed my hands underneath my own chin, lowering my head as I greeted the old woman. Smiling peacefully, she went to a nearby well and began drawing us a bucket of fresh water.

"So it is clear," said Kido as we stood on the windswept mountaintop in the shade of the canopy.

The silent nun returned and I bowed, thanking her as she handed me a stone cup filled with water. As I spoke, she served Kido as well. "Lord Privy Seal, I must tell you that in your country, nothing is ever clear."

Kido chuckled, seemingly delighted at my response. "Ah, so. Then I will help you. You must tell MacArthur that the lawyers are wrong about Prince Asaka."

He eagerly drank his water, then looked at me with an air of absolute authority. "As you can see, General Matsui accepted responsibility for Nanking long before there was a war with the Western powers. Before we had ever even heard of such a thing as the Potsdam Declaration, or war crimes trials. This shows you that as a culture we have already considered the unfortunate actions of some of our soldiers. And it should help you understand that Prince Asaka had nothing to do with it."

"There is evidence," I answered. "Our lawyers have examined many documents, including personal diaries—"

"Diaries!" he laughed. "Including mine! You cannot rely on diaries. I lie in my diary all the time."

"The majority of your other documents seem to have been destroyed," I said dryly. "General LeMay's firebombs apparently possessed a special ability to land directly on top of government files."

"The lasting effect of your bombs is remarkable, is it not?" Kido smiled brightly, ignoring my sarcasm. "But we have recently found some additional documents. I will give them to you tomorrow. They show clearly that the emperor's uncle was only present at Nanking in a ceremonial role. He was not in command. He was the emperor's representative to celebrate the conquest of the city. That is all!"

I had no doubt that the "additional documents" Kido's people had just "found" would directly contradict the evidence that Sam Genius was deriving from secondary sources. And although our investigators were having great difficulty making such distinctions, I felt certain that these new documents would also turn out to be recent forgeries. The Japanese were too well organized. If these were original documents helpful to the Japanese case, they would have been given to our staff weeks before.

I shook my head, indirectly signaling that I did not believe the lord privy seal. "We have many documents, such as your diary. Some are indicating that the killings were in fact ordered from above, and perhaps that the prince had been sent to make sure they took place."

"A total misunderstanding," sighed Kido.

"In any event, I'm sure the court will take your new documents into account," I answered obliquely.

"Do you know that our constitution precludes the prince from being charged?"

I suppressed a smile. "Then I'm sure the court will take that into consideration as well."

"I am serious!"

The tiny old nun had seen that the lord privy seal was finished with his water. She shuffled over and again stood before him, her hands pressed together underneath her chin. He abruptly handed her his stone cup. "I make this point because we agreed to end the war only if the Allied powers recognized that our system of government would remain intact. The Meiji Constitution requires that all responsibility for the exercise of the emperor's powers be assumed by the ministers of state and other organs. Prince Asaka was at Nanking only as the emperor's representative."

"What if we prove that he ordered the killings?"

Kido frowned, as if I were a dunce. "I told you, he did not! So how could such a falsehood be proved? But even if he had given improper orders on the battlefield, he could not be charged. He is the emperor's uncle. At Nanking he was protected by the emperor's sovereignty. That is our constitution! General Matsui understood this. That is why he gladly accepted responsibility."

I stared incredulously at him. "You mean that someone else must always take responsibility if the emperor or his family violates the law?"

"It is impossible for them to violate the law," said Kido. "I just explained this to you. This is our constitution!"

"The supreme commander is changing the constitution, Lord Privy Seal. You know that."

Kido grunted, staring stubbornly out toward the sea. "We must talk about that as well, Captain Marsh. Soon! General MacArthur has become—most enthusiastic on those points, but he cannot change our constitution by himself! He knows this. He can propose changes, but our government must accept them. And the emperor must agree."

"He is very adamant that he wants changes, Lord Privy Seal. But of course he wishes to make them with the emperor's concurrence."

"We shall see," said Kido. I could tell that he was working to suppress a growing irritation. "There will be time for us to work on that issue as well, you and I. But not today." He forced a smile, remembering his mission in bringing me to this mountain shrine. "For now, please remember that this debate about accountability in Nanking already took place, seven years ago! We addressed the problem. Our nation is a family. The emperor would never abuse his position to the detriment of those who serve him. It would bring him great heartache."

"But what about his uncle? I must say to you, Lord Privy Seal, that Prince Asaka has a somewhat savage reputation."

Kido sighed. "We cannot change the past, Captain Jay Marsh. You would be making a very bad mistake to be charging the emperor's uncle. It could affect many other things. Please tell this to MacArthur."

"I will do that." I handed my own cup back to the old woman. I had no need to go into this with Kido, but I knew that on this issue he had an ally in the supreme commander. "And what about General Yamashita?"

"He is in the same position as General Matsui."

"Unfortunately that is not true," I answered, thinking of Yamashita's powerful intensity during our discussion in the odorous, sweat-stained prison cell of Muntinglupa. "General Yamashita is not accepting responsibility. He is adamant that these charges insult his honor."

"I told you, he is dangerously independent."

"He said to give you his greetings," I said, feeling mischievous. "He said you were an old bastard."

"Ha!" Kido laughed abruptly, as if caught in the middle of some minor misdemeanor. "This is what I mean! Tomoyuki Yamashita is no younger than I am. That he should say such things!"

I grinned broadly, enjoying Kido's sudden discomfort. "Well, at least he didn't accuse you of being dangerously independent."

The lord privy seal grinned slyly, as if appreciating my wit. "Very good, Captain Jay Marsh. Very clever, indeed. But it does not matter. The supreme commander has removed General Yamashita's case from any Japanese participation. It has become an American military problem. So his fate is left only to General MacArthur, isn't it?"

I shrugged, dropping it. For all his apparent dislike of General Yamashita, Kido was indeed correct. By setting up the special military commission and keeping the trial in the Philippines, MacArthur had removed the case from any further Japanese argument, much less jurisdiction.

Finally I checked my watch. "We should go? It is a two-hour drive back to Tokyo. And first we must climb down from the mountain."

"Oh, going back is never a problem!" The lord privy seal was suddenly buoyant. "And anyway, we must make a stop in Atami. I have some private business to attend to."

I stifled a groan, wishing to be done with Kido and to get back to Tokyo. "I've been away for more than a week, Lord Privy Seal. I have many obligations to the supreme commander that I must catch up on."

"I will not be long."

We began walking back along the path that would take us down the steep, winding steps to the base of the mountain. Soon we passed near the shrine. The priestess watched us, kneeling on her cushion, twisting her long hair in her hands as if she were holding Rapunzel's rope. I waved good-bye to her. She smiled, tossing her hair behind a shoulder and picking up her bamboo instrument. And as the wind whistled through the trees I could hear her begin once more to sing.

Kido grinned conspiratorially to me, elbowing me as we walked. "We will be back before midnight. And I think you will not object that I have arranged for you to be entertained while I am off on my own?"

It had already turned dark when we reached Atami. The moon was behind us, just above the mountain. Looking up I saw that it was casting a glow over the goddess of mercy as she stood watch near General Matsui's Nanking shrine. The stars were coming out one at a time, so bright they seemed to crack their way into the sky. The town had already grown quiet. Long rows of paper lanterns hung in front of the inns and houses that crowded against its narrow, winding streets. The beaming lanterns marked our way, illuminating the roadside as if it were a yellow brick road.

Off to the south and east I could hear the sea waves crashing as the moon pulled in the tide. A heavy salt spray mixed with the wind, filling the air with rainlike sparkles and the smells of seaweed and dead shellfish. We turned a corner. On the left side of the road I could now see the ocean. A handful of people still walked the beach, only their silhouettes visible in the gathering dark. Seagulls and cormorants played in the air and along the edges of the water. Far in the distance I could see a pier.

Suddenly I missed my mother, with a completeness that told me she may as well be dead. The rumbling bounces of the old car, the odors of the sea in a crisp and lonesome autumn wind, the unknown of the darkened buildings we were passing, the distant, cobweb shadows of the pier, all combined to remind me somehow of the first night I had come to Santa Monica. It had only been ten years before, but that past life now seemed so surmounted as to have become unreachably in my past, even in a memory. Indeed, sitting in the old Daimler with the emperor's most trusted adviser dozing next to me, the thought of having once been a bewildered refugee out to the West Coast from Arkansas seemed even more improbable than Kido's dream that I had been chosen by the emperor's ancestors to be their vehicle for gaining the understanding of MacArthur.

Looking out at the strange but serene normality of Atami, I realized that I might never see my mother again. This was it, the Ever After, happily or not. I had gone everlastingly Asian. A part of my forever-world was passing by my window, lit only by the glow of paper lanters, just as the rest of it waited patiently for me in the sultry, flower-lush gardens of Manila. I might once have been any number of other things, from farmer to salesman to philosopher, but all that had been bombed away at Pearl Harbor. Yes, I thought, not unpleasantly, I was born at Pearl Harbor. And I was not at all unhappy with the miracle of what I had become.

The car stopped at a very old inn. The rear of the building backed up to a bluff that overlooked the sea. Below it was a grotto of rocks and sand. The surging sea waves crashed against the grotto, spewing cold salt spray high into the air. As Kido and I exited the car, the salt spray covered us like a gauzy curtain.

"Ah!" cried the lord privy seal. He fretted as we walked, seeking to brush away the wetness from his sweater. "This is Scottish wool, you know? Very difficult to find these days! But it is all right. The spirits are surging at us from the sea tonight! A good sign, Captain Jay Marsh! A very good sign."

The front doors of the inn opened before we reached them, as if the smiling, bowing old man who was its keeper had been standing patiently behind them for hours, awaiting our arrival. Yoshiko was behind him, half hidden just inside the doorway, dressed in a sea blue kimono. Seeing me, she smiled sweetly, her eyes secretly delicious in her anticipation. She bowed, then took my hand, welcoming me inside.

"Hello, Jay Marsh. I am so happy that you came tonight!"

She was beautiful, I could not deny it, and I knew the promises that lay behind the expectation in her eyes. She was the very embodiment of both good and evil, and that was my dilemma. She had a way of making me feel all-powerful at the very moment that I felt ashamed. And Father Garvey would not understand, but I also felt oddly responsible for Yoshiko. It was I, not she, who had set all this in motion. I had first chosen her with my eyes. At some level her very future depended upon Lord Privy Seal Kido's knowledge that she pleased me.

"Hello, Yoshiko. You look very beautiful tonight. How is it that you're here in Atami?"

She looked away coyly, covering her mouth as she smiled. "Sometimes I stay here for weekend relaxation."

I smiled back to her, even as I was silently cursing Kido. "Well, then we should have dinner together."

I knew exactly what would happen once I entered the inn. She would take me down a flight of stairs into a private room. She would slide a bamboo wall, opening our room up to the wild, dark beauty of the grotto and the fresh smells of the sea. There would be a deep *furo* bath carved into the stone floor. She would fill it and carefully take off her kimono. I would undress—yes, without being prodded—and sink slowly into the scalding water. She would climb into the *furo* with me and then bathe me until I was numb from the heat and from the strength of her kneading fingers. She would feed me tasty niblets as I soaked, giving me little sips of beer or sake to wash down the food. Then she would take me to a futon and make love to me until all my energy was sapped.

A part of me thrilled in this knowledge. Another, greater part angrily whispered its condemnation of my elation. But it did not matter. Walking inside the inn, I surrendered to its inevitability. This was the world I had inherited. This was my reality. I, more than Yoshiko, had become the prostitute. I was the emissary of MacArthur. I was the messenger to MacArthur. I had assumed an importance, false or otherwise, that I did not even fully understand. And until I was freed from this burden, it would be both my wages and my reward to undergo the very pleasures that I guiltily condemned.

Kido had stopped at the doorway. Now he was checking his watch. "My business will be done in two hours. That will be enough time for you to have a full and enjoyable dinner?"

She was kneeling at my feet, taking off my shoes. Her hands were strong and sure along my ankles. I did not want to feel this way, but watching the contours of her neck and the smooth lines of her back, I was already wildly aroused. "Two hours will be fine, Lord Privy Seal."

"Excellent!" he said. "And so I hope you will find the pleasures of Atami greatly to your liking."

My shoes were off. She had stood, and was taking me by the hand again. We reached the stairway that led down to our private room. The sea waves crashed and swirled inside the nearby grotto, making me feel as though she was leading me into a mysterious underwater kingdom.

Before I went downstairs I stared one last time out through the still-open doorway. Kido waved to me, climbing back into the car. Watching his knowing, possessive smile, I decided that I hated him. He was playing to my weakness. I could not deny my own responsibility. But still I vowed that, no matter what else became of me, before I left Japan I would make sure that his condescending grin forever disappeared.

CHAPTER 19

★ ★ ★ ★ ★

S omething funny happened while you were gone, monkey boy. Funny odd, not funny ha-ha."

Thus summoned, I walked into the legal office and sat comfortably across from Colonel Sam Genius. He was alone in the room, his two assistants having left for meetings outside the Dai Ichi building. His elbows were on his desk, pushing into a disorganized pile of papers. He leaned forward, working his hands over his face and along the top of his head. His uniform was so sweaty and wrinkled that it looked like he had slept in it. But he was fixing me with one of those I'm-going-to-Princeton grins that the smartest kid in the class always reserves for the competitor schoolmate who barely misses out.

I smiled back, refusing to take his bait. "Stop pulling on your hair like that, Colonel. You'll be bald by the time they send you home."

"Oh, no," he said, his smile turning glorious and secretive. "I can guarantee you I will have approximately this much hair when I leave the good General behind."

"You're getting transferred."

He shook his head, but it had been a fair surmise. Except for those few of us who were being held in Japan after our personnel files were stamped "essential to the occupation," the men who had served MacArthur during the long journey to Japan were gone. The war had ended less than two months before, but already a majority of the occupation army were soldiers fresh from the States, who had never before been overseas. And half of MacArthur's ever-burgeoning staff were new civilians, arriving fresh-faced and goo-goo eyed on every new flight from Washington. The sprawling bureaucracy he was creating inside the Dai Ichi building would soon require a 278-page phone book.

"No," answered Genius. "He's not letting me go that easily. But I'll tell you what I do have. I have the *answer*." Noting my blank stare, he leaned even further across his desk. "The puzzle," he said. "I finally solved it. The third piece fell into place."

He picked up a paper from his desk, as if wishing to tantalize me with it. "You know the rule of threes, don't you? In philosophy, I mean? Like— thesis, antithesis, synthesis?"

"Oh, sure. You mean, for instance—yin and yang?"

"Cut that shit out, Marsh. You've definitely gone Asian. Anyway, it finally makes sense. I know what the old guy is doing."

"Well that's good, because in an hour you're going to be briefing him again."

He rolled his eyes, feigning surprise. "And I thought you came down here because you missed me." Now he leaned forward, still trying to provoke me. "Don't you want to know what the third piece is?"

"I don't even know what the first two are."

"Of course you do. Nanking and Yamashita. Piece number one: he'll do anything to keep from having to go after the real perpetrators at Nanking. And piece number two: he'll do anything to hang Yamashita as fast as he can find a rope, and a tree branch to throw it over. So what's next?"

I stared at Genius for a few seconds, trying to shift into the disheveled lawyer's world. It was early in the morning of my first day back. My mind was still cluttered with thoughts of Manila and Divina Clara, of Atami and Kido and Yoshiko, of mountain shrines, perfumed gardens, tobacco-stained barracks, of steam-hot *furos* on the edges of the ocean, satin sheets in the perfumed night air, women I did not deserve and the price I knew that somehow, someday, I would have to pay.

The third piece? What the hell was he talking about? "Uh—I don't know. But I'll bet it isn't the emperor."

"Well, right and wrong." Genius chuckled, enjoying his little mystery. "You're right that he won't be going after the emperor. But you're wrong that it isn't *about* the emperor. Hey, this is Japan. Everything's about the emperor, whether MacArthur likes it or not. Here's what he figures, mark my words. First, he's doing the emperor a big favor by steering clear of Nanking. And second, the imperial court agrees with him about keeping Yamashita out of the country and away from the larger war crimes tribunal, so they're doing each other a big favor on that one." He threw his hands up into the air as if the whole thing had become simplistic. "OK, add that up. What do you have?"

"Yamashita's dead. And Prince Asaka is not."

"Think bigger!" He watched my still-puzzled face for a second, then grunted. "Clearly math is not the monkey boy's best subject. What you have is a net loss. An imbalance! Nanking is a win for the emperor. Yamashita is a wash. So what does MacArthur want?" He didn't wait for me to answer. "He wants a win, and in fact he's been planning for it all along! The emperor owes him!" Genius paused, becoming tutorial. "And where does he want this win?"

A particle of conversation with Kido during our trip to Atami floated into my consciousness. "The new constitution."

He pointed triumphantly at me. "Bingo. Exactly. All the changes he's been talking about since the day he landed at Atsugi."

"Not Atsugi," I said, remembering MacArthur's lectures during the dark, wet nights after we landed at Leyte. "Since Tacloban. His seven-point plan. Freedom of the press, giving women the vote, busting the *zaibatsu*, eliminating militarism, creating trade unions—"

"OK," said Genius, gaining energy as he watched me. "All that stuff. He's been covering the emperor in honey and oil, thinking that this was going to be easy. You know, 'I'll protect you and your family from being charged with war crimes, and in exchange for my having saved the imperial family, you back me when I reform your entire society.' But guess what? The emperor doesn't see that as a fair trade. He doesn't want to deal."

My mind had come fully alive now. "I interpreted when the emperor met with him at the embassy, remember? He scared MacArthur. I saw it. Behind that befuddled gaze is a very tough guy, Colonel."

"And I thought you said MacArthur wasn't afraid of anything."

"He didn't stay scared for long. Neither of them did."

"The great minds meet," quipped Genius, staring mockingly up into the sky. "Blood is on the floor, but deals are made. Ah, someday they will teach this in history classes around the world."

He shifted his gaze, staring acidly at me again. "Back to the ugly reality. Here's what we've got. While you were gone, MacArthur made his first move on the constitution. He published a directive called JCS 10. Kind of like a test case, you know? It doesn't change the Meiji Constitution as a document, but it overrides it during the occupation for as long as he decides it should. He's lifted all restrictions on civil, political, and religious conduct, ordered the release of all political prisoners, and abolished the secret police. He also *ordained*—you like that word? Kings use it—that newspapers can publish stories on any subject whatsoever. They can even criticize the emperor—so long as they don't in any way denounce the supreme commander." He was grinning again. "And you know what?"

"They didn't like it," I said, beginning to see where Genius was heading. "That's why Prime Minister Higashikuni resigned. I read about that in Manila."

"Exactly," said Genius. "MacArthur crossed the invisible line. The next morning, Higashikuni—remember, he ran the Japanese air force back in '37 when they ordered the mass bombings of civilians that preceded the rape of Nanking—he storms into the Imperial Palace and resigns. It was quite a show. Lots of splash in the press. But it was all play-acting, monkey boy. A symbolic gesture meant to signal that the imperial family is digging in its heels. They're never going to condone criticism of the emperor while keeping MacArthur sacred. What would that say to the Japanese people?"

"So they've got a new prime minister."

"Shidehara." Genius laughed, shaking his head in amazement. "Or shall I say, *Baron* Shidehara. And new is hardly the correct terminology. The guy's so old I think he just forgot to die. He was foreign minister back in the twenties and early thirties. The career soldiers used to call him Old Weak Knees, because his main function was to present Japan around the world as a peace-loving nation while it geared up for war. And even he didn't want the job after this new directive. It seems Hirohito had to send him a special meal, cooked in his own imperial kitchen, then personally convince him to swallow back his anti-Caucasian bile and take the job."

"You know what's amazing?" I asked. "I just spent an entire day with the lord privy seal, and he didn't mention a thing about all this."

He scoffed at me, amused. "Don't get too carried away with yourself, mister spymaster. You may be smart, but you're playing with the big boys, here. They have you just as compartmentalized as every other intelligence target. You haven't been in on the meetings up here while you were gone. Why should Kido try to pump your brain about something you didn't even observe?"

"Because I have been Japanese for two thousand years and was sent by the imperial ancestors to help MacArthur understand Japan."

"What the fuck are you talking about?"

"Ask Kido." I laughed. "Anyway, why'd they pick Shidehara?"

"Why do you think? To slow MacArthur down. That will be his whole job. Slow him down, refuse to cooperate—*bend like the young bamboo*. Then once the supreme commander loses his patience and explodes, they'll move an inch or two and Shidehara can retire again, scooping up the shame and taking it with him to his grave when he dies. Which should be soon."

I watched Genius with a fresh appreciation. "How do you know all this?"

He laughed. "You learn a lot when you're interviewing people who might stand trial for war crimes. They're not ratting each other out, understand. But they love to talk about palace intrigue. It's the national pastime."

He gathered a pile of papers from his desk, readying for the coming meeting with MacArthur. "So last week Shidehara shuffles into MacArthur's office, and your boss formally hands over a list with the changes he's decided the Japanese should make to the Meiji Constitution. Shidehara reads the list, hisses like a snake as he sucks air through his clenched teeth, then returns to the palace and does nothing. After a few days, MacArthur sends General Whitney over to offer to help them, thinking they can't figure it all out. Shidehara tells Whitney that he's, *kind of,* getting *ready* to *think* about appointing a committee to study the changes, but that once he does, they'll probably end up deadlocked between liberals and conservatives for at least a few months. MacArthur realizes that this is total bullshit and finally blows his stack. He summons Shidehara back to the Dai Ichi building and starts threatening him. And the old guy laughs! No, really! He may be Old Weak Knees but he's got balls. He just bows and suggests that maybe MacArthur should put him on the list and try him as a war criminal because he's so incompetent. And yesterday the supreme commander announced that he's going to write the new constitution himself."

"They'll love that," I said intuitively. "That's what they wanted all along. They won't dishonor themselves or their ancestors by actually writing new changes into Emperor Meiji's constitution. Just like they wouldn't actually arrest the people we're charging with war crimes. They'll find them for us, and they'll tell them where to turn themselves in to us. Same thing here. If MacArthur wants it done, he'll have to do it himself."

"Exactly." Genius shrugged, sagging in his chair. "It's been a zoo around here."

I sat in stunned silence, trying to gather my thoughts. "So I guess you know a lot more about why we're having this meeting than I do."

"Ah," teased Genius, checking his watch. "Your keen perception overwhelms me." He was giving me the I'm-going-to-Princeton grin again. "A prediction, monkey boy. My sources indicate to me—quite reliably, I might add—that your boss is going to detain a high-ranking member of the imperial family."

"Well, that should make you happy."

"Actually it infuriates me."

"Then why are you smiling?"

"Oh, now he wants answers." He checked his watch again. "We have to go soon. You know how MacArthur hates for people to be late."

"You've become quite mysterious, Colonel Genius."

"Do you know who Prince Nashimoto is?"

Genius stood, and I considered it as I stood with him. "I'm thinking something about a shrine," I finally said.

"That's very good. Nashimoto is in fact the chief priest at Ise, which as you know is Japan's most sacred shrine. He's seventy-one years old, the senior member of the imperial family, the elder brother of both Prince Higashikuni and Prince Asaka. A harmless, cheerful fellow, by all accounts." Genius snorted with disgust. "Of all the high-ranking imperial family, he's the last one anyone would want to charge with war crimes. In fact, I can guarantee that he'll never be charged."

"So why are they going to arrest him?"

"Because he'll never be charged."

"You've become very mandarin, Colonel."

"No, your boss has."

We started walking together down the corridor that led to a stairway that would take us to the supreme commander's floor. I was thoroughly confused. But Sam Genius seemed to be in utterly fine spirits. He nudged me with an elbow as we reached the stairs.

"And so, my good friend, mark my words. By tonight I will be packing my bags for home."

"Are you asking for a transfer?"

"One never asks to leave a position such as mine, you know that. Asking is death. One—makes himself available for other projects. If I were to publicly object to what they're doing, they'd destroy me."

We reached the sixth floor and walked the dark corridor that led to MacArthur's office. I was still confused. "I'm a little lost, here. What's pushed you over the cliff, Colonel?"

"A remarkable choice of words. The monkey boy is lost, but I myself have stumbled over the cliff," quipped Genius as we neared the door. "Let me put it this way. I'm not his political adviser. Do you understand what I'm saying? I didn't raise my hand and take the oath to become a member of the bar so that I could help a general turn his eyes away from justice in order to make a political deal. We're talking about two hundred thousand murdered people, here. It's my responsibility to press for the truth, or to remove myself from the case."

We were at the door. I stopped, holding the knob in my hand. "Try again, Colonel. What's going on?"

He genially slapped me on the back. "Did you ever hear of the soldiers who shot themselves in the foot, or reached their hands up in the air during a battle so they could get the famous million-dollar wound? Just watch me, monkey boy."

And then he stepped inside.

"Good day, General."

"Colonel Genius. Come on in."

The usual staff officers had been summoned. We gathered in the ever-drab, walnut-paneled office, having gone through the routine so many times before that we automatically walked to the appropriate piece of worn and scarred leather furniture and took our proper places. The gorilla-like General Willoughby nestled into his favorite armchair, frowning as he flipped through several pages of notes. General Court Whitney sat at the opposite end of the soft leather couch, winking secretly to me as if we had become lifelong friends. Colonel Sam Genius now stood near the door with an armful of papers, looking deceptively rumpled and sleepy. And Douglas MacArthur paced back and forth in front of the window that oversaw the emperor's palace grounds, playing with a pipe as he tamped fresh tobacco into the bowl.

MacArthur jumped straight to the point. "I want to scare the emperor," he said, perfunctorily pulling out a box of matches from his right trouser pocket as he paced. "It's the only way around the truculence of this new prime minister. I made an agreement with Hirohito about protecting the royal family, but implicit in that agreement was his assurance that I would have his full cooperation on matters of state."

"What are you looking for, Boss?" Court Whitney asked the question, eyeing Colonel Sam Genius as he did so.

"I want to wake him up," said MacArthur. "I want him to understand that the only reason he hasn't been charged with war crimes is that I've protected him."

"And how can we do that?" Willoughby asked the question again, as if guiding MacArthur's thought processes.

A warning bell suddenly went off deep inside my brain, and I knew that Sam Genius had been correct. It was highly unusual that MacArthur would allow a second interruption as he conducted a meeting. I was becoming uneasy, sensing that this meeting was somehow staged.

"I want to put someone close to him in jail," announced the supreme commander.

"Words of wisdom, sir! Pearls from heaven." Colonel Sam Genius grinned triumphantly, as if this were all fresh news. He began tapping the toes of his shoes into the frayed carpet as if he could not restrain his energy. "I'll be happy to oblige you, General. As you know, I've got quite a list."

MacArthur grunted, coldly surveying Genius as he lit his pipe. He looked suddenly sullen and unimpressed. "And as I told you before, I'm not sure I like your list, Colonel."

The warning bell went off again, this time loud and clear. After three years, I knew when MacArthur was conducting a meeting on more than one level. Whitney's immediate, leading questions when we all knew that the supreme commander disliked being interrupted meant that his dialogue with MacArthur had been prearranged. But for what purpose? My thoughts focused on Sam Genius. MacArthur's blunt repudiation of the frumpy lawyer, whose sole function was to find those most culpable of war crimes and attempt to prosecute them, meant that in addition to the emperor, Genius himself was somehow in MacArthur's crosshairs.

MacArthur wanted something done. But he didn't like Genius, and he didn't like his list, either. What he did not know was that Genius had somehow thought this all through in advance.

Genius grinned again, seemingly oblivious to the warning signs. He stepped forward, into what appeared to be a classic MacArthur ambush. "Well, let me just say that if you want to wake Hirohito up, I have solid evidence on every man who's ever tucked him in at night. We can charge five or six of them today and never worry about being accused of unfairness."

"I said I wanted to *scare* him," repeated MacArthur. There was a finality in his voice. He was looking at Sam Genius with a warning stare. His mood seemed carried over from the last moments of the meeting that eventually sent me down to Manila, when he had wanted to reassign the sarcastic lawyer to Borneo.

Genius seemed puzzled. He studied the supreme commander's face, as if looking for the proper clue. "Charging Princes Higashikuni and Asaka, individually or collectively, will definitely scare the emperor, General. Of that I have no doubt."

"And as you already know, that's out of the question," said MacArthur abruptly. "They're his uncles. I gave him my word."

"You gave him your word that his uncles wouldn't be prosecuted?" Genius seemed incredulous. "Then in all due respect, sir, I don't know what you want."

A real and enormous frustration breathed through Sam Genius's words. In the space of thirty seconds, the lawyer's facial expression had gone from an almost ecstatic optimism to a barely masked contempt. Watching him, I knew the gamble he was going to take and the enormous risk that it involved. There was no doubt that MacArthur was going to pummel Genius. His career was very likely going to be killed, or at least dramatically altered, within the next two minutes. I had seen it happen before. I could see it coming as clearly as if it were an approaching train.

Willoughby leaned forward, his unsolicited comments confirming my apprehension. "You have been disrespectful to the supreme commander in the past, Colonel Genius. I would advise you to watch the tone of your remarks."

Genius now alternated his seemingly amazed stare among the four of us, as if trying to make sense of the sudden hostility. "I haven't been disrespectful, sir. I'm a lawyer. It's my duty to bring the bad news."

"You're a lawyer and also a military officer, Colonel," said Whitney. "Just as I am."

"I'm a member of the bar. I have certain obligations."

Whitney guffawed. "Then maybe you'd be better off if you went back to

Queens and prosecuted pimps." MacArthur's chief political adviser now looked up from his chair to the supreme commander, as if he were a retriever dropping a shot quail at the feet of his master.

"Court," said MacArthur with false empathy, "you're being too harsh. Proceed, Colonel Genius."

Genius now stared fiercely at the supreme commander. He had crossed the line, and he was not going to back down. "Look, I've followed your orders and continued to accumulate evidence. No matter what you've said to anyone, we should charge Prince Asaka. I've documented beyond doubt that he was indeed in command for the rape of Nanking. I've placed him inside the walls of the city from Christmas Day 1937 through February tenth, 1938, which were the inclusive dates of all the mass atrocities! When he left, they stopped! Can you understand the implications of that?"

"You already told us that," grunted an unimpressed Willoughby.

Genius flipped quickly through a manila folder and pulled out a worn press clipping. "Here. This is an interview from the *New York Times*, datelined Shanghai, December twenty-ninth, 1937. Hallett Abend is talking with General Matsui, who just returned from Nanking. Matsui, according to Abend, is a 'likable and even pathetic old man.' Matsui tells the *Times* he's worried that Prince Asaka's conduct in Nanking is going to 'affect the imperial reputation.' Now, why do you suppose he said that?"

"Well, and I suppose it did," said an obviously unimpressed Court Whitney with a shrug.

Genius looked at Whitney as if he wanted to spit on him. He pulled another paper from his folder. "This is a message from Matsui to Prince Asaka's chief of staff, dated January eleventh, 1938. He's warning that the 'unlawful acts should cease, since Prince Asaka is our commander, and military discipline and morale must be more strictly maintained.' Do you understand what that means? Matsui says in writing that the prince is the commander, and he admits that unlawful acts are being carried out! How much more specific do you want me to get?"

MacArthur shook his head negatively, puffing on his pipe. "And what would happen if we charged Prince Asaka?"

"Well, for starters he'd be hanged by a rope until he's dead," said Sam Genius. "And it couldn't happen to a nicer guy."

"That's not what I mean," said MacArthur.

"Well, I guess it isn't. So why don't you help me out? What do you mean, General MacArthur?"

There, I thought, almost closing my eyes to avoid the impact that I knew was about to occur. *They got him. Or who knows? Maybe he just got them.* Genius had tiptoed over the very edge of insubordination, a precipice where Douglas MacArthur had himself lived for more than forty years, but one where members of his staff seldom lasted beyond a few seconds. And this time I knew that, whatever his motivation, Genius would not survive.

MacArthur froze the frumpy colonel with a warning glare, then suddenly waved at him as if he had become irrelevant.

"You can go, Colonel."

"Sir?" Genius seemed stunned, his soft eyes suddenly repentant. But it was too late. MacArthur had just sent another veteran home.

"I thank you for your recommendations, and we will keep them in mind. You can go."

"Go where, sir?"

"I said you're *dismissed*."

Genius sighed, as if finally understanding, and fiddled with his papers as he prepared to leave. He stood with his back to the supreme commander as he folded together the easel that held his flip charts. Unlike the others, I could see his face as he slowly worked the legs of the easel. Genius was stifling a grin. But there was something else, or perhaps a lot more, that he wanted to say before he made his final exit from MacArthur's staff. And finally he said it.

"You're a coward if you don't charge this man, General."

MacArthur's eyes bored into the colonel's back. No one had ever said such a thing in his presence, probably in his entire life, and certainly in all the time I had been on his staff. "No one calls me a coward! Turn around when you speak like that."

Genius turned slowly, trying to stand tall as he faced MacArthur. His very demeanor was so rumpled and unsoldierly, and his status so minuscule in the presence of this five-star giant, that the confrontation seemed both improbable and comical. But still Genius persisted.

"What are you afraid of, General MacArthur? With your Medal of Honor and your five stars? What are you afraid of?"

General Court Whitney jumped in, pointing a warning finger at the colonel as he spoke. "Colonel Genius, we've tolerated your insubordination for the last time. I know how emotionally involved you've become with these cases, but it is beyond the realm of military propriety for you to speak in that manner to General MacArthur."

"Calm down, Court." MacArthur had stopped pacing. From his perspective, the ambush was complete. A second round of warning shots had even been fired, telling Genius that if he were to complain to the media, he would be exposed as a disrespectful and overly emotional lawyer who became too obsessed with his cases. "Colonel Genius, I thank you for your valuable service, and I can assure you that we'll find a suitable assignment for you back in the United States."

"Just like that?" Genius seemed infuriated.

"One more word and we'll find you a jail cell in Fort Leavenworth." Willoughby's flat, accented tones gave his statement a clear promise.

"No, you won't," said Genius. He now grinned openly and defiantly, as if he had indeed snared them. "The last thing you want is for the press to start writing about a lawyer who's being tried by a court-martial for telling you that the emperor's uncle is a mass murderer."

"Who said we'd give you a trial?" warned Willoughby.

"That's just it. You're not going to," answered Genius. He was standing at the door with both arms full, prepared to depart but yet refusing to leave. He turned again to MacArthur. "I want Fort Ord."

"Fort Ord?" said MacArthur.

"San Francisco's lovely this time of year."

MacArthur looked over at Court Whitney. "Arrange for Colonel Genius to report to Fort Ord."

Whitney nodded, making a note in his legal pad. Colonel Genius gave all of us one last look, then dropped his thick manila folders onto the table in front of the couch. "I won't be needing these anymore. And I assume you'd confiscate them, anyway."

"That's very good of you, Sam," said MacArthur, as if no harsh words had been exchanged in the past ten minutes. "In fact, I did want those. And good luck at Fort Ord."

"I have a favorite bar right off the bay in North Beach. You won't want to be there when I toast you. Good day, sir," said Sam Genius. And with the slamming of the door, he was gone from MacArthur's staff.

The ambush was complete, from both sides. Sam Genius had his freedom, and he had also ceased to exist. I felt oddly sad, as if a part of my own past had faded out of the door with him. And I knew that Prince Asaka would never be charged. Indeed, in all the long months of trials that eventually took place, Asaka was never even called as a witness.

Court Whitney casually picked up the manila folders, placing them underneath his legal pad. They would no doubt disappear as well, with the sudden completeness of Sam Genius. He spoke calmly to me. "You're a witness to this insubordination, Captain."

General Whitney's pointed reminder was clearly a warning shot of a different kind: I was either in the room with the giants or out of it on my own, heading back to—where? Los Angeles? I had no idea where MacArthur might send me, or how he might be able to avenge my future, even in Manila. A part of me wanted to stand up and defend Colonel Genius, to argue that he was right, even to follow him out the door. But follow him—where? To do—what? I was a futile, tiny piece of this grand puzzle, lucky even to be observing it.

I swallowed hard, shaken by the calculated abruptness of what I had just witnessed. "Yes, sir."

"I want you to let Kido know about this exchange, so that he might inform the emperor."

"Yes, sir. I'm having dinner with him tomorrow night."

"Tell him today," interrupted MacArthur. "The emperor needs to know, so that he can understand the other things we're doing."

I swallowed hard. "Yes, sir. I'll call on him tonight."

"Don't tell him everything," warned Court Whitney. "Just let him know that the supreme commander intervened to keep Prince Asaka from being charged as a war criminal."

"Yes, sir," I said quickly. My body was tingling with an eerie fear, as if I had become a Mafia messenger. "I'll say exactly that."

"So," said MacArthur, turning to Willoughby, his chief of intelligence. "What's going on with Prince Nashimoto?"

"He is the perfect hostage. If Colonel Genius were to"—Willoughby paused a moment, looking carefully at me—"to, *accuse* us of being soft on the imperial family, the detention of Prince Nashimoto would be clear evidence that he is overly emotional and wrong in his judgment."

"This will scare the emperor?" MacArthur coaxed.

"It will scare the emperor," confirmed Willoughby. "A very powerful signal, General."

"Are there charges to be made against him?"

"Of course not, sir." Willoughby again looked carefully at me, yet another warning. "We can point out that in 1937 he did travel to China and after that conferred with Prime Minister Tojo regarding the conduct of the war. That will justify our detention. But he is clean. And he was never even near Nanking."

"Then arrest him," commanded MacArthur.

"We can do that today," shrugged Willoughby. "He'll be in Sugamo Prison by this evening."

And finally I knew that Sam Genius had been correct.

MacArthur needed a hostage, but above all the hostage had to be releasable once the emperor yielded to MacArthur's demands to change the constitution. Bringing charges against Prince Asaka would almost certainly result in a conviction. In addition, the testimony adduced at trial would create a road map that led directly to the Grand Imperial Headquarters, which had been built in the palace as the Nanking operation began. The emperor had personally followed the campaign from this headquarters, even participating in many of its day-to-day decisions. Would that make him a war criminal? The Chinese and the Australians believed so, and Sam Genius had agreed. And that was too close for MacArthur.

So sending the cheerful, rotund old Nashimoto to a cell in Sugamo Prison for a few months would be a bold stroke by MacArthur, because it also held out a silent promise. By holding Nashimoto hostage to the approval of his new constitution, MacArthur was on the one hand asserting his power and on the other assuring the emperor that he would not allow a court to scrutinize the acts of Higashikuni and Asaka. The emperor's position was secure, and MacArthur would do nothing to threaten it, including placing it in jeopardy by charging his uncles for the rape of Nanking.

Puffing on his pipe, MacArthur looked out the window for a long moment, toward the palace grounds. Just behind the Inner Palace, in a little clearing in the palace forest next to the Fukiage Gardens, was the holy of holies, the imperial family shrine. It was at this spot that Hirohito, nearly twenty years before, had stepped away from a retinue of two princes of the blood and two mere noblemen and undergone the sacred, private ritual that had made him emperor. He had placed his hands around the brocade bag that contained the green, tear-shaped jewels that represented the verdant islands of Japan. He had formally hefted a replica of the ancient sword of power, which the first emperor, the son of the Sun Goddess, was reputed to have pulled, Excalibur-like, from the tail of a dragon. And most solemnly, he had peered into an exact replica of the bronze mirror of knowledge, through which he reputedly was able to see the face of the Sun Goddess herself and thus be anointed with her wisdom.

The original of this bronze mirror, now more than two thousand years old, still lay in a vault at the Ise Shrine, on a faraway peninsula east of Osaka. The sacred shrine, to which every cabinet minister was required to report before assuming his governmental duties, overlooked the spot where the first emperor, Jimmu, had landed after crossing from a pirate's enclave called Karak at the tip of the Korean peninsula and founded the kingdom of Yamato. By sunset, the chief priest of this shrine, the protector of the mirror of knowledge, would be scrubbing toilet bowls in Sugamo Prison.

Yes, I thought, of course the emperor would eventually make a deal. For what were MacArthur's precious changes to him but words on a piece of paper, foreign scratchings that skipped like irritating little water bugs along the surface of the Japanese ethos?

"How much time will this buy us?" asked MacArthur.

Willoughby and Whitney frowned at each other, as if silently calculating the parameters of this shrewd and daring ploy. Finally Court Whitney answered. "It really depends on the emperor, Boss. There's no way he'll react immediately, because it would be too obvious that he's folding on the changes in the constitution just to get his uncle out of jail. And my bet is that the imperial family will actually gain a lot of sympathy among the masses with Nashimoto in jail for a while. But on the other hand, the longer he's in jail, the more pressure there'll be on us from the outside to bring formal charges. So I'd say we've got a few months, unless the emperor acts more quickly."

"And then where are we?"

"Well," mused the sly and calculating Whitney, "if things work out—and I think they will—you'll have your changes to the constitution, the emperor will have his favorite uncle back at the shrine at Ise, and our former allies will be screaming their heads off because it will seem you're again too soft on the issue of war crimes."

"I don't think that's going to happen," demurred MacArthur.

He moved away from the window, turning to me with a voracious look that told me I had other work to do. "Where are we with the Yamashita trial, Jay? When will it be over?"

"Over, sir?" I shrugged helplessly. "It's scheduled to begin this week, although the defense lawyers are asking for more time. My message traffic indicates that the prosecution is getting ready to bring several new charges against General Yamashita. There's no way they'll be able to examine the charges in time to start the trial."

"Poppycock," said MacArthur. "We know the dynamics of this case. Anyone who drove through the rubble of Manila knows what happened."

He began pacing again. His pipe had gone out. Now he held it in one hand like a pointer as he spoke in rapid bursts to Court Whitney. "Get Captain Marsh back down there. Have him deliver a personal, written message from me to the chief of my military commission—what is that major general's name, the fellow who just reported in from Chicago?"

"Reynolds," answered Court Whitney.

"Right," said MacArthur. "General Reynolds. The logistician. He knows what he has to do. He's taking far too long with this. We need more speed."

He turned to me. "Are you understanding me, Jay? More speed!"

CHAPTER 20

★ ★ ★ ★ ★

Major General Russell B. Reynolds, the highest-ranking officer among the five generals appointed to the Philippines War Crimes Commission, had been given the official title of president. The plump, stern-faced career officer was the commission's spokesman, responsible for its frequent public announcements and its relations with reporters who were descending upon Manila from all over the world to cover the Yamashita trial. He was also its designated "law member," which meant that he would be ruling on questions of evidence, legal procedure, and technical matters during the trial itself.

It is not an exaggeration to say that General Reynolds was owned by Douglas MacArthur, from the very moment he accepted his orders to preside over the commission. He made no attempt to hide this obeisance when I arrived at his office on the morning before the trial began. In my thick and sweaty palm was the letter that Court Whitney had drafted on behalf of the supreme commander. As instructed, I bypassed his secretary and his aides and walked directly into the general's office, where I delivered the letter into his own hands.

It was a simple letter, carefully worded. General MacArthur pointed out that he was disturbed by reports that the trial date might be continued due to the additional charges that had been filed. He stated bluntly that he doubted that the defense counsel really needed more time to prepare his case. And finally, the supreme commander wrote that the trial's preparation had already taken too long. He ended by urging "more haste."

"More haste." General Reynolds nodded comfortably, reading the end of the letter aloud, then nodded again as he looked back up to me.

"Yes, sir."

"Tell General MacArthur it's all taken care of," he said perfunctorily.

"Is that—it, sir?"

Something inside me wanted him to signal that he knew MacArthur was being ridiculous. In Europe and in Japan, the more properly constituted war crimes tribunals would not be ready to try cases for almost a year. Did it not seem peculiar to the severe, professorial Reynolds that the supreme commander was pressing him to proceed ever faster, less than two months after the formal surrender that ended the war? Did he not want to throw up his hands in exasperation and tell me of the impossibility of doing his duty without adequate preparation? Couldn't he have attacked me, lowly subaltern that I was, venting his emotions and looking for a small measure of sympathy, knowing he was presiding, cuckoldlike, over a fraudulent endeavor?

Standing before him, I found myself wishing that he would rise from his chair, yelling and screaming, even if he were finally going to obey the edict that I had dropped into his hands.

Instead, he nodded calmly one more time and put the letter carefully into a folder that lay on top of his desk.

"We're ready," said General Reynolds. "We went through a dry run this morning. The facilities are superb. The press has been fully briefed. The witnesses have all been prepared. We're starting on time. You should assure General MacArthur that we're fully sensitive to his needs."

Spoken like a true logistician, I thought, watching his impassive face. *The supply train is loaded and on the way to its destination.* He might have been moving a carload of K rations to the front instead of a Japanese general toward the gallows. "Yes, sir. I'll tell him."

He eyed me almost supinely as we walked together toward his office door, speaking with unabashed deference despite my rank. "You've been with General MacArthur since early in the war?"

"Three years now, sir."

"What an honor that must have been."

"He's a great man, sir."

"A great American. Please pass on my best wishes to him when you return to Tokyo."

"Yes, sir. I'll do that."

At the door the general hesitated, as if he might have breached some unspoken protocol. "Do you have dinner plans, Captain?"

"Actually, sir, I do."

It was an unspoken comment on the general's lack of power, even over one of MacArthur's low-ranking minions, that I had no qualms in declining to dine with him and that he took my rejection graciously.

I found Frank Witherspoon inside a Quonset hut that had been made into a gym, banging away on a sand-filled punching bag. The punching bag was hung by a chain from the hut's low ceiling. It had been made from an old canvas lister bag, used during the war for storing and treating water. Yamashita's defense lawyer was bare-chested, wearing crimson Harvard gym shorts, green jungle socks, and ugly black military tennis shoes.

I could tell he was not a fighter. He had no chest muscles. His chin was high in the air when he swung, inviting a quick knockout, and he carried his hands too low. He didn't seem to know what to do with his feet as he circled the bag. When he hit the bag he curled his wrists, beating it along the sides rather than throwing the straight, clean punches of an experienced boxer. But his face steamed with fury every time he threw a blow.

I had been on my way to the officers' mess for dinner and had seen Witherspoon through the open doorway of the gym. I stopped and watched him for a while, leaning against the door and trying not to laugh. Finally he noticed me. He grunted as he threw a few more spasmodic punches, then turned to face me.

"I'm pretending this is your boss," he said.

"Well, he's winning."

"Fuck you." Witherspoon stifled his embarrassment, breathing hard from his workout. Father Garvey would have truly enjoyed attempting to save him. He had absolutely no humility. "I fight a lot better with my brain, Marsh."

"Damn, I hope so. Otherwise you'll starve."

"All right, wise guy." He pulled off the bag gloves and tossed them to me. "You talk a good game. Go ahead."

I checked the chain above the punching bag as I slowly put on the gloves. "You don't want me to do this."

"Oh, ho. Superman speaks."

I shrugged, grinning at him, then stepped into the bag with a double jab that set it swinging, followed by a right cross that tore the chain from the ceiling. The bag ended up ten feet away, where two lieutenants were lifting weights. They howled with surprise.

"Whoa," said Witherspoon, actually appearing impressed. "Remind me not to piss you off."

"It's too late for that," I said.

"You've done this a few times before?"

"Where I come from, Witherspoon, it's a part of growing up."

"Not what I'd expect out of a general's weenie."

"I wasn't always a general's weenie, you know." I took off the bag gloves. "Want me to show you how?"

"How can you? You broke the bag! Anyway, I'm not exactly looking at this as a career." He had pulled on a green T-shirt and was now taking a few deep breaths as if recovering from a heavy workout. "I was almost done." He began walking, and nodded toward the doorway, an invitation to come with him. "What are you doing back here?"

"I thought I'd buy you dinner."

"Let's go next door," he said, grinning ironically. "It's Spam night at the local bar and grill."

Inside the officers' mess, the wispy-thin captain preceded me through the chow line and then found a table. He grunted knowingly as I carried my metal tray of food toward him. The trial preparations had worn Witherspoon down. His face carried a fatigue that made him look ten years older than when I had first met him a few weeks before. His mouth was full of mess-hall Spam as I took my seat. Finally, he swallowed.

"Actually, I heard you were back in town. So you met with General Reynolds, huh?"

"A well-intentioned officer," I said, starting to cut my food. "He even looks like a judge."

"Looks are deceiving," said Witherspoon. "How can a guy who's never even had one day of law school preside over a capital murder case? What does he even know about the rules of evidence? And he's not alone. Not one member of this commission is a lawyer!"

"I seem to recall you whining about that the last time I saw you," I said.

"Oh, so now it's irrelevant because it's old news?" Witherspoon piddled with his food. "Did I talk to you about military expertise? This case centers on the unique chaos that attends ground combat. Not one of these guys was in combat, either! Reynolds wasn't even in Asia during the war. He ran the Sixth Service Command in Chicago, making sure that logistics ran smoothly in Illinois, Wisconsin, and Michigan." Witherspoon laughed dryly. "I don't recall very many air attacks or ambushes on the supply lines in the campaign for the Great American Midwest."

I nodded quietly, sharing his cynicism. Sam Genius's recent departure had only deepened this feeling. "The supreme commander hardly sees those as problems."

"Of course not," said Witherspoon, his eyes afire with renewed anger. "He's got the perfect commission. Three major generals and two brigadiers whose future promotions and assignments depend on MacArthur! None of them with the legal background to understand the technical and procedural objections we might raise to protect Yamashita from false or unfair testimony. None of them with the combat experience that would give them credibility if they actually wanted to sympathize with the total confusion Yamashita had to operate under. So no matter what the evidence might say, none of them will *dare* to take Yamashita's side!"

I could not have argued with Witherspoon's logic even if I had wanted to. A hundred thousand Filipino civilians had been slaughtered during the retaking of Manila. There were plenty of witnesses to the rapes and the cruelties of the beleaguered, suicidal Japanese defenders. Back home, America had just begun basking in the glorious relief of a brutal war's final victory. MacArthur, for whom parks were being named and statues erected, had personally fingered Yamashita as the Asian war's most egregious perpetrator of mass slaughter. Who among these five marginally qualified general officers would dare to go against not only the supreme commander but the angry memories of their fighting soldiers and the righteous justification of the public back home? And where on this planet would such a person decide to work and to live if he did so?

"It's an odd feeling," I said. "But it's almost like General Yamashita has become irrelevant to his own case."

"What do you mean?" asked Witherspoon.

"I don't know what I mean," I answered, toying with my food. "It's just a feeling that I have."

"Well, let me personalize that feeling for you," said Witherspoon. "General Reynolds sent us a supplemental bill yesterday. *Yesterday,* two days before the trial! We thought maybe we'd get two or three new charges. No, he sent us fifty-nine. *Fifty-nine fucking charges, and now the trial starts tomorrow!* We went from sixty-four to a hundred and twenty-three, and every new charge involves new places, new people, new witnesses!"

Witherspoon was a very emotional guy, which no doubt is what had made him such a successful trial lawyer before the war. Both his hands were now in front of his face, waving at me as he spoke. "I filed for a continuance, using the exact language General MacArthur put into his directive creating the commission, stating that the accused is entitled to have the charges in advance of trial. I asked Reynolds if two days is what MacArthur intended when he wrote that. And, hey, if two days is OK for fifty-nine new charges, why not fifteen minutes? That's in advance of the trial. I reminded him that we're supposed to be operating under traditional American concepts of law, such as fairness, decency, and justice. And do you know what he told me?"

"We're in a hurry," I said.

"You're pretty good," quipped Witherspoon. "Are you the guy writing all these notes from Tokyo?"

"I only deliver them," I answered.

"General Reynolds told us his policy. Continuances will be given only for what he calls 'urgent and unavoidable reasons.' So I asked him, is there any more serious urgency than not having been allowed to prepare for fifty-nine new charges? Is there anything more unavoidable than not being ready because the charges were dropped onto my lap two days before trial? And do you know what he said?"

"Time is of the essence," I conjectured, finishing my Spam.

"You got it. He told us that we can prepare the case for the last fifty-nine while we argue the first sixty-four."

Witherspoon shook his head hopelessly, running pale, slender fingers through his shock of red hair. "Now, let's see. Beginning tomorrow, we're going into all-day sessions, six days a week, many of them already scheduled to be extended into night sessions as well. That means we'll have Sundays and our 'free' evenings to research the additional charges, interview witnesses, maybe travel to the scene of the alleged crime and prepare a defense for a man they're trying to hang. All of this at the same time we'll be trying to get ready for court the next morning on the sixty-four charges that are on the table."

He laughed dryly, almost a bark. "Did I say 'court?' Excuse me. I exaggerate. Indeed, I insult my profession. And as I am constantly reminded, with the legal calling's abysmal reputation that is very difficult to do. Anyway, all this is going to be—how shall I say it delicately—about as easy as a skunk smelling a fart in a hurricane. We've got three lawyers here—the fourth guy assigned to the defense team is in the hospital and won't be out for months. We've got one other lawyer who's already started researching how to appeal the case to the Supreme Court. Because let's face it, the verdict is already in."

"Did you say 'verdict'?"

"Very good. I think he gets the point." Witherspoon stopped, as if catching his breath. He kept peering at me with his disarming, all-seeing eyes. "So, Captain, let me ask you a very important question."

He had hardly touched his food. My plate was clean. I was sipping on a cup of piping-hot mess hall coffee. I was becoming sad, because what I was hearing was not a lecture on the railroading of General Tomoyuki Yamashita so much as a dirge that lamented the passing of my own childlike innocence. Witherspoon's bitter words, mixed in with the coffee and the smell of the mess hall, left me lonely for the long-ago evenings spent in the *Nashville's* wardroom as we steamed from Hollandia toward Leyte. Had that only been one year ago, almost exactly to the day?

"The gentleman has a question," I teased. "Ask away." I sat down the coffee cup, watching him expectantly.

"Have you ever seen General MacArthur act this weird before?"

"Now, that's complicated. Am I under oath?"

"I'm actually serious," he said, shaking his head at my apparent frivolity. "What's going on inside the man's head?"

It suddenly embarrassed me that I would dissemble at such a moment. "Sorry," I said. "You overestimate both my access and my intelligence. The General is a very complicated man."

"I'd just like to know," he said, looking around at the nearly empty dining area. "Either Douglas MacArthur has lost it, or there's something going on here that I can't figure out. And I'm not a dumb guy, Marsh. Appreciate that. I'm a student of human nature. I've made good money as a trial lawyer by being able to figure out people's motivations. All the hidden impulses that seduce their greed and assuage their fears and propel their stupid acts. That's my specialty, OK? And I've read a lot about MacArthur. The good things and the criticisms, too. I know he doesn't like Yamashita. I know how much he loved Manila. But come on. The man is truly an American hero. He's going to go down in history, and he deserves to! And now he's about to commit formalized murder, against the one guy in the entire Japanese army that he should respect above all the others. *Why is he willing to have this on his conscience?*"

"I am not MacArthur's chaplain, Captain Witherspoon. I don't know anything about his conscience."

"Come on," he said. "That's not an answer."

I held his gaze, wishing I could tell him of the meetings I had sat through and of my own disconcerted struggles. But I could not ignore the fact that Witherspoon was General Yamashita's defense counsel. Anything I might try to say to him could very well end up being used in the coming proceedings, possibly with me as a sworn witness for the defense. And above all, one did not speak to outsiders about what was discussed inside the room with the giants.

"I can't help you, Captain."

"You just did," answered the intuitive lawyer. He offered me a small smile. "I know you by now, Marsh. You're a pretty loyal guy. If there was nothing going on, you'd have said so."

He dug into his food, watching for me as if waiting for a response. "Not even a reply, huh? Damn, you're good."

"I like my job," I said.

He grunted, chewing slowly, dismissing me with his eyes. "I think you like it too much."

T he trial of General Tomoyuki Yamashita was held in the huge, ornate reception hall of the American high commissioner's residence in downtown Manila.

In preparing for the worldwide attention that the case would receive, General Reynolds, who knew a good stage prop when he saw one, had used this grand symbol of American continuity and power to its full advantage. Reynolds had placed a long rectangular table at the very front of the enormous room, where seven French doors made an arc looking out across a tropical lawn toward Manila Bay. Between the windows and the table were five leather swivel chairs, in which the commission's members would sit as they heard the case. The crossed flagstaffs of the United States and the Philippines Commonwealth stood behind the center chair. Reynolds had placed two desks in front of the table where the commission would sit, one for a court reporter and the other for the official interpreters. Further off to the right was the counsel table where Tomoyuki

Yamashita would sit, along with his attorney, Frank Witherspoon. Off to the left was a similar table for the prosecuting attorneys.

This little stage, set against the backdrop of the grand and placid bay, played out to a ballroom where chairs had been set for three hundred spectators and to a series of balconies where dozens of reporters, including moving-picture cameramen and radio announcers, would be provided the best field of vision from which to view and then tell the story of Yamashita's demise. A special section of two front rows in the ballroom was also reserved for VIPs, top-level reporters, and photographers, who would be permitted to take flash-camera photographs at any time during the proceedings.

Reynolds had been admirably thorough in carrying out the supreme commander's desire that the trial be set up to receive maximum world-wide exposure. He had put microphones at each desk and table, and had even hung large loudspeakers from the ceiling and along the walls. Mindful of the film cameras in the balcony, he had also placed spotlights along the outer edges of the room and six powerful klieg lights in the ceiling, all of them focused on the stage he had erected by the room's French doors. When the klieg lights went on, the stage area burned with a ferocious glare and the entire auditorium baked like the jungle itself from the added heat.

It was October 29, 1945. A year ago at this moment we had barely established ourselves in Tacloban, having endured the frightening near miss of Admiral Kurita's misjudgment in the Battle of Leyte Gulf. MacArthur had fulfilled an exultant promise he had made to me in the landing craft as it puttered back to the *Nashville* on the first night of his return to the Philippines while the wet rain washed our faces and we watched the torch fires that our artillery had left on the beaches of Leyte. We would be in Tokyo within a year. That's what he had predicted on that rainful but moonwashed night.

We had done better than that. We had already gone to Tokyo. We had planted the flag, claimed our victories, and even begun to discover our fallibilities. But now we were going to rewrite a portion of the history of our journey, relocate a few of the markers on the trail we had left behind, replace complexity with simplicity, assign grand blame instead of accepting the futility of a hundred thousand unavenged tragedies. For reasons that transcended this courtroom and Manila and even the conduct of the war itself, we were going to create a villain where before there had only been ugly chaos.

Nanking, I thought, entering the ballroom for the trial's opening day and taking a VIP seat in the front row. *That is why I'm here. Higashikuni. Asaka. Konoye. Hirohito. Kido. And don't forget the Meiji Constitution.*

As MacArthur had hoped, General Yamashita's trial played to a huge audience, both inside the Philippines and abroad. At precisely eight A.M. the military police opened the residence's inner doors to the public. The balconies and the front two rows of the ballroom were already taken by reporters, cameramen, and photographers. Within minutes the courtroom filled with eager spectators, most of them Filipinos with harsh memories of the Occupation of Japan. As would be the case for the next five weeks, the yard outside the residence brimmed full with hundreds and sometimes thousands of others who would wait in line all day, hoping that one spectator or another might leave, thus allowing them a glimpse inside.

General Reynolds and his subordinates arrived promptly, and regally took their seats. The lawyers then entered, followed by General Yamashita himself, along with two Japanese military officers with whom he would be allowed to consult for factual accuracy when his actions were under question. As the day progressed, formal charges would be made. After that, the arguments would be taken. Then a steady stream of witnesses would begin recounting their horrifying experiences at the hands of Japanese soldiers.

The klieg lights went on. The cameras flashed. General Reynolds coolly and dispassionately read the allegations of the United States against the accused. The charges were brief, and by their very nature vague: *"That Tomoyuki Yamashita, General Imperial Japanese Army, between 9 October 1944 and 2 September 1945, at Manila and at other places in the Philippine Islands, while commander of armed forces of Japan, unlawfully disregarded and failed to discharge his duty as commander to control the operations of the members of his command, permitting them to commit brutal atrocities and other high crimes against the people of the United States and of its allies and dependencies, particularly the Philippines, and he, General Tomoyuki Yamashita, thereby violated the laws of war."*

The crowd murmured and whispered. The photographers and cameramen took their eternal, capturing shots. The military commission's generals bickered and preened. The lawyers began to argue. The witnesses gathered in the back of the reception room and soon would be offered a weeping public catharsis. And yet the dominant figure in the room was the man who sat erect and immobile and who did not speak.

As ordered, Yamashita had worn his best green imperial army uniform, replete with knee-high cavalry boots, spurs, and four rows of campaign ribbons. Even sitting, he was a full head taller than the two other Japanese officers who had accompanied him. He was bulky, potato-faced, bull-necked. His head remained shaved, making him appear almost monster-ish. Watching him I suddenly found myself wondering if he had found a way to save a lock of hair to be sent home to his wife after his cremation.

As I watched him I thought again and again of our recent meeting in Muntinglupa's Bilibid. Yamashita dominated these proceedings without saying a word because he emanated an unusual power: *he was not afraid to die.* That certainty gave him a chilling charisma, even among the American soldiers who guarded him and the reporters who covered his case. Indeed, he had been quietly preparing to die since the very moment of his surrender. But his honor demanded that he publicly defend the reputation he would leave behind.

The prosecution presented its opening arguments. First they listed the voluminous "bills of particulars," outlining the 123 acts in violation of the laws of war that comprised the charges against Yamashita. The charges ranged from allegations that the Japanese had engaged in "a deliberate plan to massacre and exterminate a large part of the civilian population in Batangas Province" to the detailed allegations of "violence, cruelty, and homicide" as well as the "destruction of religious monuments" during the rape of Manila.

The prosecution recognized that General Yamashita neither commit-ted nor directed the commission of any of the 123 acts. But they pressed their argument that the general breached his duty to control his soldiers, thus permitting them to commit the extensive and widespread atrocities. The precise issue before the court, they argued, was Yamashita's "personal responsibility for his failure to take appropriate measures when the viola-tions resulted."

Witherspoon's opening argument on behalf of Yamashita covered all the points he had made to me during our first meeting in the chapel of the Muntinglupa Bilibid. Familiar with Western notions of military conduct, Yamashita had insisted on fair treatment of British soldiers after the fall of Singapore, a policy that had been reversed when he was reassigned to Manchuria. He had issued clear, written instructions to all Japanese forces in the Philippines, forbidding improper treatment of civilians and prison-ers of war. In Manila, he had withdrawn his own troops in order to spare the city and to concentrate his defenses farther north, leaving behind principally naval forces under dual command from Tokyo. The only order he had ever given these naval forces was to evacuate Manila rather than

destroy it, and their commander, Admiral Iwabuchi, who received different orders from Tokyo, did not obey Yamashita. With respect to American
prisoners of war, Yamashita had been reproached by his own superiors
after initially ordering that our POWs be released from captivity and given
one month's food rations, as soon as the Americans landed at Luzon.

Witherspoon was withering as he finished his opening statement. He
glared at the commission's members with unconcealed contempt as he
spoke. "Can it seriously be contended that a recently arrived commander,
beset and harassed by the enemy, staggering under a successful invasion to
the south and expecting at any moment another invasion to the north,
could gather all the strings of administration in a country as large as this?
First of all, these atrocities occurred at times and in areas that made
communication of such matters impossible! Land communication was
cut off! Japanese wireless communications at their best were worse than
ours at their worst and were reserved for matters of operational importance. And not only was General Yamashita physically unable to know of
these events but it is ridiculous to assume that those who perpetrated them
would then decide to tell him about them! They were taking place in
violation of his specific orders!"

Witherspoon took his seat. His passion had been spent on idle ears. The
heat from the klieg lights was all but unbearable. The projectors rolled
and the cameras flashed. The members of the commission nodded and
sweated and yawned. Yamashita sat unblinking and erect. The spectators
craned their necks and whispered, not understanding the legal and moral
technicalities of the angry and emotional opening statement. The witnesses rustled and fidgeted in the back of the ballroom, awaiting their
turns to show their scars and tell their nightmare stories.

And that was the last time that General Yamashita's name was even
mentioned for days. The witnesses came forth, sitting only twenty feet
away from the stoically watching defendant, giving accounts of unspeakable horror and barbarism. Prepubescent girls, raped and bayoneted and
left for dead, now revealed their ugly scars. Elderly men told of friends and
family who were forced to kneel in front of pre-dug ditches, where they
were bayoneted or decapitated and then kicked nonchalantly into the
holes. Women spoke of having babies wrenched from their arms and shot
or perfunctorily eviscerated. There were rape victims, stabbing victims,
shooting victims, children who had watched their parents die, parents who
had watched their children die, wives who had watched their husbands
and children being tortured, husbands who had watched their wives being

raped, all at the hands of Japanese soldiers. Stark photographs of gruesome scenes were held forth in the trembling hands of people whose faces promised they would never forget.

It did not matter to General Reynolds and his commission that virtually all of the true perpetrators were already dead. Or that in Tokyo, Prince Asaka was playing his usual morning round of golf with the emperor, forever absolved of the deliberate butchery of Nanking. Tomoyuki Yamashita had been hauled into the room to sit hour after hour, day after day, as the cameras captured the undeniable horror of Manila's rape. And then he would be sent out to die.

At the end of the first day, even the American journalists were grumbling about the blatantly contrived and totally predictable results. But no one seemed to understand why. Because the puzzle that they could not comprehend was the one they did not see.

Watching these proceedings, an eerie reality crept up on me. It was as though I was looking for the first time into a cruelly honest mirror at the person I had allowed myself to become. A few days before, Sam Genius had offered me a peek into that mirror, and I had shied away. But this reality was now inescapable, personalized in the Janus-like faces of Tomoyuki Yamashita and Frank Witherspoon, one decidedly serene and the other eternally enraged as the trial wore on.

What was in the mirror? Who had I become? A vacant, limpid face. An instrument to be used for the power of others. A cute-mouthed monkey boy, neither serene nor enraged, who had simply become accepting. It had happened over the course of three years, one starstruck day at a time. I had proved my worth to men who were making history, and I was proud of it. I had watched MacArthur struggle with issues that were beyond the ken of my youthful understanding. I had gladly served his vision. And in the process I had lost my own.

Sam Genius and Frank Witherspoon were standing for something. And I had come to stand for nothing.

I left the ballroom before the day's activities had finished. A great confusion washed over me as I drove my jeep toward Divina Clara's home. I could not deny that an overwhelming, truly historic burden rested on the supreme commander's shoulders. Nor did I doubt that he was better equipped than anyone else alive to harness and direct the brilliant energies of this former enemy nation called Japan. But what I was watching in the grand ballroom of the high commissioner's residence reeked with the fetid odor of unnecessary evil. *Unnecessary*, that was the reality that shamed me. The spoils of a just war, a war fought on behalf of tolerance and human decency, did not give anyone the right to murder a great man for reasons of political expedience and personal jealousy.

As I neared Divina Clara's home I found myself regretting that I did not possess the courage of Sam Genius or Frank Witherspoon either one. Perhaps their professions allowed them that courage by couching it in terms of duty. I did not know. All I knew was that I lacked it.

And there was another problem. It came to me in the black of a Manila night, on feet as quiet as cat's paws. It lingered by my bed, cloaked in a satin robe. It unknowingly pressed against me as Divina Clara dropped the robe and slid smoothly underneath my sheets. I had been reading fear in her eyes all evening. Naively I had thought she knew about Yoshiko. But her fear was directed inward, just below her heart.

Her father was on a business trip to Subic, spending a week with her grandmother while he negotiated two new construction projects with the American navy. Her mother slept just down the hallway, and her aunt was in the room below mine. The moon shone brightly through the window slats. The perfumed air of the garden outside romanced me. It startled me when Divina Clara reached my bed, for I had been dreaming about her.

In my dream I had been walking alone in the mountains overlooking Atami and had come upon the mud-glazed statue of Kanon, the Buddhist goddess of mercy. But looking up at the goddess's face, I had seen that she had now become Divina Clara. And instead of staring far away toward Nanking, she was looking down the mountain. I followed her gaze. It ended at a nearby beach, where an inn backed into a rocky grotto. Behind the inn the cold waves spewed like fountain bursts, up into the brittle sky. In the courtyard I could see Yoshiko in a blue kimono, looking up at me as I stood next to the goddess. Her smooth face was immeasurably happy, splashed with salt water and lit by the sun. Behind me I could hear the old priestess inside the shrine, beating on her strange tubular instrument, singing sadly, weeping for atonement. But it was not the Matsui shrine, it was the Jay Marsh shrine. And in my dream I knew that the goddess Kanon at my side had been baked from the mud of Manila, joined with the dust of Tokyo. And that the priestess wept for me.

Divina Clara was naked, warm, and smooth. Once in my bed she reached behind my shoulders and pulled herself against me. I was immediately aroused, but instead of kissing me she pressed her face into a safe place at the hollow of my neck. She was crying.

"Do you love me, Jay?"

"Of course I do."

"How much?"

"With all my heart."

"How do I know this?"

I gently pulled her mane of hair, forcing her to look me in the eyes. "What's the matter?"

Holding my eyes, she took my hands and slowly pressed them against her smooth stomach. "I tried to tell you this before."

With a suddenness that jolted me fully awake, I finally understood. But still I did not want to believe it. "What?"

"I'm going to have a baby."

She scrutinized me as I stumbled in silence. It's impossible, I kept saying to myself. Impossible. Not now. Not yet. We're not married. I don't even have a home. No, I don't even have a *continent.*

"Are you sure?" I finally said.

"That was the worst answer you could have given me." She buried her face into a pillow, hiding her tears. "I don't think you love me."

"I do love you!"

"Not enough."

"I do, Divina Clara!"

"I don't know what to do. I don't even know who I can tell. What do we do, Jay?"

I was reeling from the shock. I had been in the room with the giants, dealing cleverly with issues that would move or even conceal history. But at that moment I realized that I did not really understand women or even the rules that should run the rhythms of my own life. What should I do? I had no answer in the moon-swept night. MacArthur wanted me back in Tokyo. My plane left in less than six hours. But Divina Clara had been holding this secret inside her for—how long? I did not even know. How could I now simply abandon her?

She stared at me with a look that hinted of betrayal, as if not believing the truth of her own memories. "I want to know, Jay. When will we be married?"

I searched inside myself but could not come up with an answer. I felt oddly trapped by the very panic in her eyes. "I'll tell them I want out of the army," I said. "I'll tell them as soon as I get back."

"You didn't answer me."

She had stopped crying. Despite her emotions she had an almost chilling acuity. It was I who now was under the klieg lights, although it was Divina Clara whose life was at risk. *The foreigner always leaves.* It was a story told ten thousand times among the warm and trusting women of the Philippines. She had a baby inside her, and an American lover who now was in bed next to her but tomorrow would be in Japan and in a week or a month could be anywhere, from London to Los Angeles.

"Whenever you want to, Divina Clara."

"I don't like the answers you're giving me."

Tests are never obvious, that had always been Divina Clara's credo, and I lay helplessly next to her, knowing I was failing mine. Despite my love for her I felt myself harden in my confusion and resentment.

"Then maybe you should show me your script."

"That was unkind."

She was crying again. She sat up, her feet now over the edge of the bed, ready to leave. I pulled her back toward me.

"I'm sorry. I do love you, Divina Clara. I just don't know what to do."

"Have you been with another woman, Jay?"

She was facing away from me. The moon illuminated her upturned face, giving her a glow that seemed almost spiritual. Watching her I felt as though I were dreaming again and that she was fading from me like a ghost, riding out my window on a moonbeam.

"Why did you ask that?"

"Why didn't you answer it?"

"Because it doesn't need an answer." At that moment I loved her hopelessly and hated not only myself but Marquis Koichi Kido, who in his conniving brilliance had delivered into my weakness the very thing I could not refuse. "But since you asked, the answer is no."

She stared into my face for a long time, peering closely, reading my eyes in the shadows of the moon. Finally she touched my lips.

"I will believe that," she said. "Because I want to."

I tried to pull her to me but she pressed against my shoulders, holding me away. She gently kissed my forehead, then slid off the bed, picking up her robe. Her eyes continued to probe my face as she pulled the robe around her naked body.

I ached for her. "Won't you stay?"

"No," she said. "It wouldn't be honest of me to make love to you right now. And honesty is the purest form of love, don't you think, Jay?"

She is the only person I've ever met who could analyze her own emotions with such clarity. And that is why her name has always seemed so apt to me. Divina Clara. Divine Clarity. "Yes," I said. "I love you."

"When will you be back?"

"Soon," I answered. "When will we be married?"

There was an odd finality in her penetrating eyes, as if she had reached a secret resolution.

"I will think about this. And we'll talk about it when you come back."

CHAPTER 21

★　★　★　★　★

It was still dark. From my open window I could hear the jeep churning and downshifting as it made its way along the unlit street, and then its brakes squealing as it pulled up outside the villa's walls in front of the house. The driver cut the engine, slammed a door, and it became eerily quiet again. Inside the house, everyone else was still asleep. I had already shaved, dressed, and packed. Hoisting my duffel bag, I crept slowly down the hallway and into Divina Clara's bedroom, careful that the hard leather heels on my military shoes did not click too loudly on the ancient mahogany floor.

I had longed for her all through an unsleeping night, thinking of this new reality that had abruptly altered the logic of both our lives. Now I stood just inside the doorway, my eyes searching for her in the darkness. The bed was a storm-twisted pile of puffy pillows and satin sheets. Behind the bed, starshine poured through the window slats. A slight breeze lifted the white lace curtains. Suddenly she stirred, and finally I could see her. She was sitting halfway up in the bed, with her back against two pillows. She was awake, and she was looking at me.

"I feel sick," she said.

"I'm sorry, Divina Clara."

"I have morning sickness and I can't even tell my mother."

I walked to her and sat on the bed, embracing her. Outside, the jeep's driver slammed another door, started the engine, and turned on the lights, an impatient signal to me. I held her some more.

"It will be a boy," she said, nestling her head against my chest and making it sound like a question. "My grandmother always said that's what the morning sickness means."

In the jeep, the radio went on. "I wish I could stay to help you. But I have to go, Divina Clara."

"What would you like to name him?"

"I need some time to think about that."

The radio volume went up louder. A country song twanged through the window, lamenting lost love and cheating hearts, threatening to awaken the entire household.

"You always have to go. I think you always will be gone."

"I'm sorry," I said again. "I have no control over my life."

I held her more tightly. Then she abruptly pushed me away, as if my leaving were permissible if she decided that it must take place.

"Hurry up, Jay. You'll miss your plane."

"I'll be back. Soon."

"Maybe," she said.

And then she turned away from me, feigning sleep.

The courier flight that would return me to Atsugi left Nichols Field just after dawn. I was addled and melancholy as I boarded the brand-new C-54. My insides churned from the cup of bad coffee that the driver had poured for me from a thermos as I climbed into the jeep. My eyes were pasty from lack of sleep. I took my seat next to an already soundly snoring colonel, strapped the seat belt across my lap, and tried again to understand what was happening to me.

I could not stop thinking of Divina Clara pressing my hands into her smooth, hard belly as the perfumed night air wafted over us and the moon made ribbons on the bed as it shone down through the wooden window slats. Remembering her tearful face and the unspoken accusations in her simple, pointed questions left me queasy, as if I myself were going through morning sickness.

The loadmaster strolled the narrow aisle of the C-54, counting his passengers and finally signaling to the copilot that we were ready to roll. In the bluing sky above the runway the moon had just gone down. Somewhere a clock ticked over. The plane began to taxi along the runway. And again I was leaving her behind, this time holding a belly full of child.

We were not yet married, but what did that matter? She had loved me with an incomprehensible fullness. She had trusted me. We were joined now, inextricably and forever, in blood as well as spirit. She had taken me inside her and together we were going to bring new life into the world. And in the middle of the night she had asked me questions, giving me an intuitive and indecipherable test. And I had failed it.

And so I knew not only that I loved her but that I owed her. She had been living with a terrifying panic that I had dismissed as simple loneliness. Indeed, what did she possess, other than my words, that showed the strength of my commitment to her? I was now living in another country. I had been sleeping with another woman. For all she knew I might decide to go home to California or Arkansas or wherever—having never left the Philippines they were all mere words to her anyway—or perhaps simply stay permanently in Japan and never even come back to Manila to say good-bye. She had been waiting, waiting, trusting words that were uttered before the world had changed and the war had gone away, carrying the child of a man who, despite his plaintive reassurance, she might never see again.

And what of me? In one slow night the world had turned, and another mirror had been held resolutely before my face. What a glorious time I had been having in Tokyo as Divina Clara's life was being swept away by uncertainty and fear! What right did I have to my dinners and my clever conversations, to my grand thoughts about the future of Japan, when the future of Jay Marsh, and the eternal veneration of Divina Clara Ramirez, had entered this microcosmic thermonuclear crisis?

I had no choice. It was time for me to leave the army and return to Manila for good.

The plane neared the end of the runway and lifted easily into the air. I began to rehearse the words I might use, first to General Court Whitney and then to MacArthur himself, in order to expedite my discharge. I would tell them that I was a reserve officer, anyway, hardly the sort to have the words "essential to the success of the occupation" stamped into my personnel file in the first place. That I had done my part during these extraordinary three months in which history had been rewritten and the future of Japan quietly agreed upon. That it had been an honor to be trusted and to have been involved in so many momentous events. But that now they should allow me to leave.

The C-54 bounced lightly on sudden puffs of wind, rising above Manila Bay. Below me, like an old and distant dream, the still-wounded city sprawled and twisted, its long, straight streets beginning to fill with jitneys, pedicabs, and an occasional army jeep. In the bay the fishing boats were already moving languidly toward the outer banks of Bataan and Cavite. Where the bay broke into the sea the guardian island of Corregidor loomed above the water like a teardrop, still fractured from the millions of pounds of bombs and artillery that had pocked its fields and flattened its buildings. Saying good-bye to Manila was always emotional and nostalgic, especially in those sleepy, remembering moments just after dawn.

Watching all this disappear below me, I vowed that I would be back permanently by Thanksgiving. That gave me three weeks. Could I do that, with the pace the army normally worked? My heart raced. Why not? The question was how to negotiate my exit. *Exit.* The word suddenly sounded clandestine, foreign and forbidding. Leaving MacArthur seemed almost like running away from home.

Not only from home but from a calling for which he had prepared me and which I had come to love. After the past three months it seemed to me that I was born to live in the diplomatic world, with its playful, smart double-talk, historic stakes, and immersion into powerful, exotic cultures. I knew I was a natural and that the longer I played this game the more I might flourish. It was almost as though I had grown to manhood serving General Douglas MacArthur. And after this first taste, I could not imagine doing anything for Carlos Ramirez that would offer up the same intellectual satisfaction and emotional thrill as the work I had done in Japan.

But no matter, I thought again. The issue was settled. I had no choice. Divina Clara was having my child, it was as simple as that. Still, this would not be easy for me. Frank Witherspoon may have been right, after all. Perhaps I did love my job too much.

There was another consideration. Despite my lowly rank, I knew that MacArthur would resist my request. The General had a way of holding on to people who served near him. Over the past three years he had screened me, picked me, tested me, and finally come to trust me. I had been selected, brought inside the room. And I knew I was being groomed for even bigger responsibilities.

Since our first landing at Atsugi I had been told repeatedly that I was expected to remain in Japan for as long as he needed me. With MacArthur's tendencies, that could mean years. Indeed, General Willoughby had now served under MacArthur continuously since 1939, and Court Whitney had known him longer than that. Once the General decided that he trusted someone, once he had allowed a man (for it was always a man, he did not even meet with women) inside the room to hear his private thoughts and witness his manipulative genius, the staffer was expected to make the fulfillment of Douglas MacArthur's destiny his career. In particular, so long as MacArthur wished to retain an unofficial line of communication with the emperor through Lord Privy Seal Kido, he would view me as irreplaceable.

And, finally, there was something else that would drive MacArthur's resistance to my leaving. Lowly peon that I was, I could hurt him.

In subsequent years I learned that this unspoken but enormous fear is ingrained in most men of power who have trusted their private thoughts to subalterns. But even then I sensed both the importance and the danger inherent in what I had observed. I had listened to vital confidences, secret observations. I had watched intemperate outbursts of raw vanity. In short, I now possessed what Court Whitney jokingly liked to call "guilty knowledge." And in those areas that reflected on him personally, the General could not simply demand that I remain silent forever. So long as my career continued to depend at some level on these shared secrets, I could never tell them. So long as my future was shaped in some way by my relationship with Douglas MacArthur I could never betray him. But if I escaped him clean, without an obligation to continue my loyalty and with my reputation intact, he might decide that for the rest of my life I could be a threat to his reputation and his legacy.

So I knew that if I abruptly told MacArthur that I wished to leave, he might become nervous and just as suddenly decide that I could only do so with damaged credibility. When I did face him in the privacy of the walnut-paneled office at the Dai Ichi building, I knew I might need every skill I possessed to protect my reputation while breaking clean from Douglas MacArthur's grasp.

The water-swollen rice fields along the Luzon coast slowly faded behind us. The aircraft's cabin had cooled as the plane climbed. The C-54 throttled up, having reached altitude, and vibrated so strongly that my body trembled with it. The colonel next to me was hungover. He awakened and walked groggily toward the front of the aircraft, pouring tepid coffee into a paper cup from a metal container. I sat back in my chair as if locked inside a geography machine, one that would transfer me in cocoonlike sterility from Manila's stifling reality into the contrived, fairytale world of 1945 Japan.

And somewhere above the empty sea as I dozed under the rattling drone of the plane's propellers, I had an awakening.

Hadn't Sam Genius shown me the way, after all?

My eyes blinked open. I laughed aloud. My seat-partner colonel stared uncomfortably at me, sipping his coffee. I finally understood with clarity why Genius had ambushed MacArthur. Or more properly, why the irascible lawyer had simply planned his own ambush, perhaps laying the groundwork for weeks.

The more I thought about it, the more obvious it became. Genius knew MacArthur's flash point even better than I myself. Growing frustrated with the supreme commander's selective jurisprudence, like me he had decided that he wanted out. Then he had calculated all the necessary parameters with the specificity of an algebraic formula, knowing when MacArthur would decide that he had become not simply a hindrance but a threat. And he realized exactly how he might then provoke his own dismissal.

Merely asking for a transfer would have been tantamount to begging, an admission that at some level he had failed, that the problem was not the supreme commander's orders but Sam Genius's inability to carry them out. MacArthur would then have controlled the bargaining points. He could have sent Genius anywhere. He could have written whatever he wished in the colonel's fitness report. He could even have ordered Court Whitney to "find" some deficiency in Genius's performance or personal life that was unrelated to the war crimes issues, then preemptively discredited Genius and relieved him for cause. From MacArthur's perspective there would have been strong logic for doing just that. Staining the lawyer's reputation would have masked the true reason for his disenchantment and made any public criticism of MacArthur sound like mere bitterness.

Would a five-star general on the threshold of becoming an historic figure have gone to such extremes simply to insulate himself in advance from the vitriol of a disenchanted staff member? I had no need even to ponder the question. Like Yamashita himself, MacArthur knew that his reputation was his truest legacy. And like Franklin Roosevelt, that long-time adversary whom he so secretly admired, he was a master at manipulating his own persona. If he would trump up charges and coldly hang an innocent Tomoyuki Yamashita, if he would loudly lay the blame for the fall of Corregidor at the feet of the devoted Skinny Wainwright, he would have no qualms over sending Genius home as a falsely compromised capon.

But instead, Genius had struck first and through his clever boldness had become a free man. He had put himself directly into play, face to face with the supreme commander, betting his reputation in the process. And by striking quickly he had taken the game away from MacArthur, finessing all the subtle warnings and the quiet, discrediting maneuverings that might otherwise have happened. He had forced the issue of his future into the open, at the same time preserving for himself a reservoir of secrets to be kept like nuclear-tipped arrows in his own quiver, held for his protection. Not to be used but to be fired back at MacArthur only if he were fired upon.

It could have backfired, but it had not. So Genius had escaped clean. He would not spend the next two years going through the ethical drudge of prosecuting show trials that would later pass in historical comment as having held Japan accountable for war crimes. Fort Ord would be lovely in the autumn, washed by the warm desert winds as an ugly winter descended upon Japan. He could spend his weekends carefully toasting—or rather, roasting—MacArthur in his favorite bar in San Francisco. The lawyers who were left behind, or the unknowing civilians who replaced him, would carry out the counterfeit proceedings that would never include those of the highest royal blood.

Sam Genius had it made.

I played this thought over in my mind again and again. What had Genius read in MacArthur that I had missed? And finally it occurred to me. Genius had daringly played to the supreme commander's two crucial weaknesses. We all knew them. We had discussed them. First, MacArthur had a tendency to cringe before demonstrations of power. The emperor had proven as much in their closed-door meeting at the embassy a month before. But others had as well. MacArthur may have fought for years to keep the ever-loyal Wainwright from receiving his Medal of Honor, but he had felt no qualms in awarding a Silver Star to then-congressman Lyndon Baines Johnson for having participated—as a passenger—in one combat flight over enemy territory. He had approved the nation's third-highest medal for heroism for the influential politician as if it were a souvenir of his journey to the war zone, simply because Johnson had said he wanted one.

And second, MacArthur's ego was so voracious that he had an unavailing need to be worshiped. As in the case of General Sutherland, MacArthur could tolerate all manner of arrogance and even abuse of power so long as the adoration continued. But he could not stand to be served close-up by those who did not openly profess their devotion and subservience. When the veneration stopped, when the genuflections ceased, MacArthur looked elsewhere. And when he did look elsewhere, unless those who had stopped genuflecting had also found a shield, their reputations upon their exit from his staff would be shredded like confetti, as a matter of course in order to protect his own.

Sam Genius had bet that in the end the very secrets he could never tell would become his own guarantor. And I knew far more secrets than had Genius. I had heard them spoken and observed them being made. Indeed, in many cases I had discovered them myself. They were a leveler that made me equal to MacArthur, not in my impact on history but in my desire to decide my own future.

I shivered with uncertainty as the plane droned on toward Tokyo. I knew what I would have to do, although the very boldness of it all was almost more than I dared to comprehend. If I did not rescue Divina Clara I could never gaze comfortably into a mirror again. In order to do that, first I had to accept that my embryonic career as a diplomat was over. Then I had to sever my relationship with the lord privy seal, so that I would no longer be considered in any way "essential to the success of the occupation."

And finally, I would have to ambush General of the Armies Douglas MacArthur, so cleverly that he would decide that he had ambushed me.

CHAPTER 22

★   ★   ★   ★   ★

Father Garvey was standing in the middle of his tiny, dim-lit room, packing uniforms and souvenirs into two olive-drab army footlockers. The room smelled strongly of whiskey and tobacco. As Father Garvey looked over at me his usually laughing blue eyes seemed to swim longingly inside their sockets. He rubbed the top of his greying head with a small, thick hand. And then he pressed his fingers into his eyes, as if to clear them.

"Well, doesn't the dear Lord sometimes answer our little prayers, then? I've been asking Him that I might see you before I left, Jay."

"I just got in from Manila. They told me you were leaving. You're going home, Father?"

"Well I'm going back, anyway. I received my orders two days ago." He eyed me with a scarcely concealed envy. "And how was Manila?"

"Hot and wet," I answered. The rest of it was so complicated that I did not even know where to begin. "Where are they sending you?"

"I'll be out of the army."

He smiled sadly. His gaze went past my face, somewhere behind me.

"There's a Jesuit retreat in Annapolis. Just across the river from the Naval Academy, they say. I'll be there for a year or so, until they feel I've properly repaired my soul."

He was staring at me again, this time with a forced and embarrassed grin. We both knew what he meant by repairing his soul. He had told his superiors about his time in Manila.

"You're soul is in fine shape, Father. Haven't I always said that you're the only man of God I've ever trusted?"

"Yes, and look what's become of you."

"Don't scold me, Father. I told you I wasn't proud of myself."

"How could I scold you?" He turned away, continuing to load one of his footlockers. "I've never been to Annapolis, but I know how homesick it will make me feel to stroll the grounds of Manresa and look down at the river and see the boats and the sailors on the other side."

"You don't even like the navy, Father."

"I told you, I do like the navy. It's going on the ships that I hate."

"Then being on the other side of the river from them will be perfect! You can watch them and remember but you won't have to go on them. I'll come see you. We can drink wine and smoke cigars. Then we can stare across the river at the ships and talk about the way things used to be."

He chuckled softly. "And how will you do that, Jay, living in Manila?"

"It's not like I won't come back every now and then. Or you can come and visit me when your retreat is finished."

"That would indeed be the ultimate test, wouldn't it?"

A bottle of good whiskey stood on his tiny bedstand, opened and one-third gone. The Irish mistress, that was what many soldiers laughingly called hard liquor. But in Father Garvey's case the thought seemed so true that it was cruel. He was struggling to remain in God's service, and who could blame him for a drink or two? Especially I, Jay Marsh, whose autumn nights had been filled with warm sake and hot-water *furos* and a giggling, sweet-mouthed geisha while my pregnant fiancée patiently awaited my return and my good friend Father Garvey lay in his dismal army-issue cot and struggled with memories so sweet that he felt compelled to confess them and ask for forgiveness.

"Father," I said, picking up the whiskey. "Let's kill this bottle."

"Speak to me while you're sober, Jay."

I poured myself a drink. "I don't think I want to."

Father Garvey stopped packing and sat on the bed. He pointed to a nearby hard-back chair. "She's found you out, hasn't she?"

I obediently took the chair, not answering him. He shook his head, smiling with commiseration. "That's harder than telling the church, I think. For me it was weakness, an act of love. What was it for you?"

"I haven't told her, Father. She asked me and I lied."

"But she knows. I can see it in your face."

"Yes," I said. I took another swallow of his whiskey. "So let me ask you this, Father. If she knows, why do I still have to tell her?"

"Well, aren't you rationalizing, then? How can you move forward in your life together if you carry this transgression in your heart?"

"I think it would only punish her to tell her if she already knows."

"You're just afraid. Because, Jay, you cannot have love without honesty," said Father Garvey.

I laughed involuntarily, caught off guard. "Do you know that's almost exactly what she said to me? Not about being afraid, but about honesty."

"Then she's braver than you think, Jay."

"She's the bravest person I've ever met. I knew that the first time I ever saw her, sitting next to the road in a *caratela* as the bombs went off all around us."

"Ah, yes, the war again," said Father Garvey. "I feel guilty to have loved it. But where else in our lives could we ever have learned such things?"

He had almost finished packing, three years in Asia stuffed into two army footlockers. He grew sad, staring over at the footlockers as if he had neatly boxed up his entire past. "Sometimes at night I lay alone here in my cot and look up at the dark ceiling where I know only a few months ago some Japanese officer was also peering, trying to go to sleep as he waited for the end, whatever the end would be for him, a bomb on top of him or a fire that burned him up or maybe just a surrender, and then I ask myself, did all that ever really happen? And then sometimes I become filled with regret, wondering why it had to end."

Near the footlockers a cricket began to chirp. Father Garvey chuckled. "I've never been able to catch that little fellow. He's kept me awake for weeks. With my luck he'll jump into my footlocker and follow me back to Manresa. He'll have plenty to eat with my clothes in there."

He was watching after the cricket, but looking at his craggy face I knew his mind was neither in Japan nor Manresa. I took another drink.

"I have to admit something, Father. The greatest moment of my life was watching the rain come down on General MacArthur's face as we took the landing craft back to the *Nashville* that night after we landed at Tacloban and he made his radio address to the nation. We had finally done it. We had returned, and the only thing left was to win the war, and everything that was wrong in the world would turn around and suddenly be right. Do you know what I mean? He was so happy. I don't know why, but I've never felt so pure."

"Purity is a delicate thing. You cannot stay long in Asia and still keep your innocence. It is not really a Christian place."

"I wasn't talking about her, Father. She's a better Christian than I will ever be, you know."

"And neither was I," said Father Garvey.

"Then what do you mean?"

He shrugged. "And why do I always have to explain what I mean?"

I had downed several shots. My stomach burned and my fingers tingled, but my mind was still aching with the clarity I was trying to avoid. I suddenly felt bad about everything, all the loose ends of both of our lives, including now having taken half of Father Garvey's whiskey.

"I'll buy you another bottle tomorrow."

"Can't you see? I'll be gone tomorrow."

"Then I'll buy you one tonight."

"That won't be necessary, Jay. I'm all right, really. It was only a moment of weakness, the whiskey."

"She's going to have a baby."

"Somehow I knew that." He looked at me with such powerful directness that his soft words were almost a command. "God is talking to you, Jay. You must get beyond your fear and find a way to listen."

"I'll try, Father. I really will." I checked my watch. "I have to go. I have work to finish. I just wanted to say good-bye."

He stood and I rose with him. He looked shyly at me for a moment and then grasped my hand, holding it firmly in both of his for a long time, looking up into my eyes. "It's over! I just don't know what to think about that." There was a mystery in the way he said it, and suddenly I felt his sadness. "War is such a terrible thing, but it does focus the emotions. I had no idea I would love it all so much."

"Will you write to me, Father?"

"You will always be in my prayers, Jay Marsh. I'm counting on you to do great things."

I knew I was not supposed to say it but a fathomless regret hung between us like a thick, unctuous incense. We were at a secret wake, just the two of us, standing before an invisible tomb. And finally I could not remain silent. "You're in love, Father. Can't you do anything about it?"

He pinched his eyes again, now looking away from me. "I suppose I will always be in love. But I am a priest. That is my calling. I could never be anything else. When I am in my vestments I feel God's pleasure. So there is only one thing I can do, and that is to thank God for allowing me to understand how powerful this kind of love really is. I'd never known before. He punished me with its beauty, but He has made me a better priest. I now know how completely passion can take hold of someone, and how horribly it hurts to be alone. One has to be with someone before he can truly understand what it means to be by himself. So it will help me as I minister to others. Although it is my penance that others must never know."

He'd grown embarrassed as he talked, and now he looked away from me, obviously feeling he had said too much. I wanted to help him in some way, but I sensed that I had been out of place even mentioning it.

"You seem to love her so much, Father. Isn't there any other way to resolve this?"

"No," he said, now stiffening and regaining his composure. "I am at peace now. I am one small spirit in the universe, but each of us has our duties, and I know mine. This is how dreams die, Jay. And this is how sacrifices are made."

I could stay no longer. As I closed the door behind me I could hear the cricket again serenading Father Garvey in the echoing emptiness of his barren room. And I knew that for as long as I lived, I would never know a greater friend, or a more honest man.

CHAPTER 23

★ ★ ★ ★ ★

It took me more than two hours to find Lord Privy Seal Kido. It had begun to rain, cold sheets of it blown by the wind, cluttering the dark streets with vast puddles and inches of mud. I traced his evening's meanderings in my jeep, asking for him as I moved through restaurants and clubs that had become familiar haunts over the past two months, then finally catching up with him at a villa in the suburb of Roppongi. It seemed that Koichi Kido was always on the move. The electric, shock-eyed marquis cut quite a swath through the upper echelons of Tokyo's after-hours society.

I had been to this villa once before, for a private dinner at which Kido introduced me to a man he had identified only as Colonel Tsuji, who said he had served under General Yamashita during the famous attack on Singapore. As Kido nodded his concurrence, Colonel Tsuji told me that before the war he had become close to the throne while serving as a tutor for the emperor's youngest brother, Prince Mikasa. He filled me with stories of how he had used his influence with the imperial family to garner Japan's finest military units for the invasion itself, and how he, not

Yamashita, had led the key attacks that forced the hand of the British. According to Tsuji, Yamashita had resented him because of his closeness to the imperial court and eventually disciplined him out of spite for the deaths of innocent civilians as he overran a hospital. Tsuji said he had retaliated by reporting Yamashita's many disloyalties to the imperial court.

Tsuji was bright, mysterious, much younger than Yamashita, and still deeply resentful of him. It became clear by the end of the dinner that Kido was subtly trying to reinforce the imperial court's message to MacArthur that Yamashita had been disloyal and thus was expendable. When I briefed the supreme commander on the conversation he chose to interpret Tsuji's comments as evidence that Yamashita's military reputation as the Tiger of Malaya was inflated. But to me, Tsuji's boasts were proof that Yamashita had indeed disciplined his own officers for atrocities, further evidence of the unfairness of his trial. And then when I met with Yamashita in his prison barracks at Muntinglupa, he himself had mentioned Tsuji as the officer who had caused him to be censured by the imperial court.

And so Tsuji's claims became a Rorschach test for our own inner thoughts, conjuring images based on what each of us wanted to believe. And the colonel himself remained a shadow figure, a symbol of that part of the Japanese system which no one from the outside has ever penetrated, even to this day. Indeed, when MacArthur asked me to meet once again with Tsuji, Kido informed me that the mysterious colonel had somehow become "unavailable." And years later, during the Vietnam war, I read a diplomatic cable indicating that one "Colonel Masanobu Tsuji" had disappeared while on a secret mission to Hanoi on behalf of the emperor, never to be found again.

But if no one from the outside has ever penetrated that last hard kernel from which the true soul of Japan still emanates, through Koichi Kido's indulgence I had come very, very close.

I parked on a narrow street, just outside the villa's walls. The rain had stopped. The air smelled of charcoal fires and cook pots, coming from the nearby homes. A large dog barked angrily at me from the other side of the wall as I opened the gate. I entered the outer garden anyway, remembering that the dog would be locked inside a cage, and walked along a path of tiny stone steps until I reached the front door.

During my earlier visit, Kido had explained to me that the villa was home to the mistress of a friend. He had not named the friend, and I had left believing that Kido's disclaimer was actually belly talk, his own way of boasting that the villa and the mistress were his own.

The long-limbed, porcelain-skinned woman who lived in the villa gave me a secret smile as she slid open the doors of the villa's central building. She was wearing a bulky, long-sleeved housecoat that fell just below her hips, and matching striped pants. She was much older than I but had an ageless, happy face. As I entered she bowed very low. She had recognized me immediately. I returned her bow and then took her hand respectfully, for despite the question of just whose mistress she might have been, I was entering her home.

"Good evening, little sister," I said. "I am sorry to disturb you but it is very important that I see the lord privy seal tonight. Is he here?"

She squeezed my hand once, welcoming me, then knelt at my feet, starting to remove my shoes. "Oh, Mister Jay Marsh, you do me great honor by visiting my home again! The lord privy seal saw you walking from your car. He is very happy to see you. He is putting on a robe."

Kido suddenly appeared behind her, wearing a black silk robe that covered flowing blue pajamas. He bowed slightly and then laughed.

"Captain Jay Marsh, I think you are an excellent detective. Either that or I am being provided an unseen American escort wherever I travel in my own city?"

"It is possible that you are being followed." I grinned. "But your own secret police would be able to tell you far better than I myself."

Kido gestured toward the house's center room. He teased me as I walked behind him. "Ah, but as you know, the supreme commander has done away with our secret police."

"Yes," I answered, entering the center room. "And by what name do you call them now?"

He laughed delightedly, accepting my compliment without answering me. The woman was as silent as the wind as she whisked about the room, ceremoniously arranging our visit. By the time we reached the alcove area in the middle of the room she had placed two futon cushions in front of a low table. A glowing porcelain hibachi brazier was on the table, providing the only heat in the room. As we knelt on the cushions she quietly slid several wooden *shoji* doors along the floor behind us until our meeting place was closed off from the rest of the house. Then she knelt, putting her nose onto the floor, and backed out of the room.

Kido seemed enormously relaxed. He picked up a small *kiseru* pipe from the neatly arranged smoking tray that she had left in front of his cushion and sparked a long wooden match, lighting it. As he worked on his pipe I looked about the room. A tasteful *kakemono* landscape painting hung from one wall. In the alcove itself was a delicately beautiful ikebana flower arrangement. The paper windows were decorated with fine wooden grillwork. My eyes finally rested on the large, splashy *kanji* that spelled out the *gaku* above the main entrance to the room. The *gaku* that a Japanese chose for his home was very important. Often it was the subtlest way he might articulate his most strongly held passions.

"I am admiring your *gaku*," I said as the lord privy seal puffed on his pipe. "It is different than when I was here before, is it not?"

"You are most observant, Captain Jay Marsh. But I will remind you that it is not my *gaku*, because it is not my house."

"What does it say?"

The pipe was now fully lit. Kido eased back on his haunches. From his mischievous smile I could tell he was again teasing me. "But I should not read my friend's *gaku* aloud. We are both visitors here."

"I have not heard of that custom," I answered.

Kido eyed me carefully. "My friend is sometimes a very angry man. He lost a great deal in the war."

"I can understand that, Lord Privy Seal."

"Can you?" He puffed slowly on his pipe. The woman silently reentered the room, kneeling before us and setting a tray on the small, low table, and then quickly departed. The tray held a teapot, two cups, and two small bowls of *arare* appetizers. "May I pour you some tea?"

"If you allow me to pour yours, Lord Privy Seal."

"Ah, you learn so quickly," he said, pouring my tea. "But I am your host, so I will pour my own tea."

I smiled. I had caught him. "But it is not your house, so you cannot be my host. We should pour each other's tea."

He smiled back, his eyes bright and shocked behind the thick-lensed glasses, and began pouring my tea. "But for now I am the occupant of the house. And so you are right. I will also read the *gaku* for you."

I took the tea, sipping it, and nodded to him, a gesture of thanks. "That's all right, Lord Privy Seal. I've been rude. And I've lost my curiosity."

"I could lie to you anyway," he said. "You are very bad with *kanji*."

"I am terrible with *kanji*," I answered. "But I would not want you to shame yourself by lying on such a simple matter, Lord Privy Seal."

"Ah, so." We grinned at each other for several seconds, reading the messages in each other's faces and sipping our tea. Kido puffed again on his pipe. "My friend is an admirer of Sun-tzu. Do you know Sun-tzu?"

"I know him," I answered. "He was a great philosopher of war who lived more than two thousand years ago. But he was Chinese."

"Yes," sighed the lord privy seal. "Always it goes back two thousand years, and always we end up with the Chinese, do we not?" He eyed the *gaku* on the wall. "I don't mean to be mysterious. It is a simple quote."

"But if it is on your wall it must be profound."

"I told you it's not my wall!" Kido grinned. "But I will read it anyway. *'All strategy is based on deception. Pretend inferiority and encourage his arrogance.'* "

I smiled back. Kido had thought he might shock or even anger me with the quote. But I knew him too well. "Why should your friend quote Sun-tzu? He should simply listen to you, Lord Privy Seal."

"Perhaps," shrugged Kido. "But a *gaku* must be inspirational, taken from a famous man. Me, I am only a humble gate-keeper."

"Quite the contrary, Lord Privy Seal. Except for the emperor, you are the most powerful man in Japan. I have no doubt of this anymore."

He eyed me carefully now, knowing that such direct flattery was in fact an allegation, and knowing also that I would not make this allegation so bluntly without a reason. A palpable tension crept between us, instantly changing the mood of our visit.

"You are forgetting MacArthur."

"The spring will come. The snow will melt from the branches of the pines. And someday MacArthur will go home."

"And then there will be a new MacArthur."

"No, there will never be another MacArthur." I eyed him steadily. "The United States does not wish to rule Japan. In the end we desire a partner, not a colony. But you have two big problems, Lord Privy Seal. The longer you and the emperor resist his changes to the constitution, the longer MacArthur will stay. And the longer it takes to find those account-able for war crimes, the more the outside world will continue to demand that the emperor be brought to trial."

"Ah, so," he said, studying me with a newfound seriousness. "We have talked about this." He puffed on his pipe for a moment. "And how is the Yamashita trial?"

"The trial, Lord Privy Seal, is a disgrace. He'll be hung. But let me warn you: it's not going to make a difference on the issue of political war crimes. Yamashita was a field commander. Our allies are demanding that we find accountability inside the Tokyo government." I watched him for another moment. "And how is Prince Nashimoto enjoying his time in Sugamo Prison?"

"The emperor is deeply upset over the imprisonment of his favorite uncle," said Kido immediately. "I would say he is angry, but the emperor remains above anger. I will tell you personally, Captain Jay Marsh, because you have been so helpful. The emperor has been most cooperative. He has given up a great deal in order to end the suffering of our people. But if Prince Nashimoto is charged, the emperor has decided to abdicate to Kyoto and work against MacArthur."

"We must cooperate with each other to keep this from happening," I said.

"As always, I must thank you for your precious advice," said the lord privy seal.

"There is only one solution," I said.

"I am anxious to hear your thoughts," he replied.

"We must protect the emperor and his blood relatives at all costs."

"Exactly," said Kido, nodding sagely as he relit his pipe.

"But in the eyes of the world there is a debt to be paid. It will only be paid if someone near the emperor is held accountable for the advice he received which led to certain unspeakable acts."

He continued to watch me carefully, breathing slowly as he puffed on his *kiseru* pipe. The pipe had gone out again but he still sucked on it as if it were lit. "General Tojo has already been charged," he finally said.

"Not close enough. Indeed, not high enough."

"He was the prime minister."

"And who chose him, Lord Privy Seal?"

We stared silently at each other for several seconds. Kido gently placed the pipe onto its tray. He reached over and picked up the teapot.

"More tea?"

"No thank you, Lord Privy Seal, but I will light a cigarette if you don't mind."

I took out a cigarette and he struck a match, lighting it for me. In the front garden the dog barked at a passing jeep. In another part of the house a cricket began to chirp. I thought briefly of Father Garvey, now spending his last night on his canvas cot before heading back to do his penance for having fallen in love. Kido glanced briefly up at the *gaku* over his front entrance. I took another drag off my cigarette. Then finally he sighed.

"Prince Konoye's family has served as the emperors' internal advisers for more than two thousand years. But from what you are saying, he would not be protected. He is not of the imperial blood."

"He gave the advice. Bad decisions were then made. He should be charged."

"And I myself?" His voice trailed away as if it were an unfinished thought, but it came out as a question.

"To protect the emperor and his family," I said, steadily holding his seemingly astonished gaze, "Prince Nashimoto should be allowed to return to his duties at the Ise Shrine. Our allies must be silenced in their pursuit of the emperor himself."

"Are you saying we should make this offer?"

"Privately. Through me. It should be considered."

The lord privy seal took a deep breath, sucking air through his teeth for a long time. Finally he stood. I put out my cigarette and stood also, staring at him from across the small table. Then he bowed slightly, ending our visit, and gestured toward the door. His face took on a firmness as we walked. His voice was a full octave lower.

"You are sure?"

I nodded as I leaned over and began pulling on my shoes. I had begun to like this idea of the lord privy seal going to jail very much as I elaborated on it. But I was certain of nothing, except that Koichi Kido had wielded quiet and unfathomable influence with the emperor. And that a portion of my personal crisis with Divina Clara was the result of his having smoothly rewarded my most secret desires. And that my freedom from Douglas MacArthur depended also on my freedom from this medieval, symbiotic alliance.

"Regretfully, I am certain, Lord Privy Seal."

My shoes were on. He opened the door for me, bowing as I walked past him into the outside garden.

"Then I will discuss this matter with the emperor."

"A very wise decision. Good night, Lord Privy Seal. Please give my thanks to your friend."

"My friend?"

I winked, as if sharing a secret. "The owner of the house."

He smiled grimly back. "Yes, of course. My bitter friend. Good night, Captain Jay Marsh."

I began to whistle softly as I reached the jeep. Driving away in the black night air I could not help but thank General Douglas MacArthur for having trained me so well in the skills of cutthroat diplomacy. And I knew that if he found out I had negotiated on these issues without his permission, I would be on the first ship home.

As a prisoner in the brig.

CHAPTER 24

★ ★ ★ ★ ★

ood morning, General."

"Good morning, Jay. Welcome back." MacArthur paced before his window, barely glancing at me as I took my seat next to Court Whitney on the old leather couch inside his office. "Obviously, General Reynolds took my message to heart?"

An irrepressible anger welled up inside me. I tried to restrain it, nodding respectfully. "He was thoroughly prepared, sir." But I could not leave it at that. The whole so-called trial was too obscene. "As you must know, General, it's turning into quite a nightmare."

"A *nightmare?*" The supreme commander threw a harsh, disapproving look my way.

"A veritable circus, sir. A dog and pony show."

"I hope you're not talking like that in Manila."

I was in no mood to be polite. The knowledge of what I had to do, the memory of the sweltering klieg-lighted sham proceedings, the exhaustion, the thought that I was not yet even a husband but would soon be a father, all of it welled up inside me at once, impelling me finally to abandon my constant facade of contriteness. "Oh, I'm not, sir. I don't need to say a word. Everybody else is talking. Particularly the American press, in case you haven't been reading the papers."

He was scrutinizing me closely now, as if he were daring me to contradict him again. "From what I'm being told, the general is doing quite a fine job in these proceedings."

I calmly mocked him. "Depending on what you're looking for, sir. General Reynolds is clearly a well-trained—poltroon."

"Poltroon?" General Charles Willoughby glared at me from his usual chair, amazed. "I don't know what it means but it sounds offensive."

"It was meant to be, sir."

"You're speaking about a general officer in the United States Army."

"That's actually part of the problem, isn't it, General Willoughby? And I'll bet he gets promoted once this thing is over, too."

Whitney and Willoughby had been with the supreme commander for nearly an hour prior to my having been called into his office. When I entered the office, all three had seemed to be in unusually buoyant spirits. Now they were looking at one another as if I were emanating a weird body odor. I had never before directly contradicted Douglas MacArthur, and I had meant to ease into my confrontation, but it was too late. I knew from hundreds of other such meetings that if I were to back down now and apologize for my cynical and mildly disrespectful replies, then the three of them would pile on top of me so completely that I would never regain the momentum necessary to confront them. MacArthur would ridicule me, make his points, elicit my information, neglect to seek my advice, and then send me back to my own office, probably with further orders to communicate to Manila.

So after three years of playing the jester, the moment had come for me to face MacArthur like a man. He was not going to like what I had to say. At the same time I knew I lacked the devilish cleverness of Sam Genius. But I vowed that if nothing else, I would not leave his office, and probably his staff, to be remembered as a sycophantic robot.

MacArthur had recovered, although he still watched me curiously as he paced. "You may have had a—disappointing experience with General Reynolds, Jay, and we—appreciate your candor. But in all other respects, I understand the proceedings have been immensely positive. They've been fully supported by the Filipino people, widely covered by—"

"General, I'm prepared to give you a full report on the Yamashita trial, but something very important has come up."

He stopped pacing and turned to face me, clearly irritated. It was the first time I had ever talked back to Douglas MacArthur, and now I had also interrupted him.

"I was summoned to a meeting by the emperor's lord privy seal last night. They want to make a deal, and I think you need to hear what they're offering."

I kept my seat on the weathered couch, looking expectantly toward him. His whole face seemed to change as he stared down at me. With these past few exchanges I had already become a different creature in his eyes. I held his gaze, but inside I was afraid. I felt immediately stripped of his protection, somehow isolated and alone, like a suddenly rebellious teenaged son who had never before confronted his father.

"What are you talking about, Jay? The purpose of this meeting is for me to be debriefed on the Yamashita trial. And your orders with respect to the Japanese government have been clearly limited."

"Sir, I know what you're—"

But now he interrupted me. "I'm not finished! You are not empowered to negotiate with them. You are not authorized even to tell them our positions on anything. You are a listening post. Your duty is to report back to us. If a representative of the Japanese government contacts you to offer a negotiating position, it is your duty to refer them to General Whitney."

"Sir, they didn't want to talk to General Whitney."

"That's not for them to decide."

I gave him an exasperated look. "I didn't feel it was my place to say that to them. I had to make a decision, sir." There was no retreat from what I had done, and it was too late to be intimidated. "They insisted on passing this information through me. This isn't an issue for General Whitney. You need to hear this directly, sir."

Court Whitney quickly weighed in, glaring from the other end of the couch. For the first time since I had been on MacArthur's staff, he railed in anger at me. "What do you mean, it's not an issue for me? Hold on, here, Captain. You've been under strict orders! These issues are too sensitive for some twenty-five-year-old captain to be wildcatting. We're talking about the future of a country. And I'm running the entire political affairs operation for the occupation. You may believe this is a minor quibble, but you're usurping my authority."

General Willoughby was bristling with irritation. He leaned forward in his chair as if he were preparing to leap across the table and attack me. "Exactly! We have procedures," he grumbled in his thick Teutonic accent. "You are not the person to be bringing this to General MacArthur's attention. Questions must be examined and alternatives discussed before we can develop a position and take the General's time."

It was not lost on me that following Willoughby's procedures, or allowing Court Whitney to proceed formally with the Japanese, might well be the first step in my own legal proceedings. Although the intricacy of the Japanese system was its own protection against anyone firmly contradicting my story, Whitney still might learn that I had arranged the meeting with Kido and made the proposal myself. I began to wonder if I could talk Frank Witherspoon into defending me once General Yamashita's trial was over. I also began silently cursing Sam Genius for having inspired me on this quixotic path.

But there was only one way out of this. "I'm not trying to usurp anyone's authority, General Whitney. The lord privy seal came to me with a communication from the highest level of the Japanese government. From the emperor, sir!" MacArthur's eyes grew smoky at the mention of Hirohito. "What do you want me to do? I couldn't simply turn him away, particularly since you've encouraged my relationship with Kido. And bringing it to you before it came to General MacArthur would risk having it talked about among the staff."

My last comment infuriated Court Whitney even more. "Are you now attempting to insinuate that I would engage in inappropriate conduct, Captain Marsh?"

"No sir! But I didn't know who might be overhearing us if I'd brought it up in your office. I had to make a judgment call, here."

They were caught off guard, even perplexed. Watching these giants stare silently at me, I had a sense of just how deeply my loyalty was embedded in their expectations. I had sat politely in their midst for years and now was indeed like a little boy who had suddenly come of age before their eyes. This was Jay the jester, Jay the monkey boy, Jay the listening post, suddenly digging in his heels and asserting himself as a major player in their delicate negotiations. And in a way it scared them.

Whitney pointed a finger at me, an overt threat. "You could have talked to me privately. On political issues, I make the judgment calls."

"Normally I agree with you, sir. But you've put me in some really difficult situations. I didn't have time to contact you, and I decided that you'd trust me. I didn't ask for this! And I've always done my duty, sir. Always."

"That's enough, Court," said MacArthur. "He's right about that. Now, calm down, Jay."

MacArthur himself softened, turning to the other two. This was not necessarily a signal of support. He had done the same thing when allowing Sam Genius to proceed scarcely a week before, only moments before he had, in his own eyes, thrown the impish lawyer out of Japan. "We're arguing about procedure when he's been approached by the highest adviser to the emperor, with a proposal in hand. I think we at least need to hear what he has to say."

"Thank you, General."

"Don't thank me, Captain Marsh," said MacArthur coolly. "It wasn't a compliment." He turned to face me. "So what do they want?"

"They're making an offer, and I think you ought to take it." I watched Whitney bristle again at my presumptuous behavior but continued on. "You're going to get what you want, General. This is the way to go."

Willoughby could not restrain himself. "I will remind you again," he said angrily. "You are a provider of information, Captain. A *listener*. A conduit. We are not interested in whether you think the offer should be accepted."

I raised my chin, looking him full in the eyes. I was no longer afraid, no longer chained by the manacles of my rank, no longer even appreciative. I had earned my place inside this room, given them my loyalty and every ounce of my dedication. I was weary of the turf battles and fragile egos that gave the supreme commander's staff the aura of a medieval court. And on this matter I knew far more than they did.

"General, don't you find it odd that you'd trust me to communicate privately with the most powerful man in Japan other than the emperor himself, but when I come to you with a solution you expect me to behave like I'm some silly little recording secretary? I'm not just a pair of ears! I have a solution, sir! Don't you even want to hear it?"

MacArthur had been eyeing me closely, taking in every twitch of my face, every movement of my hands and body, measuring me against some hidden referent borne of more than four decades of such meetings. I could tell he was seeing something in me that he felt he had missed before. But I could not ascertain what or why.

"Leave him alone," he said, waving off both Whitney and Willoughby with the sweep of a hand. "All right, Jay, let's hear it."

"It's very simple, General," I began. "A very simple solution."

"Nothing in Japan is simple," interrupted Court Whitney.

"Court," said MacArthur, this time commandingly. "Hear him out."

I wheeled toward Whitney. "In all due respect, General Whitney, you may be an expert on the Philippines, but Tokyo isn't Manila. I was a student of Japan even before the war began, sir. I understand how complicated this culture is far better than you do."

I was breathing heavily again. My pulse was racing. Sweat was dripping from my armpits. But I held Court Whitney's eyes for a long moment, until he dropped his own.

I turned back to MacArthur. "Sir, you want two things. You want the changes to the constitution, and you want to resolve the issue of political war crimes without having to charge either the emperor or any of his immediate family. Particularly Prince Asaka, who as you well know is guilty as hell."

"We want a lot of things," argued Willoughby. "And I will remind you that this talk about the emperor's immediate family is highly classified!"

"Yes, General Willoughby, but can you deny that what I'm saying is true?" I now faced Willoughby directly. "I've been in the room with you for a long time, General. I've listened to the debates. I've run your errands. I've taken notes. Lots of notes. How can you imagine that I'm not aware of what you're trying to do?"

There, I thought edgily. It's done. I've said it. *I've taken notes.* In my simple words was the cautionary reminder that I not only shared their guilty knowledge but had recorded it, and that I would be forever, from this point forward, either a collaborator or a threat. Their choice.

"Let him talk," commanded MacArthur again.

"Thank you, General."

This time he did not ridicule me for thanking him. I gathered myself and began again. "OK, sir, two things. You can keep Prince Nashimoto in jail for a while, and I'm sure you'll eventually win on the changes to the constitution. By now the emperor probably sees them as a small price to pay. Speaking personally, sir, they'll have their little ways of finding loopholes to get around most of what you're proposing so that it doesn't go too far. On the surface the country will be implementing your changes, but underneath it will remain Japanese. That's the way they've always worked, for thousands of years. Did you know they even took their famous tea ceremony from the Chinese? But they made it Japanese. The Chinese don't even recognize it anymore. They'll do the same thing with your constitution. It'll take a while but they'll absorb it, process it, refine it, and make the parts they don't like evaporate before your eyes."

And now MacArthur himself flashed, launching into one of his famous stentorian lectures. "Captain Marsh, on this I am *certain* that you are wrong. This document is beyond doubt the most liberal constitution ever written. It will be the single most important accomplishment of our occupation. We are lifting them up from the ashes that the arrogance of their old system brought down on them. This constitution will bring the Japanese people freedom and privileges which they have never before known."

But then he stopped, as if suddenly running out of words, joining Whitney and Willoughby as they all quietly stared at me. It was clear that he wanted me to continue.

"Yes, sir," I answered, gathering myself again. "I was merely trying to give you an observation from the Japanese perspective."

"Then don't say 'personally,'" warned Whitney.

"Right, sir," I answered. "Not personally. Let's try 'culturally.' But here's the point." I burrowed my eyes into the supreme commander's, ignoring the other two officers, determined that I not be sidetracked again. "You have taken a royal hostage, and it's worked quite effectively. But if you trade Prince Nashimoto merely for the changes in your constitution, what do you have? Not much. You have American words in a Japanese constitution. That's it. Prince Nashimoto is back tending the Sun Goddess's Mirror of Knowledge at the Ise Shrine. And our allies are still screaming that you haven't done enough on the issue of war crimes."

"No," said MacArthur. "We'll have General Yamashita's conviction to take care of that."

"*It's not going to work, General!*" I was trying to keep my composure, but his cavalier dismissal of what he was ordaining for General Tomoyuki Yamashita as a bargaining chip had suddenly enraged me again. "It won't work, sir! Not by itself! The Yamashita case is not going well for you."

"That's not what I'm hearing. He will be convicted, Captain!"

"Yes he will. And I know how happy that makes you. *But it's becoming a horrifying sideshow, that's all! It doesn't make a goddamn bit of difference on the points I'm talking about, sir!*"

MacArthur stared at me, stunned and obviously angry, like a king slapped down by a lowly serf.

"I will not have you take the Lord's name in vain in my presence."

I was panting. My hands were trembling. Whitney and Willoughby were looking at each other with an unprecedented mutual rage, as if I had lost my mental capacities. I took a deep breath.

"I'm sorry, sir. I apologize for swearing."

MacArthur checked his watch. I knew he was not worried about the time. "Finish what you were saying, Captain."

"Yes, sir. I'm trying to."

My very words brought back the haunting image of Colonel Sam Genius struggling to convince MacArthur about the importance of holding Prince Asaka accountable for the rape of Nanking. I knew that I myself was dangling over a dangerous precipice. And I wasn't doing very well in my own little ambush. Maybe they had learned from Genius's antics. I hadn't thought about that. Or maybe I just wasn't as clever. Or maybe Genius hadn't even wanted to go to Fort Ord, and I had totally misread what had happened to him. But it did not matter, not any of it, because there was no way I could now reverse myself anyway.

"Let me try again, sir. If you simply trade Prince Nashimoto for the changes in the constitution, it is—*highly likely*—that the issue of political war crimes will remain on the table. General Yamashita's conviction won't solve that problem. He's a theater commander and a commoner. Even trying General Tojo in front of a proper tribunal next year won't solve the problem. He's a general who was picked to serve as prime minister by the imperial court. If you want to protect the emperor, then you *must charge someone who was close to the throne.* And since you don't want to charge the emperor's blood relatives, that leaves two people. That's it, General! *Two people.* Prince Konoye, who is the emperor's hereditary internal adviser, and Koichi Kido, the lord privy seal."

The three silently looked at one another for several seconds. I waited for an answer, drenched in sweat. There was no answer. Either I had given them fresh grist for their thinking, or I had so offended them that they were mentally preparing my coffin.

Finally I continued. "Two people, sir. There is no alternative. Make it a package deal. Trade them for Nashimoto and the constitution. Then you're done, sir. You have it all. You have the constitution, and you've charged the emperor's two closest advisers."

"And what are the charges?" asked MacArthur, now looking out his window toward the palace grounds.

"Accountability for all the emperor's decisions during the war. You've got Kido's diaries, use them! Kido and Konoye gave the emperor the bad advice. They picked the people who ran the government. They approved the policies that put Asia into full-scale slaughter. It's one or the other, General. Either the emperor did it, or they did."

This time I knew their silence was a form of stunned acceptance, as if they had never expected me to be capable of such shrewdness. The three generals stared at one another for a long time, deep in thought. Finally Court Whitney probed me.

"They came to you with this?"

"Kido came with the proposal," I said. "The analysis is my own."

I particularly enjoyed that little lie, for it was one that the lord privy seal himself might have been proud to tell. Lies to him were never lies if they prevented shame, and Kido more than anyone wished to insulate the emperor from shame. So in an odd, thoroughly Japanese way I was telling the truth. "They have come to understand that it is the only way to protect the imperial family. And as you know, they have dedicated their lives to protecting the imperial family."

"Will they make that offer officially?" asked the skeptical Willoughby.

"They have made the offer officially to the emperor," I answered. This time I knew that I probably was correct. Kido had said as much as I left the house of his mistress. "But they would never officially offer up one of their people to the Americans to be charged with a war crime, General. You know that, sir. It is their position that no single Japanese committed war crimes of a political nature, that the country acted as a collective family, that if you charge one Japanese with a political war crime, then you should charge the entire nation."

"They should communicate this to us directly," said Court Whitney.

"They have. That's what the meeting last night was all about." Again I held his piercing, unsettled stare. "They would never pass this on to your staff, General Whitney, because they fear it would make them lose face if you used the information improperly, or decided to expand on it by somehow using it as evidence of an admission of guilt by the imperial family. There will be no witnesses and no paper trail. Kido trusts me. He believes I was sent by the imperial ancestors to help Japan as it moves into the future."

"The silly little bastards," quipped a suddenly chuckling Willoughby.

"Jay the Duck, a spirit sent by the ancestors," laughed Court Whitney.

"I thought I sent you here, Captain Marsh," joked the supreme commander.

They laughed together for several seconds, enjoying the thought of my supposed ancestral mission. I did not join them. Instead, I persisted. "I'm not asking you to believe what they believe, and for my part I'll be very happy to be sent back to Manila as a civilian. But this is a serious offer. And in my opinion it will remove any criticism you might otherwise receive once you free Prince Nashimoto. So what more are you looking for, sir?"

MacArthur was smiling widely at me now, as if I were that same, formerly rebellious son who had just graduated first in his class from college. Watching his face I could not contain my own inner sense of elation and pride. It was as if a miracle had occurred, for in my adamance I seemed to have earned his full respect.

"It's an exceptional idea. A brilliant solution to a terrible dilemma! So what is there left to do, Jay?"

I took a deep breath, staring directly at him and speaking with forced conviction. "Charge them, sir."

"That's all?"

"They're expecting it."

MacArthur paced for a while, staring as he so often did across the near moat toward the emperor's residence, playing with his unlit pipe. Then he turned and pointed to Court Whitney.

"Charge them."

Whitney's mood had quickly changed. He glanced at me, then winked, a gesture of forgiveness. He even smiled as he furiously wrote notes in his legal pad.

"Bold stroke, Boss."

"Indeed." MacArthur turned back to me. "All right, now tell me about the Yamashita trial. It's clear that you're not as enthusiastic as other people who have been reporting to me."

I tightened my lips and sat full up in my chair, a gesture of final defiance. "I told you how I feel about it, sir. I want out."

"What do you mean?"

"I want out of the army. I can't go along with it anymore."

I could almost hear his mind calculating as he watched me, again taking in every nuance—the way I sat on the couch, where I kept my hands, how directly I was gazing back at him. He puffed up his chest, raising his chin as if somewhere nearby a camera was rolling. But he did not fool me. Looking into his eyes I realized that no matter what he would say, inside his heart he knew that at some level he was wrong.

"It is not easy for me to pass judgment on a defeated adversary, Captain

Marsh. But rarely has so cruel and wanton a record been held up for public scrutiny."

"I can't imagine you'd say that if you've been reading the transcripts, General. You're hanging the wrong man, sir. This is an emotional time, but all wars end emotionally. General Grant didn't seek to hang General Lee after the Civil War just because he lost, did he?"

MacArthur bridled at that, his mouth tightening with disgust. "General Lee did not sanction the killing of innocents. Nor did he pillage and destroy an ancient Christian city."

I took a deep breath, but said it anyway. "No, I guess we'd have to go to the rape of Georgia and the burning of Atlanta for that. But that was the Union army, and General Sherman was on the winning side. So I guess we're not supposed to mention it?"

I was trying to force his hand, to get him so angry that he'd be done with me, fire me and send me off. After all, as soon as Sam Genius had become personal, he was gone. But for some reason the supreme commander held back. A small, teasing smile crept onto his face. "An interesting point, but you realize that you are treading on very thin ice, Captain! My father was a soldier in that march."

"I well know that, sir. And I make no judgments, although I suppose he did feel some air of conciliation in marrying your mother, a daughter of the Confederacy?"

Surprisingly, MacArthur's smile broadened with appreciation at my knowledge of his family history. His eyes went far away. "To the great distress of her family, I might add. But that is the spirit of America." He seemed to catch himself, to forcibly bring his mind back to the present. "But I can understand that you are ready to resume your civilian career. And what is it that you want to do with your life, Jay?"

"I want to return to Manila, sir. I have an offer to join a family business there."

Court Whitney leaned forward, joining the conversation. "You will recall that Captain Marsh is engaged to a Filipina woman, Boss. From the Ramirez family. A good family. They do construction and food services. Very active in Subic and Manila."

"The girl. Yes, of course I remember." MacArthur's eyes softened, again chasing memories and dreams, perhaps of a life he himself might have lived if duty had been different and destiny had not been a blood obligation. "So you haven't forgotten her, up here in the land of geishas? You still want to marry her. And what is her name?"

"Consuelo, sir."

He visibly jolted, coming out of the past to stare hard at me. He knew why I had said it. It was a private joke, perhaps a hidden threat. For a brief second his face held a mix of pained memories, undefined jealousies, and vague fears. But I was the only one who comprehended this, because I was the only one who knew. And finally he smiled blandly.

"An interesting name."

"Actually it's a middle name," I lied. "They call her Divina Clara."

He scrutinized me further, as if finally accepting me as something of an intellectual equal. "You would make an excellent businessman, Jay. But I should counsel you never to join a Filipino family as a junior partner. You would lose your position of high respect in their community if you do that."

I had never thought of that. And although I could not measure the sincerity of his advice, it occurred to me that he might be right. "Thank you for saying that, General. But it will give me some time to look at other options."

"If you need time, then I will help you find some time." MacArthur turned grandly to General Whitney. "Court, we need to send Jay back to the Philippines. He should be down there for the Yamashita trial, anyway."

My heart sank. "But sir, I want out of the army!"

MacArthur held back a smile. "In due course, Jay. When the trial is over. We need you to provide us with a continuing update, and to see it— to its conclusion. Thank you for your excellent observations with respect to the Japanese. We will charge these people. It was an astute recommendation. And, good day." And now he smiled grandly, dismissing me with the simple nodding of his head toward the door.

"Good day, sir."

I rose slowly from my seat, stunned and deflated. I had tried to ambush him, but I knew that he had just mousetrapped me instead. For so long as General Tomoyuki Yamashita was alive, I would remain his hostage. One false word, one loud protest that might resonate in the media, and I would be recalled from Manila and posted by MacArthur to anywhere in the world that he might decide.

As I neared the door he called to me.

"Oh, Jay—"

I turned to face him. "Yes, sir?"

"I want your notes."

Another mousetrap. I could not help but grin. "Yes, sir. Of course."

He grinned back, in full control. There was a playful mystery in his eyes. "And there's a gentleman waiting outside to meet me by the name of Thorpe Thomas. Would you bring him in?"

"Yes, sir."

Thorpe Thomas was sitting on a chair in the corridor just outside MacArthur's office. He was a tall, crisp-looking man of about sixty, with wavy white hair and a quick smile that revealed perfect teeth.

"Excuse me, sir. Are you Thorpe Thomas?"

"Indeed I am."

"General MacArthur will see you now."

He stood, walking toward the door with me. "Well, that's wonderful."

He was wearing a grey woolen pinstriped suit, a red silk tie, and the most expensive pair of Florsheim shoes I had ever seen. He moved with an air of easy self-confidence that seemed only to emanate from those who have become irreversibly and supremely successful. I found myself instinctively liking him.

MacArthur was standing at the door itself as I opened it. His face was brimming with a regal, welcoming charm.

"Thorpe, old man! It's good to see you."

"Douglas, you're looking well, for an old warrior."

As they shook hands I began to leave, but instead MacArthur took my elbow and held me in their presence. For the first time in my life he put an arm around my shoulder, embracing me and turning me to face Thorpe Thomas.

"Here's a top prospect for you, Thorpe. And you know I've never made an introduction without personally backing it up. Captain Marsh has given me unprecedented service for three years, now. I can't tell you how valuable he's been over the past few months here in Japan. He's a Japanese-speaker, a born diplomat, and very, very smart about Asia. Despite his junior rank I've had him working on his own, negotiating at the top levels of the Japanese government! But I'm going to be losing him soon. He wants to leave the army and get into business."

Thomas smoothly took my hand, never losing his smile as he took in every aspect of my appearance with cool, appraising grey eyes. "Have you thought about investment banking?" he asked.

I felt flattered, but at the same time stunned, unprepared, even small. I had never even contemplated such an immensely rewarding future. I looked uncertainly from Thomas to MacArthur and then back again. "I haven't ruled it out," I finally managed to say.

"This region is going to explode with American capital," said Thomas. He reached into a pocket and came out with a business card. I examined it as he talked. "Japan, the Philippines, Hong Kong, Singapore! They're all waiting to be rebuilt, and American business is going to lead the way. We're looking for bright young men with energy and insight who also have some knowledge of the area."

"You won't find a better man," said MacArthur, giving me a fatherly pat on the back. "I will stake my own reputation on that."

The business card read *Managing Director, International Investment, Bergson-Forbes Group, New York.* An uncontrollable thrill now shimmered through me. I was as breathless as the first time I had ever seen a naked woman. New York. Hong Kong. Japan. Singapore. And Manila as well! I knew vaguely what investment bankers did. They lived well, traveled to great places, and made millions of dollars.

"Are you interested?" asked Thomas.

And why not? MacArthur had planted a powerful and accurate seed of uncertainty about working for the Ramirez family in Manila, no matter what happened between Divina Clara and myself. "I'd, uh—I'd be happy to talk with you about it, sir."

"Do you have a card?" asked Thomas.

"Jay is being posted back to Manila for an exceptionally important assignment," interrupted MacArthur. "He'll be there for a few months. I will make sure you know how to reach him."

"I'm planning to be in Manila soon, anyway," said Thomas. He shook my hand again. "I'll give you a call!"

"That would be fine, sir."

"Excellent!" said this mysteriously kind and elegant man.

I was sky-high as I walked out of the supreme commander's office. I even managed to ignore the secret smirk on Court Whitney's face as I closed the door behind me. Making my way down the darkened corridor past rooms where an ever-increasing preponderance of strangers from Washington now toiled at peacetime tasks, it did not even bother me that Douglas MacArthur had mousetrapped me three separate times in my naive attempt to ambush him once.

I had not broken away clean, but neither had I totally lost. Compared to where the world had been only twenty-four hours before, I now had reason to be happy. Kido would be charged and sent to jail. I was still in the army, but I would have my time in Manila. True, I was surrendering my notes, swallowing back the bile of General Yamashita's kangaroo court, and being lured into a position that might forever buy my silence.

But I already knew that, thanks to the recommendation of General MacArthur, Thorpe Thomas was going to give me the chance to become a very rich, and even a very powerful, man.

CHAPTER 25

★ ★ ★ ★ ★

I had waited in the cold night air for half an hour, standing on the front steps of the Dai Ichi building, my eyes continually searching the faintly lit, heavily treed Imperial Palace grounds on the far side of the palace plaza. Here and there a light glowed from the Household Ministry buildings and the Outer Ceremonial Palace, but otherwise the grounds were black and devoid of motion. Kido had said ten-thirty, and usually he was irritatingly prompt. I checked my watch, huddling my shoulders against the frostbitten air. It was now nearly eleven. I paced along the steps, shoving my hands deep inside my pockets, and began to wonder if the lord privy seal had changed his mind.

And then finally I saw the headlights. Two cars were slowly making their way along an inner road toward the nearby Cherry Field gate, their path twisting back and forth, negotiating moats and tree lines like mice inside a maze. My heart raced. Kido was coming. History was being made, propelled into action by my own cunning. I walked quickly across the street toward the gate. In one of those delicious little ironies that seemed only to happen with Kido, he had asked me to be his personal escort when he gave himself up to the American authorities.

At the gate the two cars stopped. Nearing them I could see that the emperor had again offered up his personal plum-colored Daimlers for our short journey. Kido was going to prison in style, far more grandly than when MacArthur and his entourage had entered the country in the now-famous charcoal-burner convoy that took us from Atsugi to Yokohama. Kido was in the lead car, sitting in the back seat. Through the window I could see that he was as usual dressed quite elegantly, wearing the striped pants and cutaway coat that had been his normal working uniform. He waved to me, indicating that I should open the door and sit next to him.

"We have plenty of time," he said, declining to apologize for his tardiness as I climbed into the car. "Omori is not that far." Even in the darkness his eyes burned into me. "But why did you say we should arrive at midnight, Captain Jay Marsh?"

"Because MacArthur announced that you should turn yourself in today," I answered. "And I thought you should have every minute that was available to you."

"Ah, so. An excellent gesture," said Kido, as if he were somehow still in charge. "A good sign." He looked back with undisguised longing at the palace grounds. The Daimler pulled smoothly onto the empty street, immediately picking up speed. "I very much appreciated the opportunity to say my farewells properly. And I'm sure the emperor was pleased as well."

"It is a noble thing that you are doing, Lord Privy Seal."

"I am no longer the lord privy seal, Captain Jay Marsh. You must now call me Marquis Koichi Kido." He covered his obvious sadness with a sarcastic smile. I could tell that he had been drinking. "That is, until the supreme commander strips us all of our royal titles as well."

"I will always call you the lord privy seal."

"You may do that only if you wish to insult the emperor."

"I'm sorry, Marquis Koichi Kido," I said pointedly. A part of me actually empathized with the enormity of his loss. "I have no wish to insult the emperor."

"No," he said, looking out the window. "Not you, of all people. But anyway you are wrong to call my actions noble. Do you understand *majime?*"

"Perhaps if I study for the rest of my life I will understand *majime*, Marquis Kido. For now I am too young and immature."

He twinkled with delight at my response. "Very good, Captain Jay Marsh. I am going to miss you." He looked out the window again. "I have lived my life in service of the emperor. That has been my outer truth. My inner life must feel the same truth or I have no *majime*. And so I am happy to have volunteered to make this simple journey."

We rode silently for a while, staring out at dark, empty streets. I looked behind us. "Why do you have two cars, Marquis Kido?"

"It was the emperor's wish," he said simply. His eyes went far away, and the pride of a recent memory washed over his face. "We had a long and comfortable meeting in his private study, talking about many things, from the time of the emperor's childhood. I was his eldest Big Brother from the time he was very young, you know."

"Yes, I know."

"And then there was a wonderful dinner. Many friends from the—old days. Many stories. Ah, yes, there were great days in the past, Captain Jay Marsh! It is impossible to explain to you how complete my honor has been, to serve my emperor from the time of his childhood. And then Empress Nagako presented me with a most beautiful antique table on the occasion of my—departure. And a tray of doughnuts that she baked herself!"

"You are indeed a lucky man—*Marquis* Koichi Kido."

The Daimler raced along the city streets, uninterrupted by traffic. Omori, which had once been a prisoner of war camp for Allied soldiers, was to our south and indeed not far away. After a few minutes Kido glanced carefully at me. "I must ask you a cultural question. My son-in-law is a graduate of Harvard and something of an expert on American ways. He has advised me that if I simply accept responsibility for the conduct of the war, the Americans will somehow believe that I am only protecting the emperor. But he says that if I claim I am not responsible for these things and wish to argue them at my trial, it will for some reason protect the emperor. I do not understand this logic. Is this true?"

I thought about it for a moment. "It is possible, Lord Privy Seal."

"I told you, I am not the lord privy seal."

His stubborn adamance about his recently abandoned title seemed tragically humorous, even at this moment of humiliation. Despite myself I fought back a grin. "I am sorry, Marquis. But it is possible that your son-in-law is correct. If you readily admit that you are responsible, American minds might seek to pierce through your defenses, deciding that they were offered only as a cover-up for the emperor's acts. But if you deny any responsibility at all, Americans might decide that there is no reason to look beyond you to the emperor, and that they should look in other places for the culprits."

"You have a very strange society," Kido mused, looking out the window.

"We believe an individual has the right to maintain his innocence until he is proven guilty," I said. "It is very unusual for someone to turn himself in and admit his error."

Kido stared at me, suddenly bitter and bemused. "That encourages people to deny responsibility for their own actions," he said.

"But aren't you taking responsibility for the emperor and his uncles, and not yourself?"

"I told you all this already!" He was looking at me with great exasperation, as if I were a failed student. "The emperor has accepted responsibility on behalf of the entire nation. But it is impossible for the imperial family to violate the law. Any law. That is the reason your earlier advice to me was so sound."

"You must never tell the Americans that I gave you such advice, Marquis Koichi Kido. You must tell them only that you decided to turn yourself in after being charged by the supreme commander."

"Yes," he said. "Of course."

"To protect the supreme commander," I said.

He peered deeply into my eyes, as if he were able to read the unspoken meaning in my words. I stared back, slowly smiling. At that moment we both knew the convoluted, hidden truth. And I also knew that Kido would never admit that I had tricked him into this perfect journey. He was comfortable with his sacrifice. It would indeed protect the emperor, and it would also free Prince Nashimoto. He had been given his farewell meal and his antique table and his tray of doughnuts. How could he now complain that his journey was set into motion by a young, scheming captain?

"You are much smarter than I thought, Captain Jay Marsh."

"I was sent by the imperial ancestors, Marquis Koichi Kido, for the good of Japan. This was meant to happen."

"Yes," he said, his voice going soft and vague. "You have been Japanese for two thousand years." For some reason he smiled and stared back out the window. "I had always wondered. But now I know how you won this war."

Ahead of us the high, dark walls of the Omori Prison compound came slowly into view. A small entourage of American military officials had gathered at the main gate, awaiting Kido's arrival. He saw them and began fidgeting nervously in his seat. Another, involuntary smile crept onto his face. I could tell that this time it was motivated by a sense of shame.

"My captors await me."

"Yes," I said. "They have been waiting for some time."

"You must take care of Yoshiko," he said as we neared the gate.

"How?" His comment startled me fully awake. I had not thought about her for days and had no idea what he meant.

His eyes bore relentlessly into me. "She has—extended herself on your behalf, Captain Jay Marsh. She is a geisha but she has never been a prostitute. She is a delicate girl and as you know highly schooled. But now she will always be remembered as having been your—escort."

"Yes, but she was—introduced to me by you, was she not?"

"Of course she was. In the restaurant that night I could see that you liked her. It was my honor. And hers. But now I am gone. Others might not look so kindly on her—service."

"Your culture is not like that," I protested softly. "It protects the individual who is acting for the—greater good. She was seeing me with your full encouragement."

"My culture does not fully appreciate foreigners, Captain Jay Marsh. Or women who have made love to them."

"I am leaving in two days for Manila. I will be married there."

"But you do believe in obligations, do you not?"

He smiled at me with a comfortable vindictiveness. Yoshiko had been my reward and now she had turned into his own little payback. He knew he was skewering me with my Western culture's sense of guilt as he predicted Yoshiko's Oriental shame.

"What should I do?"

"Take care of her."

"How?"

He did not answer. The car slowed, then came to a halt. Near us, the group of military police and senior officers seemed to collectively stiffen all at once, waiting for Kido to exit the car. He touched me warmly on the shoulder, smiling with what I knew was a heartfelt sincerity.

"It has been great fun, Captain Jay Marsh. I hope I will see you again once I am—free from this sacrifice."

"Yes it has, Lord Privy Seal."

"You must learn to stop saying that."

Behind us, four tuxedoed imperial chamberlains crawled quickly from the Daimler that had been following us. Now they gathered outside the car door on Kido's side. One older man ceremonially reached out and opened the door. Then all four bowed deeply as Kido stepped from the car and faced the group that would take him into custody. I opened my own door and walked to the other side of the car, joining Kido as he moved toward the Americans.

In the darkness I was surprised to see General Court Whitney among them. "Well, I'm glad he showed up," said Whitney. "Prince Konoye wasn't as cooperative."

"What's the problem, General?"

"He killed himself."

"The guy had style," said a tall, acne-scarred colonel I did not recognize, stepping up next to Whitney. "He threw a big party last night at his villa, supposedly to celebrate his arrest. Everyone says he was the perfect host. Then after they left he slipped into his silk pajamas, swallowed down a dose of poison, and went to bed."

Behind us, the two Daimlers pulled slowly away, leaving Koichi Kido alone in the midst of his captors. He spoke quickly to me in Japanese. "I heard the general mention Konoye. Is he here yet?"

"No," I said to Kido in Japanese. "It seems that Prince Konoye is dead."

"Ah, so," said the former lord privy seal, his face awash in a knowing sadness. "*Majime* again. Now do you understand? For more than two thousand years, his family has never betrayed the emperor. He had warned me that he would not testify."

"Time to bring the Big Boy inside," interrupted the colonel, nodding toward Kido.

Whitney handed me a piece of paper. "Konoye left a letter. We need to get it translated."

I stared at the *kanji* for a few seconds, then stopped the colonel as he neared Kido. "Give me a minute, Colonel."

I handed the letter to Kido. Both of us smiled knowingly. "As you know, I am terrible with *kanji*, Marquis Koichi Kido. But it would be useful to hear what the prince wished to say?"

Kido bowed slightly, then brought the letter very close to his face, reading aloud it in the dark. " '*I have committed certain errors in handling state affairs since the outbreak of the China incident. I believe my real intentions are even now understood and appreciated by my friends, including not a few friends in America. But the winner is too boastful and the loser too servile. World public opinion, which is at present full of overexcitement, will in time recover a more normal calmness and balance. Only then will a just verdict be rendered.*' "

"What did he say?" asked Whitney.

"The winner is too boastful, and the loser is too servile," I answered. "And some embellishment."

"And so he kills himself? How servile can you get?" The colonel snickered, shaking his head as if Konoye's act of honor were completely absurd. And to him I suppose it was.

I turned to Kido, bowing to him in farewell. "You must go now. Good luck to you, Marquis Koichi Kido."

He returned my bow. "I will miss you, Captain Jay Marsh. The others do not understand us."

"It has been an honor."

The colonel took Kido by the arm, and the other soldiers surrounded him. Whitney stood alongside me, watching as they marched Kido inside the prison gate.

"Good job, Jay. Sorry about Konoye, but this will indeed fix the problem."

"Thank you, sir." I felt suddenly exhausted, as if I needed to sleep for years. And I cannot deny that I felt a pang of remorse, thinking of Konoye's death and watching the sly and brilliant Kido disappear inside the cold grey prison walls.

Whitney pointed toward a nearby jeep. "That one's yours. See you tomorrow."

I could hear the water running even before I opened the door to my room. Inside, the air was wet and hot. The covers of my bed had already been turned back. She was in a grey cotton shift, kneeling at the edge of the *furo* bath, her hair hanging loose and silky down her back. Hearing the water running and seeing the long, slim lines of her body I was overcome with such a mix of elation and dread that I stood paralyzed for a long moment in the doorway.

As I lingered in the doorway she seemed to sense my presence, turning from the *furo* and watching me carefully. She stood and slowly walked toward me. Behind her, the water was still running, sending up a mist of steam that filled my unheated room like fog. A hopeful smile crept upon her face. Her nipples were hard against the fabric of the shift. The fabric caught against the top of her thighs as she walked, giving her hips a smooth and tantalizing fullness. She tossed her head and then shook it with her chin held high, settling her hair behind her shoulders. And finally she bowed.

"I waited outside for a long time," she said. "And the landlord finally let me in. I hope you are not angry with me, Jay-*san*."

"No," I answered. "You shouldn't have to wait outside, Yoshiko. It's become very cold."

She glowed thankfully, then knelt at my feet, beginning to take off my shoes. "I watched for your jeep," she said. "And finally you returned! After so long a day you must take a very hot bath."

I said nothing. The shoes came off, one by one. She stood again, looking up into my face as if trying to read my mood. Finally she tried to tease me. "I think maybe you don't want a bath."

"Yoshiko, I have to talk to you. We must speak honestly."

She studied my face some more, comprehending my seriousness. "I should turn off the water, then?"

"Yes. Turn off the water."

I removed my coat, tossing it across the desk, then loosened my shirt and sat on the edge of the bed. In the bathroom the water stopped running. Yoshiko stood before me for a second, uncertain of what I wanted, and then sat next to me on the bed. Her almond eyes were wide with apprehension.

"Marquis Kido is now in jail."

"Yes," she said, staring acutely into my face, as if for clues. "He is no longer the lord privy seal. We were told this."

"And I must leave Japan in two days."

"For good?"

"Yes."

Her face fell. She ran a hand along her chin and then behind her head, grasping her long hair. "May I tell you that I will miss you—very much, Jay-*san*?"

"I will miss you, too." I felt disloyal to Divina Clara saying it, but it was the truth. She looked quickly at my face as if there might be more to what

I was saying, but my eyes told her that there was not. "The lord privy seal—I'm sorry—the Marquis Kido—is worried that you might—have some problems since he is in jail and I will be gone."

"I will not have *many* problems," she said carefully. Her voice had become silky and flat. "And when he returns, I will be fine."

"He is worried that there might be some retaliation against you, since I am an American. Since we were lovers."

She smiled slowly, her eyes filled with an accepting sadness, and I knew that Yoshiko had indeed been on a kamikaze mission. "Japanese men do not like that."

"He said that I might be able to help you."

"Yes," she answered. "You might help me."

I took out my wallet, opening it. "Yoshiko, I don't have much money, but—"

"No!" Her hand insistently closed the wallet and held it firmly. "You must never give me money."

I quickly understood that I had threatened to shame her. "I'm sorry, Yoshiko." I put the wallet away. "How can I help you?"

She stared at me for what seemed to be a long while, her very silence taking on an unusual power. And then she decided. "Please lay back on the bed, Jay-*san*."

Hesitantly, I stretched out on the bed, resting my head on a pillow.

"Now, you must hold me." She climbed into my arms, resting her head on my shoulder. I could feel her relax. Her eyes closed. She began running a hand over my stomach and chest. "When I am very old I will look back and remember you like this."

We lay still on the bed for a long time. Finally she spoke again. "If you wish to help me, then you must make sure my superiors understand that I did not make you happy."

She felt warm and comfortable alongside me. I could not deny my feelings for her, and I felt badly for the turmoil I had brought into her life. "But you did make me happy, Yoshiko."

"No," she said, now looking cleverly up into my face. Her lips were smiling but her eyes were pleading. "I have brought great shame upon myself, Jay-*san*. I did not carry out the lord privy seal's wishes that I bring you comfort and recreation."

And then I understood.

The next afternoon I visited the restaurant where I had first met Yoshiko, seeking out the older geisha who had then greeted me at the door. The restaurant had not yet opened for dinner, but she bowed deeply to me as I entered, recognizing me immediately.

"You are here to visit Yoshiko?" she asked knowingly.

"No, elder sister," I said. "I wish to speak to you in Yoshiko's presence."

She watched me for a moment, confused and mildly frightened. Then she gestured with a hand toward the kitchen area. "You will please follow me, sir?"

Yoshiko sat with five other geisha in a small side room near the kitchen. The girls stood when I entered, then bowed. A few of them were smiling expectantly at Yoshiko, who was feigning a deep surprise at my unannounced arrival.

I wasted no time. "Elder sister, tomorrow I will be leaving for the Philippines. I wish to thank you for the kindness and the courtesies you and your staff have given me over the past few months. But I must also be honest with you about my deep disappointment. I did not bring up this matter before, because I believed it might cause the lord privy seal to lose face. After all, it was he who selected Yoshiko to be my—escort, and cultural adviser."

The older woman was now looking harshly at Yoshiko, knowing that I had in some way been displeased. And in the other girls' faces I could see surprise and even fear. But Yoshiko was now staring hotly back at me, as if with open dislike.

"I must tell you first," I continued, "that I found Yoshiko to be highly intelligent, and an expert in explaining all manner of Japanese customs and traditions. And also, I cannot deny that I found her to be beautiful. With the right man, she will no doubt be a wonderful mistress, or even a wife."

They all were now looking at me with complete confusion. I forced a frown, stiffening as I stared at her, and putting my hands onto my hips. "But despite the lord privy seal's personal encouragement to me, I found that Yoshiko had no interest in making love to me. And in fact, I believe she dislikes Americans."

"No!" said the elder sister, having softened her visage but still seeming to be upset. "I am very sorry for whatever displeased you, Captain Jay Marsh. And I must tell you I am surprised by this report, since both Yoshiko and the lord privy seal had informed me that you were happy. But I can promise you that whatever the problem might have been, all of us like Americans very, very much!"

"Then perhaps she simply disliked me," I said with finality. "Because—

and I say this even though I know I am losing face—I tried many times to make love to Yoshiko. And she wanted nothing to do with me!"

The other girls were now laughing, their hands covering their mouths as if to hide their delight. Yoshiko continued to stare silently at me, her chin held high in mock defiance. The older geisha was frowning at Yoshiko, but her eyes were merry, and I could see relief in her face as well.

"Captain Marsh," said the elder sister, "I promise you we will work very hard with Yoshiko to improve her attitude."

All of them knew by now that I was pretending, but by the time I left the restaurant, Yoshiko's esteem had soared in their eyes. How deeply she must have pleased me, and how much I truly must have cared for her, that I would take such pains before I departed to visit her fellow workers and reconstruct her purity! My strutting, blatant lie had lifted away any shame that might have someday been visited upon the gentle and loving geisha.

Yes, I had taken care of Yoshiko. But driving back toward my *ryokan*, the inconsistency of how I had done this left me troubled. For some reason I kept thinking of Father Garvey's final admonition as I returned to my room and packed for my return to Manila. *You cannot have love without honesty, Jay.*

And I knew that it would be much more difficult for me to resolve this matter with Divina Clara.

CHAPTER 26

★ ★ ★ ★ ★

Two days later I was back in Manila, on my final military assignment. MacArthur, ever brilliant and sometimes cruel, had dangled the ugliest and yet most tantalizing of carrots before me. The very thing that I had told him should not happen would be the ticket to my freedom. Once General Tomoyuki Yamashita was dead, Jay Marsh could begin again to live, and yes, to prosper in a manner he had never before dreamed. MacArthur had handcuffed me to the proceedings, causing me to wish that they would simply end so that I could get on with my civilian life. Yes, this was MacArthur at his imperial best, making me wait impatiently for the very act I condemned in order to be personally set free.

And how quickly those next few weeks went by!

The supposed purpose of my presence was to report in detail each night to Tokyo, offering a summary of Yamashita's trial. And so I spent my days in the crowded, oven-hot ballroom as the trial pressed relentlessly forward. The prosecution was winding up its case when I rejoined it. Victim upon victim was bearing scars and telling tales of Japanese atrocities, until the very word "atrocity" became mind-numbing, redundant, devoid of meaning or emotion.

Once the last mutilated child had exposed her wounds, once the last old man had told of the murder of his family, Frank Witherspoon began his defense. He started with General Muto, Yamashita's chief of staff, who laid out in great detail the insurmountable problems of divided command, poor communications, and lack of supplies that Yamashita had faced as the field commander in the Philippines. He introduced voluminous American army intelligence and operational reports that verified Muto's testimony. He flew in seven character witnesses from Japan who described Yamashita's great popularity among Japanese commoners and the frequent disagreements between the general and the imperial government over whether to fight the war at all and how to fight it once it had begun.

And finally Yamashita himself took the stand, speaking patiently and persuasively without notes for three full days, including an eleven-hour period of cross-examination. Through this whole interrogation the general sat at a stiff attention under the relentless lights in the witness chair. Sweat continually dripped down his face and neck, drenching his khaki uniform. Now and then he would reach over to a small table and take a long drink of water. Other than that, he remained acutely focused on his questioners, just as he had remained focused on the testimony of each witness during the prosecution's case. Behind him the prosecution had placed a large map of the Philippines. The map was covered with more than a hundred red disks. Each disk represented the location of a major atrocity.

His testimony remained simple and consistent. He had inherited this army, arriving in the Philippines only days before the Americans landed at Leyte. He was directing a complex mobile defense against insuperable odds. He had given repeated, explicit written instructions regarding the conduct of war and the treatment of civilians. Once the Americans landed in Luzon, neither he nor his top officers had the ability to make inspection trips to remote Japanese units. He had never been told of atrocities occurring, and he vigorously condemned the atrocities that had indeed taken place.

In the eleven hours of cross-examination the chief prosecutor, Major Robert Kerr, who in civilian life was an experienced trial lawyer, had been unable to break down any element of the general's testimony or to find any inconsistencies or falsehoods. Finally in frustration he pointed to the map.

"Do you deny to this commission that you knew of, or ever heard of, any of these killings?"

Yamashita continued to stare at the prosecutor without emotion. He spoke emphatically. "I never heard of nor did I know of these events."

"I find that impossible to believe." Major Kerr paused dramatically, then pointed a finger at Yamashita and shouted into his face. "This is your opportunity to explain to this commission, if you care to do so, how you could have failed to know of these killings!"

He failed to know of the killings. This, in one sentence, was the entire case against General Tomoyuki Yamashita. Either he knew, in which case he was directly culpable. Or he did not know, making him criminally negligent and thus responsible for the climate that permitted the killings.

Speaking slowly through a simultaneous interpreter, for forty-two minutes General Yamashita explained in detail why he had not known. Witherspoon had already outlined the reasons, but Yamashita stated them once again, all the military considerations and human difficulties of his isolated, heavily pressured journey into the mountains near Baguio that were in one respect a complete validation of the American and Filipino forces who had done their duty so well and fought so hard to pressure and destroy the Japanese army. Finally the Tiger took a deep breath. For the first time he spoke with emotion.

"I believe under the circumstances that I did the best job that could be done. If I could have foreseen these things I would have concentrated my efforts to prevent them. If the situation permits, I will punish the people who did them to the fullest extent of military law. I absolutely did not order these things. Nor did I receive the order to do them from any superior authority. Nor did I ever permit such a thing, or if I had known would I have condoned such a thing. I will swear to heaven and earth concerning these points. That is all I have to say."

The cameras clicked and rolled. The klieg lights finally went out. Those in the audience murmured and stood from their chairs, exhausted and relieved. Yamashita was escorted out of the room by his entourage of military police. The "trial" was finally over. All that was left would be the reading of the verdict at two o'clock the following afternoon.

It was December 6. MacArthur, with his penchant for anniversaries, had arranged for the verdict to be read to the world during a live, fifteen-minute radio address on Pearl Harbor Day. That night the twelve American, British, and Australian journalists who had covered every moment of the trial were polled by the International News Service in a secret ballot. Asked if the evidence presented at the trial warranted Yamashita's conviction, all twelve voted Yamashita innocent.

Yamashita's verdict came quickly, and it was no surprise to anyone. At precisely two o'clock on the afternoon of December 7, the gargantuan general stood at attention, facing the table of five general officers who had heard his case. Flanked by Frank Witherspoon and Colonel Hamamoto, his Japanese interpreter, Yamashita's back was to the mulling crowd as General Russell B. Reynolds read the findings and the sentence of the military commission.

It was a grand, theatrical moment. The cameras clicked and rolled again. A clutch of microphones was just before General Reynolds. He cleared his throat, his furrowed face steeped in sober judgment. Manila Bay glimmered through the window behind him. In front of him the historic ballroom was packed with spectators and media. They whispered to one another, staring forward, craning their heads with a hushed excitement that normally might indeed have been reserved for the final act in a play.

Reynolds read his statement carefully, mindful of his worldwide audience. "General Yamashita, the commission concludes the following: that a series of atrocities and other high crimes have been committed by members of the Japanese armed forces under your command; that they were not sporadic in nature but in many cases were methodically supervised by Japanese officers and noncommissioned officers; and that during the period in question you failed to provide effective control of your troops as was required by the circumstances."

Now he paused, looking slowly around the room before reading the sentence itself. "Accordingly, the commission finds you guilty as charged and sentences you to death by hanging."

If this had indeed been a play, there might have been a round of applause for the perfect manner in which General Reynolds had portrayed a judge. But it was real, and instead the packed, sweltering ballroom fell into a hush, as if aware for the first time of the consequences of their public catharsis. Yamashita himself merely nodded silently and calmly turned to leave. He was escorted back to his prison cell, and later that afternoon was transferred to the Los Banos Bilibid, where he was to stay until he died.

But Frank Witherspoon was not done. The wiry, flame-haired lawyer marched lividly out of the building and filed an appeal to the U.S.

Supreme Court. Among the charges in Witherspoon's petition was the claim that "General MacArthur has taken the law into his own hands, is disregarding the laws of the United States and the Constitution, and has no authority from Congress or the president."

MacArthur, hurrying to be done with Yamashita, just as immediately approved the commission's sentence, wanting to hang the Tiger before the end of the week. On December 9 the secretary of war intervened, "suggesting" to MacArthur that he delay Yamashita's execution until the Supreme Court decided on Witherspoon's appeal. MacArthur, angry and imperious, radioed back to the secretary, who by law was his superior, refusing to take the "suggestion" and claiming that the Supreme Court did not have any jurisdiction in this "purely military" affair. And finally the secretary of war directly ordered MacArthur to stay the execution.

And so I would be stuck in the Philippines for at least another month, awaiting the actions of the U.S. Supreme Court. Once freed from the army, I would be trained in New York City under the guiding hand of Thorpe Thomas. More important, I would return home alone. This had not been my plan when I had flown happily back to Manila after my final meeting with MacArthur. Nor was it my choice. It simply became my fate. Or shall we call it the consequences of Father Garvey's creed of honesty?

Perhaps for some of us every piece of good news has its price, because it all had begun with Thorpe Thomas. MacArthur's investment-banker friend had flown down from Tokyo a few days after my own flight, then offered me a position with his firm after one lengthy dinner. Carlos Ramirez clearly felt that he had lost great face among many of his Filipino business associates. Even worse, he viewed my decision to join Thomas in New York as a betrayal, a rejection of the greatest gift he could have offered me other than Divina Clara herself. As the Yamashita trial sped by he grew increasingly hostile to me. In his eyes I had made promises as solemn as a wedding vow. I had violated the unspoken terms of his blessing, then humiliated him among his peers by rejecting full membership in his family.

Toward the end of the trial I learned that I would be required to return to New York for the first part of training by myself, and would have to wait several months before I could send for Divina Clara. Carlos became overtly suspicious, often visibly angry. He seized on this small turn of events to insinuate that I was again manipulating his family. Not even my offer to move up the wedding date could assuage him. Divina Clara was his favored child, the very jewel in his crown. It became clear to me that he no longer wanted a wedding at all. In his view our relationship was forever spoiled. Divina Clara was either going to be deserted as part of a lover's hoax, a form of sexual poaching that would bring an even greater insult to his family pride, or to be gone from him forever, living in a country so far away that he probably would never live to see it. Suddenly I was no different than the Subic sailors who perennially made empty promises and sailed away, never to return. He abruptly announced that I could not stay overnight in their house anymore, a clear first step in breaking off the engagement.

We had not yet garnered the courage to tell him that she was with child. That night on the bench in her family garden, as the moon shone down on us and the perfumed air swirled slowly against our faces, we talked anxiously in hushed tones about how to tell him in the face of his fresh hostility. As we huddled and whispered, Carlos came repeatedly to the upstairs window, staring down at us with his arms folded in disapproval. And finally, awash in a logic driven from a place within her that I could not fully comprehend, Divina Clara decided that since the next day was Sunday, she would pray all night, so that in church God might provide her the answer.

That night I tossed unsleeping in my military bed at the transient officers' barracks. I missed her immensely. I was trying to picture her in her own bed, praying for the answer that God might bring her. And I was struggling with another problem: my own need for expiation. For I had not been able to tell her about Yoshiko, either.

My thoughts drifted to Father Garvey, now back in his Jesuit retreat at Manresa. Was he praying for me as he remembered his forbidden but treasured nights in Manila? Had I betrayed his trust, ignoring his final warning? *God is talking to you, Jay*, that was what Father Garvey had told me on the night before he sailed for home. *You must have the courage to listen. How can you move forward in your life if you carry this transgression in your heart?* And as dawn began to brighten my drawn window shades, I resolved that I must tell her.

And so as we walked to church the next morning I told her the rest of it. I told her I had been weak, that at first I had been trapped by Lord Privy Seal Kido in my drunkenness and lack of sophistication, and that later I had been unable to make a clean break with Yoshiko because I had been required to continue my relationship with Kido. Coming out of my mouth it sounded cynical, horrible, and wrong. I knew immediately that there was no way I could explain what had been in my heart as I splashed in Yoshiko's *furos* and nibbled food from her playful fingers. How could I justify to Divina Clara that there was no sin in Tokyo, only shame, and that part of what I did was to shield Yoshiko herself from shame?

Watching her mortified face as we walked I knew that I had been wrong to tell her. She was horrified, speechless. She physically retreated from me, pulling her arms into herself and tucking her chin onto her chest. And for the first time I comprehended that raw honesty does not always bring unmitigated happiness, that indeed, as Lord Privy Seal Kido so easily understood, there are times when a lie can be more honest than the truth. Because I was losing her. She was vanishing before my eyes. All I could do was keep saying over and over that it had meant nothing, nothing at all. But it had meant everything.

She hurried before me when we reached the chapel and did not look at me when we took our seats. She wept throughout the Mass and was still weeping and stumbling as she went forward to take Communion. Kneeling before the altar of Christ, shuddering with tears, she raised her head to take the Communion wafer from the priest. And as his hand neared her lips he dropped the wafer.

Perhaps he was distracted by her weeping. Perhaps her lips moved as she sniffled and choked. But the wafer fell before her, onto the chapel floor. There it lay like a filthy, shameful omen, Christ's body having traveled from the priest's hand only to miss her lips, denying her its blessing, now in the dirt at her knees. The priest quickly retrieved the wafer, washing the spot where it had fallen with holy water, then took it outside, where in the Filipino Catholic custom it would later receive a formal burial.

And so God had spoken to her, physically rejecting her, turning His flesh away just as He neared her quivering lips. She would not even look at me when she returned to our pew. For the rest of the service she remained on her knees, praying and crying. Outside the chapel a small boy was selling *kasuy*, the young leaves of the cashew tree. Still ignoring me, she bought a bag of leaves from the boy. Back at her house, she began slowly, obsessively eating them, dipping them one at a time into a shrimp paste that the servants had prepared for our afternoon *merienda*.

Her mother watched her carefully as she ate the *kasuy* leaves. Finally she ventured a tentative, double-edged joke. "You are lucky you are not pregnant, Divina Clara. Many people believe that too much *kasuy* can cause a miscarriage, you know."

Divina Clara said nothing, looking down at her plate of shrimp paste. But the stunned bewilderment that flashed across my face was more telling than a scream. Her father looked from her to me, and then he did begin to scream. He screamed at me to leave his house. He screamed at her to pack a bag. He screamed at a servant to prepare the car. I stood firm, beginning to resist him. But Divina Clara herself suddenly looked up and pointed toward the door.

"You must leave now, Jay," she said. "I need to be with my family."

I was on the edge of panic. "We need to talk about this," I said.

"You must leave!" she said, pointing again. "*Leave!* We will talk about this some other time."

I left, but I did not go far. I drove my jeep to a nearby side street and waited, thinking I would follow them. Soon their car approached, but I had not fooled old Carlos Ramirez. The car stopped near my jeep. Carlos and the driver both stepped out, walking quickly to me. Carlos leaned casually toward my window, speaking now in soft but serious tones.

"If you follow me, I will kill you," he said.

And as he spoke his driver punctured both of my front tires with two quick swings of a machete.

It was dark when the car returned. I was still sitting in my jeep, having left it only to flag down a passing army truck and arrange for a motor-pool mechanic to drive out and fix the tires. I was dozing. The sound of the approaching car startled me suddenly awake. A servant boy magically appeared at the gate, opening it, and the car entered the inner yard.

By now my shock had turned into anger. Something beautiful had vanished, and I wanted it back. It was mine. I may have abused it through my stupidity but I had loved it immensely, sacrificed for it, planned my life around it. I strode into the yard, brushing off the servant boy with a whisk of my hand, and walked up to the car.

She was not inside. Carlos slowly climbed out. He now was trembling with his own unsuppressed rage. Waiting for him as he walked toward me, I had a clear sense that one or the other of us might soon die. And for the first time in my life I did not care if it was I myself.

"Where is she?" I shouted.

He neared me, not slowing his pace. His head came only to my shoulders and now it was bent forward, as if he were going to butt into my stomach. My hands were balled into fists. I was bigger, stronger, younger, angrier, ready to beat him into oblivion, to pummel him until he told me where I might find her.

He had the fastest hands I have ever seen. He brought the banana knife to my face and thrust it so hard that it went all the way through my cheek, shattering teeth and cutting the edge of my tongue. Then he pulled the knife forward, slashing my cheek open almost to my mouth. It happened so quickly that by the time I raised my hands he had already pulled the knife out and brought his hand back to his side.

I straightened and pulled away, gagging from the shock and the sudden gush of blood, and he quickly kicked me in the groin. I was curled over, choking and spitting from the knife wound, nauseous from the blow to my groin. He stood in front of me, now looking down into my face. He was breathing heavily, his eyes glowing in the dark, beaming his hatred. Slowly, just to make the point, he reached up and wiped the blade of his banana knife on my shirt. Then he folded it and put it back into a pocket.

"The next time you come to this house you will be dead. I am not playing a game. Eleven men who tried to prove me wrong are already waiting for you in hell."

Pieces of teeth and a constant stream of blood poured onto my chest as I tried to speak. "I love her! Can't you understand that? She's having our baby, Carlos, and there's nothing you can do about it!"

"She is having no one's baby, not anymore. *No one's.*"

He was taking deep breaths, glaring at me with an eternal anger. At that moment I sensed that it was all he could do to keep from taking out his knife and finishing the job. Something terrible had happened, even beyond the nightmare of a few hours before. A different knife, a wrong twist in another place, a disaster far worse than the gash that had split open my face.

"The most beautiful object on this earth," continued Carlos, as if his words themselves might stab me. "*I created her!* And now what does she have? What hope do I have for her? A lying American and a doctor that I trusted. One I have known since my childhood! And what does she have? Nothing!"

"Where is she? What did you do?"

He lowered his head as if trying to restrain himself, then wheeled and kicked me again in the groin. I fell to my knees, suddenly vomiting through the blood that kept pouring from my mouth.

"What did I do? What did *you* do?" He stood over me. "I should cut your balls off. Then you would know how she feels. I should do that. But if

I did that, she would forgive you. That is her purity! That is the way she thinks! No, I must simply promise you that if you come back here I will kill you as a spying, unwelcome intruder. I can justify that, not only to her but even to God."

He deliberately pushed two fingers into my bleeding cheek, then wiped his hand on my shirt. "This is what I think of you. A bleeding pussy on your face. You can't run away from it. It will follow you. And wherever you go, Mister big-time banker, every morning when you wake up and shave you can look into the mirror and think of me. Because every morning she will wake up childless and think of you."

And thus began my years of hopelessness. The times I tried secretly to find her as my piercing injury healed and I awaited Yamashita's hanging. The dozens of letters I sent her, none of them returned or answered. Her complete disappearance from my life, as if she had been ripped apart from me at the moment of my greatest need. If she had died I might have grieved and then resolved our tragedy. But knowing she remained alive and yet being cut away from all contact with her became my greatest punishment, renewed each morning when I looked into the mirror and shaved.

No, I had not returned to Manila with the thought of abandoning everything and leaving the Philippines for New York by myself. To put it bluntly, I struggled to remain different from Douglas MacArthur. And regrettably I failed.

CHAPTER 27

★ ★ ★ ★ ★

So, finally it would be over. I simply could not believe that in one day I would be gone.

I left Manila at midnight, driving south toward Cavite along the cluttered main highway. Even at that hour the city's streets were choked with a mix of pushcarts, jeepneys, military trucks, and horse-drawn *caratelas*, all traveling at different speeds, cutting in and out of the traffic, mixing among one another, their drivers waving and cursing and beeping their horns, most of them packed to capacity with somnolent, thin-limbed Filipinos. Between Manila and Cavite the traffic thinned and the memories began. The wreckage of war still littered the roadside from the battles of a year before. The shell-pocked carcasses of trucks, tanks, and airplanes lay here and there, half covered with jungle vines, their innards picked clean, buzzardlike, by local scavengers.

On the other side of Cavite the world seemed to change. In another mile the road became desolate, as if the whole countryside had suddenly gone home to sleep. It was peaceful here, quiet and redolent and warm. My mind wandered, lost in the memories, as if I were cataloging them for the final time. It seemed that I had grown into adulthood along such roads. I had even fallen in love just at the edge of the bombarded highway, thirty miles to the north. The slumbering little nipa shacks that dotted the countryside with their tiny, twisting night fires and the smell of water buffalo from the pens behind them had become the very norms of my existence. And after nearly four years in the Pacific it was difficult to comprehend that this would be my last journey into a mud-slung Asian countryside, perhaps forever.

A blanket of evil-looking clouds began to swirl just above the trees, blotting out the moon. I shuddered as I drove, looking at the leaden sky. Typhoon season had recently passed, but in the Philippines one never knew when a wall of unremitting rain would rush in from the sea, making instant swamps and wheel-high pools of mud. If a hard rain came I might not even make it to Los Banos. Or worse still, I might reach the camp and then be stuck there in the mud and mire, unable to catch the troopship that would take me back to America.

But the rain did not come, and finally I saw a large olive-drab sign protruding from the far side of the road. The sign's bright yellow letters marked the turnoff that I was to follow into the jungle. My headlights flashed across it as I eased my way onto the smaller, gravel road.

LOS BANOS

U.S. ARMY PRISON CAMP

KEEP OUT!

Once I turned onto the prison road the seething, fetid jungle swallowed me whole, as if I were driving into a long, tubular corridor toward the caverns of the dead. Moist black air clung to me in the open jeep. Gravel crunched steadily underneath my tires. Nearby tree limbs swayed slowly in the wind, drooping like shrouds across my path. My mind cleared. The nostalgia had for the moment disappeared. I was here for an unhappy reason. I became all business, searching steadily to my front, knowing that somewhere beyond the tangles of brush and trees was a field of barbed wire that would mark the outer perimeter of the prison compound.

Finally the road took a long, slow turn. On the other side, the jungle suddenly cleared. A huge compound spread out in front of me, scraped away a few months before by teams of American military bulldozers. Vast rows of barbed wire glinted in my headlights. Their spikes reflected up-ward, like a million dots of snowflakes that had forgotten to fall. Behind the wire I could see the dim silhouettes of five hundred tents, slumping and flapping in the wind. Here and there among the rows of tents was the soft glow of a bare electric lightbulb. Nothing seemed to move. It was deathly quiet. I had arrived at Los Banos.

Los Banos was the final remaining processing facility for those Japanese soldiers now under American supervision. Some had surrendered en masse after the emperor's radio address of the previous August. Others had trickled in from their far-flung defensive positions over the six months since the war ended. Most had already been debriefed, deloused, and sent home. But thousands still remained behind, awaiting final clearance from American occupation authorities, as well as berthing spaces aboard military transport ships so that they could return to Japan.

And here, tonight, they would hang General Tomoyuki Yamashita.

On January 7, 1946, the Supreme Court had heard Frank Witherspoon's appeal, and on February 4 it rendered its opinion. Despite a scathing dissent by Justices Rutledge and Murphy, the Court declined to intervene in the case. The Court began by maintaining it was "not concerned with the guilt or innocence" of the accused but could only consider the "lawful power of the commission" to try him for the offenses charged. Significantly, the Court's majority mentioned that the Supreme Court did not have the constitutional authority to reverse military cases "merely because they have made a wrong decision on disputed facts." As a consequence, General Yamashita's fate turned on a narrow legal technicality: since the war would not officially be over until formal peace documents were signed, MacArthur still retained the power to convene a military commission "so long as a state of war exists."

The dissent of Justices Murphy and Rutledge was written in language dripping with anger. The two justices claimed that despite MacArthur's power to convene the commission, its very makeup denied General Yamashita the most basic constitutional protections of due process of law. "No military necessity or other emergency demanded suspension of the safeguards of due process," wrote Justice Murphy, who prior to becoming a Supreme Court justice had served as governor-general of the Philippines. "Yet General Yamashita was rushed to trial under an improper charge, given insufficient time to prepare an adequate defense, deprived of the benefits of the most elementary rules of evidence, and summarily sentenced to be hanged. In all this needless and unseemly haste there was no serious attempt to prove that he committed a recognized violation of the laws of war. He was not charged with personally participating in the acts of atrocity, or with ordering or condoning their commission. Not even knowledge of these crimes was attributed to him. This indictment in effect permitted the military commission to make the crime whatever it willed."

Then in words that would bedevil American military commanders during the Vietnam war, Murphy made a haunting prediction. "Such a procedure is unworthy of our people," he wrote. "The high feelings of the moment doubtless will be satisfied. But no one in a position of command in an army, from sergeant to general, can escape these implications. The fate of some future president and his chiefs of staff and military advisers may well have been sealed by this decision."

Justice Rutledge echoed Murphy's concerns, then finished with his own warning to the ages. "He that would make his own liberty secure must guard even his enemy from oppression. For if he violates this duty he establishes a precedent that will reach himself."

Undeterred, MacArthur scheduled General Yamashita's execution without even reading the Supreme Court opinions. Announcing that "Yamashita's transgressions are a blot on the military profession, a stain upon civilization, and constitute a memory of shame and dishonor that can never be forgotten," the supreme commander ordered that the Tiger be "stripped of uniform, decorations, and other appurtenances signifying membership in the military profession" and set his hanging for 3:00 A.M. on February 23.

And here I was, on a dark jungle road at midnight, carrying out the last and most odious assignment of my military career: to watch the Tiger die, so that I myself might be freed.

As I neared the gate a military policeman stepped from a small sentry booth and stood in front of my jeep. His too-young face was falsely scowling underneath his white helmet. He raised an M2 carbine and pointed it directly at my windshield. I slammed the brakes, knowing that the baby-faced corporal was no doubt fresh meat, in from the States. Having missed the war by only a few months, he would be even more hungry for a reason to shoot an obstreperous intruder while on assignment in this foreign land. For how else could he bring a war story home?

He barked at me as my jeep slowed. "You! Cut your lights!"

I brought the jeep to a dead stop and turned off the headlights. He walked to the driver's side and shined a flashlight into my eyes. Then he noticed my rank.

"Sorry, Captain." He shouldered the rifle, giving me a brisk salute.

"We've had some pretty strange people trying to get in here tonight, sir. Reporters, photographers, and all that, wanting to cover the execution. I've got orders to turn all visitors back. The hanging's a private matter. By direction of General MacArthur himself."

"Well, General MacArthur happens to be the person who sent me," I said. I handed him my military identification card and my written orders. "To observe."

"Holy Moley," he said, examining my papers under the flashlight's beam. "He wants you to just come down here and watch a Jap general die? Too bad for you, huh, sir?"

"General MacArthur is a very thorough man," I answered dryly. "He is very much concerned with details. He wants a full report."

"We could've sent him pictures, or something." The corporal caught himself. "No disrespect intended, sir." He gave me a snaggletoothed grin, unable to contain his awe. "You work directly for the supreme commander?"

"Three years," I said. "This is my last show. I'm on the troopship out of here tomorrow."

"And thank God for that, I'll bet. Off this goddamn pile of mung." He interpreted my sudden silence as agreement and grew even more familiar. "How does a solider get picked to work for General MacArthur, if you don't mind my asking, sir? I wouldn't mind that." His flashlight beam bounced off the deep scar on my cheek. "Nasty scar. Wow! Must have pulled you in from the field after you were wounded, huh?"

"Are you on duty, Corporal?" The scar was none of this little pissant military cop's business. He had passed from politeness to an irritating coziness. I felt suddenly done with him. "I've got a job to do. Give me my papers and open up the gate."

"Sorry, sir. No disrespect intended, you understand." Abashed, he quickly handed me my papers. Then he moved toward the gate and began to swing it open.

I turned the headlights back on and put the jeep into gear. As the gate swung open I drove forward. The corporal saluted me again. I called to him as I drove through the gate.

"Call the camp commandant. Tell him I want to see General Yamashita. *Immediately!* On orders from MacArthur."

The camp commandant, a leathery-faced, humorless colonel, did not conceal his irritation at my demand to visit with the Tiger so soon before his hanging. Even the invocation of MacArthur's orders did not deter the colonel from a petulant display of his own power. Meeting me at the gate, he perfunctorily ordered me to park my jeep in front of his Quonset hut. Then he brought me into his office, leaving me standing as he took a seat behind his small field desk. He slowly, deliberately smoked an unfiltered Camel cigarette, pretending to meticulously examine my papers. Finally he grunted his assent, unimpressed.

"I don't know why we're making such a big goddamn deal out of this thing. For Christ's sake, how many Americans died in the war? How many Filipina women did the assholes rape in Manila? How many babies did they bayonet? They should've just taken the fucker out back and shot him six months ago."

He tossed my papers dismissively across the desk. "Hamamoto's already awake. Surprise, surprise. They all are. It's like locusts out there in the tents. The whole camp's buzzing, knowing the old guy's gonna die. Anyway, I'll get him for you."

"I don't need an interpreter."

The surprise on his face was mixed with a veiled contempt. "Jap speaker, huh?" I nodded. "Fluent?" I nodded again, and he sneered again. "I see. One of those real Asia guys." He stubbed out his cigarette. "You can have this fucking place. The sooner they send me back to Kansas the happier I'll be."

I thought I'd try a pleasantry or two. "So you're from Kansas, Colonel?"

"No, I'm from Chicago. But once we've sent all these slope-heads home I'm going to go back to Fort Leavenworth. I've already got my orders. To the jail, that is, not the post." He smiled. "I like putting people away. And I enjoy keeping them there."

The colonel had a thoroughly felonious grin. I began to wonder on which side of the prison bars he really belonged. I made a mental note to include my uneasiness with him in my after-action report to MacArthur. And then I remembered that I would no longer be writing after-action reports to MacArthur.

I could feel the colonel peering eagerly at my face under the dim light of the bare bulb that hung above us. "Captain, that is one miserable-looking scar. Where the hell did you pick that up?"

I checked my watch. "Is that it, Colonel? Would you like to frisk me, to make sure I'm not going to slip General Yamashita an escape weapon?"

He lit another cigarette. The wicked grin reappeared on his face. "That won't be necessary, Captain. Go ahead and give the Jap a weapon. I'll just have both of you shot on the spot. And I guarantee you I've got hand-picked boys here who wouldn't mind doing it."

I could hear the prison tents buzzing with whispered anticipation as I walked across the camp in the sultry darkness. The Tiger's imminent death was on the lips of every Japanese soldier in Los Banos. These were, after all, Yamashita's troops. Or at least the fraction of them that had survived nearly a year of vicious fighting, from Leyte to Lingayen Gulf and then all the way to the northern mountains. They had been defeated, but Yamashita had brilliantly maneuvered them against overwhelming odds. They were fiercely loyal to the Tiger. And few of them would sleep tonight.

Yamashita's tent was on a small hill in the center of the prison camp, surrounded by a second field of concertina wire. By the time I reached it the Tiger was waiting for me, standing at the front flap. He smiled brightly and his eyes were clear, but he looked terrible, even for a man about to die. He had lost at least thirty pounds since I had last seen him in early December. His usually shaved head was covered with a shaggy mat of unkempt hair. He had grown a scraggly, white-flecked beard. On orders from MacArthur they had taken away his uniforms, making him wear a set of worn blue army fatigues. He looked to me like a very old man who had just escaped from a cancer ward.

I greeted him in Japanese as I stepped inside the barbed wire. "You're awake, General."

He laughed, amused. "Captain Marsh. And I suppose you thought I would be resting up for my hanging?"

I reached him. We bowed slightly to each other, then shook hands. He caught the surprise in my eyes and knew immediately that it embarrassed me to be inspecting him in the muted darkness.

"I am fine," he said, preempting my questions. "It is just that your colonel is afraid that I will kill myself before he has the opportunity to do it for me. And so they took everything from me that I might use. My razor. My nail clippers. My pen set." He laughed, pointing at his face. "Even my glasses! Did he think I would slash my wrists with the lenses?"

"The colonel does not understand the Japanese," I said.

"I could never kill myself," said the general simply. "It would be disloyal. The emperor ordered me to surrender."

"I know that," I answered. "But things look differently to the colonel. If you did kill yourself he would lose face. Then they would never send him back to Kansas to work at the prison of his dreams."

"The colonel is a soldier. He is only doing his duty." Yamashita shrugged, no longer concerned. Then he pointed beyond the barbed wire at the rifle-toting sentry who was standing guard at the break in the wire that led to his tent. "The corporal has become my little nephew. He sneaks me my glasses for an hour every night so that I might read my Chinese poetry. He watches me while I read, then he takes the glasses back." He grinned impishly. "I wonder sometimes what he thinks when he watches me reading. Why does a Japanese soldier about to die wish to read Chinese poetry? I don't know enough English to explain it to him. And anyway, it doesn't matter. He has been kind to bring me the glasses."

The sentry could not understand what we were saying, but looking at him I could see compassion in his eyes. Abruptly I left the general and strode up to him.

"Get me a razor and some scissors," I said.

"Captain, I can't do that," he protested. He was looking nervously toward the colonel's Quonset hut.

"Hurry up."

"Captain, the colonel—"

"Fuck the colonel," I said. "I have orders from MacArthur."

Within five minutes the corporal had delivered Yamashita's razor, scissors, and manicure kit. Inside the general's tent I took a long time cutting off his hair. After that he shaved, first his face and then his scalp, and clipped his fingernails. Once we finished he carefully made a pile of the cuttings and folded them inside a handkerchief. He had grown emotional as I cut his hair, as if I were a devoted attendant. Now he bowed, far too deeply, handing me the handkerchief that contained his hair and fingernails.

"You remembered, Captain Marsh. I am deeply grateful. They took everything from me when I transferred from Manila to Los Banos."

I took the handkerchief from him and stuffed it into my pocket. An unspoken promise passed between us, that in the Japanese tradition I would ensure that these clippings were sent back to his family along with his cremated ashes.

"I will take care of this, General."

"Why do you bother with these things?" He stood close to me, gazing curiously into my eyes. Outside I could hear vehicles approaching. It sounded like two jeeps and a truck. I knew they were coming for him and that within an hour he would be dead.

"Because I respect you," I finally answered. "And I know that you did nothing dishonorable."

"I cannot complain about my fate," he said. "But I still do not understand this trial."

"Did you know that General MacArthur received a petition last week, signed by eighty-six thousand Japanese, asking that your sentence be commuted?"

The Tiger smiled, obviously moved, then shrugged. "But a thing such as that would never change his mind."

"No," I said, looking steadily at him. "I must tell you the truth, General. A thing such as that could only guarantee that his mind would never change."

Yamashita chuckled knowingly. Outside, the vehicles braked to a halt, their engines running. Several car doors slammed. A host of voices barked nervously to one another. And so he had no chance to answer me, for in seconds the tent flaps opened and four armed military policemen strode inside.

"Good evening, Captain," said a bulky, hard-eyed sergeant, giving me a false grin. "Or should I say good morning, sir? It's now zero-two-thirty hours. Anyway, I assume you're done with your little visit, here?"

"In a minute," I said.

The sergeant impatiently checked his watch. "We've got a schedule, sir, and we—"

"*In a minute, Sergeant!*" I towered over him. I was thick-muscled and ugly-scarred and totally unafraid. My lips had tightened into a threatening scowl. "What difference does five minutes make? He'll be dead soon enough. Now, get the hell out of the tent."

"Ah—right, sir."

The four soldiers looked at one another for a moment, then backed slowly out of the tent. Only then did Yamashita relax his stoic expression into an amused grin.

"These are your own soldiers, Captain Marsh. You should show them more respect."

"Respect has nothing to do with it anymore."

My words seemed to jolt him. He suddenly put a hand on my shoulder, moving his face to within inches of my own. He was the only Japanese I had ever met who was taller than I, and even in his wasted condition he exuded a physical power that filled the tent.

"Captain Marsh, I am a defeated soldier. I will soon be dead. But you have been good to me, and so I would like to leave you with one last thought. In fact, you are the last person I may ever talk to. So you are hearing my final words."

He paused as if waiting for my agreement. I watched him silently, feeling moved but also very guilty. I was in his tent because of my own personal sympathy, but I was attending his hanging under orders. And why did I deserve this advice, having stopped fighting on his behalf a few months before?

"It always matters." He peered into my eyes, trying to see if I had understood him. "Respect," he added. "For one another. For oneself. Is there anything more important to leave behind? I don't think so. Why did so many of our soldiers fight to the death rather than surrender? Because respect is more important than life." He continued to watch me. "That is why MacArthur did this. To destroy my respect. Is it not?"

I held his stare, deciding that he deserved the truth. "Not only MacArthur," I answered. "Also the imperial court."

He shrugged, unsurprised. "Oh, of course many members of the imperial court would want me dead. This should not trouble you, Captain. I understand the complications if I were to return and confront them."

"You are right. So now you know. Good-bye, General." There was, after all, nothing left to say. "This may sound strange, but it has been an honor knowing you."

He gave me a slight bow, indicating his farewell. "Please do not think ill of the emperor."

The sergeant reappeared, pushing aside a tent flap and again standing silently just before us. The colonel followed him inside the tent, looking at me as if I were a collaborator with the enemy. Nearing Yamashita, he flicked his cigarette onto the tent floor and ground it out with the toe of his boot. Then he fixed me with his evil grin.

"Time for a hanging, Captain. I didn't know you were in love with the old guy."

I fixed him with a threatening glare. "In four weeks I'm going to be a civilian, Colonel. No disrespect intended, you understand, but I think I might just stop by Fort Leavenworth and kick your sorry ass."

He gave off a dry, unconcerned laugh. "You can try if you want. My boys will be waiting for you. Handpicked." He gestured toward General Yamashita. "Now if you don't mind, it's time to do the dirty deed."

Eight soldiers and a very nervous-looking Japanese officer whom I recognized as Colonel Hamamoto were silently gathered at the base of the scaffolding that had been erected to hang the Tiger. The officers ignored Hamamoto, speaking to one another in whispers as they waited in the thick black night. There were no reporters present. Instead, the media would be fed the official story of Yamashita's hanging by a thirtyish major who introduced himself as the press officer for Lieutenant General Wilhelm Styer, Commander of Army Forces, Western Pacific. The major nervously latched on to me as I joined the group, happy to see another general's flunky. I shook his hand, then did my best to ignore him.

At exactly three o'clock, Yamashita was led up a half dozen wooden steps to the center of the platform. His hands were tied behind his back. A masked soldier fixed a noose around his neck. The Tiger looked calmly above all of us as the hangman worked, ignoring these crude preparations, peering out into the jungled darkness.

At the base of the scaffolding another colonel, the camp commandant's superior, called to him in a flat, emotionless voice. "Do you have any last words, General Yamashita?"

Hamamoto translated into Japanese, looking up apologetically at the Tiger. General Yamashita glanced for a moment at the colonel, then seemed to dismiss him from his thoughts. He bowed deeply, facing the north, toward Tokyo, where at that moment the emperor and General of the Armies Douglas MacArthur both slept peacefully.

"I will pray for the emperor's long life and his prosperity forever."

The higher-ranking colonel nodded. Behind him, the camp commandant sneered. The masked soldier cinched the rope up tight. He took two steps back, breathing deeply. Then he yanked hard on a lever. The trapdoor sprung. General Tomoyuki Yamashita dropped abruptly through the floor of the platform, bounced hard against the rope, and then immediately hung limp and lifeless. Dangling before us, the general's head arched strangely sideways, like a wooden mannequin snapped loose from its neck post.

And that was it. For some reason the way the general swayed on the rope reminded me of the deer my father used to hang from a tree behind our cabin after he had shot and gutted them when I was a child. The Tiger of Malaysia was no longer a person. He was a hunting trophy, waiting to be cut down and incinerated and sent home in a jar. And I knew there was no sense in thinking about this moment any longer.

The camp commandant barked at me as I began walking away. "Did you like that, Captain? Clean and quick, huh?"

"Very clean, Colonel," I said. "So I'll be going now. And fuck you." More than anything else, I was now finally ready to return home.

He laughed at me in the thick night air, refusing to let it go. "Tell me. Whose army are you in, anyway?"

"Not yours, Colonel. So like I said, fuck you."

The public relations major called after me. "Captain Marsh! What did Yamashita say? His final words. What were they? I have to file a press release."

"Ask Hamamoto," I answered, walking ever more briskly toward my jeep.

The tents in the camp were hushed as I walked back toward the colonel's Quonset hut, as if the snapping of Yamashita's neck when the trapdoor sprung had echoed so loudly that each of the soldiers inside had heard it and retreated into an accepting silence. It had been a long war, filled with bitter endings. There was nothing left to talk about, just as there was nothing left to think about. The Tiger had faced death bravely. And now he had joined his ancestors.

I felt an odd freedom as I drove back to Manila in the sorrowing darkness. Not the freedom that comes from hope but rather a permanent sense of disentanglement, a knowledge that there was no remaining aspect in my life where I would ever again be required to confront the dangerous unknown of my untested innocence. It was undeniably liberating, knowing I had failed on so many levels and yet still survived. No, I thought, survival was not even strong enough a word. I had prevailed, despite consistently betraying my inner instincts. I had a bright future, and the only place I had reached for it was down. I was going to be rewarded with a plush life, a demigod named MacArthur's compensation for betraying myself.

Then I decided that perhaps I was being too harsh. I had been so young to be making such difficult moral decisions. Although I had repeatedly dared the fantasy of my conscience only to run away when confronted with reality, my strivings had been honorable. Father Garvey had tried to help me, and yet in the end I lacked what Koichi Kido called *majime*, the wisdom and courage to eliminate any distinctions between my actions and my inner thoughts. One was not born with *majime*. He gained it through years of thought and struggle.

Someday, I thought, I might gain that perfect balance between my inner and outer self. But no matter what rewards I received I would also forever pay, every morning when I looked into the mirror and saw the ugly scar that creased my face like a jagged bolt of lightning, and every night when I turned back empty sheets to go to bed. Yes, I decided as I watched the sun glimmer over Manila for the last time. I was now twenty-five years old. A part of me had grown old in the sixteen months since I had first seen the sun scorch the eastern jungles of the Philippines. And a part of me had forever died. But finally it was all over.

Yamashita had been hanged. Prince Konoye had committed suicide. Lord Privy Seal Kido was in jail. The emperor was now protected from the wrath of our avenging allies. Prince Asaka was free to continue his golf game. The rape of Nanking had been marginalized. The way was clear for the able and intricately prepared Shigeru Yoshida to become prime minister. The new Japan could now proceed toward its destiny. And, not incidentally, the part of Captain Jay Marsh that had survived could finally leave all of this behind and find the life that it had dealt him.

EPILOGUE

FEBRUARY 23, 1997

Afternoon

I

☆ ☆ ☆ ☆ ☆

And it became a good life, prosperous, challenging, rewarding not only to myself but to those who trusted me. In joining the Bergson-Forbes Group I had found the perfect venue for my gift of diplomacy and my instinct for intricate negotiation. I quickly became respected for my judgment, relied upon for my vision of East Asia's future, and, not incidentally, rich.

And as my career ascended ever upward, I often looked back at that crucial moment in the supreme commander's office that so inalterably changed the direction of my life. I had faced MacArthur wanting only my freedom and my future with Divina Clara. I had left his office doomed on both counts but launched toward semigreatness. With every success I would secretly ask myself where I might have been if I had acted differently. But the answer, inevitably, was that my very speculation was moot. For I would not have acted differently.

MacArthur was smarter than I was. And in most ways I benefited from his genius.

How sweet is the siren of seduction, and how empty are the promises of virgins who know their time has come. To have escaped MacArthur only with the right to forever denounce his actions would have been a hollow, Pyrrhic victory. What indeed would my dignity have purchased? And when all was said and done, how could I think ill of the man who so generously rewarded my service to him by handing me over like a valuable baton to the likes of Thorpe Thomas?

Indeed, confronting MacArthur so strongly in that final meeting had provided me the luckiest moment of my professional life. Perhaps it was because he had always known the power of my intellect and the dedication I had brought to serving him. Perhaps he had admired the fortitude that I had shown that morning, having kept it so hidden before. More likely, I had also succeeded at some level in scaring him. But no matter. MacArthur had opened the door, ushering me from one secret room into another.

And Thorpe Thomas became my truest mentor. He taught me the business of investment banking, continued my education as a negotiator and diplomat, refined my mannerisms and even my dialect until within ten years I myself might have been born in Darien and schooled at Groton. And always at the bottom of his respect for me was the knowledge that I had given his great friend General Douglas MacArthur crucial and valuable service during the Southwest Pacific campaign, and in the all-important first months of the Occupation of Japan.

And so as the years slipped by and my memories became leavened with the pleasures that MacArthur's reward made possible, I would have been the last person to criticize him. And in fact, it soon became both my duty and my passion to actively defend him. In 1950, war suddenly engulfed the Korean peninsula. After his quiet partnership with Emperor Hirohito and Prime Minister Yoshida brought about the near miracle of Japan's resurgence, at the age of seventy the supreme commander was pulled from his dreamlike sinecure and thrust into command of the United Nations combat forces. It was there that he demonstrated his greatest battlefield genius. And it was also there that he underwent his deepest, and final, personal defeat.

Korea for MacArthur had all the elements of Greek tragedy. I was one of his greatest cheerleaders as he defied everyone, including a reluctant Joint Chiefs of Staff, and directed the dangerous and risk-filled amphibious invasion of Inchon. In one of the most brilliant battlefield maneuvers in American history, MacArthur cut off the North Korean army's logistical support far to their rear and then turned south and pounded its combat units all the way to the Pusan perimeter. I was an ardent, vociferous defender after he then turned north and chased the remnants of that army not only out of South Korea but all the way to the Chinese border.

His brilliance was even more profound when one considered that this soon-to-be seventy-one-year-old general still had the vigor and the fighting vision to have so completely destroyed an attacking army. He was dogged and on his own during those maneuverings, innovating day by day, seeking but not receiving clear directions from a Truman administration that was swept with confusion and indecision after the suddenness of the war's outbreak. I took his side as the nation argued the consequences of the Chinese army then pouring across the Yalu River into North Korea, enlarging the war and prompting the supreme commander's disgrace when President Truman abruptly relieved him of command.

The tragedy was that in five short years the nature of war had changed in a way so fundamental that no battlefield commander, not even MacArthur, would be able to comprehend for decades. MacArthur, who had preached repeatedly that in war there is no substitute for victory, had been hamstrung by a new modifier—the word "limited." The battlefield itself now had limited objectives. Military forces would be subjected to limitations in their use of power. MacArthur did not know it, and indeed neither did we for many years, but President Truman had secretly assured the British, who were worried about possible Chinese retaliation in Hong Kong, that under no circumstances would we ever cross into China. A communist spy ring inside the British government had then tipped the Chinese that it was risk-free for them to send soldiers into Korea. MacArthur, whose bold move to the Chinese border had been coupled with numerous options to threaten any Chinese intervention, was in the end mousetrapped by a betrayal he never comprehended, begun unwittingly by the very president who disgraced him, relieved him of command, and brought him home.

Yes, I was proud to come to Washington and shake his hand after his eloquent, spine-tingling "Old Soldiers Never Die" speech before a teary-eyed joint session of Congress once President Truman had humiliated him. And more than a decade after that, as he lay wasting on the edge of death at the Walter Reed Army Hospital, I, like so many others who had served him over a career that spanned nearly fifty years, paid him an emotional, nostalgic homage.

I sat for a full hour next to his bed in my grey woolen suit and silk tie and Florsheim wing-tip shoes, listening to his frail-voiced stories that recalled exactly all the jungle-hot, rainwashed, moonlit moments of our years together. Merely sitting next to him made me feel inalterably young again. I was forty-four, on my way to Thailand, just posted as ambassador. He glowed with a father's pride as we discussed my coming duties. His eyes were still bright with energy. Then as the hour wound down he checked his watch and reached over and gripped my arm tightly for a long time. It was the warmest gesture he had ever made to me.

"We did great things, Jay. We moved the world."

"Yes, sir," I answered, choking with a quiet nostalgia. "We did."

"I must tell you," he said in his now-trembling, husky voice, looking carefully into my face, "that the end of life is quite educational. Illuminating, if you would. I marvel that it has not been studied more fully. As I sit here and feel it falling away from me, I can somehow see all the points of my life with the same clarity. It is an odd experience, at the same time shackling and liberating. I can feel the heat and the warm rain of Leyte and Samar as it steamed my body sixty years ago. I can smell the gas and feel my feet freezing in the mud-filled trenches of France as we stepped out for the attack on Côte de Chatillon. I can hear the Japanese artillery thumping overhead as I walk in the dank tunnels of Corregidor. The salt air of the Pacific is on my face and the wind blows and the ship tosses and rolls like an anxious tiger, and we are on our way again to Leyte! Yes, Leyte! And then Manila. And after that Japan. All rolled up together, happening to me at the same time. And the morning when I landed at Inchon just after the assault. My stomach was roiling with uncertainty, until finally I threw up. I can still feel my nerves tingling. I had sent our troops into the riskiest amphibious salient in history and they had rewarded our nation with their unbounded courage! All these moments! They are with me now, although they are so unreachably far away! And when I die they will be the country's, to cherish and remember if it so chooses."

Now he gave me a warning look. There was purpose in his rasping voice. "But the other things? The private, desperate, sometimes blundering negotiations that are essential to history's progress? The personal moments filled with loss and desire and unfathomable regret, which I don't need to tell you tore at my heart beyond the capacity of words to explain?"

He paused, a thin smile on his aged face. "They are mine, Jay. They belong only to me. And to those few who shared them. And so it will be with you. You don't realize it yet. But in time you will."

"And how about General Yamashita?" I asked. "In what category does he fit, General?"

His eyes grew smoky. Even at the end of his dotage MacArthur could chill a visitor with one cool look. "You'll never forget that, will you?" He raised his chin. "I go to my God with clean hands."

He let go of my arm and turned his face away from me, indicating that our last meeting had ended. I rose and turned to leave.

"Good-bye, General. You'll be in my prayers, sir."

"Good-bye, Jay." Suddenly he turned back to me, giving me a knowing, mischievous smile. He was bent on teasing me, even from the caverns of his ever-dimming retreat.

"I forgot to ask," he said. "How is Consuelo?"

It was his own private joke, a final burst of incorrigibility, his little way of reminding me that at some level we both had traveled the same emotional journey.

"I don't know," I answered, stunned at his recollection and suddenly hurt once again by the memory of it all. For I did not know. My only answer was an equally provocative riposte. "How is she, General?"

He smiled and nodded, ever in control, as if I had indeed answered his question. "That's the way it is at the end, Jay," he answered, his eyes strong and warm behind the fading face. "We don't know."

Yes, even our last meeting was filled with barbs and cant, as if it were one more opportunity to teach me. I was addled when I left him, confused by his very certainties. It had been nearly twenty years since that final moment in his Dai Ichi office, but still I had felt my blood pressure rise and my fists begin to clench when he had obliquely made reference to the compromises his generosity had brought me. He knew that since that moment I have always lived with a pit of darkness in my conscience, an echo of sorrow in my heart. For in accepting the truth of MacArthur's vision and the favor of his eternal blessing I ceased to be the proud young spirit who believed anything was possible. And I not only lost the dream that fires youth's less forbidding aspirations but I destroyed the very treasure I had been working so assiduously to retain.

He knew that. And had this also been his fate? Watching his eyes twinkle at me as he lay in his old West Point bathrobe wasting slowly into his eternity, I sensed that much. He had taught me how to trade, Faust-like, and in this sense I had become his spiritual successor. We both knew the extent of that loss, because in our lives we both had chosen to trade precious things for the rewards of large ambition.

But what he never comprehended was how hard I had tried to keep just that from happening. And at that moment, I decided that someday I would indeed find out the answer to his question.

How was she? Where was she? What had she become? I wanted very much to know.

And it took me more than thirty years to find out.

11

✯ ✯ ✯ ✯ ✯

The Carmel of the Saint Therese of the Child Jesus convent is located on Gilmore Avenue in Quezon City. Home to perhaps a hundred nuns, the Gilmore convent is less than half a mile from the Mount Carmel church on Broadway avenue, where there also stands another, larger convent for Carmelite priests. Built in 1925, the convent grounds cover an entire city block. Inside its mildew-stained walls are a well-manicured, tree-strewn yard, a small chapel where the nuns meditate and pray, a graveyard and catacomb where they know they will someday be put to rest, and the plain-walled, two-story convent house where they eat, pray some more, do their chores, and sleep.

Although the Gilmore convent is located in a well-kept residential area of gentle hills, redolent flowers, and sprawling trees, the modernization of metro Manila has begun creeping inexorably toward it. Across Gilmore Street on one side of the convent's entrance is a Burger Machine fast-food franchise. On the other side is a busy Shell Oil gas station. A block away are two huge production plants, one that refines and packages dairy products and another that bottles and ships Pepsi-Cola throughout the metropolitan area. Office towers are beginning to dot the horizon. The traffic is starting to pick up on Gilmore Avenue and especially on nearby Aurora Boulevard, upon which a large shopping mall has recently been constructed.

But for the nuns of the Carmel of the Saint Therese, life has a beatific simplicity that has not changed markedly since the Carmelite order was first founded by Pope Honorius III on October 1, 1226. The residents of the Gilmore convent are Discalced Carmelites. In the church they are known as contemplative nuns. Their diet is vegetarian. They take vows of poverty, chastity, and obedience and with few exceptions must observe a code of strict silence. Outside visitation is permitted only in rare circumstances.

The single rooms in which each nun sleeps are known as cells. Each cell is by tradition about nine feet by twelve feet, and its contents are identical. Against one wall is a small, narrow bed. Next to the bed is a plain wooden night table. On top of the table is a lamp. Underneath it is an unpadded wooden pew, to be taken out for morning and evening prayers. A simple wooden cabinet stands on the wall opposite the bed. The walls themselves are barren, except for a crucifix that hangs above the bed.

The nuns arise every morning at four-thirty. At five they meet in the chapel for an hour of meditative prayer, then after breakfast return to chapel for a full Mass. Morning chores follow, usually washing, cleaning, cooking, and gardening, after which they return again to the chapel for formal prayers before they go to lunch. Following lunch they are allowed a brief recreation period, in which they may speak quietly to one another. Then after more prayer, they return to work. Once the day's work is finished there follows a period of private reading, more meditative prayer, dinner, further meditative prayer, a recitation of the *Angelus* in the chapel, always accompanied by the ringing of bells, thirty minutes of recreation, and finally more than an hour of evening formal prayers. The nuns then return to their cells and are in bed each night at nine o'clock.

When a woman joins the Carmelite order, she must leave her given names behind, taking on instead the names of two favorite saints. It is not required that the new names even be female. Her old names are never used, just as her past is never mentioned. In fact both are protected, particularly from inquisitive outsiders.

And thus despite my wealth and my many positions of importance it took me more than twenty years to locate Sister Thaddeus Anthony of the Carmel of the Saint Therese of the Child Jesus. And once I discovered her location, it took another seven to negotiate a visit. Particularly unhelpful and often disruptive during this period were her immediate family, who had wealth and power of their own, and who of course were far more influential in both the government and church bureaucracies of the Philippines than was I. For even though Sister Thaddeus Anthony's parents had long since died by the time I intensified my quest to see her, the decades had not lessened the vitriol and hatred among her siblings that had marked my long-ago departure for New York.

I have never been so nervous as when I stepped out of my hired car and stared through the front gates of the Gilmore convent. I stood frozen, as if in shock, an old man leaning forward on hobbling knees, taking deep breaths to control the trembling that had overtaken my hands from a sudden rush of adrenaline. Watching the nuns in the yard before me as they glided slowly through their afternoon tasks, for the first time in nearly thirty years I questioned whether I even wanted to know what awaited me on the other side of the iron gates, inside the meticulously kept grounds.

For is it not true that the furious intensity of searching for something is often merely a mask for our fear of actually finding it?

In my insistent quest I had lived inside the dream of what might have been. But now I was facing the stark reality of what the past had brought us, at a time in our lives when we both lacked a future in which to change it. Yes, inside one of these ankle-length, long-sleeved brown tunics, with her hair, ears, and even her once-lovely neck hidden by a white coif headdress, labored the brilliant and beautiful woman who still represented my life's greatest love and at the same time its most inescapable tragedy.

I waited for her in a small garden, surrounded by blooming, aromatic flowers, underneath a white marble statue of Saint Therese. I recognized her immediately when she exited the front door of the chapel and looked across the paved courtyard toward the garden. Even her hands were hidden as they clasped a crucifix behind the brown scapular that went over her shoulders, covering her tunic front and back. I could see nothing of her except the circle of her coifed face and her leather-sandaled feet. But the tilt of her head when she surveyed the courtyard and the certainty of her firm stride as she headed toward me were unmistakable, even after fifty years.

Finally, finally, it was she.

I stood speechless and awkward, waiting for her to reach me. Oddly, at this moment I found myself thinking again of MacArthur. Not MacArthur the General, who brought me to the moment where I had discovered her, or even MacArthur the supreme commander, who tore me from her and set into motion the ignominious seductions and rewards that caused me to lose her. But MacArthur in his deathbed, telling me in his rasping voice how in those final, helpless months he could somehow feel all the great events of his life at the same time, so sensually that they were real, and yet so unreachable that examining them was a form of cruelty. Because as she neared me the past forced itself forward until it became indiscernible from the present, and she herself became ageless.

Perhaps it was the heat. My knees were trembling and I was growing light-headed. Perhaps it was my age, for I had waited so long to see her that I knew there would be little time left to savor the rediscovery. But as she walked toward me I could see in her eyes the same unflinching, bold curiosity and bright intelligence of the first time I had come upon her in my jeep, as she sat proud and erect in her *caratela* while her small pony lay in the mud twisting and snorting and the bombs burst around us and her servant boy nervously prepared to shoot the animal.

And suddenly it all erupted before me. Divina Clara in the *caratela*, lush and fecund even with her breasts bound, demanding my name and service number, then lecturing me about courage as we drove to Pampanga, and finally inviting me to dinner in her home. Divina Clara in the yawing, overfilled Papa boat as we crossed the river on the way to Subic, laughing as she invited all the passengers to ride in my jeep, then merrily instructing us on the mysteries of love. Divina Clara with her grandmother, explaining the certainty of her feelings for me, announcing that truth and even love are like the wind, unviewable but somehow tangible. Divina Clara swaying gorgeous and full above me on the soft sheets of my bed as the moon burned through the window, smelling faintly of *sampaguita* from the garland her mother had woven into her hair, then crying when I left again for Japan, then pulling my hands into her ever-filling belly upon my return. Divina Clara struggling to believe, bursting with such honesty that the truth itself somehow made her fragile, forced her to see more than was before her eyes, to feel less than was in my heart, until finally the very power that had impelled her love caused our world to permanently implode.

Yes, even old nuns were young once. And some of them have lived wondrous, unrewarded dreams.

I reached my hands out to her. *"Divina Clara."*

She stopped abruptly a few feet in front of me, looking wide-eyed at my hands. "I'm sorry but you cannot call me that. You must call me Sister Thaddeus Anthony. And I am not permitted to touch you. I have been instructed to tell you that if you will not obey the rules of the convent they will not let us talk. And you will have to leave."

She said it kindly but firmly, in a soft voice just above a whisper. I became uncertain and for a moment thought that she actually might have wanted me to leave. But looking into her eyes I could see that they were inviting, somehow swollen with gladness.

"I've waited all this time," I said. "Of course I will obey the rules."

"I knew you would."

She was smiling softly now, almost possessively. In that moment I could tell that she had never stopped knowing me, that her memory of me was as clear as the day I had left, and more important, that my answer had confirmed for her that her memories had not deceived her.

I shrugged helplessly, looking around for someplace where we might sit. "What shall we do?"

"We have to go inside. Those are the rules."

She turned and began walking toward the convent house, and I dutifully followed. It was so quiet that even the sound of the cars on Gilmore Avenue seemed too near, vulgar and intrusive. Watching her from behind I suddenly remembered our tearful, uncertain predawn farewell before I had first left for Japan, sitting in my jeep and seeing her disappear through the vine-covered walkway that led into her house. In a way, that parting had been the last pure moment, the last breath of simplicity in my life. And what had it been for her?

We walked under a pillared archway, onto a concrete corridor that connected the chapel and the convent house. Reaching the house, she opened a near door. Only then did she turn around to see if I had followed. Saying nothing, but smiling happily at my nearness, she then led me into the dim-lit, concrete-floored visitors' lounge.

Her very happiness caused me to be overcome with regret. I had sought this simple meeting for decades but there was a tragedy in my victory, one that I could not properly define. How many people had she been permitted to see and converse with over the last half century? In this darkened void that was her home my own last fifty years leaped before me, all the grand flourishes, great debates, and bitter defeats that had informed my life as she swept and planted, ate and prayed. All I knew was that we were two lives that might have been lived together, split like an atom by anger and misunderstanding until one was propelled into constant motion and the other driven into permanent retreat. And that I had never stopped thinking about her, not even for one day.

A low wall ran across the visitors' room, dividing it. Atop the wall was a prisonlike, grilled partition. She walked to the other side of the wall and then waited expectantly, smiling at me from behind the wooden grill as if there were a normalcy in such meetings. Her hands were back inside the scapular, holding the hidden crucifix. Her eyes were intent, ravenous, feasting on me as I slowly approached her, taking in every piece of me from my shoes to my thinning hair, as if she were furiously working a camera, capturing all the details to be gone over again and again like a scrapbook for the remainder of her years as she meditated and prayed and remembered.

"I am so proud of you, Jay," she finally said. "You became a very famous man!"

Her compliment conjured up an emptiness inside me, a lament that I could not even articulate. "I have never stopped loving you," I said, searching her face.

"Please. You are not allowed to say that. Those are the rules. And my love is now in Christ." Her eyes caught the deep scar that still creases my right cheek. "That is where he cut you?"

She asked me as if it had happened yesterday. Without thinking, I absently touched my cheek, where every morning I must pause when shaving to work around the cleaving. Yes, every morning, just as he predicted when he sliced me deep and ragged, I must stop for a moment and think about her father.

"Yes."

"I never saw it—before."

"I know."

"He should not have done that."

She held my eyes. I tried to search behind her face for something that might tell me how she felt, or used to feel. I wanted to ask her. We were alone in the room. But there were, as she kept reminding me, the rules. "How did you pick your names?" I finally managed to say.

"Saint Thaddeus is the patron saint of lost causes," she answered simply. Then she hesitated, a small cloud passing before her eyes. "And Saint Anthony is the patron saint of barren women."

My knees began knocking again. My hands were trembling anew. I wanted more than anything to reach through the grill and clasp her to me, to try again to explain, to beg her for forgiveness. I knew it was fruitless at this point but still I felt a call for justice, an anger that life does not always reward the right intentions, that the cycles of days and years and seasons lull us into thinking that in all things there will be second chances, and even thirds, when in some things we have only one. And sometimes we never know we had that single chance until it disappears.

"The reason that he cut me. The reason that you—became sick. It was not what it sounded like," I said. "It's important to me that you understand that."

"You should not carry this burden in your heart," she said simply. "I have forgiven you, Jay. But you should also forgive my father."

Suddenly I relaxed. I felt myself smiling, because I knew now that it had been right for me to come. I knew that behind the layers of clothing, inside the heart and brain of the person before me, was indeed Divina Clara, ever logical and constant, always trying to mend and to heal, even here, so near to the end. We stared at each other through the impenetrable wooden grill and across the unrecoverable years. Outside the church bells began ringing. I sensed that soon she would have to leave. Her nearness, the ringing of the bells, the sweet smell of flowers, my fingers pressing into the scar upon my cheek, the very city in which we had loved so fiercely, all combined to surround me with the memory of the day our lives had so completely turned.

"I forgive him for what he did to me," I said. "Because I know that you were precious to him, and he had his pride. But I have never been able to forgive him for what he did to you."

"Please," she said, almost as if she were counseling me. "We are not permitted to talk about this." And so for a long moment I stopped speaking. But although we could not speak about it, it was indeed before us, tangible and alive, held in the space between our staring eyes.

"I tried to find you. They kept me from you."

"I did not know that."

"You didn't know?"

"No." In her eyes I saw not regret, for what good would that emotion have accomplished? Instead she slowly smiled, her face overcome with gladness, as if I had vindicated some distant, undisturbed memory. "But anyway, now you are here."

Indeed I was. She stood before me, too distant and too late, but mine at least to see, if only for one brief moment that might confirm the grandeur of our loss. She continued to smile at me through the grill, then reached through it to briefly touch my hand. In her cloistered world it was an act of utter boldness. "I have always prayed for you. Every day."

I held her fingers briefly, remembering their touch with an aching clarity. Surprised by the intimacy of my gesture, she pulled them away. "Do you really believe there is a reason for everything?" I asked.

"It does no good to question the will of God." She eyed me carefully. "You do have children, do you not?"

"Yes," I answered, almost embarrassed to speak of them in front of her. "Two." I watched her pleased smile and knew she was happy for my good fortune. "I married late in my career." I took a deep breath. "It took me a very long time, you know."

"Like MacArthur!" she suddenly said. She seemed happy in her discovery, as if it brought a final balance to her life. "Did you know that Consuelo Trani did not die until the year after MacArthur did? Yes! It is still a grand love story in the Visayas. For the rest of her life she prayed after him and remembered him and looked after his soul. Even though she could not have him."

I found myself smiling sadly with her, for I knew that she was not simply talking about Consuelo. "*Waray waray*," I said.

Her face brightened. "You remember, even after all these years! Yes, that is the way of our people. To the last drop of blood. To the last breath of air. To the last beating of the heart. This is how we fight. This is how we pray. This is how we love."

Listening to her and watching her smooth, full face become so animated as she spoke left me overwhelmed with the greatest certainty of my life. "I will always love you. Always, always."

Her face became firm, but in her eyes I could see a young girl, forever handing me her heart. "You are not permitted to say that!"

"I know. But how can I wait this long and still keep it inside me?"

Outside a clock began to chime. The bells rang again and from the chapel I could hear soft female voices beginning to chant the Angelus.

"*Angelus Domini nuntiavit Mariae . . .*"

"I am late," she said. There was duty in her voice but also regret. Her eyes were scanning me again, soaking up memories that might have to last her forever. For who knows, on the far side of seventy, how quickly God might take us?

She walked with me along the concrete drive way until we reached the iron gate that for a half century now had defined the boundaries of her life. Behind us the bells and the chanting voices called her. In front of me my driver waved, jumping down from his perch on the front hood of my hired car and running to open a door. Divina Clara stood next to me, just as she might always have stood had I not been pulled away from her into the chaos of war-bombed but ever-resilient Japan.

If it had not been for MacArthur I would not have lost her, I thought. And then I stopped. For I had done it to myself. And if it had not been for MacArthur I would never have found her, either.

We reached the gate, and I could control myself no more. I turned suddenly and embraced her, no longer caring about the rules. Surprisingly, she held me tightly, and from deep within her I heard an involuntary groan. She was still firm, even at this age, but far too slender. I thought I might tell her to eat more food, to take care of herself, but then I realized how silly that all would sound.

She sought to push me away but I held on to her, not wanting her to see me weeping. "I will never stop loving you, Divina Clara."

"My name is Sister Thaddeus Anthony," she said simply, now freeing herself from my embrace. She wiped my eyes with the front of her scapular, as if tending to me. "You will have to get used to that, Jay. Now, I must go."

I watched her from the gate as she walked back toward the chanting voices. "Divina Clara!"

She stopped for a moment and turned back to me as if to scold me.

"You are my guardian angel," I said.

She waved sadly to me. Her dark eyes were swarming with unquenchable memories. "I have thought about that," she said.

Then she walked away from me. And as I watched, she disappeared inside the chapel.